Ellery Queen's Crookbook

28th Mystery Annual

"If Crime comes, can Crooks be far behind?"

RANDOM HOUSE   NEW YORK

Ellery Queen's Crookbook

25 stories from
*Ellery Queen's
Mystery Magazine*

EDITED BY

Ellery Queen

Library of Congress Cataloging in Publication Data

Queen, Ellery, pseud., comp.
    Ellery Queen's crookbook.

    (Mystery annual, 28)
    CONTENTS: Queen, E.   Introduction.—Daniels, H. R.
Three ways to rob a bank.—Asimov, I. The acquisitive
chuckle. [etc.]
    1. Detective and mystery stories, American.
2. Detective and mystery stories, English.   I. Ellery
Queen's mystery magazine.   II. Title.   III. Series:
EQMM annual, 28.
PZ1.A1Er vol. 28 [PS648.D4]   823'.0872   73–5418
ISBN 0–394–48850–4

Manufactured in the United States of America
First Edition

9   8   7   6   5   4   3   2

Acknowledgments

The editor hereby makes grateful acknowledgment to the following authors and authors' representatives for giving permission to reprint the material in this volume:

Isaac Asimov for *The Acquisitive Chuckle*, © 1971 by Isaac Asimov

Mary Barrett for *Déjà Vu*, © 1972 by Mary Barrett

Brandt & Brandt for *The Niece from Scotland* by Christianna Brand, © 1972 by Christianna Brand; and *Jericho and the Two Ways to Die* by Hugh Pentecost, © 1972 by Hugh Pentecost

Curtis Brown, Ltd., for *The Other Side of the Wall* by Stanley Ellin, © 1972 by Stanley Ellin; and *Winner Takes All* by Patricia McGerr, © 1972 by Patricia McGerr

Collins-Knowlton-Wing, Inc., for *A Kind of Madness* by Anthony Boucher, © 1972 by Phyllis White

John Coyne for *A Game in the Sun*, © 1972 by John Coyne

John Cushman Associates, Inc., for *The Panic Button* by Michael Gilbert, © 1972 by Michael Gilbert; and *Pickup on the Dover Road* by Julian Symons, © 1972 by Julian Symons

Harold R. Daniels for *Three Ways to Rob a Bank*, © 1972 by Harold R. Daniels

Celia Fremlin for *The Coldness of a Thousand Suns*, © 1972 by Celia Fremlin

Tonita S. Gardner for *A Girl Can't Always Have Everything*, © 1972 by Tonita S. Gardner

Anthony Gilbert for *A Day of Encounters*, © 1971 by Anthony Gilbert

Joyce Harrington for *The Purple Shroud*, © 1972 by Joyce Harrington

Edward D. Hoch for *The Theft from the Empty Room*, © 1972 by Edward D. Hoch

Fritzi Franz Lumen for *The Prayer Wheels*, © 1972 by Fritzi Franz Lumen

Dana Lyon for *The Good Companions*, © 1972 by Dana Lyon

Florence V. Mayberry for *So Lonely, So Lost, So Frightened*, © 1972 by Florence V. Mayberry

McIntosh & Otis, Inc., for *Woodrow Wilson's Necktie* by Patricia Highsmith, © 1972 by Patricia Highsmith

Scott Meredith Literary Agency, Inc., for *The Island of Bright Birds* by John Christopher, © 1971 by John Christopher

Robert P. Mills, Ltd., for *Don't Worry, Johnny* by Robert L. Fish, © 1972 by Robert L. Fish

David Morrell for *The Dripping*, © 1972 by David Morrell

Francis M. Nevins, Jr., for *Open Letter to Survivors*, © 1972 by Francis M. Nevins, Jr.

Harold Ober Associates, Inc., for *The Resurrection Men* by Lillian de la Torre, © 1972 by Lillian de la Torre

Contents

Six Best "First Stories" of the Year

Contents

Six Best "First Stories" of the Year

Introduction

Dear Reader:

Here is the gourmet recipe for *Ellery Queen's Crookbook*, the twenty-eighth volume in this series of annual anthologies:

INGREDIENTS

- 25 mysteries (chilled)
- 25 suspenses (and suspensions of disbelief)
- 23 crimes (assorted)
- 11 detections (mixed)
- 1 espionage (salted and peppered to taste)

with toppings of:

    terror

    violence

    horror

    murder

Slice a story by Stanley Ellin into shivers (remember his "specialty of the house"?), adding generous pinches of Edward D. Hoch. Toast a tale by Lillian de la Torre, grill the Gilberts (Michael and Anthony), spooning in Hugh Pentecost. Fillet Robert L. Fish, with cuts of John Christopher, moistening with Patricia McGerr and a measure of Florence V. Mayberry, melted. After heating Patricia Highsmith, baste with Christianna Brand, then brush lightly with Mary Barrett. Ladle off Dana Lyon slowly. Stir in Isaac Asimov and let simmer. Flavor with Celia Fremlin, dot with diced Harold R. Daniels, sprinkle Julian Symons, and garnish with Anthony Boucher.

Serve before midnight—and shake well after reading.

Bon appétit!

                             ELLERY QUEEN (*chef de cuisine*)

Ellery Queen's
Crookbook

THREE WAYS TO ROB A BANK

by Harold R. Daniels

It is more than six years since Harold R. Daniels has written a story for Ellery Queen's Mystery Magazine. *Welcome back to the fold, Mr. Daniels, with a decidedly unsheepish story—with, indeed, as impudent and amusing a story as we've read in perhaps six years . . .*

THE manuscript was neatly typed. The cover letter could have been copied almost word for word from one of those "Be an Author" publications, complete with the proforma "Submitted for publication at your usual rates." Miss Edwina Martin, assistant editor of *Tales of Crime and Detection*, read it first. Two things about it caught her attention. One was the title, "Three Ways to Rob a Bank. Method 1." The other was the author's name. Nathan Waite. Miss Martin, who knew nearly every professional writer of crime fiction in the United States and had had dealings with most of them, didn't recognize the name.

The letter lacked the usual verbosity of the fledgling writer, but a paragraph toward the middle caught her eye. "You may want to change the title because what Rawlings did wasn't really robbery. In fact, it's probably legal. I am now working on a story which I will call 'Three Ways to Rob a Bank. Method 2.' I will send this to you when I finish having it retyped. Method 2 is almost certainly legal. If you want to check Method 1, I suggest that you show this to your own banker."

Rawlings, it developed, was the protagonist in the story. The story itself was crude and redundant; it failed to develop its characters and served almost solely as a vehicle to outline Method 1. The method itself had to do with the extension of credit to holders of checking accounts—one of those deals where the bank urges holders of checking accounts to write checks without having funds to back them. The bank would extend credit. No papers. No notes. (The author's distrust of this form of merchandizing emerged clearly in the story.)

Miss Martin's first impulse was to send the story back with a polite letter of rejection. (She never used the heartless printed rejection slip.) But something about the confident presentation of the method bothered her. She clipped a memorandum to the manuscript, scrawled a large question mark on it, and bucked it to the editor. It came back next day with additional scrawling: "This is an awful piece of trash but the plan sounds almost real. Why don't you check it with Frank Wordell?"

Frank Wordell was a vice-president of the bank that served Miss Martin's publisher. She made a luncheon date with him, handed him the letter and the manuscript, and started to proofread some galleys while he looked it over. She glanced up when she heard him suck in his breath. He had turned a delicate shade of greenish white.

"Would it work?" she asked.

"I'm not quite sure," the vice-president said, his voice shaking. "I'd have to get an opinion from some of the people in the Check Credit Department. But I think it would." He hesitated. "Good lord, this could cost us millions. Listen—you weren't thinking of publishing this, were you? I mean, if it got into the hands of the public—"

Miss Martin, who had no great admiration for the banking mentality, was noncommital. "It needs work," she said. "We haven't made a decision."

The banker pushed his plate away. "And he says he's got another one. His Method 2. If it's anything like this it could ruin the entire banking business." A thought came to him. "He calls this 'Three Ways to Rob a Bank.' That means there must be a Method 3. This is terrible! No, no, we can't let you publish this and we must see this man at once."

This was an unfortunate approach to use with Edwina Martin who reached out her hand for the letter and manuscript. "That is our decision to make," she told him coldly. It was only after he had pleaded the potential destruction of the country's economy that she let him take the papers back to the bank. He was so upset that he neglected to pay the luncheon check.

He called her several hours later. "We've held an emergency meeting," he told her. "The Check Credit people think that Method 1 *would* work. It might also be legal but even if it isn't it would cost us millions in lawsuits. Listen, Miss Martin, we want you to buy the story and assign the copyright to us. Would that protect us against him selling the story to someone else?"

"In its present form," she told him. "But there would be nothing to prevent him from writing another story using the same method." Remembering his failure to pay the luncheon check, she was not inclined to be especially cooperative. "And we don't buy material that we don't intend to publish."

But after an emergency confrontation between a committee of the City Banking Association, called into extraordinary session, and the publisher, it was decided to buy Nathan Waite's story and to lock the manuscript in the deepest vault of the biggest bank. In the interest of the national economy.

Economy, Miss Martin decided, was an appropriate word. During the confrontation a Saurian old capitalist with a personal worth in the tens of millions brought up the subject of payment to Nathan Waite. "I suppose we must buy it," he grumbled. "What do you pay for stories of this type?"

Miss Martin, knowing the author had never been published and hence had no "name" value, suggested a figure. "Of course," she said, "since it will never be published there is no chance of foreign income or anthology fees, let alone possible movie or TV rights." (The Saurian visibly shuddered.) "So I think it would be only fair to give the author a little more than the usual figure."

The Saurian protested. "No, no. Couldn't think of it. After all, we won't ever get our money back. And we'll have to buy Method 2 and Method 3. Think of that. Besides, we've still got to figure out a way to keep him from writing other stories using the same methods. The usual figure will have to do. No extras."

Since there were thirty banks in the Association and since the assessment for each would be less than $10 per story, Miss Martin failed to generate any deep concern for the Saurian.

That same day Miss Martin forwarded a check and a letter to Nathan Waite. The letter explained that at this time no publication date could be scheduled but that the editor was very anxious to see the stories explaining the second and third ways to rob a bank. She signed the letter with distaste. To a virgin author, she knew, the check was insignificant compared with the glory of publication. Publication that was never to be.

A week later a letter and the manuscript for "Three Ways To Rob a Bank. Method 2" arrived. The story was a disaster but again the method sounded convincing. This time it involved magnetic ink and data processing. By prearrangement Miss Martin brought it to Frank Wordell's office. He read it rapidly and shivered. "The man's a genius," he muttered. "Of course, he's had a lot of background in the field—"

"What was that? How would you know about his background?" Edwina asked.

He said in an offhand manner, "Oh, we've had him thoroughly checked out, of course. Had one of the best detective agencies in the business investigate him—ever since you showed me that first letter. Couldn't get a thing on him."

Miss Martin's voice was ominously flat. "Do you mean to tell me that you had Mr. Waite *investigated*—a man you only learned of through his correspondence with us?"

"Of course." Wordell sounded faintly surprised. "A man that has dangerous knowledge like he has. Couldn't just trust to luck that he wouldn't do something with it besides write stories. Oh, no, couldn't let it drop. He worked in a bank for years and years, you know. Small town in Connecticut. They let him go a year ago. Had to make room for the president's nephew. Gave him a pension though. Ten percent of his salary."

"Years and years, you said. How many years?"

"Oh, I don't remember. Have to look at the report. Twenty-five, I think."

"Then naturally he wouldn't hold any resentment over being let go," she said drily. She put out her hand. "Let me see his letter again."

The letter that had accompanied the second manuscript had cordially thanked the publisher for accepting the first story and for the check. One paragraph said, "I assume you checked Method 1 with your banker as I suggested. I hope you'll show him Method 2 also, just to be sure it would work. As I said in my first letter, it's almost certainly legal."

Miss Martin asked, "Is it legal?"

"Is what legal?"

"Method 2. The one you just read about."

"Put it this way. It isn't illegal. To make it illegal, every bank using data processing would have to make some major changes in its forms and procedures. It would take months and in the meantime it could cost us even more millions than Method 1. This is a terrible thing, Miss Martin—a terrible thing."

Method 2 caused panic in the chambers of the City Banking Association. There was general agreement that the second story must also be bought immediately and sequestered forever. There was also general agreement that since Method 3 might be potentially even more catastrophic, there could be no more waiting for more stories from Mr. Waite. (Miss Martin, who was present, asked if the price of the second story could be raised in view of the fact that Mr. Waite was now, having received one check, a professional author. Saurian pointed out that Waite hadn't actually been published, so the extra expense was not justified.)

A plan was adopted. Miss Martin was to invite Mr. Waite to come up from Connecticut, ostensibly for an author-editor chat. Actually he would be brought before a committee chosen by the City Banking Association. "We'll have our lawyers there," Saurian said. "We'll put the fear of the Lord into him. Make him tell us about that Method 3. Pay him the price of another story if we have to. Then we'll work out some way to shut him up."

With this plan Miss Martin and her fellow editors and her publisher went along most reluctantly. She almost wished that she had simply rejected Nathan Waite's first submission. Most particularly she resented the attitude of the bankers. In their view, Nathan Waite was nothing more than a common criminal.

She called Nathan Waite at his Connecticut home and invited him to come in. The City Banking Association, she resolved to herself, would pay his expenses, whatever devious steps she might have to take to manage it.

His voice on the phone was surprisingly youthful and had only a suggestion of Yankee twang. "Guess I'm pretty lucky selling two stories one right after the other. I'm sure grateful, Miss Martin.

And I'll be happy to come in and see you. I suppose you want to talk about the next one."

Her conscience nipped at her. "Well, yes, Mr. Waite. Methods 1 and 2 were so clever that there's a lot of interest in Method 3."

"You just call me Nate, Miss. Now, one thing about Method 3: there's no question about it being legal. The fact is, it's downright honest. Compared with 1 and 2, that is. Speaking about 1 and 2, did you check them with your banker? I figured you must have shown him Method 1 before you bought the story. I was just wondering if he was impressed by Method 2."

She said faintly, "Oh, he was impressed all right."

"Then I guess he'll be really interested in Method 3."

They concluded arrangements for his visit in two days and hung up.

He showed up at Miss Martin's office precisely on time—a small man in his fifties with glistening white hair combed in an old-fashioned part on one side. His face was tanned and made an effective backdrop for his sharp blue eyes. He bowed with a charming courtliness that made Miss Martin feel even more of a Judas. She came from behind her desk. "Mr. Waite—" she began.

"Nate."

"All right. Nate. I'm disgusted with this whole arrangement and I don't know how we let ourselves be talked into it. Nate, we didn't buy your stories to publish them. To be honest—and it's about time—the stories are awful. We bought them because the bank—the banks, I should say—asked us to. They're afraid if the stories were published, people would start actually using your methods."

He frowned. "Awful, you say. I'm disappointed to hear that. I thought the one about Method 2 wasn't that bad."

She put her hand on his arm in a gesture of sympathy and looked up to see that he was grinning. "Of course they were awful," he said. "I deliberately wrote them that way. I'll bet it was almost as hard as writing good stuff. So the banks felt the methods would work, eh? I'm not surprised. I put a lot of thought into them."

"They're even more interested in Method 3," she told him. "They want to meet you this afternoon and discuss buying your next story. Actually, they want to pay you *not* to write it. Or write anything else," she added.

"It won't be any great loss to the literary world. Who will we be meeting? The City Banking Association? An old fellow who looks like a crocodile?"

Miss Edwina Martin, with the feel for a plot developed after reading thousands of detective stories, stepped back and looked at him. "You know all about this," she accused him.

He shook his head. "Not all about it. But I sort of planned it. And I felt it was working out the way I planned when they put a detective agency to work investigating me."

"They had no business doing that," she said angrily. "I want you to know that we had nothing to do with it. We didn't even know about it until afterwards. And I'm not going to the meeting with you. I wash my hands of the whole business. Let them buy your next story themselves."

"I want you to come," he said. "You just might enjoy it."

She agreed on condition that he hold out for more money than her publisher had ostensibly been paying him. "I sort of planned on charging a bit more," he told her. "I mean, seeing they're that much interested in Method 3."

At lunch he told her something of his banking career and a great deal more about his life in a small Connecticut town. This plain-speaking, simple man, she learned, was an amateur mathematician of considerable reputation. He was an authority on cybernetics and a respected astronomer.

Over coffee some of his personal philosophy emerged. "I wasn't upset when the bank let me go," he said. "Nepotism is always with us. I could have been a tycoon in a big-city bank, I suppose. But I was content to make an adequate living and it gave me time to do the things I really liked to do. I'm basically lazy. My wife died some years after we were married and there wasn't anybody to push me along harder than I wanted to go.

"Besides, there's something special about a small bank in a small town. You know everyone's problems, money and otherwise, and you can break rules now and then to help people out. The banker, in his way, is almost as important as the town doctor." He paused. "It's not like that anymore. It's all regimented and computerized and dehumanized. You don't have a banker in the old sense of the word. You have a financial executive who's more and more just a part of a large corporation, answerable to a board of directors. He has to work by a strict set of rules that don't allow for any of the human factors."

Miss Martin, fascinated, signaled for more coffee.

"Like making out a deposit slip," he went on. "Used to be you walked into the bank and filled out the slip with your name and address and the amount you wanted to deposit. It made a man feel good and it was good for him. 'My name is John Doe and I earned this money and here is where I live and I want you to save this amount of money for me.' And you took it up to the cashier and passed the time of day for a minute."

Nate put sugar in his coffee. "Pretty soon there won't be any cashiers. Right now you can't fill out a deposit slip in most banks. They send you computer input cards with your name and number on them. All you fill in is the date and amount. The money they save on clerical work they spend on feeble-minded TV advertising. It was a TV ad for a bank that inspired me to write those stories."

Miss Martin smiled. "Nate, you used us." The smile faded. "But even if you hold them up for the Method 3 story, it won't hurt anything but their feelings. The money won't come out of their pockets and even several thousands of dollars wouldn't mean anything to them."

He said softly, "The important thing is to make them realize that any mechanical system that man can devise, man can beat. If I can make them realize that the human element can't be discarded, I'll be satisfied. Now then, I suppose we should be getting along to the meeting."

Miss Martin, who had felt concern for Nathan Waite, felt suddenly confident. Nate could emerge as a match for a dozen Saurians.

A committee of twelve members of the City Banking Association, headed by the Saurian, and flanked by a dozen lawyers, awaited them. Nathan Waite nodded as he entered the committee room. The Saurian said, "You're Waite?"

Nate said quietly, "Mr. Waite."

A young lawyer in an impeccable gray suit spoke out. "Those stories that you wrote and that we paid for. You realize that your so-called methods are illegal?"

"Son, I helped write the banking laws for my state and I do an odd job now and then for the Federal Reserve Board. I'd be happy to talk banking law with you."

An older lawyer said sharply, "Shut up, Andy." He turned to Nate. "Mr. Waite, we don't know if your first two methods are criminal or not. We do know it could cost a great deal of money and trouble to conduct a test case and in the meantime, if either Method 1 or 2 got into the hands of the public it would cause incalculable harm and loss. We'd like some assurance that this won't happen."

"You bought the stories describing the first two methods. I'm generally considered an honorable man. As Miss Martin here might put it, I won't use the same plots again."

Gray Suit said cynically, "Not this week, maybe. How about next week? You think you've got us over a barrel."

The older lawyer said furiously, "I told you to shut up, Andy," and turned to Nate again. "I'm Peter Hart," he said. "I apologize for my colleague. I accept the fact that you are an honorable man, Mr. Waite."

Saurian interrupted. "Never mind all that. What about Method 3—the third way to rob a bank. Is it as sneaky as the first two?"

Nate said mildly, "As I told Miss Martin, 'rob' is a misnomer.

Methods 1 and 2 are unethical, perhaps illegal, methods for getting money from a bank. Method 3 is legal beyond the shadow of a doubt. You have my word for that."

Twelve bankers and twelve lawyers began talking simultaneously. Saurian quieted the furor with a lifted hand. "And you mean it will work just as well as the first two methods?"

"I'm positive of it."

"Then we'll buy it. Same price as the first two stories and you won't even have to write it. Just tell us what Method 3 is. And we'll give you $500 for your promise never to write another story." Saurian sank back, overwhelmed by his own generosity. Peter Hart looked disgusted.

Nathan Waite shook his head. "I've got a piece of paper here," he said. "It was drawn up by the best contract lawyer in my state. Good friend of mine. I'll be glad to let Mr. Hart look it over. What it calls for is that your association pay me $25,000 a year for the rest of my life and that payments be made thereafter in perpetuity to various charitable organizations to be named in my will."

Bedlam broke loose. Miss Martin felt like cheering and she caught a smile of admiration on Peter Hart's face.

Nate waited patiently for the commotion to die down. When he could be heard he said, "That's too much money to pay for just a story. So, as the contract specifies, I'll serve as consultant to the City Banking Association—call it consultant in human relations. That's a nice-sounding title. Being a consultant, of course, I'll be too busy to write any more stories. That's in the contract too."

Gray Suit was on his feet, yelling for attention. "What about Method 3? Is that explained in the contract? We've got to know about Method 3!"

Nate nodded. "I'll tell you about it as soon as the contract is signed."

Peter Hart held up his hand for quiet. "If you'll wait in the anteroom, Mr. Waite, we'd like to discuss the contract among ourselves."

Nate waited with Miss Martin. "You were tremendous," she said. "Do you think they'll agree?"

"I'm sure they will. They might argue about clause 7—gives me the right to approve or disapprove of all TV bank commercials." His eyes twinkled. "But they're so scared of Method 3 I think they'll agree to even that."

Five minutes later Peter Hart called them back to face a subdued group of committee members. "We have decided that the association badly needs a consultant in human relations," he said. "Mr. Graves"—he nodded toward a deflated Saurian—"and myself have signed in behalf of the City Banking Association. By the way, the contract is beautifully drafted—there's no possibility of a legal loophole. You have only to sign it yourself."

Gray Suit was on his feet again. "Wait a minute," he shouted. "He still hasn't told us about Method 3."

Nate reached for the contract. "Oh, yes," he murmured, after he had signed it. " 'Three Ways to Rob a Bank.' Method 3. Well, it's really quite simple. *This* is Method 3."

THE ACQUISITIVE CHUCKLE

by Isaac Asimov

The first of a brand-new series—about the Black Widowers and the piquant problems that challenge them monthly . . . In this opening adventure Bartram, the private detective, tells the Black Widowers the details of an old case that the detective had never been able to solve. Could the five members—patent lawyer Geoffrey Avalon, code expert Thomas Trumbull, writer Emmanuel Rubin, organic chemist James Drake, and artist Mario Gonzalo— solve the mystery? . . . Can you?

HANLEY BARTRAM was the guest, that night, of the Black Widowers, who met monthly in their quiet haunt and vowed death to any female who intruded—for that one night each month, at any rate.

The number of attendees varied: on this occasion five members were present.

Geoffrey Avalon was host for the evening. He was tall, with a neatly trimmed mustache and a smallish beard, more white than black now, but with hair as black as ever.

As host it was his duty to deliver the ritual toast that marked the beginning of the dinner proper. Loudly, and with gusto, he said, "To Old King Cole of sacred memory. May his pipe be forever lit, his bowl forever full, his fiddlers forever in health, and may we all be as merry as he all our lives long."

The six cried "Amen," touched lips to drink, and sat down. Avalon put his drink to the side of his plate. It was his second and was now exactly half full. It would remain there throughout the dinner and not be touched again. He was a patent lawyer and he carried over into his social life the minutiae of his work. One and one-half drinks was precisely what he allowed himself on these occasions.

Thomas Trumbull came storming up the stairs at the last minute, with his usual cry of "Henry, a Scotch and soda for a dying man!"

Henry, the waiter at these functions for several years now (and with no last name that any Black Widower had ever heard used), had the Scotch and soda ready. He was sixtyish but his face was unwrinkled and staid. His voice seemed to recede into the distance even as he spoke. "Right here, Mr. Trumbull."

Trumbull spotted Bartram at once and said to Avalon in an aside, "Your guest?"

"He asked to come," said Avalon, in as near a whisper as he could manage. "Nice fellow. You'll like him."

The dinner itself went as miscellaneously as the Black Widowers' affairs usually did. Emmanuel Rubin, who had the other beard—a thin and scraggly one under a mouth with widely spaced teeth—had broken out of a writer's block and was avidly giving the details of the story he had just finished. James Drake, with a rectangular face, a mustache but no beard, was interrupting with memories of other stories, tangentially related. Drake was an organic chemist but he had an encyclopedic knowledge of pulp fiction.

Trumbull, as a code expert, considered himself to be in the inner councils of government and took it into his head to be outraged at Mario Gonzalo's political pronouncements. "Damn it," he yelled, in one of his less vituperative moods, "why don't you stick to your idiotic collages and burlap bags and leave world affairs to your betters?"

Trumbull had not recovered from Gonzalo's one-man art show earlier that year, and Gonzalo, understanding this, laughed good-naturedly, saying, "Show me my betters. Name one."

Bartram, short and plump, with hair that curled in tiny ringlets, clung firmly to his role as guest. He listened to everyone, smiled at everyone, and said little.

Eventually the time came when Henry poured the coffee and placed the desserts before each guest with practised legerdemain. It was at this moment that the traditional grilling of the guest usually began.

The first interrogator, almost by tradition, was Thomas Trumbull. His swarthy face, wrinkled into perennial discontent, looked angry as he began with the invariable opening question: "Mr. Bartram, how do you justify your existence?"

Bartram smiled. He spoke with precision as he said, "I have never tried. My clients, on those occasions when I give satisfaction, find my existence justified."

"Your clients?" said Rubin. "What is it you do, sir?"

"I am a private detective."

"Good," said James Drake. "I don't think we've ever had one before. Mannie, you can get some of the procedures correct for a change when you write your private-eye stuff."

"Not from me," Bartram said quickly.

Trumbull scowled. "If you don't mind, gentlemen, as the appointed grillster please leave this to me. Mr. Bartram, you speak of the occasions on which you give satisfaction. Do you always give satisfaction?"

"There are times when the matter can be debated," said Bartram. "In fact, I would like to speak to you this evening concerning an occasion that was particularly questionable. It may even be that one of you might be useful in that connection. It was with this in mind that I asked my good friend, Jeff Avalon, to invite me to a meeting, once I learned the details of your organization. He obliged and I am delighted."

"Are you ready now to discuss this dubious satisfaction you gave or did not give, as the case may be?"

"Yes, if you will allow me."

Trumbull looked at the others for signs of dissent. Gonzalo's prominent eyes were fixed on Bartram as he said, "May we interrupt?" Quickly, and with an admirable economy of strokes, he was doodling a caricature of Bartram on the back of a menu card. It would join the others which memorialized guests and which marched in brave array across the walls.

"Within reason," said Bartram. He paused to sip at his coffee and then said, "The story begins with Anderson, to whom I shall refer only in that fashion. He was an acquisitor."

"An inquisitor?" Gonzalo asked, frowning.

"An *acquisitor*. He acquired things, he earned them, he bought them, he picked them up, he collected them. The world moved in one direction with respect to him—it moved toward him, never away. He had a house into which this flood of material, of varying value, came to rest and never moved again. Through the years it grew steadily thicker and more amazingly heterogeneous. He also had a business partner, whom I shall call Jackson."

Trumbull interrupted, frowning, not because there was anything to frown about, but because he always frowned. He said, "Is this a true story?"

"I tell only true stories," Bartram said slowly and precisely. "I lack the imagination to lie."

"Is it confidential?"

"I shall tell the story in such a way as to make it difficult to be recognized; but if it were recognized, it would be confidential."

"I follow the subjunctive," said Trumbull, "but I wish to assure you that what is said within the walls of this room is never repeated, or referred to, outside its walls. Henry understands this, too."

Henry, who was refilling two of the coffee cups, smiled a little and bent his head in agreement.

Bartram smiled also and went on, "Jackson had a disease, too. He was honest, unavoidably and deeply honest. The characteristic permeated his soul as though, from an early age, he had been marinated in integrity.

"To a man like Anderson it was most useful to have honest Jackson as a partner, for their business, which I carefully do not describe in detail, required contact with the public. Such contact was not for Anderson, for his acquisitiveness stood in the way. With each object he acquired, another little crease of slyness entered his face, until it seemed a spider's web that frightened all flies at sight. It was Jackson, the pure and the honest, who was the front man, and to whom all widows hastened with their mites, and orphans with their farthings.

"On the other hand, Jackson also found Anderson a necessity, for Jackson, with all his honesty, perhaps because of it, had no knack for making one dollar become two. Left to himself he would, entirely without meaning to, lose every cent entrusted to him and would then quickly be forced to kill himself as a dubious form of restitution. Anderson's hands were to money, however, as fertilizer is to roses, and together he and Jackson were a winning combination.

"Yet no paradise continues forever, and a besetting characteristic, left to itself, will deepen, widen, and grow more extreme. Jackson's honesty grew to such colossal proportions that Anderson, for all his shrewdness, was occasionally backed to the wall and forced into monetary loss. Similarly, Anderson's acquisitiveness burrowed to such infernal depths that Jackson, for all his morality, found himself occasionally twisted into questionable practices.

"Naturally, as Anderson disliked losing money, and Jackson abhorred losing character, a coolness grew between the two. In such a situation the advantage clearly lay on the side of Anderson, who placed no reasonable limits on his actions, whereas Jackson felt himself bound by a code of ethics.

"Slyly Anderson worked and maneuvered until, eventually, poor honest Jackson found himself forced to sell out his end of the partnership under the most disadvantageous of conditions.

"Anderson's acquisitiveness, we might say, had reached a climax, for he acquired sole control of the business. It was his intention to retire now, leaving its everyday running to employees, and concerning himself no further than was required to pocket its profits. Jackson, on the other hand, was left with little more than his honesty, and while honesty is an admirable characteristic it has small direct value in a hockshop.

"It was at this point, gentlemen, that I entered the picture. Ah, Henry, thank you."

The glasses of brandy were being passed around.

"You did not know those people to begin with?" Rubin asked, his sharp eyes blinking.

"No," Bartram said, sniffing delicately at the brandy and just touching it to his upper lip, "though I think one of you in this room did. It was some years ago.

"I first met Anderson when he entered my office in a white heat. 'I want you to find what I've lost,' he said. I have dealt with many cases of theft in my career and so I asked, naturally, 'What is it you have lost?' And he answered, 'Damn it, man, that's what I've just asked you to find out.'

"The story came out rather raggedly. Anderson and Jackson had quarreled with surprising intensity. Jackson was outraged, as only an honest man can be when he finds that his integrity is no shield against the conniving of others. He swore revenge, and Anderson shrugged that off with a laugh."

"Beware the wrath of a patient man," quoted Avalon, with the air of precision-research that he brought to even his least portentous statements.

"So I have heard," said Bartram, "though I have never had occasion to test the maxim. Nor, apparently, had Anderson, for he had no fear of Jackson. As he explained, Jackson was so psychotically honest and so insanely law-abiding that there was no chance of his slipping into wrongdoing. Or so Anderson thought. It did not even occur to him to ask Jackson to restore the office key—something all the more curious since the office was located in Anderson's house, among all that knickknackery.

"Anderson recalled this omission a few days after the quarrel when, returning from an early evening appointment, he found Jackson in his house. Jackson carried an attaché case which he was just closing as Anderson entered—closing with startled haste, it seemed to Anderson.

"Anderson frowned and said, 'What are you doing here?'

" 'Returning some papers which were in my possession and which now belong to you,' said Jackson, 'and returning the key to the office.' With this remark he handed over the key, indicated papers on the desk, and pushed the combination lock on his attaché case with fingers that Anderson could swear trembled a little. Jackson looked about the room with what appeared to Anderson to be a curious, almost a secretively satisfied, smile and said, 'I will now leave.' And he proceeded to do so.

"It was not until Anderson heard the motor of Jackson's car whirring into action and then retreating into the distance that he could rouse himself from a kind of stupor that had paralyzed him. He knew he had been robbed and the next day he came to me."

Drake pursed his lips, twirled his half-empty brandy glass, and said, "Why not to the police?"

"There was a complication," said Bartram. "Anderson did not

know what had been taken. When the certainty of theft dawned on him he naturally rushed to the safe. Its contents were secure. He ransacked his desk. Nothing seemed to be missing. He went from room to room. Everything seemed to be intact as far as he could tell."

"Wasn't he certain?" asked Gonzalo.

"He couldn't be. The house was inordinately crowded with every variety of object and he didn't remember all his possessions. He told me, for instance, that at one time he collected antique watches. He had them in a small drawer in his study—six of them. All six were there, but he was nagged by the faint memory of having had seven. For the life of him he could not remember definitely. In fact, it was worse than that, for one of the six present seemed strange to him. Could it be that he had had only six but that a less valuable one had been substituted for a more valuable one? Something of this sort repeated itself a dozen times over in every hideaway and with every sort of oddment. So he came to me—"

"Wait a while," interrupted Trumbull, bringing his hand down hard on the table. "What made him so certain that Jackson had taken anything at all?"

"Ah," said Bartram, "that is the fascinating part of the story. The closing of the attaché case, and Jackson's secretive smile as he looked about the room, served to rouse Anderson's suspicions, but as the door closed behind him, Jackson chuckled. It was not an ordinary chuckle—but I'll let Anderson tell it in his own words, as nearly as I can remember them.

" 'Bartram,' he said, 'I have heard that chuckle innumerable times in my life. I have chuckled that way myself a thousand times. It is a characteristic chuckle, an unmistakable one, an unmaskable one. It is the acquisitive chuckle; it is the chuckle of a man who has just obtained something he wants very much at the expense of someone else. If any man in all the world knows that chuckle and can recognize it, even behind a closed door, that man is myself. I cannot be mistaken. Jackson had taken something of mine and was glorying in it!'

"There was no arguing with the man on this point. He virtually slavered at the thought of having been victimized and, indeed, I had to believe him. I had to suppose that for all Jackson's pathological honesty he had finally been lured, by the once-in-a-lifetime snapping of patience, into theft. Helping to lure him must have been his knowledge of Anderson. He must have known Anderson's intent hold on even the least valued of his belongings, and realized that the hurt would extend far deeper and far beyond the value of the object taken, however great that value might have been.

"There you have the problem. Anderson wanted me to find out what had been taken, for until he could identify a stolen object and show that that object was, or had been, in the possession of Jackson, he could not prosecute—and he was most intent on prosecution. My task, then, was to look through his house and tell him what was missing."

"How would that be possible, if he himself couldn't tell?" growled Trumbull.

"I pointed that out to him," said Bartram, "but he was wild and unreasoning. He offered me a great deal of money, win or lose; a very handsome fee, indeed, and he put down a sizable portion of it as a retainer. It was clear he resented beyond measure the deliberate insult to his acquisitiveness. The thought that an amateur non-acquisitor like Jackson should dare beard him in the most sacred of his passions had driven him, on this one point, mad, and he was prepared to go to any expense to keep the other's victory from being final.

"I, too, am human. So I accepted the retainer and the fee. After all, I reasoned, I had my methods. I took up the question of insurance lists first. All were outdated, but they served to eliminate the furniture and all the larger items as possible objects of Jackson's thievery; for everything on the lists was still in the house."

Avalon said, "They were eliminated anyway, since the stolen object would have had to fit into the attaché case."

"Provided that it was the attaché case that was used to transport the item out of the house," Bartram pointed out patiently. "The attaché case might easily have been a decoy. Prior to Anderson's return, Jackson could have had a moving van at the door and taken out the grand piano had he so chosen, and then snapped the attaché case in Anderson's face to mislead him.

"But never mind that. I agree it wasn't likely. I took him around the house room by room, following a systematic procedure of considering the floor, walls, and ceiling, studying all the shelves, opening every door of every piece of furniture, going through every closet. Nor did I neglect the attic and the basement. Never before had Anderson been forced to consider every item of his vast and amorphous collection in order that somewhere, somehow, some item would jog his memory of some companion item that was *not* there.

"It was an enormous house, a heterogeneous one, an endless one. It took us days, and poor Anderson grew more befuddled each day.

"I next tackled it from the other end. It was obvious that Jackson had deliberately taken something unnoticeable, probably small; certainly something that Anderson would not easily miss and therefore something to which he was not greatly attached. On the other hand, it made sense to suppose that it was something Jackson would *want* to take away, and which he would find valuable. Indeed, his act would give him most satisfaction if Anderson also considered it valuable—once he realized what it was that was gone. What, then, could it be?"

"A small painting," said Gonzalo eagerly, "which Jackson knew to be an authentic Cezanne, but which Anderson thought was junk."

"A postage stamp from Anderson's collection," said Rubin, "which Jackson noted had an error in the engraving." He had once written a story which had hinged on this precise point.

"A book," said Trumbull, "that contained some hidden family secret with which, in due time, Jackson could blackmail Anderson."

"A photograph," said Avalon dramatically, "showing the likeness of an old sweetheart which Anderson would give a large sum to buy back."

"I don't know what business they were in," said Drake thoughtfully, "but it might have been the kind where some unvalued gimcrack might actually be of great value to a competitor and drive Anderson to bankruptcy. I remember one case where a formula for a hydrazo-intermediate—"

"Oddly enough," Bartram broke in firmly, "I thought of each of these possibilities, and I went over each one with Anderson. It was clear that he had no taste in art and such pieces as he had were really junk, and no mistake. He did not collect stamps, and though he had many books and could not tell for certain whether one were gone, he swore he had no family secrets anywhere that were worth the skipped beat of a blackmailer's heart. Nor had he ever had any old sweethearts, since in his younger days he had confined himself to professional ladies whose photographs he did not prize. As for his business secrets, they were of the sort that would interest the government far more than any competitor, and everything of that sort had been kept from Jackson's honest eyes and were still in the safe, or long in the fire. I thought of other possibilities, but one by one they were knocked down.

"Of course, Jackson might betray himself. He might blossom into sudden wealth and in ferreting out the source of the wealth we might learn the identity of the stolen object.

"Anderson himself suggested this and paid lavishly to have a twenty-four-hour watch put on Jackson. It was useless. The man kept a dull way of life and behaved precisely as you would expect someone minus his life savings to behave. He lived parsimoniously and eventually he took a menial job, where his honesty and calm demeanor were desirable assets.

"Finally I had but one alternative left—"

"Wait, wait," said Gonzalo, "let me guess." He tossed off what was left of his brandy and said, "Would any of you care for a cigar?" Only Trumbull reached for one.

Gonzalo lit the cigar, signaled Henry for another brandy, and said, "You asked Jackson what he stole!"

"I was strongly tempted to," said Bartram ruefully, "but that would scarcely have been feasible. It doesn't do in my profession to even hint at an accusation without evidence of any sort. Licenses are too fragile. And in any case he would simply deny theft, if accused, and be put on his guard against any self-incrimination."

"Well, then . . ." Gonzalo said blankly, and petered out.

The other four furrowed their brows, but only silence ensued.

Bartram, having waited politely, said, "You won't guess, gentlemen, for you are not in the profession. You know only what you read in romances and so you think gentlemen like myself have an unlimited number of alternatives and invariably solve all cases. I, myself, being in the profession, know otherwise. Gentlemen, the one alternative I had left was to confess failure.

"Anderson paid me, however. I'll give him that much credit. By the time I said goodbye to him he had lost some ten pounds. There was a vacant look in his eyes and as he shook hands with me they moved round and round the room he was in, still looking, still searching. He muttered, 'I tell you I couldn't possibly mistake that chuckle. He took something from me. He took something from me.'

"I saw him on two or three later occasions. He never stopped looking; he never found the missing object. He went rather downhill. The events I have described took place nearly five years ago, and last month he died."

There was a short silence. Avalon said, "Without ever finding the missing object?"

"Without ever finding it."

Trumbull said, with disapproval, "Are you coming to us for help with the problem?"

"In a way, yes. The occasion is too good to miss. Anderson is dead and whatever is said within these walls will go no further, we all agree, so that I may now ask what I could not ask before. Henry, may I have a light, please."

Henry, who had been listening with a kind of absentminded deference, produced a book of matches and lit Bartram's cigarette.

"Let me introduce you, Henry, to those you so efficiently serve. Gentlemen, may I introduce to you—Henry Jackson."

There was a moment of clear shock and Drake said, "*The* Jackson."

"Exactly," said Bartram. "I knew he was working here and when I heard it was at this club that you met for your monthly meetings I had to beg, rather shamelessly, for an invitation. It was only here that I could find the gentleman with the acquisitive chuckle, and do so under conditions of both bonhomie and discretion."

Henry smiled and bent his head.

Bartram said, "There were times during the course of the investigation when I could not help but wonder, Henry, whether Anderson might not have been wrong and whether there might possibly have been no theft at all. Always, however, I returned to the matter of the acquisitive chuckle, and I trusted Anderson's judgment."

"You did right to do so," Henry said softly, "for I *did* steal something from my one-time partner, the gentleman you have referred to as Anderson. And I never regretted the act for a single moment."

"It was something of value, I assume."

"It was of the greatest value and no day has passed without my thinking of the theft and rejoicing in the fact that the wicked man no longer had what I had taken away."

"And you deliberately roused his suspicions in order that you might experience the greater joy."

"Yes, I did."

"And you did not fear being caught?"

"Not for a single moment."

"By God," roared Avalon suddenly. "I say it again. Beware the wrath of a patient man. I am a patient man, but I am tired of this endless cross-examination. Beware my wrath, Henry. What was it you carried off in your attaché case?"

"Why, nothing," said Henry. "The attaché case was empty."

"Heaven help me! Where did you put whatever it was you took from him?"

"I didn't have to put it anywhere."

"Well, then, what did you take?"

"Only his peace of mind," Henry said gently.

WOODROW WILSON'S NECKTIE

by Patricia Highsmith

A rare type of story nowadays—contemporary American Grand Guignol—shocking, sensational, horrifying . . . a story you won't forget—even if you try to, even if you try very hard to . . . Patricia Highsmith's newest crime story is destined, we believe, to be an anthology favorite for years to come . . .

THE façade of Madame Thibault's Waxwork Horrors glittered and throbbed with red and yellow lights, even in the daytime. Knobs of golden balls—the yellow lights—pulsated amid the red lights, attracting the eye and holding it.

Clive Wilkes loved the place, the inside and the outside equally. Since he was a delivery boy for a grocery store, it was easy for him to say that a certain delivery had taken him longer than had been expected—he'd had to wait for Mrs. So-and-so to get home because the doorman had told him she was due back any minute, or he'd had to go five blocks to find some change because Mrs. Smith had had only a $20 bill. At these spare moments—and Clive managed one or two a week—he visited Madame Thibault's Waxwork Horrors.

Inside the establishment you went through a dark passage—to be put in the mood—and then you were confronted by a bloody murder scene on the left: a girl with long blonde hair was sticking a knife into the neck of an old man who sat at a kitchen table eating his dinner. His dinner consisted of two wax frankfurters and wax sauerkraut. Then came the Lindbergh kidnaping scene, with Hauptmann climbing down a ladder outside a nursery window; you could see the top of the ladder out the window, and the top half of Hauptmann's figure, clutching the little boy. Also there was Marat in his bath with Charlotte nearby. And Christie with his stocking, throttling a woman.

Clive loved every tableau, and they never became stale. But he didn't look at them with the solemn, vaguely startled expression of the other people who looked at them. Clive was inclined to smile, even to laugh. They were amusing. So why not laugh?

Farther on in the museum were the torture chambers—one old, one modern, purporting to show Twentieth Century torture methods in Nazi Germany and in French Algeria. Madame Thibault—who Clive strongly suspected did not exist—kept up to date. There were the Kennedy assassinations and the Tate massacre, of course, and some murder that had happened only a month ago somewhere.

Clive's first definite ambition in regard to Madame Thibault's Waxwork Horrors museum was to spend a night there. This he did one night, providently taking along a cheese sandwich in his pocket. It was fairly easy to accomplish. Clive knew that three people worked in the museum proper—down in the bowels, as he thought of it, though the museum was on street level—while a fourth, a plumpish middle-aged man in a nautical cap, sold tickets at a booth in front. The three who worked in the bowels were two men and a woman; the woman, also plump and with curly brown hair and glasses and about forty, took the tickets at the end of the dark corridor, where the museum proper began.

One of the inside men lectured constantly, though not more than half the people ever bothered to listen. "Here we see the fanatical expression of the true murderer, captured by the supreme wax artistry of Madame Thibault"—and so on. The other inside man had black hair and black-rimmed glasses like the woman, and he just drifted around, shooing away kids who wanted to climb into the tableaux, maybe watching for pickpockets, or maybe protecting women from unpleasant assaults in the semi-darkness. Clive didn't know.

He only knew it was quite easy to slip into one of the dark corners or into a nook next to one of the Iron Molls—maybe even into one of the Iron Molls; but slender as he was, the spikes might poke into him, Clive thought, so he ruled out this idea. He had observed that people were gently urged out around 9:15 P.M., as the museum closed at 9:30 P.M. And lingering as late as possible one evening, Clive had learned that there was a sort of cloakroom for the staff behind a door in one back corner, from which direction he had also heard the sound of a toilet flushing.

So one night in November, Clive concealed himself in the shadows, which were abundant, and listened to the three people as they got ready to leave. The woman—whose name turned out to be Mildred—was lingering to take the money box from Fred, the ticket seller, and to count it and deposit it somewhere in the cloakroom. Clive was not interested in the money. He was interested only in spending a night in the place and being able to boast he had.

"Night, Mildred—see you tomorrow," called one of the men.

"Anything else to do? I'm leaving now," said Mildred. "Boy, am I tired! But I'm still going to watch Dragon Man tonight."

"Dragon Man," the other man repeated, uninterested.

Evidently the ticket seller, Fred, left from the front of the building after handing in the money box, and in fact Clive recalled seeing him close up the front once, cutting the lights from inside the entrance door, then locking the door and barring it on the outside.

Clive stood in a nook by an Iron Moll. When he heard the back door shut and the key turn in the lock, he waited for a moment in delicious silence, aloneness, and suspense, and then ventured out. He went first, on tiptoe, to the room where they kept their coats, because he had never seen it. He had brought matches—also cigarettes, though smoking was not allowed, according to several signs—and with the aid of a match he found the light switch. The room contained an old desk, four metal lockers, a tin wastebasket, an umbrella stand, and some books in a bookcase against a grimy wall that had once been white. Clive slid open a drawer and found the well-worn wooden box which he had once seen the ticket seller carrying in through the front door. The box was locked. He could walk out with the box, Clive thought, but he didn't care to, and he considered this rather decent of himself. He gave the box a wipe with the side of his hand, not forgetting the bottom where his fingertips had touched. That was funny, he thought, wiping something he wasn't going to steal.

Clive set about enjoying the night. He found the lights and put them on so that the booths with the gory tableaux were all illuminated. He was hungry, took one bite of his sandwich, then put it back in the paper napkin in his pocket. He sauntered slowly past the John F. Kennedy assassination—Mrs. Kennedy and the doctors bending anxiously over the white table on which JFK lay. This time, Hauptmann's descent of the ladder made Clive giggle. Charles Lindbergh, Jr.'s face looked so untroubled that one would think he might be sitting on the floor of his nursery, playing with blocks.

Clive swung a leg over a metal bar and climbed into the Gray-Snyder tableau. It gave him a thrill to be standing right *with* them, inches from the throttling-from-behind which the lover of the woman was administering to the husband. Clive put a hand out and touched the red-paint blood that was seeming to come from the man's throat where the cord pressed deep. Clive also touched the cool cheekbones of the victim. The popping eyes were of glass, vaguely disgusting, and Clive did not touch those.

Two hours later he was singing church hymns, "Nearer My God to Thee" and "Jesus Wants Me for a Sunbeam." Clive didn't know all the words. And he smoked.

By two in the morning he was bored and tried to get out by both the front door and back, but couldn't—both were barred on the outside. He had thought of having a hamburger at an all-night diner between here and home. However, his enforced incarceration didn't bother him, so he finished the now-dry cheese sandwich and slept for a bit on three straight chairs which he arranged in a row. It was so uncomfortable that he knew he'd wake up in a while, which he did—at 5:00 A.M. He washed his face, then went for another look at the wax exhibits. This time he took a souvenir—Woodrow Wilson's necktie.

As the hour of 9:00 approached—Madame Thibault's Waxwork Horrors opened at 9:30 A.M.—Clive hid himself in an excellent spot, behind one of the tableaux whose backdrop was a black-and-gold Chinese screen. In front of the screen was a bed and in the bed lay a wax man with a handlebar mustache, who was supposed to have been poisoned by his wife.

The public began to trickle in shortly after 9:30 A.M., and the taller, more solemn man began to mumble his boring lecture. Clive had to wait till a few minutes past ten before he felt safe enough to mingle with the crowd and make his exit, with Woodrow Wilson's necktie rolled up in his pocket. He was a bit tired, but happy—though on second thought, who would he tell about it? Joey Vrasky, that dumb cluck who worked behind the counter at Simmons' Grocery? Hah! Why bother? Joey didn't deserve a good story. Clive was half an hour late for work.

"I'm sorry, Mr. Simmons, I overslept," Clive said hastily, but he thought quite politely, as he came into the store. There was a delivery job awaiting him. Clive took his bicycle and put the carton on a platform in front of the handlebars.

Clive lived with his mother, a thin highly strung woman who was a saleswoman in a shop that sold stockings, girdles, and underwear. Her husband had left her when Clive was nine. She had no other children. Clive had quit high school a year before graduation, to his mother's regret, and for a year he had done nothing but lie around the house or stand on street corners with his pals. But Clive had never been very chummy with any of them, for which his mother was thankful, as she considered them a worthless lot. Clive had had the delivery job at Simmons' for nearly a year now, and his mother felt that he was settling down.

When Clive came home that evening at 6:30 P.M. he had a story ready for his mother. Last night he had run into his old friend Richie, who was in the Army and home on leave, and they had sat up at Richie's house talking so late that Richie's parents had invited him to stay over, and Clive had slept on the couch. His mother accepted this explanation. She made a supper of baked beans, bacon, and eggs.

There was really no one to whom Clive felt like telling his exploit of the night. He couldn't have borne someone looking at him and saying, "Yeah? So what?" because what he had done had taken a bit of planning, even a little daring. He put Woodrow Wilson's tie among his others that hung over a string on the inside of his closet door. It was a gray silk tie, conservative and expensive-looking. Several times that day Clive imagined one of the two men in the museum, or maybe the woman named Mildred, glancing at Woodrow Wilson and exclaiming, "Hey! What happened to Woodrow Wilson's tie, I wonder?"

Each time Clive thought of this he had to duck his head to hide a smile.

After twenty-four hours, however, the exploit had begun to lose its charm and excitement. Clive's excitement only rose again—and it could rise two or three times a day—whenever he cycled past the twinkling façade of Madame Thibault's Waxwork Horrors. His heart would give a leap, his blood would run a little faster, and he would think of all the motionless murders going on in there, and all the stupid faces of Mr. and Mrs. Johnny Q. Public gaping at them. But Clive didn't even buy another ticket—price 65 cents—to go in and look at Woodrow Wilson and see that his tie was missing and his collar button showing—his work.

Clive did get another idea one afternoon, a hilarious idea that would make the public sit up and take notice. Clive's ribs trembled with suppressed laughter as he pedaled toward Simmons', having just delivered a bag of groceries.

When should he do it? Tonight? No, best to take a day or so to plan it. It would take brains. And silence. And sure movements—all the things Clive admired.

He spent two days thinking about it. He went to his local snack bar and drank beer and played the pinball machines with his pals. The pinball machines had pulsating lights too—*More Than One Can Play* and *It's More Fun To Compete*—but Clive thought only of Madame Thibault's as he stared at the rolling, bouncing balls that mounted a score he cared nothing about. It was the same when he looked at the rainbow-colored jukebox whose blues, reds, and yellows undulated, and when he went over to drop a coin in it. He was thinking of what he was going to do in Madame Thibault's Waxwork Horrors.

On the second night, after a supper with his mother, Clive went to Madame Thibault's and bought a ticket. The old guy who sold tickets barely looked at people, he was so busy making change and tearing off the stubs, which was just as well. Clive went in at 9:00 P.M.

He looked at the tableaux, though they were not so fascinating to him tonight as they had been before. Woodrow Wilson's tie was still missing, as if no one had noticed it, and Clive chuckled over this. He remembered that the solemn-faced pickpocket-watcher— the drifting snoop—had been the last to leave the night Clive had stayed, so Clive assumed he had the keys, and therefore he ought to be the last to be killed.

The woman was the first. Clive hid himself beside one of the Iron Molls again, while the crowd ambled out, and when Mildred walked by him, in her hat and coat, to leave by the back door, having just said something to one of the men in the exhibition hall, Clive stepped out and wrapped an arm around her throat from behind.

She made only a small *ur-rk* sound.

Clive squeezed her throat with his hands, stopping her voice. At last she slumped, and Clive dragged her into a dark, recessed corner to the left of the cloakroom. He knocked an empty cardboard box of some kind over, but it didn't make enough noise to attract the attention of the two men.

"Mildred's gone?" one of the men asked.

"I think she's in the office."

"No, she's not." The owner of this voice had already gone into the corridor where Clive crouched over Mildred and had looked into the empty cloakroom where the light was still on. "She's left. Well, I'm calling it a day too."

Clive stepped out then and encircled this man's neck in the same manner. The job was more difficult, because the man struggled, but Clive's arm was thin and strong; he acted with swiftness and knocked the man's head against the wooden floor.

"What's going on?" The thump had brought the second man.

This time Clive tried a punch to the man's jaw, but missed and hit his neck. However, this so stunned the man—the little solemn fellow, the snoop—that a quick second blow was easy, and then Clive was able to take him by the shirtfront and bash his head against the plaster wall which was harder than the wooden floor. Then Clive made sure that all three were dead. The two men's heads were bloody. The woman was bleeding slightly from her mouth. Clive reached for the keys in the second man's pockets. They were in his left trousers pocket and with them was a penknife. Clive also took the knife.

Then the taller man moved slightly. Alarmed, Clive opened the pearl-handled penknife and plunged it into the man's throat three times.

Close call, Clive thought, as he checked again to make sure they were all dead. They most certainly were, and that was most certainly real blood, not the red paint of Madame Thibault's Waxwork Horrors. Clive switched on the lights for the tableaux and went into the exhibition hall for the interesting task of choosing exactly the right places for the three corpses.

The woman belonged in Marat's bath—not much doubt about that. Clive debated removing her clothing, but decided against it, simply because she would look much funnier sitting in a bath wearing a fur-trimmed coat and hat. The figure of Marat sent him off into laughter. He'd expected sticks for legs, and nothing between the legs, because you couldn't see any more of Marat than from the middle of his torso up; but Marat had no legs at all and his wax body ended just below the waist in a fat stump which was planted on a wooden platform so that it would not topple. This crazy waxwork Clive carried into the cloakroom and placed squarely in the middle of the desk. He then carried the woman—who weighed a good deal—onto the Marat scene and put her in the bath. Her hat fell off, and he pushed it on again, a bit over one eye. Her bloody mouth hung open.

Good lord, it *was* funny!

Now for the men. Obviously, the one whose throat he had knifed would look good in the place of the old man who was eating wax franks and sauerkraut, because the girl behind him was supposed to be stabbing him in the throat. This took Clive some fifteen minutes. Since the figure of the old man was in a seated position, Clive put him on the toilet off the cloakroom. It was terribly amusing to see the old man seated on the toilet, throat apparently bleeding, a knife in one hand and a fork in the other. Clive lurched against the door jamb, laughing loudly, not even caring if someone heard him, because it was so comical it was even worth getting caught for.

Next, the little snoop. Clive looked around him and his eye fell on the Woodrow Wilson scene which depicted the signing of the armistice in 1918. A wax figure sat at a huge desk signing something, and that was the logical place for a man whose head was almost split open. With some difficulty Clive got the pen out of the wax man's fingers, laid it to one side on the desk, and carried the figure—it didn't weigh much—into the cloakroom, where Clive seated him at the desk, rigid arms in an attitude of writing. Clive stuck a ballpoint pen into his right hand. Now for the last heave. Clive saw that his jacket was now quite spotted with blood and he would have to get rid of it, but so far there was no blood on his trousers.

Clive dragged the second man to the Woodrow Wilson tableau, lifted him up, and rolled him toward the desk. He got him onto the chair, but the head toppled forward onto the green-blottered desk, onto the blank wax pages, and the pen barely stood upright in the limp hand.

But it was done. Clive stood back and smiled. Then he listened. He sat down on a straight chair and rested for a few minutes, because his heart was beating fast and he suddenly realized that every muscle in his body was tired. Ah, well, he now had the keys. He could lock up, go home, and have a good night's rest, because he wanted to be ready to enjoy tomorrow.

Clive took a sweater from one of the male figures in a log-cabin tableau of some kind. He had to pull the sweater down over the feet of the waxwork to get it off, because the arms would not bend; it stretched the neck of the sweater, but he couldn't help that. Now the wax figure had a sort of bib for a shirtfront, and naked arms and chest.

Clive wadded up his jacket and went everywhere with it, erasing fingerprints from whatever he thought he had touched. He turned the lights off, made his way carefully to the back door, locked and barred it behind him, and would have left the keys in a mailbox if there had been one; but there wasn't, so he dropped the keys on the rear doorstep. In a wire rubbish basket he found some newspapers; he wrapped up his jacket in them and walked on with it until he found another wire rubbish basket, where he forced the bundle down among candy wrappers, beer cans, and other trash.

"A new sweater?" his mother asked that night.

"Richie gave it to me—for luck."

Clive slept like the dead, too tired even to laugh again at the memory of the old man sitting on the toilet.

The next morning Clive was standing across the street when the ticketseller arrived just before 9:30 A.M. By 9:35 A.M. only four people had gone in; but Clive could not wait any longer, so he crossed the street and bought a ticket. Now the ticket seller was doubling as ticket taker, and telling people, "Just go on in. Everybody's late this morning."

The ticket man stepped inside the door to put on some lights, then walked all the way into the place to put on the display lights for the tableaux, which worked from switches in the hall that led to the cloakroom. And the funny thing, to Clive who was walking behind him, was that the ticket man didn't notice anything odd, didn't even notice Mildred in her hat and coat sitting in Marat's bathtub.

The other customers so far were a man and a woman, a boy of fourteen or so in sneakers, alone apparently, and a single man. They looked expressionlessly at Mildred in the tub as if they thought it quite "normal," which would have sent Clive into paroxysms of mirth, except that his heart was thumping madly and he could hardly breathe for the suspense. Also, the man with his face in franks and sauerkraut brought no surprise either. Clive was a bit disappointed.

Two more people came in, a man and a woman.

Then at last, in front of the Woodrow Wilson tableau, there was a reaction. One of the women, clinging to her husband's arm, asked, "Was someone shot when the armistice was signed?"

"I don't know. I don't *think* so," the man replied vaguely.

Clive's laughter pressed like an explosion in his chest; he spun on his heel to control himself, and he had the feeling he knew *all* about history, and that no one else did. By now, of course, the real blood had turned to a rust color. The green blotter was now splotched, and blood had dripped down the side of the desk.

A woman on the other side of the room, where Mildred was, let out a scream.

A man laughed, but only briefly.

Suddenly everything happened. A woman shrieked, and at the same time a man yelled, "My God, it's *real!*"

Clive saw a man climbing up to investigate the corpse with his face in the frankfurters.

"The blood's *real!* It's a *dead* man!"

Another man—one of the public—slumped to the floor. He had fainted.

The ticket seller came bustling in. "What's the trouble here?"

"Coupla corpses—*real* ones!"

Now the ticket seller looked at Marat's bathtub and fairly jumped into the air with surprise. "Holy Christmas! *Holy* cripes!—it's *Mildred!*"

"And this one!"

"And the one here!"

"My God, got to—got to call the police!" said the ticket seller.

One man and woman left hurriedly. But the rest lingered, shocked, fascinated.

The ticket seller had run into the cloakroom, where the telephone was, and Clive heard him yell something. He'd seen the man at the desk, of course, the wax man, and the half body of Marat on the desk.

Clive thought it was time to drift out, so he did, sidling his way through a group of people peering in the front door, perhaps intending to come in because there was no ticket seller.

That was good, Clive thought. That was all right. Not bad. Not bad at all.

He had not intended to go to work that day, but suddenly he thought it wiser to check in and ask for the day off. Mr. Simmons was of course as sour as ever when Clive said he was not feeling well, but as Clive held his stomach and appeared weak, there was little old Simmons could do. Clive left the grocery. He had brought with him all his ready cash, about $23.

Clive wanted to take a long bus ride somewhere. He realized that suspicion might fall on him, if the ticket seller remembered his coming to Madame Thibault's often, or especially if he remembered Clive being there last night; but this really had little to do with his desire to take a bus ride. His longing for a bus ride was simply, somehow, irresistible. He bought a ticket westward for $8 and change, one way. This brought him, by about 7:00 P.M., to a good-sized town in Indiana, whose name Clive paid no attention to.

The bus spilled a few passengers, Clive included, at a terminal, where there was a cafeteria and a bar. By now Clive was curious about the newspapers, so he went to the newsstand near the street door of the cafeteria. And there were the headlines:

Triple Murder in Waxworks
Mass Murder in Museum
Mystery Killer Strikes: Three Dead in Waxworks

Clive liked the last one best. He bought the three newspapers, and stood at the bar with a beer.

"This morning at 9:30 A.M., ticket-man Fred J. Carmody and several of the public who had come to see Madame Thibault's Waxwork Horrors, a noted attraction of this city, were confronted by three genuine corpses among the displays. They were the bodies of Mrs. Mildred Veery, 41; George P. Hartley, 43; and Richard K. McFadden, 37, all employed at the waxworks museum. The two men were killed by concussion and stabbing, and the woman by strangulation. Police are searching for clues on the premises. The murders are believed to have taken place shortly before 10:00 P.M. last evening, when the three employees were about to leave the museum. The murderer or murderers may have been among the last patrons of the museum before closing time at 9:30 P.M. It is thought that he or they may have concealed themselves somewhere in the museum until the rest of the patrons had left . . ."

Clive was pleased. He smiled as he sipped his beer. He hunched over the papers, as if he did not wish the rest of the world to share his pleasure, but this was not true. After a few minutes Clive stood up and looked to the right and left to see if anyone else among the men and women at the bar was also reading the story. Two men were reading newspapers, but Clive could not tell if they were reading about him, because their newspapers were folded.

Clive lit a cigarette and went through all three newspapers to see if any clue to him was mentioned. He found nothing. One paper said specifically that Fred J. Carmody had not noticed any person or persons entering the museum last evening who looked suspicious.

". . . Because of the bizarre arrangement of the victims and of the displaced wax figures in the exhibition, in whose places the victims were put, police are looking for a psychopathic killer. Residents of the area have been warned by radio and television to take special precautions on the streets and to keep their houses locked."

Clive chuckled over that one. Psychopathic killer! He was sorry about the lack of detail, the lack of humor in the three reporters' stories. They might have said something about the old guy sitting on the toilet. Or the fellow signing the armistice with the back of his head bashed in. Those were strokes of genius. Why didn't they appreciate them?

When he had finished his beer, Clive walked out onto the sidewalk. It was now dark and the streetlights were on. He enjoyed looking around in the new town, looking into shop windows. But he was aiming for a hamburger place, and he went into the first one he came to. It was a diner made up to look like a crack railway car.

Clive ordered a hamburger and a cup of coffee. Next to him were two Western-looking men in cowboy boots and rather soiled broad-brimmed hats. Was one a sheriff, Clive wondered? But they were talking, in a drawl, about acreage somewhere. Land. They were hunched over hamburgers and coffee, one so close that his elbow kept touching Clive's. Clive was reading his newspapers all over again and he had propped one against the napkin container in front of him.

One of the men asked for a napkin and disturbed Clive, but Clive smiled and said in a friendly way, "Did you read about the murders in the waxworks?"

The man looked blank for a moment, then said, "Yep, saw the headlines."

"Someone killed the three people who worked in the place. Look." There was a photograph in one of the papers, but Clive didn't much like it because it showed the corpses lined up on the floor. He would have preferred Mildred in the bathtub.

"Yeah," said the Westerner, edging away from Clive as if he didn't like him.

"The bodies were put into a few of the exhibits. Like the wax figures. They say that, but they don't show a picture of it," said Clive.

"Yeah," said the Westerner, and went on eating.

Clive felt let down and somehow insulted. His face grew a little warm as he stared back at his newspapers. In fact, anger was growing quickly inside him, making his heart go faster, as it always did when he passed Madame Thibault's Waxwork Horrors, though now the sensation was not at all pleasant.

Clive put on a smile, however, and turned to the man on his left again. "I mention it, because I did it. That's my work there." He gestured toward the picture of the corpses.

"Listen, boy," said the Westerner casually, "you just keep to yourself tonight. Okay? We ain't botherin' you, so don't you go botherin' us." He laughed a little, glancing at his companion.

His friend was staring at Clive, but looked away at once when Clive stared back.

This was a double rebuff, and quite enough for Clive. He got out his money and paid for his unfinished food with a dollar bill. He left the change and walked to the sliding-door exit.

"But y'know, maybe that guy ain't kiddin'," Clive heard one of the men say.

Clive turned and said, "I *ain't* kiddin'!" Then he went out into the night.

Clive slept at a YMCA. The next day he half expected he would be picked up by a passing cop on the beat, but he wasn't. He got a lift to another town, nearer his hometown. The day's newspapers brought no mention of his name, and no mention of clues. In another café that evening, almost the identical conversation took place between Clive and a couple of fellows his own age. They didn't believe him. It was stupid of them, Clive thought, and he wondered if they were pretending? Or lying?

Clive hitched his way home and headed for the police station. He was curious as to what *they* would say. He imagined what his mother would say after he confessed. Probably the same thing she had said to her friends sometimes, or that she'd said to a policeman when he was sixteen and had stolen a car.

"Clive hasn't been the same since his father went away. I know he needs a man around the house, a man to look up to, imitate, you know. That's what people tell me. Since he was fourteen Clive's been asking me questions like, 'Who am I, anyway?' and 'Am I a person, mom?'" Clive could see and hear her in the police station.

"I have an important confession to make," Clive said to a deskman in the front.

The man's attitude was rude and suspicious, Clive thought, but he was told to walk to an office, where he spoke with a police officer who had gray hair and a fat face. Clive told his story.

"Where do you go to school, Clive?"

"I don't. I'm eighteen." Clive told him about his job at Simmons' Grocery.

"Clive, you've got troubles, but they're not the ones you're talking about," said the officer.

Clive had to wait in a room, and nearly an hour later a psychiatrist was brought in. Then his mother. Clive became more and more impatient. They didn't believe him. They were saying his was a typical case of false confession in order to draw attention to himself. His mother's repeated statements about his asking questions like "Am I a person?" and "Who am I?" only seemed to corroborate the opinions of the psychiatrist and the police.

Clive was to report somewhere twice a week for psychiatric therapy.

He fumed. He refused to go back to Simmons' Grocery, but found another delivery job, because he liked having a little money in his pocket, and he was fast on his bicycle and honest with the change.

"You haven't *found* the murderer, have you?" Clive said to the police psychiatrist. "You're all the biggest bunch of jackasses I've ever seen in my life!"

The psychiatrist said soothingly, "You'll never get anywhere talking to people like that, boy."

Clive said, "Some perfectly ordinary strangers in Indiana said, 'Maybe that guy ain't kidding.' They had more sense that *you!*"

The psychiatrist smiled.

Clive smoldered. One thing might have helped to prove his story—Woodrow Wilson's necktie, which still hung in his closet. But these dumb clucks damned well didn't deserve to see that tie. Even as he ate his suppers with his mother, went to the movies, and delivered groceries, he was planning. He'd do something more important next time—like starting a fire in the depths of a big building or planting a bomb somewhere or taking a machine gun up to some penthouse and letting 'em have it down on the street. Kill a hundred people at least, or a thousand. They'd have to come up in the building to get him. *Then* they'd know. *Then* they'd treat him like somebody who really existed, like somebody who deserved an exhibit of himself in Madame Thibault's Waxwork Horrors.

A DAY OF ENCOUNTERS

by Anthony Gilbert

Two women, complete strangers to each other, meet in the waiting room of St. Barnabas' Eye Clinic—and thereby hangs a tale. And is there anyone in the mystery field who can write more convincingly about certain types of women than Anthony Gilbert? Always there was that special touch . . .

I NOTICED the woman the minute she came into the clinic—St. Barnabas' Eye Clinic where I go every six weeks about a little trouble I have. I'm Martita Browne and you've probably seen my books all over the place. Eggheads despise them, but I consider myself a benefactress. Even in the Affluent Society lots of women lead pretty dreary lives. So my books are like a magic mirror that reflects them as they see themselves, not as they appear to husbands or families—beautiful, loyal, courageous, even though they may scream at the sight of a mouse, and above all irresistible to men; and, naturally, only to be had at the cost of a wedding ring. Services like that are worth paying for, and, to do my readers justice, they pay at the rate of substantial royalties to me every year.

This newcomer—I realized at once I'd never seen her before, you get to know the regulars—didn't resemble my heroines in any way. For one thing, she was past forty, not good-looking, though she had a lively face that was somehow demure, too, which wasn't without attraction. But though her clothes were good—her crocodile bag alone had set someone back about £60, her scarf was pure heavy silk, and her shoes handmade—she lacked something, a kind of vitality perhaps. There was a man with her, presumably her husband, a fair, quiet sort of fellow, but not living on the breadline—far from it. An expensive house in the suburbs, I thought, with central heating, a double garage, storm windows, at least one trip abroad every year, and not a package tour at that.

I usually sit in a sort of alcove that holds only three or four chairs, and hardly anyone else ever chooses them. The patients have an idea that if they sit in the middle of the room they'll be seen sooner, but, of course, it doesn't help; it's all poppycock— you're seen when the doctor's ready for you and not before. I'd brought the proofs of my new book with me—*Not Wooed but Won*—and I thought I might get quite a lot of work done while I waited. I could see it was going to be a busy clinic this afternoon.

I was a bit surprised when the newcomer came to sit beside me. "Is it always as crowded as this?" she asked. "Willy said he'd be back in an hour and he does hate waiting." Then before I could reply she saw the proofs on my lap—I hadn't begun, so the title page was on top. "Are you Martita Browne?" she asked. "Did you write that?"

I knew what was coming, of course. She'd always longed to write, but there'd never been time; her life story would make a wonderful plot, and since she'd never use it—and of course I'd disguise the names. If I've heard that once, I've heard it a hundred times. I was wondering how I could suggest that none of my readers would be interested in a woman in her forties when she gushed on, "People say that sometimes your heroes are too good to be true, but of course that's nonsense. I know because—well, you might say I married one of them. You might have taken Victor for your model."

"I thought you said his name was Willy," I murmured.

"Victor was my first husband. Willy's as different as chalk from cheese. Victor had everything—good looks, a marvelous figure, tall, dark, alluring—it wasn't surprising all the women were after him. I'm sure they must all have gasped when they heard it was me he was going to marry. I wasn't even young—twenty-eight— you'd never have a heroine of twenty-eight, would you, Miss Browne?"

Well, she knew I wouldn't. My readers never see themselves as more than twenty-five at the very most.

"I wasn't in the least like one of your heroines," the voice babbled on. "My father—he was a minister with a great sense of fun—everyone said so—used to call me Miss Brains-Before-Beauty. Count your blessings, he'd say. Brains are often a better investment. And I put mine out to usury like that man in the Bible, whose ten talents turned into twenty talents. I never really thought I'd get married."

"But there was Victor?" I remarked.

"Yes. He came into this office where I was working—actually, it was my own business—and it was like the sun coming in. He was a bit younger than me, but he said he preferred mature women. Girls never had any conversation except hairdos and what he called 'parish pump' subjects."

"What was his job?" I asked. It was quite automatic. I couldn't have even a minor character in a story without knowing his background, and obviously Victor wasn't going to be minor.

"Oh!" For the first time she sounded evasive. "He was a sales representative—went round to the big industrial houses."

"A success?" I bored on. You might say it was none of my business, but the woman had thrust herself on me and I had a right to some return. Anyway, you can never be sure where you'll find plot and character ideas.

"You'd have thought with those looks and that charm he couldn't fail, though he always warned me it was cutthroat competition, and I suppose he wasn't ruthless enough. Still, at first everything went all right, and then he started going 'on the road.' You know what that means? The firms—and they weren't always the same firms—sent him to the outlying districts. He made a joke of it. Someone's got to carry news to the heathen, he'd say, but—oh, Miss Browne, it was like playing Shaftesbury Avenue and then finding yourself sent out with a second-class repertory company. Luckily I wasn't called Miss Brains-Before-Beauty for nothing. I'd sold my business when I got married, so I had a nice little nest egg put by, and believe me, it came in very useful."

Candidly, I didn't think this was getting me anywhere. A plain woman had been married for her money—that's what it amounted to. But of course there had to be a third party, otherwise there was no story at all. And even I couldn't believe *she* would turn up with a lover.

"So what happened?" I encouraged.

Her reply startled me. "Oh, he died."

"Victor died?"

"Yes. It was a bit sudden."

I had a fresh idea. "Sudden enough to attract the attention of the police?"

She took off her handsome gloves and folded them carefully on her knee. Her rings would have paid my rent for a year.

"Anyone could tell you *are* a writer. You know all the answers."

But did I? There'd been an odd note in her voice when she said, "Oh, he died." Not grief, not relief either, but a sort of lack of confidence, as if she couldn't be certain. But that was nonsense. You either know your husband's dead or you don't. Or perhaps she knew he wasn't, and he was blackmailing her. It seemed pretty obvious she'd struck it rich in her second marriage. I was so deep in calculations that I missed the next few sentences, but what I did hear nearly blew me out of my chair.

"You couldn't call it murder, could you?" the voice pleaded. "I've waited eight years to hear someone say that, only there was never anyone to tell. I don't even have a sister."

And wouldn't tell her if you had, I thought grimly. Not if you've got the sense you were born with.

I realized now, of course, that she had no doubts about dear Victor's death—a posh funeral and wreaths three foot deep, most likely. No, it was the way of it that worried her. But—murder? I hadn't time to think straight.

"What did the police make of it?" I asked. "I mean, who mentioned murder?"

"There were only three alternatives—accident, suicide, or murder—and no one could believe it was an accident."

"Why should it be a suicide?"

"Well, there was this girl—Elizabeth Sinclair."

Inwardly I heaved a sigh of relief. So we'd got to the heart of the story at last—the third side of the triangle, without which there's no story at all.

"People used to ask me sometimes—aren't you afraid of someone trying to steal your handsome husband now that he's away from home so much? But I wasn't. Oh, there might be incidents, but a sensible wife shuts her eyes to them. He was away three or four days on end sometimes. Frankly, I didn't see how he could afford to leave me. It's a cruel thing to say about a dead man, Miss Browne, but—well, charm's like anything else: it gets tarnished, and thirty-six is different from twenty-four, which was his age when we married. It appeared he'd met this girl—she was barely twenty-one—and it had been love at first sight for both of them."

"I thought you said he couldn't afford to keep a wife. Or did Elizabeth have money?"

"She was the only daughter of a very rich man—the only child—and she'd get everything."

"Unless Daddy married again." I took for granted he was a widower.

Her mouth hardened. "You didn't know Victor. He'd have insisted on a prenuptial settlement—and he'd have got it. I don't say Daddy would have approved, but Elizabeth was the kind no man can resist. Now, *there* was a heroine for you, Miss Browne. Dark and slender and—glowing. You remember Shelley's moon-maiden, with white fire laden? She made me think of that. I only saw her the once, you know."

"You mean he brought her?" Victor was proving himself less and less like one of my heroes.

"She brought herself. 'I thought if I came in person, perhaps you'd understand,' she said. 'Oh, how can you want to hold onto him when you know it's me he loves? Why won't you divorce him, Mrs. Hughes? You've had twelve years—'

"And, of course, Victor could live another thirty. But not with this girl, I decided. If I'd been tempted to yield before, I was iron-hard now.

"'Surely she made you see—' That was Victor talking, when he came home.

"'So it was your idea?' I said. 'I might have guessed it. You must be mad if you think I'd make it possible for you to ruin that girl's life,' I said warmly. 'She's made for better than secondhand goods.'

"'I won't give her up,' Victor said.

"'There's no law to stop your setting up house,' I agreed. 'But would Daddy like that?' He raged, but he didn't move me. 'You'll only marry her over my dead body,' I said. Have you ever noticed, Miss Browne, how often clichés come home to roost?"

"But it was Victor's dead body," I pointed out.

"Yes."

"And there was talk of murder."

"It's what the police would have liked to believe," she said bitterly. "I suppose you can hardly blame them. You don't get promotion by arresting motorists for illegal parking."

"You want to be careful," I advised her sharply. "You never know who may be sitting next to you in a place like this. There's an ex-Superintendent Humbolt who comes here sometimes." He was one of the few useful contacts I'd made at the clinic; he'd helped me out of knotty problems once or twice when my heroines had been more feather-brained than usual. I knew what he'd say about Victor. Never trust charm, it's the most powerful weapon in the devil's armory. I've heard him say that more than once. "But why should anyone think it was murder?"

She went off at a bit of a tangent. "If you saw someone who'd cheated you sitting on a balcony, say, and a chimney pot started to topple, and you knew it would hit him and you didn't yell out, would that make you a murderer?"

It wasn't the sort of problem I've ever been called on to solve. Murder's taboo in my kind of tale. "Accessory before the fact?" I hazarded.

"Ah, but whose accessory? You can't be accessory to a force of nature—but what else caused the chimney pot to fall?"

"A good question," I agreed. I wondered what the pious would say. An Act of God? Not very complimentary to God, of course. Not that I supposed a chimney pot had actually played any part in this story. And of course it turned out to be just an analogy.

But talk about clichés! The truth was almost as incredible—the truth as she told it, that is.

It seems that it was Victor's custom to make their after-dinner coffee.

"And you let him do it, even after you'd refused him a divorce?" My most addle-pated heroine would have had more sense than that.

"If he'd meant to—to do away with me—he'd never have chosen anything so obvious."

"Sometimes the most obvious thing is also the most subtle."

"Anyway, that night—it was a few days after our conversation about Elizabeth and I thought he was accepting the situation—he'd just brought in the coffeepot and tray when the phone rang. I went to answer it, expecting it to be for me. But it was for Victor. When I came in he'd just poured out the coffee. 'Well, that was quick,' he said. 'Or was it a wrong number?' 'It's for you,' I told him.

" 'Chaps do choose the most inconvenient times,' he grumbled, looking at his coffee. 'He might have waited another five minutes.'

" 'It'll take five minutes to cool—or are you afraid I might lace it with arsenic while you're out of the room?' I said.

"He stared. 'That's a nice thing for a wife to say to her husband.' He jammed the cup down. 'Don't let yours grow cold. I poured it out'—and he went off, shutting the door behind him. It's funny, Miss Browne, how trifles can hold your attention. I hadn't thought anything about his pouring out both cups till he called my attention to it, and it made me wonder. You see, he knows—knew—I love everything piping hot, and if it had been Leila Hope on the phone—the call I'd expected—well, it's always ten minutes before she hangs up.

"I'd picked up my cup, but now I put it down and crept over and opened the door. The telephone was in an alcove in the hall, so that I could hear without being seen. Victor was laughing and joking, then suddenly his voice changed. 'I'm very anxious about her,' he said. 'She gets these moods, you can't reason with her, and she's inclined to be morbid. I can neither laugh nor argue her out of it.'

"I shut the door and came back to my chair. So that was his game, I thought. I was to be represented as being eccentric, so that anything might be expected of me. Automatically I picked up the coffee, and then the notion came to me. I'm not a writer, Miss Browne, though I'm quite a reader. And being alone so much I'd had time to think. And I wondered why he'd been so anxious that I drink my coffee hot. It wasn't like him to worry about things like that. And then his saying I was morbid."

I interrupted rather brutally. "So you decided he'd poisoned the coffee and then gone off to telephone. But how did he know it was going to ring then?"

"He could have arranged it, knowing I'd probably answer. Oh, I didn't think he intended murder. He knew the surviving partner would be the first suspect, and there was no one but ourselves in the house. But don't you see, that meant he could tell any story he liked! I thought he'd put in enough of whatever it was to make it necessary to call a doctor, who'd say it was attempted suicide, and then later, if, for instance, I fell under a subway train or something—I don't drive a car—everyone would remember the first time."

"Why didn't you pour the coffee out of the window?" I suggested sensibly.

"I didn't think of that, only of upsetting the table, and that would have meant breaking the cups; but then I'm not clumsy, so I'd have aroused his suspicions at once. Besides, I didn't see why he shouldn't be—what's the phrase?"

"Hoist on his own petard?"

"That's it. Biter bit. So—oh, Miss Browne, I switched the cups. I thought it would serve a dual purpose—make him uncomfortable and let him see I knew what he was up to. I thought of it as a self-protective measure."

"And when he came back?"

"I'd finished my cup, and he drank his—well, mine really. Then we each had a refill, and soon after he said he was tired and how about bed? Happy dreams, he said. Those were the last words I ever heard from him. When I went in next morning with a cup of tea—we had separate rooms by then, since I'd found out about

Elizabeth—oh, it was clear he wasn't going to be interested in tea any longer.

"The doctor said he must have been dead for quite some time; and he couldn't give a death certificate, he'd have to inform the coroner. That's when the horror suddenly became real. You're very clever, Miss Browne, not to have crimes in your books. People who like violence can get it in the newspapers. The police were in and out of that house like—like mites in a cheese."

"What was it he'd taken?"

"One of the barbiturates. I don't understand about medicine—I'm never ill, neither of us ever was. I hardly take an aspirin six times a year. Of course, they searched everything, almost took the paper off the walls, but they couldn't find even an empty vial. And seeing that I practically never went to a doctor they couldn't have traced the stuff to me, however much they'd wanted to."

"Where did they think he got it from?"

"No one knows, but he did travel for a firm of pharmaceutical chemists at one time. He could easily have got it that way, though I've heard you *can* get hold of drugs even without a doctor's prescription. But that was only the beginning. Accident was ruled out—which left suicide or murder. Everyone said he wouldn't have committed suicide, and I didn't think he would myself."

She paused, but I wasn't letting her stop there. It's not often an hour-and-a-half wait in a clinic can bring you a plum like this. "So it *had* to be murder?"

"Only it couldn't be. What advantage did I gain from his death, I asked them. I didn't inherit a penny—in fact, after the funeral I had to pay a large tailor's bill—he was very dandified about his clothes. If I'd wanted to be rid of him I had only to walk out. I had my own means, you know."

"You didn't think of telling them the simple truth?"

Her eyes stared at me, as round as pennies. "Well, naturally I thought of it; and naturally I held my tongue. There was no proof and if I let them know I had a suspicion—well, there was only my word for it that *I* hadn't doped the coffee. They wouldn't have got a conviction, I know that, but the mud would have stuck to me for life. Anyway, the verdict was death from barbiturate poisoning, with insufficient evidence to show how it had been administered.

"But that was bad enough. I was conscious of very odd looks wherever I went, and people in shops suddenly and mysteriously didn't have the things I wanted. A little later I changed back from Ruth Hughes to Ruth White—they're neither of them conspicuous names, are they?—and I came south. In London they might never have heard of Victor Hughes and quite likely they hadn't. Anyway, it's like that hymn you learn at school. 'They fly forgotten as a dream—' "

"And in London you met Willy?"

"Well, that was three years ago. I still had my capital and I went into partnership with a woman who ran an agency. I supplied the competence and she supplied the charm, which seemed to me quite a fair division of labor. When I met Willy—he was so different from Victor they might hardly have belonged to the same species."

"And yet they say that when people marry again, they always choose the same type," I reminded her.

"I suppose there has to be an exception to every rule. Victor had been so popular, but Willy seemed so—so neglected. He'd been a widower for years, had a bookshop, and was the studious type. The shop had great potentialities, but, oh, Miss Browne, the confusion in it, everything so hugger-mugger it would take a week to find anything a customer wanted. Willy lived—very uncomfortably—in two rooms above the shop. The first time I invited him back to my apartment for a meal he said, 'This is what I call a home. I've seen nothing like it since Edna died fifteen years ago.'

"He was so vague—if he'd been in Victor's shoes the police wouldn't have found any trouble at all in believing he'd taken the stuff himself thinking it was saccharine. I had a sense of responsibility towards him. That was the start. Of course, it was never like Victor, but I was forty-five by then, an age when your ardor has cooled off. And then, when once you've been married—

even if it hadn't worked out too well—well, it seems unnatural to be living alone.

"Anyway, we got married. I kept up my interest in the business—Willy had the shop, you see, and it wasn't as though we were likely to have a family—and weekends we worked among the books. I tell you, Miss Browne, you wouldn't recognize the place now. It's got quite a reputation. We can tell customers right away if we've got what they want in stock, and, if not, where we can get it and how long they must wait. A few months ago we put in a manager, a very capable fellow of about forty-five—sometimes I say to Willy, I don't know how we'd get on without Mr. Brett. It means Willy isn't tied down so much, he can go to book sales, have a bit of private life. Mr. Brett's a bachelor—it doesn't seem to matter to him how long hours he works."

I only had time for one more question before her name was called. "Did you tell Willy about Victor?"

She looked astounded, as though her eyes would drop out of her head.

"Of course not! All that happened to Mrs. Victor Hughes, and to me at least she's as dead as her husband. Nothing whatever to do with Willy."

Then her name was called and she jumped up with the eagerness of all new patients. I saw that she'd left her umbrella leaning against the chair, but I supposed she'd come back for it. I got down to my proofs at last; a while later I heard a creak as some heavy body descended alongside mine.

A voice said, "Well, Miss Browne, still at it, I see?"

I looked up and there was my old friend, ex-Superintendent Humbolt, though he doesn't insist on his former title any more. Pulling rank, he calls it.

"This is a day of encounters," I said. "I haven't seen you for a long time."

"Come for my semiannual checkup," he told me. "Fact is, my sight's not what it used to be. There's one disease none of the doctors can cure, and that's *Anno Domini*. And a good thing for the race it can't. We'd all be living in trees like chimps—there wouldn't be anywhere else to live."

"Oh, come on," I jollied him. "You're not that old. I was wondering if you could give me some advice."

"I knew it," he said mournfully. "All you ever want of me is a chance to pick my brains."

"It's a point arising from a story," I explained, carefully not saying it was one of mine. "If you'd been married to a man who tried to murder you, and later on you decided to marry again, would you tell Husband Number Two about Number One?"

"I'd never put the notion of murder in any husband's mind," he replied promptly.

"That solves my problem," I told him, and then he shook out his newspaper and I got to work.

A bit later a rather diffident voice said, "I was looking for my wife, and I believe this is her umbrella." And I looked up to see the rather vague-looking man who'd come with the "late" Mrs. Victor Hughes.

"It's quite a relief," he told me. "I thought I'd lost her."

An odd sound, like a bear chuckling to itself in a sardonic sort of way, came from behind the open newspaper.

"You want to be careful you don't make a habit of it, Willy." The newspaper was lowered. Ex-Superintendent Humbolt might appear to be grinning but his voice was the voice of Jehovah. "This 'ud be the third, wouldn't it? It never pays to overdo things. People get such strange ideas. Funny, you know."

"I don't call that very funny," said Willy. "I'm surprised at you, Mr. Humbolt."

"Your wife's seeing one of the doctors," I intervened quickly. "I don't suppose she'll be long."

"Don't want to get caught up in the rush hour on the underground," Humbolt went on, and Willy said, "I've got the car. We live out at Sheepshot now, and Ruth doesn't drive. Still, it's a nice house and a big garden. My wife enjoys gardening."

"Nothing wrong with gardening so long as you don't dig too

deep." I had never thought that Humbolt could be so malicious. And then *she* came hurrying back, saying, "Oh, Willy, did I keep you long? I had to wait, and the doctor thinks I should come again in six weeks."

"It'll be Harley Street for you next time, my dear," said Willy.

"You must meet Miss Browne, Martita Browne, the famous writer. You know." She didn't pay any attention to Humbolt. After all, she'd never set eyes on him before.

"Why did you say that, about losing wives?" I demanded, as soon as the couple was out of earshot. I simply had to know. If an angel had summoned me with a trumpet at that moment, I wouldn't have heard.

"The object of the police is to try and prevent crime," Humbolt said in his deceptively quiet way. "Poor Willy! He's lost a couple of wives already. Such a careless fellow—or could I be wrong? I mean, no doctors, no deathbeds. Number One was drowned in the South of France. They'd only been married two years. Something went wrong, the boat overturned, he kept swimming round and diving for her; they saw him from the shore, but he couldn't find her. She was under the boat, and they said she must have hit her head on something that knocked her out.

"Then about three years later he married again. It was the Costa Brava this time, and he was miles away, sunbathing. She'd taken the car—she brought that and some other very nice bits of goods you'd not turn your nose up at, Miss Browne, to the marriage—and had gone to visit friends. When she didn't come back he got anxious, phoned the friends' house, but she'd never arrived. Then he called the authorities, but you know how it is in Spain. *Mañana!*" He looked at me questioningly.

"I understand," I assured him. "Never do today what you can put off till tomorrow."

"She'd been dead for hours when they found her, under the wreck of the car. One of the Spanish police said, 'What a waste!

Such a beautiful motor!' Nothing about the lady, but I daresay when they found her she wasn't so beautiful."

"What did they think had happened?"

"No one could tell for sure, the car being in the state it was—something gone wrong with the steering, perhaps. Only— she had been proud of that car, had had it completely overhauled only the week before, when they'd left England. Still, there were no witnesses and a car can't talk. The advantage of coming to a sticky end in a warm foreign climate is you can't hang about waiting for relatives—"

"You mean, she was buried in Spain?"

"Both wives were buried abroad. Good sense really. The authorities make a lot of hoo-ha about shipping a corpse home—much less trouble and, of course, much more economical to have it buried on the spot. Wonder if the new Mrs. Willy likes to travel."

"I don't think she said. Just that she'd met him by way of business. Gone to his shop to buy a book, I suppose." That surprised me. She looked the sort who would expect to get her reading from the Public Library.

Humbolt shook his head. "They met at her place of business, not his."

"She said she ran some sort of agency with another woman."

"That's right. Marriage bureau. Fact, Miss Browne. They'll tell you there's one born every minute, and you don't have to be a policeman to know it's true. Convenient for chaps like Willy: you get all the statistics about the lady, age, looks—they have to supply a photograph and not one taken twenty years ago at that—financial position—the agency does all your homework for you. It's my belief if a chimp walked into one of those places they'd match him up with a woman chimp."

He thought a moment, then went on, "I suppose it occurred to Willy he could hardly do better than to marry the boss. To my way of thinking he's no matinee idol, but somehow he gets the women. That quality called charm, I suppose. She kept on with her interest in the agency, and he had the shop—got a very good name now, I understand, quite a little gold mine."

"I thought you were retired," I remarked maliciously.

"Once a copper always a copper. I'll retire when they start ringing the church bell for me. Still, as you say, no skin off my nose."

"It proves one thing," I said. "Women do always go for the same type. Willy may not look remotely like Victor, but they're chips from the same block."

I saw I'd really got his attention now. "Who's Victor?"

"Victor Hughes—her first husband."

"First time I heard she had one before she married Willy. Sure she's not pulling your leg?"

"After he died—"

"How was that?"

"You could call it a sort of accident."

"With or without wifely assistance?" The Day of Judgment will hold no shocks for that man.

"Let's say that she took a chance and it came off." I told him in detail about her switching the cups. "And if you don't believe me," I said, "there's bound to be a record. I'm not sure where it happened, but somewhere up north."

He shook his head. "Not me, Miss Browne. You've just reminded me, I'm retired and if there wasn't a trial—or was there?"

"There wasn't enough evidence to charge her. They never seemed to think of the fourth alternative—that he might have been the one with the murderous impulse."

"You bet they thought of it, but the police can't go on feminine intuition, not the way ladies do. No witnesses, no proof she'd ever handled a barbiturate in her life, and, like she said, no motive. Anyway, it wasn't my manor and the Chief Constable wouldn't thank me for raking up an old case. I've no fresh evidence. You might say it's a good thing she knows how to take care of herself, seeing who she's married to now."

"But you can't leave it at that," I exclaimed. "She could be in danger this very minute."

Humbolt has one of those India-rubber faces that can change under your eyes. Now he looked like a bloodhound—sad, a bit bloodshot, long drooping jowls. "You don't have to worry about her, Miss Browne, now that Willy knows we've met her. Even he 'ud be hard put to it to explain a third tragedy. Of course, if I was to drop dead, or you—but you take it from me, there'll be no need to search the newspapers for her name this side of Christmas."

Only the ex-superintendent was wrong. About four months later I picked up my *Morning Argus*—the posh papers are no good to writers like me—and there he was on the front page: *Well-Known Bookseller Falls to His Death*. It was in France—that was true to type, I thought—they'd been staying in one of these big old-fashioned hotels with a balcony and steps leading to a courtyard, a fountain, flowers, that sort of thing.

There was a gate in the trellis you could unbolt if you wanted to go down. The widow said they'd been talking and she went back into the bedroom for a cigarette, and the next minute she heard a scream and a sort of muffled crash and the trellis gate was swinging. It was two stories to the courtyard and Willy never recovered consciousness.

Everyone in the hotel was shocked—such an affectionate couple! Only they changed their tune when some busybody dug up the story of his previous wives. Then they started to talk about the mills of God grinding slowly, Providence seeing to it that he'd fallen into the pit he'd dug—meaning he'd opened the gate intending to give her a fatal shove, and then forgotten he'd opened it.

Her story was they'd been in the courtyard earlier, looking at the fish in the fountain, and he must have forgotten to bolt the gate after them. No, there was no family tomb, and burial on the spot, she was sure, was what he'd have preferred.

A few weeks ago I happened to be passing the bookshop. It was just about closing time, and Ruth came out with a tall dressy sort of fellow—forty-five or forty-six, I'd say.

When she saw me Ruth said, "Fancy meeting you again! Do you still go to that eye clinic? Do you remember me telling you about Mr. Brett? You did read about Willy, I expect? Wasn't it terrible? But he was always so absent-minded. I don't know what I'd have done without Malcolm."

It was easy to see who Malcolm was—easy, too, to realize she probably wasn't going to have to do without him.

I haven't seen Mr. Humbolt since—perhaps he doesn't come to the clinic any more. Of course, I'm only a writer of romantic tales, not works of logic or mystical speculation; but I do sometimes wonder, if there really is a Hereafter, what Victor and Willy are thinking now.

THE ISLAND OF BRIGHT BIRDS

by John Christopher

Quotes from reviews of John Christopher's novels: "strange, though always believable" . . . "terrifying story" . . . "written with fluency, color, and elegance" . . . "sensitive character development" . . . "insights often alarming" . . . "special kind of excitement" . . . "for best effects, read after midnight" . . . and "if the H. G. Wells of the fantastic stories has any true successor, it is fellow Englishman, John Christopher" . . .

We think you will find "The Island of Bright Birds" moving and disturbing, and chillingly neogothic . . .

THE first time she heard him speak, he was describing how he made his own bread, a fairly ordinary subject for a Chelsea party of this kind. But there was something in the voice, a strength, which was not so usual, and she half turned from her own group to identify him.

He was a short, slenderly built man who yet contrived to look powerful. He was about fifty, she thought, with silver-gray hair and a clipped silver-gray mustache, and it was plain that he kept himself in good physical condition. He moved his head, as though conscious of her gaze, and their eyes met. His were very blue, and direct, and she was the first to look away.

Later he spoke to her, catching her skillfully between groups, and getting her to himself.

"My name's Merronish, Adrian Merronish," he said. "Friend of John's. We knew each other in the war."

John and Helen Warrington were their hosts.

"I'm Angela Blake," she said.

"I wanted to talk to you," he said, "because you are so beautiful. But also because you are happy. I should think you are in love."

His sentences were short, but not clipped. Rather they carried an implication of flow, a wavelike hypnotic quality. What he said surprised but also pleased her. She said, laughing, "The last part's true."

"Is he here?"

She pointed. "Over there. The tall one with the fair curly hair."

He nodded in appraisal. "You make a handsome pair."

Peter, and her love for him, were the supremely important things in her life at that time.

"We are to be married next month," she said. "As soon as he has finished his present job, up in the wilds of Scotland. He's a development engineer."

Merronish said, "A development engineer. It sounds like an exciting profession. I don't do anything but live on an island. An island full of bright birds. Someday you must visit it."

She laughed again, glorying in a world that could offer islands and bright birds and her own true love.

"We'd love to," she said.

She spoke of him to Peter, as they went home together.

"Yes, I know," Peter said. "A rather interesting chap."

"Did he talk to you about his island?"

"Not much. He talked about my job mostly." He paused, considering this. "I suppose that's why I thought him interesting."

"He goes to the root of things," she said. "He told me I was happy, because I was in love."

Peter bent down to her, as a gust of breeze from the river ruffled the early summer leaves of the Embankment trees. With his mouth against her hair he asked her, "True?"

She squeezed his arm with her two hands. "So true."

Merronish called on her two weeks after the funeral. She opened the door, saw and recognized him, and remembered what he had said at their first meeting. There was no danger, she thought bitterly, of anyone saying that now. She did not look much in mirrors these days, but she knew her hair was lank and untidy, her skin blotched from crying.

"What is it?" she said stiffly.

"May I come in?"

"If you like."

He carried a great bunch of chrysanthemums and roses. She stood aside and he came in and put them on the hall table. He had the discreet solemnity of a professional mourner, she thought, but his blue eyes were still direct, seeking and holding.

"I saw John, and he told me," he said. "I'm sorry."

"Thank you. For the flowers." She stared at them, hoping she would not cry again. "Can I get you a drink?"

She was sure he would say no, but he said yes, and took the seat she offered him. He sat there, watching patiently, while she got the drink; and afterward. He was waiting for her to talk. She had run from all company, even her family, since it happened, but now she felt it growing in her—the urge to tell her misery as once she had told her happiness.

She said, conscious of the dryness of her voice, "I don't know how much John told you. It was a hit-and-run accident. There was a good trout stream near where he was working, and he used to go fishing in the evening. They found him dead by the side of the road. No one saw it happen—no one even saw the car. There was a bend in the road. No footpath, of course. The police said the car must have come round very fast, and hit from behind."

She paused, seeing it again, as she had seen it so often. Merronish said, "Go on," in a gentle voice, and the tears came. She was alone again, in a melting universe of weeping, an ocean of which she could not remember the beginning or imagine the end.

At one point he gave her a handkerchief, but he might have been a robot serving her. When the outburst came to a sobbing, gasping end, she was almost surprised to find him still sitting there.

He waited until she was breathing steadily, and said, "Now go and get yourself ready and I will take you out to dinner."

She shook her head. "No. It's kind of you, but no. I want to stay here." She added petulantly, "I'm not hungry."

"Come all the same," he said. "Have a glass of wine while I eat. It will do you good not to be alone."

She thought about that for a moment, and knew it was true. Obediently she got up and went to her bedroom to make up her face.

She learned things about herself during the next weeks and months, and about grief. The bouts of wild angry misery were fewer, but as time stretched between them she became aware of a new horror that in some ways was worse. The nearest description she could put to it was boredom, but it was boredom of a kind new to her, a yawning listless pointlessness that staled and fouled her very being. In it she contemplated suicide for the first time, but knew she could not command the energy even for that nihilistic resolve.

She had an overpowering need of something, anything, to distract her ears and eyes. She watched television in lethargic and fascinated irritation, and sometimes when the programs had ended she found herself staring for long periods at the empty screen.

Merronish returned two weeks later, and after that at more or less weekly intervals. He would come up to London one day and go back the next; he would not leave his island for longer than that at one time. She was guarded at first, but soon was simply glad of his kindness and attention, his unfailing patience with her.

She was becoming aware again of other people in the world, but with more irritability than pleasure. They talked when she did not want them to talk, and were silent or vapid when she needed speech and comfort.

Merronish was the remarkable exception. He sensed her moods and responded to them, talking at the right time and listening with the right, unobtrusive attention. From being apathetic about his visits, she grew to welcome them, and at last began to count the days between them. Autumn blurred into winter, and there were times when, because of bad weather and rough seas, he was late in visiting her. Thrown back on the unsatisfactory others, and on contemplation of the wound of grief, which still could bleed, she found herself missing him quite sharply.

The great reassuring thing, of course, was that nothing that could remotely be called sexual came between them. If there had been the slightest hint of desire in his attitude, she would have been repelled and would have turned him away. But there were only kindness and patience. He never attempted even to kiss her good night, and scarcely touched her beyond a handshake. Once or twice she wondered about this, seeking a motive behind his kindness; but for the most part she was content to accept it. And to let it nourish her.

He talked a lot about the island, and a picture of it grew in her mind. Rose-pink granite rocks, lulled by blue or lashed by gray-green seas—rabbit-cropped grass burnt by long days of sun—a wood sparkling with rain after a shower, and echoing with birds. A place of peace and beauty, remote from the world's miseries, armored by the waves against shock and change. And yet, she realized one day with a small tremor of surprise, she really knew very little about the island. His descriptions had been general, not particular. The thought whetted her curiosity; the next time he came, she would ask him questions.

But the answers she got were vague, and the picture remained as it had been—a mosaic of impressions, more a description of dream than reality. She could not be sure if it was a failure of communication or a deliberate evasiveness on his part. She even toyed with the idea that the island might not exist—might merely be some fantasy he had created for himself.

One day, on the telephone to Helen Warrington, she asked her about it, as tactfully as she could. Helen's reply was not helpful. No, she said, she did not know much about it. She and John had never been there. There had been talk of their going, but somehow it had never happened.

And Angela, putting down the telephone, realized that, although Merronish had talked of the place so much, he had never, since that first encounter, spoken of her visiting it.

It was spring again, the days lengthening and brightening, the earth stirring from its sleep, new green budding from old brown. She decided she would not ask him anymore, kept to her resolve, and as soon as he had gone away, regretted it. There were spring storms, and it was nearly three weeks before he came again. Almost as soon as she saw him, she said, "The island—I would like to see it."

He smiled at her. "Of course."

"How soon?"

"In the summer." He brushed the silver-gray mustache down

with the side of his finger. "The summer is the best time to visit the island."

As the train gathered speed leaving the station, she asked curiously, "Do you always travel down by train?"

He nodded from the facing seat in the first-class compartment which they had to themselves.

"Invariably. Motoring is no longer a pleasure. Except for one occasion I haven't driven since the war."

She looked out of the window. The sky was blue and empty over the sweltering city.

"It's a good day," she said, "to be leaving London."

"Yes. A good day to be going to the island."

"Tell me about it."

"No. Seeing is best. And you will see it soon."

"How soon? How long is the journey by boat?"

"Not much more than half an hour. We can do better than twenty knots on a day like this."

"You have a speedboat?"

"A twin-engined diesel. 'Hermes.'"

"Do any other boats go to the island?"

"There's a young fisherman who brings over any heavy stuff I need. No one else."

"Might people not go there while you're away?"

"It's unlikely. We're too far out for the small boats. And there's only one landing place, and that's a tricky one. Some nasty rocks, and the whole area's due for recharting."

"So you preserve your isolation."

"Yes. And hope to go on doing so."

In the late afternoon there was some cloud in the sky, but it was still hot. England was a haze on the horizon; the sea was smooth and glassy except for the bubbling, widening furrow of their wake.

She stared at the island, which now lay full ahead. A hummock of pink and green rising out of the calm blue waters—the pink of rock, the green of trees and grass. So it was true. It existed. She had not been sure till now.

"It's strange," she said.

"What?"

She raised her voice to be heard above the roar of the diesels. "I don't see any gulls."

"There are none."

"Why is that?"

"You'll see."

The landing place was round the other side and, as he had said, tricky. There was a tortuous and not very wide channel through rocks, and a short concrete jetty concealed behind a prow of granite. He handled the boat with a skill and confidence, bringing her in to bump her rubber fenders gently against the jetty wall. There was an iron ladder by which they climbed ashore. He tied up and they climbed the hill to the house.

It was built of the island's granite, and had been scarcely noticeable from the sea; as they approached she realized it was larger than she had expected—a rambling place with more than a dozen windows on this side. The immediate approach was through a garden, and one in surprisingly good heart for land which, in rough weather, would probably be touched by the salt spray blowing up from the inlet. She saw roses and honeysuckle, and a cabbage palm bursting into white spiky flower. They entered the house through a terrace where there were various flowering shrubs, and ropes of clematis dropping their large blue blossoms from a covering lattice.

The house, undistinguished from outside, was beautifully appointed within. The furniture was good, of several different periods but in harmony, and the decor was in quiet splendid taste. While he was getting them a drink, she rubbed the wallpaper gently with the back of her hand. It was heavy, silky stuff, the Regency stripes strongly embossed. There were paintings on the walls: a Stubbs, a Fragonard, and two of Russell Flint's studies of nude girls bathing.

There was a change in him, she thought, since they had come ashore, a quickening into enthusiasm. He did not let her sit down with her drink, but took her at once on a tour of the ground floor. There was a library, with three walls shelved and glassed, and behind the glass, gold leaf winking from dull greens and blues and reds of leather. Another fairly small room, looking out over the sea, was empty except for a few chairs, a table, and a harpsichord. The harpsichord was in light walnut, and the room was paneled to match. The kitchen, on the other hand, was all steel and plastic, with an electric mixer, a cooker, a deep-freeze, and a large blue refrigerator humming to itself.

"What about power?" she asked.

"A generator. I leave it on while I am away. It can run a week or more without attention."

"And who cleans and tidies?"

"I do. Not difficult. I am a tidy person by nature."

She said, "It's a lovely house."

He nodded, accepting this. "Leave your glass there. I want to show you the rest of the island."

She followed him obediently. They went up steps, along a path hemmed in by the blinding yellow of gorse and the white spears of sloe. The path branched and he pointed downward.

"My pool."

It was a tiny cove, with a minuscule beach of golden sand. A wall, which had been built between the two enclosing arms of rock, held in the water—full tides would wash over and refresh it. It looked very blue. Beyond it, higher land seemed to have been cut away in an inverted saddle.

"It is open to the setting sun," he said, "but I wanted the sun in the morning, as well. One can swim at dawn and watch the sun rise."

They took the upward path. The wood started farther up, but below it there was a place, about 50 by 100 yards, where the ground was level, covered with short grass and pocked with holes. In the center of this small plateau a bird was perched on a padded hoop.

At the sight of it she exclaimed, "An eagle?"

"A falcon, but not an eagle. The earl's bird. An eagle for an emperor, a peregrine for an earl. A tiercel."

"Tiercel?"

"The male of the species. A third smaller than the female, but more powerful."

"And you go away and leave him tethered?"

"His rein takes him to the edge of the wood." He gestured toward the holes which she saw were littered with droppings. "He gets at least one fat rabbit, morning and evening."

"But why?" she asked. "Why a falcon here?"

"For protection," he said simply. "To guard my bright birds."

As they approached the wood she saw them—flashes of emerald, of blue, of yellow. She did not recognize them at first, but then their harsh chatter identified them. They were grass parakeets—budgerigars. She saw more and more, of many different colors and combinations of colors—turquoise, opaline, pearl-gray, mauve, olive, cobalt.

"They live here wild?"

"Yes. I have put up nesting boxes, and I give them seed. Apart from that they are on their own. The losses were heavy at first. Some died, some stupidly flew out to sea. I brought in more, and they adapted."

"But I thought other birds attacked them?"

"There are no other birds."

She realized that she had not seen any, that she had heard only the parakeets.

"They were attacked at the beginning," he explained. "That was when I brought the peregrine in. I tamed and trained him. He cleared the sky in a couple of months, and I restocked. Some gulls come in from time to time, and he kills them."

They were in the wood, the path still winding up. The colored birds flashed overhead.

"You killed them all?" she said in horror.

"It was the only thing to do."

The wood was a tonsure round the island; its summit and center were open. They came out into meadow grass. The birds were here, too, hanging onto the long grass and pecking at the seeds. There was a summerhouse, quite substantially built, with a veranda.

When he opened the door she saw that it was furnished with cushioned wicker chairs, a couch, a low table. He pressed a button just inside the door and to her amazement there was music, the precise ecstasy of a piano.

"*The Art of Fugue,*" he said. He smiled. "No magic. A land line to a tape recorder in the house. I switched it on before I left." He looked at her searchingly. "Do you like my island?"

She said, "It's . . . magnificent."

"It wants one thing." Their eyes were locked still. "A mistress."

She looked away.

After a pause he said, "There is something else to show you." But the enthusiasm had gone, his voice was cold. "Over here."

She followed him. It emerged suddenly from the high grass, which had concealed it. It was roughly square, its sides precipitously steep, a hole chiseled out of the rocky core of the island. About twenty feet across, perhaps fifteen feet deep on the far side, twenty-five on this. The walls, like the floor, were granite.

"They got the stone from here," he said, "to build the house. Not long after Waterloo. The man who owned the island was a sea captain, and he had the use of French prisoners. Quite a few died."

Imagining the past she averted her head.

"There is another story—something that happened fifty years later. The owner is said to have been in love with a beautiful girl.

He brought her here by a trick, and when she defied him he had his servants put her down there. The story goes that, since she still would not yield, he sent down drugged wine, and when she was senseless he climbed down a rope ladder and violated her. If so, he was a crude and stupid man. Patience would have brought him to a better end. Privation, exposure, the place itself, would have tamed her."

She stared into the barren granite hole. A little rainwater had collected in a hollow at one point. She could visualize the degradation of sucking at it, on hands and knees, with a face watching above, with the music of Bach faint on the air.

He said, "The moment I saw you I knew you would crown the island."

She could not look at him. She thought of his patient, hideous resolution. A hillock carved to let him see the dawn while he swam. Bird life destroyed to make way for his parakeets. Bach brought up to the island's crest for his pleasure. And so he had seen a woman, and wanted her.

What was it he had said in the train? "Except for one occasion I haven't driven since the war." One occasion. A hunting down, a waiting, and a car driven into a defenseless man on a lonely road . . . And then the slow, sexless wooing of a girl crazed by grief.

She turned to him, smiling, opening her arms. For a moment he was surprised, and then triumphant. He took her in his arms, felt her body melt toward his, and tried to guide her back to the summerhouse.

She shook her head.

"No, here," she whispered. "Here. Now!"

They lay in the grass, a foot or two from the lip of the granite hole. The sun slanted through the tops of the trees.

"Sleep," she crooned. "Be at rest, my darling. Sleep. Sleep."

He was about twenty-five, dark, strong, with a stubble of beard, the local fisherman who had brought oil for the generator.

"Lucky there was plenty of food in the place," he said. "Of course, if you'd known how to handle the boat . . . But better not, I reckon. These are nasty waters for those that don't know them."

She had led him up to the crest and they stood by the edge of the granite hole.

Looking down, he said, "It's a long enough drop to kill anyone. You wouldn't think he would miss his footing, would you, knowing the place so well? But that's how it happens—you get overconfident."

In three weeks the sun had bleached it and rain had rotted it. One could see the white gleam of bone.

"Funny that," he said. "The way he's fallen. He looks as though he's trying to climb out. Well, there's nothing we can do, I reckon."

He looked around, at the waving empty grass, at the silent wood.

"Used to be full of budgies, this place," he said. "Lovebirds, you know. Hundreds of them."

"They're dead."

He looked at her, puzzled. "Dead?"

"It was the falcon," she said. "I could not bear to see him tied, so I cut the tether. He killed them all, all the bright birds."

Suddenly, uncontrollably, she began to weep. Sobbing she turned her face up toward the sky's bright blue. High up, almost invisible, the patient falcon hung, waiting.

PICKUP ON THE DOVER ROAD

by Julian Symons

A pickup in the rain on a dark road late at night can be dangerous for a traveler. Julian Symons tells us about a case in point in a masterly study of suspense . . .

Now, join Donald en route to a gay holiday in France when suddenly he becomes involved in a deadly battle of wits . . .

THE milestone, just visible in the rain, said Dover 41. Donald's mouth pursed and he began to whistle "The Song of the Skye Boatmen":

Speed, bonny boat, like a bird on the wing,
Over the sea to Skye.

Carry the man who was born to be King
Over the sea to Skye.

Not to Skye, but to Calais. In a light pleasant voice he fitted words to the tune:

"Carry the man who was born to be young
Over the sea to France."

To be young, he thought, to be young and happy. He remembered for a moment the row with Charles, but nothing could keep down for long the bubble of his high spirits. Rain splashed on the car's windshield, the tires made sucking noises on the wet road, the wipers echoed his thoughts by saying *a new life, a new life.*

Quite wrong, of course; he would return to England—this was nothing but a short holiday. He said aloud, "One of the *things* about you, Donald, is that every time you do something fresh you think it's the beginning of a new life."

Perfectly true, but a little silent reproach was in order. He knew that talking to himself was a bad habit, so he turned on the radio and found the plum-voiced announcer halfway through the news:

"*. . . yet another government scandal. Mr. Michael Foot called on the government to resign.*" Pause, slight change of tone. "*A murder in Kent. An elderly woman, Mrs. Mary Ford, was found murdered this evening in her house on the outskirts of the village of Oastley in Kent. She had been brutally attacked and beaten, and the house had been ransacked. Mrs. Ford was something of a recluse, and it is believed that she kept a considerable sum of money in the house. Police investigations are continuing.*"

Oastley, he thought, can't be more than five miles from there now. He was listening abstractedly to an interview with a beauty queen when he became aware of something in the road and in the next moment he realized that the something was human. He began to go into a skid, corrected it, stopped, opened his window, and shouted, "What the hell do you think you're doing?"

A grinning face appeared, wet, snubnosed, cheerful. "Flashing a torch."

"I didn't see it. I might have—"

"Can you help me? I've had a breakdown." There was no car visible in the headlights. As though answering an unspoken question the man said, "Down that side road you've just passed. I think the rear axle's gone," he said and laughed again, the sound loud and meaningless. His voice was deep, coarse. "Look, can you give me a lift? There's a café a few miles down the road. If you drop me off there I can make a phone call."

Donald felt a momentary reluctance to let the man into the car, overcame it, leaned over, and opened the passenger door. The man took off a wet raincoat, threw it on the back seat, and got in. The interior light showed him as a rather squat figure, perhaps in his late twenties, a little younger than Donald, with thick brows and the corner of a thick mouth turned up in what seemed a perpetual smile. Then the door closed, the light went out, and he became just a darkly anonymous figure in the next seat.

"Dripping all over your car," he said. "Sorry."

Donald did not reply. The incident had somehow disturbed his serenity. He drove off and found himself whistling the song again. Then the voice beside him revived the euphoria he had felt a few minutes ago by saying, "Going far?"

"Into the sunset and beyond," Donald said gaily. "That's if it weren't night and raining. Dover, then across to France. Driving off the quay in another country, that's a wonderful feeling."

"Must be. Never done it myself. You can do with a bit of a change in this weather."

Sheer pleasure in what lay ahead made Donald talk. "You know, in England we always talk about the weather. I do it myself, it shows what a boring nation we are. In France that sort of thing simply couldn't happen—there are a thousand better things to talk about. God, I shall be pleased to get out of this smug country."

As soon as the words had been spoken he regretted them. "Not that I'm unpatriotic, mind you. This is just a holiday. Still, I shan't be sorry to get out of England in March. It's just that I know everything will be different in France—hotels, food, even the weather."

"I know what you mean. Wish I was coming with you. Haven't been abroad for five years, and then it was just for the firm to a sales conference in Frankfurt. Trouble is, when you've got a wife and two kids it comes expensive, going abroad. So it's Littlehampton instead. Every year. Relatives there. You married?"

"No," Donald said, a trifle sharply.

"Lucky man." Again that laugh, loud and meaningless and somehow unlikeable.

"Why lucky?"

"Don't know, really. It's just when I think of you single chaps, with a flat in London, time your own, do what you like, go where you like, I feel envious sometimes."

"I didn't say I had a flat in London." Again Donald spoke more sharply than he had intended. "And I work, too. I'm a writer. A freelance journalist."

"Freelance, there you are. Freelance, freedom." A smell of drying clothes pervaded the air. Donald could almost feel them steaming. "This breakdown's serious for me, I can tell you. I'm a knight of the road."

"What's that? I didn't quite—"

"Commercial traveler, old man, and the bus is my steed, as you might say. Without it I'm sunk. Point is, I've got to get to Folkestone tonight—got an appointment there in the morning. If they can get my car going, well and good, but I doubt it and if not I'm in trouble. I was wondering." Donald sensed what was coming. "I was wondering if you could drop me off at Folkestone. Not out of your way, and it would be the most tremendous help to me."

There was something about the man that did not seem genuine, and instinct told Donald to refuse; but that seemed churlish. "I suppose if your car's still out of action—well, all right."

"Very very decent of you, old man. We'll just look in at that café for five minutes so I can phone a garage. Must go through the motions."

Something was troubling Donald and suddenly he realized what it was. "What do you travel in?"

"Woolens, all sorts of woolens."

A flurry of rain blurred his vision. Headlights loomed up dazzlingly and were gone. "Samples?" Donald asked.

"How d'you mean?"

"You've got no samples."

The pause was fractional. "Left my case in the car. Overnight bag, too. Didn't want to drag 'em up the lane. You get used to traveling light, you know, in my game." Another pause, a longer one this time. Then, as though to divert Donald's attention from the missing sample case, the stranger said, "Shocking business, that murder."

For a moment Donald could not believe his ears. "What murder?"

"Just a few miles away, place called Oastley. Old woman had her head bashed in, nasty business from the sound of it. They'll get the chap though. I wouldn't mind betting somebody saw him leaving the house, and then we shall get 'Police are anxious to interview Joe Doakes,' and we all know what that means."

Donald said absently, "You seem to know a lot about it."

"Only what I've heard. But I'm interested. I'll tell you why. Murder is easy." He gave that mechanical laugh, then said in a different tone, almost of alarm, "What are you stopping for?"

"You should keep your eyes open." Donald could not keep a tinge of malice out of his tone. "There was a sign that said single lane traffic. Part of the road's under construction."

"Oh, is that all?? Well, as I say, murder's easy. I mean, look at the two of us. You give me a lift, you don't know me from Adam. Nobody sees me get in. I put a gun in your ribs, tell you to pull over and stop. I shoot you, toss you out of the car, drive off, leave the car somewhere, take two or three train and bus rides to get rid of the fuss, and I'm away. With whatever's in your wallet, of course. Don't worry, old man." His loud bark sounded like the rattling of keys. "But it's been done, you know. Think of that A.6 job."

"Hanratty, you mean? They caught him."

"If he was the one who did it." The laugh again, but this time it was only a chuckle. Then Donald felt a pressure on his arm from which he jerked away. "Sorry. Am I putting you off your stroke?"

"Every murderer makes a mistake. Fingerprints, footprints."

"I ought to have put my gloves on." The laugh now was like a donkey's bray. "You've got to forgive me, it's just my sense of humor. That café's round the next bend if I remember right, on the left, stands back a bit. But murder is fascinating, don't you agree?"

Donald did not reply. I want to get the night ferry, he told himself; whatever he says I must avoid becoming involved. He found himself whistling the song in an attempt to drown the other man's words.

"I mean, the psychology of it," his passenger said. "A chap goes in a house, bashes up an old woman in the hall, gets her money, fifty or a hundred quid. Do you reckon it's going to worry him, what he did? I don't."

Along the road to the left, lights shone. It had stopped raining. There was no sound when he switched off the wipers, except the engine's throb and the suck of the tires. Donald cut off the tune in mid-whistle.

"A case like that," the other man went on, "it could be the good old tramp at the door who leaves his dirty paw marks or footprints over everything. Or it could be the real artist, the kind of thing that interests me. But as I say, this one doesn't impress me that way. I reckon it was just run-of-the-mill and we'll be reading that the police want to talk to a one-eyed farm laborer from Rutland." He broke off and said in a tone of some anxiety, "Hey, here it is, here's Joe's."

Donald took the car into the open space in front of the café. He sat with his hands on the wheel, uncertain what to do.

"Thought you'd missed it." His companion stepped out. "Coming?"

Donald decided there were things wrong with the man's story. He would have to do something about it. Reluctantly, he got out. The night air was fresh, cool. As he followed the other man into Joe's he could not help noticing his shoes. They were thickly caked with mud. Had that come just from walking up a lane?

Plastic-topped tables with sauce bottles on them, a few truck drivers sitting on tubular chairs, a smell of frying food— Joe's was not the sort of place to which Donald was accustomed. His companion, however, seemed quite at home. "Two cups of tea, nice and strong. And can you do us sausages and chips?"

The man behind the counter had a squashed nose and a cauliflower ear. "Right away."

As his passenger turned, red-faced and smiling, Donald felt angry. "Nothing to eat, thank you."

"We'll both feel better with something hot inside us." Sitting down at a corner table, smiling across it, his face was revealed as round and ingenuous. It was given a slightly sinister look by a cast in the left eye.

"I told you," Donald said, "I don't want anything to eat. And anyway, I never eat sausages." He was dismayed to hear his own voice come out as shrill, pettish.

"Right, old man, don't fret. Just one order of bangers and chips, not two," he shouted across the room. The ex-boxer raised a hand like a veined slab of beef in acknowledgement. "The name's Golightly, by the way. Bill before it, but friends call me Golly."

That is a familiarity to which I should never aspire, Donald thought. The phrase pleased him. He said rather less aciduously, "I thought you came in here to telephone."

"That's right." Golightly got up, but seemed reluctant to leave the table. "I'll just make that call, ask Joe there if he knows a garage." He went over and spoke to Joe, nodded, and crossed to a telephone in a corner. Was he really intending to make a call? Would it be a good thing just to walk out and leave him, or would that be too barbarously uncivilized? Donald liked to think of himself as above all a civilized man, and as Joe brought over the sausages and chips, with two cups of tea in thick mugs, he remembered something Golightly had said that jarred on him.

"Do you have an evening paper, by any chance?" Donald asked the café owner.

"Yeah, a driver brought one in. Late edition you want, is it, got the racing results?" Donald said that was what he wanted. Joe waddled across the room, came back with the paper, leaned over the table, and said confidentially, "Had Rolling Home for the second leg of a double. Third at a hundred to eight. Still, you can't beat the bookies all the time, can you? Know what I took off 'em last week? Forty nicker."

"Oh. Congratulations. You said this is the last edition?"

"That's what I said, mate."

He really did not know how to talk to people like Joe. He looked through the paper carefully, then folded it, still not knowing quite what to do. Was Golightly—if that was his ridiculous name—telephoning or just standing there pretending to do so? Donald pursed his mouth in thought, stopped himself from whistling, sipped his strong tea. Golightly came over, rubbing his hands and smiling.

"Bangers and chips, I love you." He poured purplish sauce around and over them, began to ply knife and fork, spoke between mouthfuls. "Tried a couple of garages—the second one's going to tow my old bus away and look after it for the night. I'll go on to Folkestone with you, since you were kind enough to offer. I mean, it's going on for eleven now, and I don't want to get stranded."

"What are you going to do, stay at a hotel?"

"Not exactly. I've got a friend there."

"Like your relatives in Littlehampton?"

"No, no." Golightly did not seem to appreciate that this was sarcasm. He closed the eye with the cast in it. "This is a lady friend. A commercial traveler's a bit like a sailor, you know, a girl in every port. As a matter of fact, that's the real reason I want to get to Folkestone tonight, and can you blame me? Why should you single men have all the fun? I suppose you've got a little bit o' fluff waiting for you across the Channel? Or perhaps you're not that way inclined."

"What do you mean?"

"Nothing. No offense meant and none taken, I hope. Talking too much. I always do. Shan't be a couple of minutes now." There was sweat on Golightly's forehead.

"I'm not taking you," Donald said flatly.

"Not taking me!" The knife and fork clattered on the table. The hand that held the cup shook slightly. Donald felt calm, in complete control of the situation.

"Don't worry," he said. "I'm not going to do anything about it. I've thought it out and I don't want to get involved."

There was a blast of cold air as the door opened to let in two truck drivers in overalls. Golightly looked down at the table and spoke in a low voice. "What d'you mean, involved?"

"I mean you've been telling me a pack of lies. Come along now, admit it." Donald cocked one leg over the other, admired the sheen on his shoes.

"How d'you make that out, old man?"

"I'll tell you, *old man*. You say you're a commercial traveler and you've got an important appointment tomorrow morning. Now, I've met one or two commercial travelers, and I've never known one who let himself be parted from his sample case. Natural enough, because without it they've got nothing to show. But you not only leave it in your car—so you say—but you don't even bother to have the garage that's collecting the car drop the bag in here."

"I shan't need the samples tomorrow." Golightly spoke without conviction.

"And then you don't really *sound* like a traveler. All that knight-of-the-road and girl-in-every-port stuff, it's out of date. You sound like an actor, not a very good one, *pretending* to be a commercial traveler. I don't believe you've got a car, let alone a sample case. What's your car number?"

"AKT 113 H."

"Make?"

"Triumph Herald."

"Firm?"

"Universal Woolens."

"Prove it." Donald uncrossed his legs. "Show me your business card."

Slowly Golightly's hand went into his jacket. He kept his eyes on Donald, those slightly crossed eyes, until he had drawn out a wallet. He looked through the contents, wiped his brow with his sleeve, then, "No business card."

"No card! Why, without a card a commercial traveler doesn't exist."

"All right, I haven't told the exact truth, but I still want to get to Folkestone. I still need a lift."

It was the moment at which Donald had planned to walk out, but something about Golightly's manner made him abruptly change his mind. "Come on then."

His reward was the other man's startled look. "You're taking me?"

"That's what it looks like, doesn't it??"

Golightly said nothing more. He paid the bill and they walked to the car in silence, with Donald a couple of steps behind. The ruddiness had drained from Golightly's face, leaving it pale. Donald, as he drove away, said, "There's more to come."

"How do you mean?"

"About you. Who you are, what you've been doing. I want an explanation."

"I don't know what you're talking about."

"Your shoes. The mud on them. That hasn't come from walking up a lane. More like walking, or maybe running, across fields."

"It was a muddy lane."

Donald took his right hand from the wheel, felt in his jacket pocket, then took it out again. "I pick you up near Oastley where that old Mrs. Ford was murdered. You tell me this cock-and-bull story about being a commercial traveler and you talk about murder in a very queer way. How did you know about the murder?"

"Read it in the paper."

"No. I borrowed the last edition in the café and there was nothing in it. How could there be, when it didn't happen till seven o'clock. I heard it on the ten o'clock news, on my car radio. But how about you?"

"Must have heard it the same way. On my car radio."

"That won't wash. I picked you up a couple of minutes after I heard it. And I'll tell you something else. On the radio they didn't say anything about her being killed in the hall."

Silence. The lights showed Ashford ahead, the Folkestone bypass to the left. They took the left turn to the dual highway. Donald thought triumphantly: that's shown him, that's shaken him up, now perhaps I'll get the truth. And sure enough, it was in a tone much less boisterous than usual, in a tone almost meek, that Golightly said, "I made a mistake there, didn't I?"

"You certainly did." Donald began to whistle sweetly, melodiously. And then—he could hardly believe it—Golightly's voice took on a jeering tone.

"You think I was the one who did for her, so why not tell the police then?"

Donald was so shaken that he could not reply.

"All right, I did it. I killed the old girl," Golightly said.

"You—"

"Let's say I did. So why not ring the police from Joe's, when you've got it worked out so nice and logical?"

"I'll tell you why," Donald said. His voice shook with the emotion he had been suppressing. "I hate England—everything about this smug country, the filthy weather, places like that disgusting café, people like you. If I call the police it means I'll have to make a statement, give evidence. I shan't be able to leave for—oh, perhaps not for days, weeks. So I don't care, I just don't care what you've done."

"Very decent of you, old man." Still that jeering tone. "We haven't been introduced, have we? I mean, you know my name, you haven't told me yours. But I think I know it."

"What is it?"

"Donald Grant, right?"

With anger that was half assumed and half real Donald said, "You've been looking at my logbook."

"I haven't, you know." Somewhere in the far distance there was furious hooting, then it stopped. "I'll tell you a bit of a story, shall I? About an old lady named Mrs. Ford. Quite a nice old lady, but a bit close with her money. No sons, no daughters, so what did it matter, who cared? Nobody, you might think."

Donald pressed his foot on the accelerator. He did not usually drive fast, but it was as if pushing up the needle from seventy to eighty and nearly to ninety helped him to get away from the voice, although of course in fact it didn't; the voice was like a needle digging into his skin.

"One person did care, though. That was her nephew. I expect the sort of thing she said was, 'You'll get everything when I'm gone, dear, now here's a five-pound note to be going on with.' Very annoying to a young man, especially one without much money. He was a sort of freelance writer, though people don't seem to think he made much of a living at it. Not enough to keep up the nice little pad he shared with his boyfriend.

"So one fine evening—a wet evening, as a matter of fact—Mrs. Ford is murdered. Quite a nasty murder—everything turned upside down to try and make it look like a hurried job. Wasn't, though." With a sound like a sigh he added, "I don't have to tell you the name of the nephew."

Donald's mind was empty of thought, except that of the need for action. Golightly went on talking.

"We found out quite a bit about you when we rang your flat, and the young man you share it with—Charles is his name? He said you'd decided to take off quite suddenly on a holiday abroad. Seemed peeved you didn't take him along, too—quite a row you had, according to him. So we've been looking for you. You'd have done better to stay put. Didn't know which road you'd take, so there was poor Golly, Detective Sergeant Golightly as you'll have guessed by this time, getting wet. Could have taken you in for questioning, but I thought you might have a gun. Have you, by the way?"

Behind were the lights of a car, flashing on, off, on again. Donald's fingers moved over the hard curves of the metal in his pocket, and he kept one comforting hand there while he said in a distressed falsetto: "Why shouldn't I go abroad? It's not a crime."

"No, but you made one or two mistakes. Not deliberate ones like mine. You said Mrs. Ford was killed around seven o'clock. So she was, but it didn't say so on the radio."

"Your word against mine. I should deny saying it."

"Something else. A witness saw you leave the cottage. Didn't know you, but gave us a description, said he'd know you again."

"One witness. A good counsel would—"

"You were whistling that catchy little tune. Favorite of yours, isn't it? The witness got it loud and clear." Golightly began to sing, loudly, but in tune:

Carry the man who was born to be King
Over the sea to Skye.

Two things happened together. The car that had been flashing drew level, switched on a spotlight, began blaring away with a hooter. And Golightly, in a quite different voice, loud and angry, cried, "Give me that gun," and threw himself across the steering wheel, pinioning Donald's right arm to his pocket.

Donald just had time to realize that he was not able to control the car with his left hand, and to think about the bad luck that seemed to have dogged his whole life, and then there was nothing . . .

Golightly woke up in a hospital bed. The Superintendent was glaring down at him. "You're a fool, Golly. Only cuts and bruises, but you're lucky to be alive. Grant isn't."

"He bought it?"

"A sliver of glass through the neck when you crashed. You had no need to get into his car, no need at all. Just let us know what road he was on, that's all you had to do."

"Yes, sir. It seemed a good idea at the time."

"And why the hell did you have to leave that café with him?"

"He'd have taken me along anyway, sir. I'd been needling him. and I made a slip. He was on to me."

"Don't expect any medals. What was the slip?"

Golightly told him. "He made one, too—mentioned the time she was killed; but of course he'd have denied it. He broke when I told him we had a witness who'd seen him leave the house and heard him whistling that song—you know, song of the Skye boatmen. One of the villagers said he was fond of it."

"We had no witness."

"No, sir. But he didn't know that. And he *was* fond of that song, kept whistling it in the car." Virtuously Golightly said, "I don't like whistling. Bad manners, bad habit. Can get you into trouble."

DÉJÀ VU

by Mary Barrett

In her accompanying letter the author wrote: "My new story started out to be a women's liberation ghost story and ended up having nothing to do with either phenomenon."
Now you have exactly the same head start your editor had . . .

MRS. OLIVER was puzzled. She always liked to pay cash, not that she could, and she no longer kept in touch with anyone out of town. Therefore she received almost no mail. The package which the mailman handed her was a surprise, and, like many surprises, unwelcome.

"There must be a mistake," Mrs. Oliver said uncertainly.

"No mistake, lady." And the mailman walked away.

Mrs. Oliver inspected the parcel. It was wrapped in brown paper and sealed with tape. Her name and address were clearly spelled out in neat block letters. The stamps were canceled with the local postmark.

She put the parcel down on the dining table. For some reason she was reluctant to open it. At the edge of awareness, the sensation gnawed at her that she had experienced this same event before. *Déjà vu.*

Don't be a fool, Mrs. Oliver said sternly to herself. She hoped that she wasn't getting eccentric, living alone as she had been since John died. Surely a package in the mail was nothing to be so upset about.

She pulled at the sealing tape. Under the paper was a plain white box bearing no identification. Its very impersonality somehow increased Mrs. Oliver's uneasiness.

The box was lined with white tissue paper. Lying in the center, like a cherished treasure, was a little music box with a dainty lady dancer on top.

Mrs. Oliver gasped. She picked up the box. She wound the little key. The lady dancer turned slowly, gracefully, and the music box tinkled "The Blue Danube."

It was impossible!

Mrs. Oliver sat down. Her hands were suddenly cold and her heart was beating fast.

It was the very first gift that John had sent to her. It came before they were married, when John was still courting her. The little Bavarian music box had arrived, then as now, in a parcel in the mail. Then, as now, it had been carefully wrapped and sealed. John was always a careful man.

She looked again at the address on the wrapping paper. It told her nothing. The printed words were impersonal, unrevealing.

Panic hit Mrs. Oliver like a sonic boom. She knew very well

where she had last seen the music box—in Mr. Stover's store, where she had taken it to be sold.

She stood up shakily and forced herself into action.

"Mr. Stover, I would like to see the Bavarian music box which I sold to you."

Mr. Stover had been afraid of this. How much of the truth could he tell her? He looked at her closely. No, he decided, she was too agitated; even part of the truth would be too great a shock.

"I remember it," he said. "Had a little dancing girl, didn't it? That was sold some time ago."

Mrs. Oliver was uncertain whether to feel relief or apprehension.

"Do you remember who bought it?"

"No. I didn't know the man. He was a stranger who happened in. A young fellow. Didn't quibble about the price."

Mrs. Oliver felt dizzy. That would have been John's style.

"A young man, you said?"

"That's right. In his early thirties, I'd say."

Mrs. Oliver slept restlessly that night. She had distressing dreams from which she woke perspiring, her heart pounding, the thought of her dead husband vivid in her mind.

John. *He* was in his early thirties when they first met. He was handsome and ambitious, already a successful lawyer. It was inevitable that he would become an important man in state politics.

He was a good catch for any woman. And how persuasively he had courted her, showering her with attention and presents!

He had this house built for her, and had it furnished with the finest things. She appreciated all this. There was no passion on her part, but she couldn't, finally, resist him. Her family was an old one, far more distinguished than his; but their money had long ago trickled away. She could not afford not to marry for money. So it might as well be John.

If he was ever disappointed he was too gentlemanly to let it show . . .

She hid the music box in a drawer under the linen tablecloths and tried to forget it. It was not that simple. Whoever was manipulating Mrs. Oliver's state of mind was not only very clever but astonishingly well informed.

Only a week after the arrival of the music box another parcel was delivered. It, too, was carefully wrapped and sealed. The box was, again, disquieting in its impersonality.

Mrs. Oliver opened it and felt her knees go weak. Deep in tissue paper the box held the exquisite emerald brooch which John had given her on the day they were married. It was a lovely thing, of superb craftsmanship. Mr. Stover had given her a very good price for it. Now it lay in her hand, as sparkling as it was the day John had pinned it so tenderly on her bridal dress.

Mrs. Oliver tried to slow the beating of her heart. It wasn't good for her to be so upset. The doctor would be cross with her.

If this eerie procedure continued, she would receive many packages. John had been very generous with gifts. His practice brought in a great deal of money. To outside observers she seemed a very lucky woman. She had only to drop the smallest hint and John would buy her whatever she wanted.

Still, as time went by, she had felt more and more like a kept slave. She yearned for a little cash of her own. Not much. Just enough so that she could be free to buy some small things for herself. He never let her have a personal checking or bank account, and he gave her a minimum of pocket money.

"I would rather take care of you myself, dear," he said.

John overlooked nothing. He established charge accounts with the grocery store, the milkman, the dry cleaners. He bought all her clothes himself. In all the days of her marriage she never had more than a five-dollar bill of her own. Of course, John paid all the bills himself . . .

The packages continued to come. Mrs. Oliver lived in a state of constant agitation. The parcels arrived with no regularity, and she never knew on which day one would be delivered. There was, however, one thing she could be certain of ahead of time—the contents of each box. For the presents were coming back to her in the exact order John had given them to her.

Her birthday present, the diamond bracelet, was followed by the matching earrings John had given her for Christmas.

At first, when she was a new bride, she had been charmed by John's generosity. She had never owned beautiful things before, and the shower of extravagant gifts was like a dream come true. It was only in time that the longing for the illusion of financial independence came to sit on her soul like a lead weight; and in time the longing became an obsession.

John refused even to consider the possibility of her looking for a job.

"We're rich, dear," he said. "It would be ridiculous for you to work. You know that I'll get you anything you want."

As time passed, John's gifts brought her no joy. They seemed merely symbols of her bondage. She even had trouble pretending to be pleased.

Now, receiving them a second time, she felt even less pleasure. She felt only horror and repugnance. As each gift arrived she quickly hid it away.

His anniversary present of silver demitasse spoons came only shortly before the handblown crystal vase which John had brought back from a short trip out of town.

Mrs. Oliver's panic was now beginning to overwhelm her. There was only one gift left—the last one John had given her. She knew what it would mean if that one came back. And she knew with dreadful certainty that although it had been, in life, John's last gift, it would not now be. She knew that the final gift would come to her from the grave.

Mrs. Oliver, never a hardy woman, was not well. She hardly ever slept. When, finally, she did drop off, her dreams were terrifying, and she often woke up screaming.

She no longer had any appetite. She had lost so much weight that her dresses hung like bags. She hardly recognized herself in the mirror. Her eyes stared back at her from sunken sockets like glass globes in a skull.

The package came.

John's last gift.

She knew very well what the package contained even before she opened it. He had brought this gift on no special occasion—it had been a sudden whim. He had seen it in a store window and, on impulse, had gone in and bought it for her.

Her hands shook. She could hardly tear off the paper. Inside the white box lay the gift. It was a beautiful little emerald pillbox, made by an expert craftsman. It was truly a work of art. Mrs. Oliver put it out of sight as quickly as she could.

She tried to brace herself for what she knew was bound to come next. But what could she do? There was no way to anticipate how it would come, or in what form. There was no way to protect herself.

That night she went to bed early and lay there, wide-awake. Her eyes were open, staring unseen at the ceiling.

There was a knock at the door. It was not imperative—simply firm and sure.

Mrs. Oliver stepped into her bedroom slippers and put on her robe. She went silently down the stairs. She could no more have ignored that self-assured knock than she could have left the packages unopened. She was moved by an irresistible compulsion.

The knock sounded again—no louder than before, but still firm and self-confident.

Mrs. Oliver went to the door. She stood there, dizzy. Her hand was on the doorknob.

She was faint with panic and fatigue. Her body shook, out of control. She sank to the floor and her face pressed against the hard wood of the door.

Again the knock sounded.

There was a pounding in her ears. The hall seemed to tilt, first one way, then another.

"John," she whispered, "how did you know?"

It *was* John on the other side of the door. She was certain of that. And somehow he had learned the truth.

She had taken the poison out of the little enamel pillbox. She had put it in his demitasse. She was sure he hadn't seen her do it. She had sat there calmly and watched him drink the coffee, and die. And, finally, she had money of her own.

She should have known better, she thought fuzzily. She should have known she couldn't outwit John, that he would never stop giving her things.

She lay, a crumpled disorderly heap, on the floor of the hall. She was shrunken and unadorned. She looked old. She sighed, a long sigh, and then she died.

There was a final knock on the door, and then the sound of footsteps going away.

Mr. Stover was disappointed. He had waited until he had sent back all her lovely things, in the same order she had sold them, to tell her he loved her. Well, he would call again tomorrow.

THE OTHER SIDE OF THE WALL

by Stanley Ellin

Once each year Stanley Ellin writes a story especially for Ellery Queen's Mystery Magazine, *and each year readers and critics look forward eagerly to this new story as a mystery event. This year's story is about a psychotherapist and his deeply disturbed patient. "Did you never wonder," the doctor asked his patient, "what lay on the other side of that wall?" . . . Was it the ultimate experience or the ultimate truth?*

"SO," Dr. Schwimmer said. "So. It comes to this at last. The inevitable. Confrontation, penetration, decision making, action. Wait."

The office door was partly open. Through it could be heard the sound of a typewriter being pecked at slowly and uncertainly. The doctor rose from behind his desk, crossed the room, and closed and locked the door. He returned to the swivel chair behind the desk. The desk was long and wide, a polished slab of walnut mounted on stainless steel legs and without drawers. Arranged on it were a crystal ashtray; a cardboard box of straw-tipped Turkish cigarettes ("I don't even enjoy smoking," the doctor remarked, squaring the edge of the box with the edge of the ashtray, "but these help the image, you understand. The exotic, somewhat mysterious image I cultivate to impress the impressionable females in my clientele."); a razor-edged, needle-pointed letter opener of Turkish design ("Also part of the image, naturally. Again the exoticism of the Near East, with its suggestion of the menacingly virile."); a cigarette lighter; a small brass tube like a lipstick container, which did not contain lipstick but a breath deodorant that left the mouth reeking of peppermint; and a neat little tape recorder, an XJE-IV Memocord, not much larger than the box of Turkish cigarettes.

"So." The doctor leaned toward the tape recorder. He hesitated, then sat back in his chair. "No. No need to put any of this on tape, Albert."

"Why, Doctor? Is it too intensely personal to be recorded for posterity?"

"I am a psychotherapist, Albert. All the business transacted in this room is intensely personal."

"Never to this extent though, is it? And that name Albert. Must you continually address me by it? You know how I detest it."

"Too bad. But I will address you as Albert. This is necessary. It is a way of establishing identities and relationships. And consider the distinguished men who bore that name. Einstein. Schweitzer. They seemed to survive it reasonably well, didn't they?"

"I still detest it. There wasn't even a sensible reason for being saddled with it. No one in the family ever had it. Mother was enamored of the figure on the tins of tobacco father smoked, that's all. An incredible woman. Imagine naming one's firstborn after a pipe tobacco. Or was she so viciously foresighted that she knew this was the perfect name for a child who was doomed to become a bald, potbellied, blobby-nosed little man with weak vision and a perpetually nagging sinus condition?"

"So. Suddenly we are faced with the ghost of the mother?"

"Why not, Doctor? I didn't manufacture my own ugliness, did I?"

"Albert, if I were a Freudian, we could have such a good time with this mother image. We could make it your sacrificial goat, stuff all your problems into it, and slaughter it. So. But luckily for us, I am not a Freudian. Your dead mother deserves better than to be declared guilty of your misfortunes. Consider how she made it her duty to bolster your shaky ego every day of her life. Your academic brilliance, your professional success, your devotion to her—it was like a catechism to her, the recitation of her admiration for you day after day."

"It was a trap. It was a pit I lived in like a captured tiger, feeding on those greasy chunks of admiration she flung to me."

"So. Very dramatic. Very colorful. But an evasion, Albert. Only an evasion."

"Is it? Then what about the father image? The big, handsome, loudmouthed father. And the two handsome, muscular brothers. The overwhelming males in my home. And me the runt of the litter."

"You were, Albert. But never overwhelmed. Consider the facts. Your father died when you were a child. His absence may have affected you, but never his presence. And that pair of clods, Albert, those two handsome, muscular brothers, stood in awe of your intellect, were wary of your cold self-restraint, terrified of your unpredictable explosions of temper. They quickly learned not to step over the lines you drew. Do you remember how one earned a broken leg when he was tripped up by you at the head of the staircase for trying a little bullying? How the other found himself playing a game where he was locked in a trunk and almost smothered in payment for a small insult? Yes, yes, a few such episodes and they soon came to understand that one did not carelessly tread on the toes of this small, fat, pale older brother with the thick eyeglasses and the sniffle. They are still afraid of you, Albert. They are two of your very few triumphs. But it is your failure alone that concerns us. Let us get on with it."

"My failure? Am I the only one in this room stamped with failure? My dear Doctor, what about the way you've managed to destroy a splendid practice in a few short months? Eccentricity is one thing, Doctor. Patients like a little eccentricity in their therapists. But they also draw lines. A therapist who lives in a daze, who sits lost to the world when patients are trying to communicate with him, who angrily sends them packing when they resent this—what did you think was bound to happen to this practice in short order? And what course did you think your fellow professionals would take when they observed your grotesque behavior? Your inexplicable compulsions? Did you really expect them to continue to refer patients to you? No, Doctor, there is no need to rush through this consultation. No need to look at clocks and measure out your time in expensive little spoonfuls any longer. The clocks have stopped. We have all the time to ourselves now we can possibly use."

"Albert, listen to me. This room is not meant to be an arena where we turn our cruelty on each other. We are not antagonists. We will achieve nothing through antagonism."

"You're a coward, Doctor."

"We are both cowards about some things, Albert. Do you think I disparage you when I say you are essentially a creature of emotion? Believe me, I do not."

"I don't believe you. You're much too clever with words, Doctor, to be believed in that regard. Creature of emotion. What you mean is incorrigible romantic, don't you? An ugly little wretch stuffed to the bursting point with romantic visions. Made self-destructive by them. A fifty-year-old man flung back into adolescence and unable to claw his way out of it. Why shouldn't you disparage him?"

"Because, Albert, you are not playacting your condition. You are not pretending you face a crisis. This condition is real. The crisis is real. One does not disparage a reality."

"A reality based on dreams? On sexual fantasies dredged up from my unconscious while I lie snoring in bed?"

"All these are realities, too. Are scientific laws and material objects the only reality? No, no, Albert. Your mistake from the start was in not recognizing the validity of those dreams. Of the situation they depicted."

"But the situation was all in my own mind."

"In your emotions. Your emotions, Albert. If tests were made while you were asleep and dreaming of this woman, they would clearly indicate physiological reactions. A quickened breathing, an increase in blood pressure, sexual excitation."

"Just as I told you. All the symptoms of delayed adolescence. The pimply high school boy's nightly dreams of his nubile girl friend. The only difference is that in the daylight he joins her in some noisy roost where they happily share a nauseous concoction of ice cream and syrup and hold hands under the table. While all I could do was turn night dreams into day dreams."

"Slowly, Albert. Confrontation, penetration, decision making, action. Each in its turn. So far we have barely begun the penetration. We have merely put aside the clichés of the possessive mother and bullying siblings and turned to the image of the dream woman herself. We have a distance to go before the decision making."

"Girl, Doctor. Maiden, if you will. Not woman."

"So? Is it important that she has not reached full womanhood?"

"Yes. I don't like women. Something happens to a girl the instant she becomes one. In that instant she becomes too knowing, too wise, too self-sufficient to provide happiness for any man."

"Not any man. Perhaps only men who are afraid they don't

measure up. Tell me, Albert. What kind of man were you in your first dreams of this girl? Still the small, fat, fifty-year-old lump of self-hatred? Or heroic in dimensions?"

"I don't know. It's hard to remember."

"Think. Penetrate."

"I'm trying to. Not heroic. That much I'm sure of. Beyond that, I still don't know. I wasn't aware of my body, my appearance, my deficiencies. Only of my sensations when I saw her there. Ecstatic recognition. Passionate desire for her. And I remember my own astonishment that I should feel this. I hadn't ever known I was capable of such feelings. All my life I've paid for my female companionship. Paid to satisfy my physical needs. There was never a suggestion of emotional involvement in the transactions. Now here I was, being drowned in emotionalism. I woke up suffocating with it."

"So. And you knew on waking that this dream girl was based on an actuality? That she had a flesh-and-blood counterpart?"

"Not then. Not the first time. Only later when I realized the dream was recurrent. And then only when in one of the later dreams I realized that I knew her name. Sophia. When I woke that morning it struck me that of course she was the counterpart of a real Sophia. The inept child I had recently hired as my receptionist."

"She resembled her?"

"More and more, once I knew her name. At first she was shadowy. She was only the suggestion of a beautiful Greek maiden. After I knew her name she took on clearer and clearer definition. Still shadowy, because we always met at night in dim lighting, but now as if a veil had been removed from her face. No more chiaroscuro, but every delicate curve of feature revealed. Sophia. I can even remember the idiotic imagery, the coinage of every bad poet, that crossed my mind in that dream when I stood there looking at her in full recognition for the first time. Doe-eyed, raven-haired, swan-necked. My God, I didn't even blush at my own puerile poeticizing of her. I rejoiced in it."

"You think this girl in the dream was aware of your feelings?"

"She must have been. How could she help it? I tell you, Doctor, I yearned toward her with such intensity that she must have felt the current surging from me. This was before I even recognized her identity. I walked into this room, a bedroom lit by a small lamp somewhere, and she stood silent and unmoving in the middle of the room dressed in a white gown—the classically simple Greek gown—and with what seemed like an almost transparent veil covering her hair and face. A tender, living goddess. I was stricken by the sight of her. The emptiness in me, my lifetime of emptiness, was suddenly filled with a white-hot lava of emotion. You see? Again I am poeticizing like a fool, but what other way is there to describe it? In psychologic jargon? In those deadly words: *I fell in love?* Although, believe me, Doctor, coming from me, those words mean infinitely more than they would coming from the ordinary man."

"I do believe you, Albert. But are you sure you never knew such an emotion before?"

"Never."

"Think, Albert. You were not born middle-aged. In your youth there must have been some woman—girl—who excited this emotion in you."

"Never. I never permitted myself to feel anything like this. I knew the response my size, my ugliness, my sweaty, tongue-tied ineptitude in conversation would draw from any girl I thought desirable. Why invite disaster? Better to freeze the heart into a block of ice than have it torn to pieces."

"And you did not experience any of this when you confronted the dream Sophia? When you let her feel the current of emotion surging from you?"

"No. I seemed to have no room in me for anything but that aching desire."

"Sexual desire?"

"That would have been later. In the early dream, all I wanted to do was touch her. Just touch her shoulder gently with my fingertips. To reassure her, perhaps. Or myself. I moved toward her with my hand outstretched, and she moved away a little, barely out of my reach. Then suddenly we were someplace else. I recognized where at once. The hallway outside the room. The hallway of my brownstone house."

"Yes?"

"The old brownstone. My living tomb. My office downstairs, the bedrooms on the second floor where we stood. All those empty bedrooms. I was jubilant. This lovely, veiled creature was with me in my domain, I was not trespassing on hers. I looked and saw her standing now in the middle of that long gloomy hallway. While I watched she held out a hand as if inviting me to clasp it in mine. She pressed her other hand against the wall there, the blank, wallpapered expanse between two doors, and an opening showed in it. She moved through the opening, it closed behind her, and she was gone. I was frantic. Wild with despair. I ran to the wall and searched for some clue to the opening, but there was none. I struck my fist against the wall, but my fist had no substantiality, no strength. It moved in slow motion against the wall, it met it with hardly the impact of a feather brushing against it. That was all. I woke up drenched with sweat, weak with a sense of futility.

"I knew at once it had been a dream. I knew that the logical thing to do was either lie there and dispassionately analyze it or to clear it completely from my mind. But I knew that either way would purge me of the glorious new emotions I had discovered in the girl's presence. I was in love. For the first time in my life—at the age of fifty, mind you—I was willingly and hopelessly in love. I had the sense of it in my every nerve.

"It was dawn now. Incredibly, I got out of bed in that gray light and went out into the hallway, searching along its wall for the mysterious opening in it, desperately running my hands over its smooth surface. I went into the room on the other side of the wall there, my youngest brother's room, empty of all its furniture since his marriage, and it was as empty as ever, a fine dust on its floor and that was all. I knew then that the only thing left to me was the recurrence of the dream, a reentry into the shadowy world where the girl might be waiting for me. Would surely be waiting for me."

"So." Dr. Schwimmer rested his head against the back of his swivel chair and closed his eyes. "Then from the very start, Albert, you surrendered to this girl completely."

"Completely."

"You asked nothing in return. You expected nothing in return."

"At the start, nothing. Only her presence."

"And later?"

"Later, as the dream recurred again and again, I wanted her response. Her acknowledgement that she felt for me at least a part—a little—of what I felt for her. I wanted her not to retreat from me every time I reached toward her. But I forgave her for it each time she did. I knew it was because this experience was as strange and novel for her as it was for me. She was very young. Untouched. Timid. She was to be wooed gently, not taken by force. And I was willing to be patient, because my fingertips came infinitesimally closer to her each time. I settled for that."

"So. And when you realized that this girl of the dreams was, in reality, the pretty little receptionist who sat in your outer office every working day of the week it did not break the spell?"

"No, because it didn't end the dreams. At night I had the Sophia of the dreams; in daylight I had the Sophia of reality nearby where, whenever I chose, I could look at her, speak to her.

"And the living reality, as it turned out, made the dreams that much more exciting. Every detail of the flesh-and-blood Sophia was transmitted to the dream image I loved. Now that image removed its veil and showed me the glowing eyes and parted lips and curve of cheek of the enchanting child I employed in my office. The length of leg, swell of breast, everything became substantial in the dreams."

"But you did not transfer your emotions to this flesh-and-blood girl? Then or ever?"

"No."

"Are you sure of that, Albert? Consider this very carefully. It is important."

"I still say no. I didn't want to risk it. I didn't have to. It was more than enough that I had the dream Sophia to woo and win. In the daylight there were mirrors in the house where I would catch sight of myself at unexpected moments. A self that invited rejection. In the dimly lit room and hallway of the dreams there were no mirrors. I had no view of myself then. I never gave thought to what I looked like. Above all, somehow I knew that the brownstone house stood all alone in the dream world and that there was no one else in it besides the girl and me. I was the only man in her existence, she had no freedom of choice. Ultimately she would have to give herself to me."

"A quaint way to phrase it, Albert. Almost Victorian. And what does it connote? She allows you to touch her at last? To press your lips to her blushing cheek? Or more?"

"More. Much more."

"Yes?"

"She would be my slave. My willing slave. Grateful that she could be possessed by me. She would not so much love me as worship me."

"So. And all this, Albert, in the light of your futile pursuit of her through dream after dream? The nightly confrontation in the bedroom, the scene in the shadowy hallway where, at the crucial moment, she disappears through that blank wall? Now tell me. Did you never wonder what lay on the other side of that wall?"

"I didn't have to. I was sure I knew what was there. Her room. The small room with carpeted walls and floor where she lay on a bed under some diaphanous covering breathlessly waiting for me to find my way to her. Afraid of the moment when I would, but eagerly anticipating it. Her room. Her solitary, sweetly scented refuge."

"So there it is, Albert. That preconception was your great mistake. Your tragic misjudgment."

"The room was there. I entered it. I found it exactly as I had imagined it."

"No, you did not. Otherwise, would there be this crisis? This anguish? You should have been prepared, Albert, for more than you bargained for. You should have known yesterday when you first saw your real Sophia's young man in her office, when she proudly introduced him to you, that there was a crisis brewing. Admit it. Didn't your hackles rise when you met that young man? When you took his measure?"

"All right, yes. Yes. But I didn't make anything of it then. Why should I? All my life I've hated these hulking Adonises, these huge, handsome, brute images of masculinity. My hatred for this specimen was innate. Why should I think it had anything to do with the adoration my infatuated, flesh-and-blood Sophia aimed at him?"

"Hard words, Albert. But the dream Sophia is cast in the image of the flesh-and-blood Sophia. There was one danger signal. The other was at the instant in your dream last night when you pressed a hand against that wall, that barrier to her hidden room, and at last it opened to you. Didn't you wonder why, at long last, it should suddenly open? Didn't it enter your mind that it might be a means of providing you, not with the ultimate experience, but with the ultimate truth?"

"No. And you yourself know this only through hindsight. When I entered that room I felt jubilation. Utter ecstasy. Nothing else. I had no premonition I would find them on that bed together, she and that hulk. I had no idea until that incredible moment that this room was their refuge, not hers alone. Or, worst of all, that when caught shamelessly sprawled beside him in their lovemaking, she would only smile pityingly at me.

"How could I be prepared for any of that? After all, those dreams were mine. How could I ever imagine they would be invaded by any gross stranger? And now—"

"Yes?"

"Now that I know the truth I can't turn my mind away from it. Awake or asleep, all I can think of is that she was taken from me. Violated. And with her eager consent. God almighty, since I found my way into that room I've lived only with the picture of them in my mind. I can't live with it any longer."

"So. Then it must be exorcised, Albert, must it not?"

"Yes."

"At last we come to the decision making. And is it to be my decision to make, Albert? Mine alone?"

"Yes."

"You will accept it without question?"

"Completely."

"Good. Then I will state the case directly. It is obvious that someone must pay the penalty for your betrayal, Albert. As a sane and intelligent man you must know that a blood sacrifice offers the only possible solution in a case like this. The only one. Under any conditions it would be impossible for you to be released from your agony while your betrayers maintain their obscene relationship. Yes. One or the other must be eliminated. But which? The intruder?"

"And then what, Doctor? Another such intruder to take his place in that room? Another crisis? Now that I know what the girl really is—what she's capable of—can I expect more than that?"

"True. Then you plainly see she herself must be sacrificed."

"Yes."

"So. And you also understand how it must be done?"

"Yes. With a blade, naturally."

"Naturally. A blade of the finest steel. That is traditional, and there are times when one sees the wisdom behind these timeworn traditons." The doctor picked up the letter opener from his desk and regarded it with admiration. He turned it slowly back and forth so that sunlight from the window flowed up and down the blade. "The finest steel, a tradition in itself. More than eight inches of it, Albert. More than enough for its purpose.

"And you realize, of course, that the first killing blow deep between the lower ribs does not mean the completion of the ritual. There must be total release of the emotions immediately afterward. A frenzied hacking until the lovely image is made a horror. A full measure of blood must flow to wash away betrayal. Remember, Albert, the therapeutic value of the act lies in that."

"Yes. Of course."

"Then," said the doctor, "all that is left is action."

He unlocked the door and opened it slightly on the drafty ground-floor corridor of the old brownstone. And, when in answer to his call, Miss Sophia Kaloosdian, doe-eyed, raven-haired, swan-necked, a large wad of chewing gum working rhythmically in her jaws, left her desk in the outer office and came to see what he wanted, he was waiting for her with smiling confidence, the hilt of the letter opener gripped tight in his fist and hidden behind his back.

The confidence was not misplaced. Dr. Albert Schwimmer may have been short, fat, nearsighted, and with a perpetual sniffle, but he was very strong.

A KIND OF MADNESS

by Anthony Boucher

So far as we know, Anthony Boucher wrote only two stories that have not yet appeared in print. One was a Nick Noble short story which Ellery Queen's Mystery Magazine *purchased in October 1943, but which, for reasons that cannot be disclosed at this time, was never published.*

The second unpublished story was discovered after Boucher's death in 1968. Evidence indicates that the story was written in 1961 and was probably the last crime story that Anthony Boucher wrote. For unknown—perhaps unknowable—reasons Boucher put the manuscript aside, never getting around to sending it to Ellery

Queen's Mystery Magazine, *or even to giving the story a title; the present title was chosen by your editor.*

Here, then, is a find for mystery fans in general and for Boucher fans in particular. It is a story about Jack the Ripper—but a Ripper "revelation" with, as one would have expected from Anthony Boucher, a "difference" . . .

IN 1888 London was terrified, as no city has been before or since, by Jack the Ripper, who from April through November killed and dissected at least seven prostitutes, without leaving a single clue to his identity.

The chain of murders snapped abruptly. After 1888 Jack never ripped again. Because on July 12, 1889 . . .

He paused on the steps of University College, surrounded by young ladies prattling the questions that were supposed to prove they had paid careful attention to his lecture-demonstration.

The young ladies were, he knew as a biologist, human females; dissection would establish the fact beyond question. But for him womankind was divided into three classes: angels and devils and students. He had never quite forgiven the college for admitting women nine years ago. That these female creatures should irrelevantly possess the same terrible organs that were the arsenal of the devils, the same organs through which the devils could strike lethally at the angels, the very organs which he . . .

He answered the young ladies without hearing either their questions or his answers, detached himself from the bevy, and strolled toward the Euston Road.

For eight months now he had seen neither angel nor devil. The events of 1888 seemed infinitely remote, like a fever remembered after convalescence. It had indeed been a sort of fever of the brain, perhaps even—he smiled gently—a kind of madness. But after his own angel had died of that unspeakable infection which the devil had planted in him—which had affected him so lightly but had penetrated so fatally to those dread organs which render angels vulnerable to devils . . .

He observed, clinically, that he was breathing heavily and that his hand was groping in his pocket—a foolish gesture, since he had not carried the scalpel for eight months. Deliberately he slowed his pace and his breathing. The fever was spent—though surely no sane man could see anything but good in an effort to rid London of its devils.

"Pardon, m'sieur."

The woman was young, no older than his students, but no one would mistake her for a female of University College. Even to his untutored eye her clothes spoke of elegance and chic and, in a word, Paris. Her delicate scent seemed no man-made otto° but pure *essence de femme*. Her golden hair framed a piquant face, the nose slightly tilted, the upper lip a trifle full—irregular but delightful.

"Ma'm'selle?" he replied, with courtesy and approbation.

"If m'sieur would be so kind as to help a stranger in your great city . . . I seek an establishment of baggages."

He tried to suppress his smile, but she noticed it, and a response sparkled in her eyes. "Do I say something improper?" she asked almost hopefully.

"Oh, no. Your phrase is quite correct. Most Englishmen, however, would say 'a luggage shop.'"

"Ah, *c'est ça*. 'A luggage shop'—I shall remember me. I am on my first voyage to England, though I have known Englishmen at Paris. I feel like a small child in a world of adults who talk strangely. Though I know"—his gaze was resting on what the French politely call the throat—"I am not shaped like one."

An angel, he was thinking. Beyond doubt an angel, and a

° A word only Anthony Boucher would use. Originally he wrote "attar"; but he crossed that out and substituted "otto."

delectable one. And this innocently provocative way of speaking made her seem only the more angelic.

He took from her gloved fingers the slip of paper on which was written the address of the "establishment of baggages."

"You are at the wrong end of the Euston Road," he explained. "Permit me to hail a cab for you; it is too far to walk on such a hot day."

"Ah, yes, this is a July of Julys, is it not? One has told me that in England it is never hot, but behold I sweat!"

He frowned.

"Oh, do I again say something beastly? But it is true: I do sweat." Tiny moist beads outlined her all but invisible blonde mustache.

He relaxed. "As a professor of biology I should be willing to acknowledge the fact that the human female is equipped with sweat glands, even though proper English usage would have it otherwise. Forgive me, my dear child, for frowning at your innocent impropriety."

She hesitated, imitating his frown. Then she looked up, laughed softly, and put her small plump hand on his arm. "As a token of forgiveness, m'sieur, you may buy me an ice before hailing my cab. My name," she added, "is Gaby."

He felt infinitely refreshed. He had been wrong, he saw it now, to abstain so completely from the company of women once his fever had run its course. There was a delight, a solace, in the presence of a woman. Not a student, or a devil, but the true woman: an angel.

Gaby daintily dabbed ice and sweat from her full upper lip and rose from the table. "M'sieur has been most courteous to the stranger within his gates. And now I must seek my luggage shop."

"Mademoiselle Gaby—"

"Hein? Speak up, m'sieur le professeur. Is it that you wish to ask if we shall find each other again?"

"I should indeed be honoured if while you are in London—"

"Merde alors!" She winked at him, and he hoped that he had misunderstood her French. "Do we need such fine phrases? I think we understand ourselves, no? There is a small bistro—a pub, you call it?—near my lodgings. If you wish to meet me there tomorrow evening . . ." She gave him instructions. Speechless, he noted them down.

"You will not be sorry, m'sieur. I think well you will enjoy your little tour of France after your dull English diet."

She held his arm while he hailed a cab. He did not speak except to the cabman. She extended her ungloved hand and he automatically took it. Her fingers dabbled deftly in his palm while her pink tongue peered out for a moment between her lips. Then she was gone.

"And I thought her an angel," he groaned.

His hand fumbled again in his empty pocket.

The shiny new extra large trunk dominated the bedroom.

Gabrielle Bompard stripped to the skin as soon as the porter had left (more pleased with her wink than with her tip) and perched on the trunk. The metal trim felt refreshingly cold against her flesh.

Michael Eyraud looked up lazily from the bed where he was sprawled. "I never get tired of looking at you, Gaby."

"When you are content just to look," Gaby grinned, "I cut your throat."

"It's hot," said Eyraud.

"I know, and you are an old man. You are old enough to be my father. You are a very wicked lecherous old man, but for old men it is often hot."

Eyraud sprang off the bed, strode over to the trunk, and seized her by her naked shoulders. She laughed in his face. "I was teasing you. It *is* too hot. Even for me. Go lie down and tell me about your day. You got everything?"

Eyraud waved an indolent hand at the table. A coil of rope, a block and tackle, screws, screwdriver . . .

Gaby smiled approvingly. "And I have the trunk, such a nice big one, and this." She reached for her handbag, drew out a red-and-white girdle. "It goes well with my dressing gown. And it is strong." She stretched it and tugged at it, grunting enthusiastically.

Eyraud looked from the girdle to the rope to the pulley to the top of the door leading to the sitting room, then back to the trunk. He nodded.

Gaby stood by the full-length mirror contemplating herself. "That silly bailiff, that Gouffé. Why does he dare to think that Gaby should be interested in him? This Gaby, such as you behold her . . ." She smiled at the mirror and nodded approval.

"I met a man," she said. "An Englishman. Oh, so very stiff and proper. He looks like Phileas Fogg in Jules Verne's *Le Tour du Monde*. He wants me."

"Fogg had money," said Eyraud. "Lots of it."

"So does my professor . . . Michi?"

"Yes?"

Gabrielle pirouetted before the mirror. "Am I an actress?"

"All women are actresses."

"Michi, do not try to be clever. It is not becoming to you. Am I an actress?"

Eyraud lit a French cigarette and tossed the blue pack to Gaby. "You're a performer, an entertainer. You have better legs than any actress in Paris. And if you made old Gouffé think you love him for his fat self . . . Yes, I guess you're an actress."

"Then I know what I want." Gaby's eyelids were half closed. "Michi, I want a rehearsal."

Eyraud looked at the trunk and the block and tackle and the red-and-white girdle. He laughed, heartily and happily.

He found her waiting for him in the pub. The blonde hair picked up the light and gave it back, to form a mocking halo around the pert devil's face.

His fingers reassured him that the scalpel was back where it belonged. He had been so foolish to call "a fever" what was simply his natural rightful temperature. It was his mission in life to rid the world of devils. That was the simple truth. And not all devils had cockney accents and lived in Whitechapel.

"Be welcome, m'sieur le professeur." She curtseyed with impish grace. "You have thirst?"

"No," he grunted.

"Ah, you mean you do not have thirst in the throat. It lies lower, hein?" She giggled, and he wondered how long she had been waiting in the pub. She laid her hand on his arm. The animal heat seared through his sleeve. "I go upstairs. You understand, it is more chic when you do not see me make myself ready. You ascend in a dozen of minutes. It is on the first floor, at the left to the rear."

He left the pub and waited on the street. The night was cool and the fog was beginning to settle down. On just such a night in last August . . . What was her name? He had read it later in *The Times*. Martha Tabor? Tabby? Tabbypussydevil?

He had nicked his finger on the scalpel. As he sucked the blood he heard a clock strike. He had been waiting almost a half hour; where had the time gone? The devil would be impatient.

The sitting room was dark, but subdued lamplight gleamed from the bedroom. The bed was turned down. Beside it stood a huge trunk.

The devil was wearing a white dressing gown and a red-and-white girdle that emphasized its improbably slender waist. It came toward him and stroked his face with hot fingers and touched its tongue like a branding iron to his chin and ears and at last his lips. His hands closed around its waist.

"Ouf!" gasped the devil. "You may crush *me*, I assure you, m'sieur. I love that. But please to spare my pretty new girdle. Perhaps if I debarrass myself of it . . ." It unclasped the girdle and the dressing gown fell open.

His hand took a firm grip on the scalpel.

The devil moved him toward the door between the two rooms.

It festooned the girdle around his neck. "Like that," it said gleefully. "There—doesn't that make you a pretty red-and-white cravat?"

Hand and scalpel came out of his pocket.

And Michel Eyraud, standing in the dark sitting room, fastened the ends of the girdle to the rope running through the block and tackle and gave a powerful jerk.

The rope sprang to the ceiling, the girdle followed it, and the professor's thin neck snapped. The scalpel fell from his dead hand.

The rehearsal had been a complete success.

Just as they planned to do with the bailiff Gouffé, they stripped the body and plundered the wallet. "Not bad," said Eyraud. "Do actresses get paid for rehearsing?"

"This one does," said Gaby. And they dumped the body in the trunk.

Later the clothes would be disposed of in dustbins, the body carried by trunk to some quiet countryside where it might decompose in naked namelessness.

Gaby swore when she stepped on the scalpel. "What the hell is this?" She picked it up. "It's sharp. Do you suppose he was one of those types who like a little blood to heighten their pleasures? I've heard of them but never met one."

Gaby stood pondering, her dressing gown open . . .

The first night, to the misfortune of the bailiff Gouffé, went off as smoothly as the rehearsal. But the performers reckoned without the patience and determination and génie policier of Marie-François Goron, Chief of the Paris Sûreté.

The upshot was, as all aficionados of true crime know, that Eyraud was guillotined, nineteen months after the rehearsal, and Gaby, who kept grinning at the jury, was sentenced to twenty years of hard labour.

When Goron was in London before the trial, he paid his usual courtesy call at Scotland Yard and chatted at length with Inspector Frederick G. Abberline.

"Had one rather like yours recently ourselves," said Abberline. "Naked man, broken neck, left to rot in the countryside. Haven't succeeded in identifying him yet. You were luckier there."

"It is notorious," Goron observed, "that the laboratories of the French police are the best in the world."

"We do very well, thank you," said Abberline distantly.

"Of course." The French visitor was all politeness. "As you did last year in that series of Whitechapel murders."

"I don't know if you're being sarcastic, Mr. Goron, but no police force in the world could have done more than we did in the Ripper case. It was a nightmare with no possible resolution. And unless he strikes again, it's going to go down as one of the greatest unsolved cases in history. Jack the Ripper will never hang."

"Not," said M. Goron, "so long as he confines his attention to the women of London." He hurried to catch the boat train, thinking of Gabrielle Bompard and feeling a certain regret that such a woman was also such a devil.

SO LONELY, SO LOST, SO FRIGHTENED

by Florence V. Mayberry

The Las Vegas scene and a young divorcée—young, scared, eager, beautiful, with "moonbeams for hair," still pure and innocent, her ideals untarnished. Then along came Frank—a contemporary Prince Charming, a modern knight in a white car—big, strong, perfectly tailored, wealthy. What was there to be frightened of? . . .

"HELLO," said this man's voice on the telephone. "This is Eddie. Hey, pretty girl, how about a whirl up and down the Strip tonight? Have us a ball. Sinatra's dropping in and out of the spots and with the fellow we'll be with, if we run into Sinatra, who knows, maybe we'll end up buddies. How about it, chickie-dee?"

Well, why not? I had no boyfriend. No husband any more, after coming to Nevada. All I had was a job at the Las Vegas daily paper typing up bills and things. Boring. I was tired of it, and tired of me. I had found out I don't like divorced girls. They're torn in two, scared and eager at the same time. And I was one of them.

"Okay," I said. I tried to place this Eddie, especially an Eddie who might know somebody who might be buddies with Sinatra. There had been an Eddie, a long-haired blond with a blond mustache in the newspaper gang I had gone out with one night. Not my date. And vaguely I recalled another Eddie who clerked at the hotel where I had stayed two nights when I first came to Las Vegas. Dark bangs to his eyebrows which intensified the droop of his eyelids. The vague memory of him bothered me a bit. He had always looked at me as if he knew more about me than I knew about myself.

"By the way, your date is this fellow with me. Lucky you! You hit the jackpot, kid, a great guy, really great. Loaded. And with good—know what I mean?—good connections around Vegas. Name's Frank. Okay, chickee, pick you up in front of your place in an hour."

Ye gods, I thought, could this Eddie whichever-one-he-is be talking in a roundabout way about Sinatra himself?

Frank, as I waited for the car to pick me up, I was shaking. I really thought you might be Sinatra. Isn't that a laugh?

But it was you, Frank. No laughing matter.

It was the Eddie who worked in the hotel. "Tabby, meet Frank," Eddie said, leaning out the back window of your car.

You were coming around the car to help me in. I felt wooden as I stepped inside, as if maybe I couldn't bend when I tried to sit down. That was the first time I ever rode in a white car like yours, so long and beautiful and expensive. And the first time I ever met a man like you. Your silk and linen suit, so perfectly tailored, the big diamond ring, along with that strong look as if maybe you ran the world by pushing buttons. You even smelled rich, so clean with a faint bite of perfume. I suppose that's the way all rich people with saunas smell.

Over your shoulder you said to Eddie, "Eddie, why didn't you tell me the truth? You said she was the prettiest girl in Vegas." My heart went thud. Like, wow, this fellow is really living up to his name, be frank, tell the bitter truth, he's seen prettier. "But this little Tabby is the prettiest girl in the world. What's Tabby short for, little one? You're not a tabby cat, you're a princess."

"Tabitha," I said, blushing.

"What would be your pleasure tonight? Which big name star would you especially like to hear?"

"Perhaps you have someone in mind," I said. I didn't want to let on I was so dumb about the Strip, its big hotels and entertainers, that I didn't know which entertainers were in town. Sure, I had been on the Strip a few times. But the fellows I dated just took me into cocktail lounges with no cover charge, so I didn't know much about the big shows.

You said, "Eddie, I've been stashed away in Houston for a long time. Who's playing the Strip tonight?"

Do you remember? One of the stars was Peggy Lee. She really knocks me out. The way her voice throbs makes me want my heart to break along with hers—or maybe she just sings the way my heart already felt. At her show I didn't realize I was crying until you took out your handkerchief and patted it on my cheek. Frank, did you figure out how good that would feel to a girl who thought she might really have a broken heart? I mean, was it real? Or a man on the make?

Somewhere along the Strip Eddie and his girl friend faded out. In a kind of blur I saw you whisper to Eddie as we left the Peggy Lee show to catch another show at another hotel. And pretty soon Eddie and his girl were gone. It pleased me, like bubbles of champagne in my mind, because you wanted to be alone with me.

I love your eyes. Bright blue, kind and smiling. Most of the time. You know something crazy, Frank? You have the eyes of a good, loving father. You told me you weren't married, that is, any more. That you never had children. But do you suppose you were meant to be a good father and the trouble was, you never had the chance?

Your nose is a little long and your lips are too thin. If it weren't for your eyes you would have frightened me. You were so big and rich and overpowering, six feet of you towering over my five feet one. And there was a mystery in you that frightened me, like a person in a dark room who hears footsteps that shouldn't be there.

I really was awed, Frank. I felt so young, and you were so grown up. How old were you? Thirty-five? Forty? You never said exactly. I was twenty-two.

When you asked me that first night to go to your hotel with you I wasn't angry. I didn't go, but I wasn't mad. I cried, sure. But it made me face facts. I had been wishing you were my father. Then, when you asked me that, it was clear you were a man and I was a woman, and I might as well stop wishing for a father.

To make up for thinking that way, as I left your car I took your face between my hands, looked into your wise eyes and kissed you. "You're really a good man," I said. Wasn't that a dumb thing to say? Right after what you'd asked me? But I meant it. "You're such a good man," I said. Then I ran into the cottage apartment where I lived.

I peeked through the curtain of the front window without turning on the lights. You sat out there in your car a long time. I could see the light of your cigar. Once you got out and started toward my door.

But you turned around, got back in your car and drove away. "Good-bye," I whispered. One more blind date struck out. Bye-bye. Fellows on blind dates usually don't like girls who kiss and run.

You know why I ran? Not because I didn't like you. It was because of the way my grandmother, who raised me, taught me. I was kind of an orphan, my folks divorced, and then my mother died and my father sort of disappeared. Anyway, my grandmother said keep yourself pure for marriage, that's what God wants. I believed her. I still do. But when marriage goes wrong and one's mind and emotions feel like they've been operated on, it's harder to remember what one believes, or should believe.

So that night, after you drove away, I wished I knew which hotel you were in. So I could telephone you and tell you to come back.

"Hello, little Tabby," you said. I had just come out of the newspaper office after work, wondering whether to get a hamburger and a milk shake someplace or go home first and take a shower. It was midsummer in Vegas, and midsummer in Vegas is like sitting on a hot stove in a dry frying pan.

You were in your big white car, calling to me. I ran to you as if you were Santa Claus and I was about five years old. "I never thought I'd see you again," I said.

You chuckled. "Funny," you said. "*I* knew I would see *you* again. If I lived. Get in the car, sweetheart. You look tired. Let's go have dinner."

"Oh, please, I need to shower and change first!" What would I wear—my white pants suit?—no, maybe that new long pale-blue lace, with the ribbon around the waist.

Naturally you came in my apartment while I changed—you couldn't sit out there in the heat. So you waited in my living room, flipping through magazines. I locked the door of my bathroom, very softly so you wouldn't hear. But you never moved. Crazy thing, I was disappointed you didn't even move.

I wore the long pale-blue dress and pinned up my hair because I thought it made me look older. I was always running into trouble at the clubs; they were afraid I was too young to come in. I bleach my hair, I told you that a long time ago. And you said, "I don't want to hear about it. All I want is to believe you have moonbeams for hair." Well, with that kind of hair and blue eyes—no, actually they're violet—and being small, I guess—

You took a deep breath when I came out of the bedroom ready to go. You stood up, put your hands on my shoulders, bent down, and kissed my forehead. "Honey, you're not real. Wherever we go tonight, they'll think I'm bringing my baby-dollie with me."

Where did we go that night? Dinner, yes. Yes, I remember. In an elegant quiet room with quiet dreamy couples scattered around it. That kind of place. I knew you had to be somebody special to know about a place like that in Vegas when all most people know about are the loud, slot-machine hotel kind.

Later we went to the big clubs, all of them I think. It made me giggle, how the head waiters bowed so low and smiled and led us to special tables beside the dance floor. And I felt so important to be with you when executive-looking men came to our tables saying things like, "Good to have you back in Vegas. Hope you stay with us." And you saying, yes, good, but you'd be back and forth. I tried to worry about that "back and forth," but giggles bubbled out of me all the time as if they were champagne and I was a glass.

As we drove away from the last club, the bubbles stopped. Nothing was left in the glass except a sad worry that you and the whole evening were not real, only a dream. I told you that, that night. But you said it would last forever, it wasn't a dream, it was the only real thing in your life.

Later, when you insisted I quit my job, I asked what had been on my mind all along. "You mean, we're going to get married?" It was pretty embarrassing. I mean, even with a man I knew as well as you, it should be the man asking the girl.

"As soon as possible," you said. "Right now I'm under heavy pressure. Business. And I'm in a business where pressure isn't—good. At this stage in my affairs it's better for you to be involved as little as possible. Tabby, with a man like me, marriage takes time and caution."

"What kind of business are you in?" I asked.

"We won't talk about it now," you said. "Let me do the

worrying and you do the playing. Little girls with moonbeam hair and violet eyes shouldn't bother about a man's business troubles. Then, if anybody asks questions, you won't know any answers."

I knew you were doing the worrying, your face had become so strained. It didn't ease up when you said we were going on a vacation, to Acapulco; your face became even more tight and your eyes more watchful. So I knew we were leaving because of something frightening about your business. But I never asked about it, not even when you had me fly alone from Las Vegas one early morning to Los Angeles, and from there to Acapulco. Not even after those long hours of waiting for you in the Acapulco airport.

But then you came and everything was wonderful. Except, it wasn't a vacation. You leased a house and paid a year's rent in advance.

Acapulco was so beautiful, so soothing that I forgot to worry. Soft guitars, tropical birds singing, flowers everywhere. The Mexican people were so warm, loving, yet so exotic, their voices rising and falling in the mysterious gaiety of a foreign language.

And this house you rented, high-ceilinged with wide windows and doors facing the sea. White walls, lime-colored drapes with blue-green flowers floating on them. The furniture white and gold, hand-carved. Goatskin rugs scattered over the tiled floors for me to pad over with my bare, manicured feet. Before I went to Mexico I never dreamed manicurists came to houses just to do fingernails and toenails. A silly thing, but it made me feel so rich and beautiful, so cared for.

Best of all was good strong Mamacita who ran the house, bossed her two daughters and the gardener, and taught me Spanish. I depended so much on Mamacita, especially the times you went away on business, back to Las Vegas or wherever.

Which place did you go to this last time, Frank? The Bahamas, New York, or just out on some godforsaken nowhere road? Where did these terrible things happen to you?

Even though this last time you were away longer than usual, I wasn't frightened until those men came to our house. Two of them. One blond, one medium, but both with dark faces. Not dark from being tanned in the sun. Dark from something deep inside.

I was frightened the moment they stepped into our living room, even though I didn't yet know how they shoved past Mamacita at the entrance door. The gardener had been working out front and they gave him a hundred pesos to unlock the street gate—Mamacita made him admit it later. She followed the two men and stood in the door of the living room, her big brown eyes flashing and her jaw set.

When they said they were your friends and asked to see you, I invited them to sit down and sent Mamacita for fruit juice. She tossed her head and when she came back, one of her daughters was with her and I was vaguely aware that now the gardener was trimming shrubs with his machete just outside the open French doors.

I told those men the truth. That I didn't know where you were, that you never told me, never wrote letters. That you said you would be back within the month, but now the month was up.

The way they watched me, still and probing, reminded me of you, Frank. Sometimes you looked like that in Las Vegas when you met your business friends. Only their eyes were flatter, deader than yours ever were. Frank, I was scared to death.

Finally they said the papers they had for you to sign could wait until you returned. "But I don't know when he will be back!" I said. I sounded desperate because I was desperate. "Perhaps— perhaps he's looking for you somewhere in the States. If he needs to sign papers, perhaps he's up there waiting for you."

Their eyes flicked over me. "Waiting for us?"

"In Vegas, or somewhere. Just waiting while you're here looking for him. He may wait until you come. Only I hope not, he's been gone such a long time already. I'm—I'm anxious about him."

They smiled, as if something funny had suddenly struck them. "Don't worry, little lady," one of them said. "We'll send a wire to our associates so he won't need to wait any longer. One of them will see that he gets the papers."

They thanked me and left, Mamacita bouncing angrily behind them to the outside gate and then locking it with a big flourish.

When she returned to the house I ran to her, put my arms around her, and cried, "Mamacita, *tengo meido, tengo meido!* I have fear, I have fear for my Senor."

"*Si, si,* poor little Senorita. Don't have fear, Mamacita will take care of you. Did not the Senor tell me to?"

She suddenly left off patting my back and vanished toward the kitchen. "One little moment, Senorita," she called over her shoulder.

She returned holding a long thin kitchen knife, polished down by use until it was almost a stiletto. She waved it in a circle, then gave a sudden jab through the circle. "This, in case of thieves. Or if those wicked men come back and make trouble." She pulled out a drawer in the white-and-gold cabinet beneath the framed mirror in the entrance hall. "Look, Senorita, remember it is here. In case I should not be near. The knife is here." She nodded with satisfaction and walked off about her work, her lovely broad hips swaying.

I could hear her flaying the gardener with fierce words because he was a scoundrel and took money to open the gate; no need to confess to the priest for that evil deed, she would take it out of his hide. Her daughters, all ears, were idling in the background; she ordered them back to work. Everything was normal once more and I tried to laugh, pretending what had happened was only funny. Like some crazy movie with make-believe villains. But the laugh stuck in my throat.

Frank, you were away so long that the money you left gave out. There was no worry about the house, the rent was paid. The manicurist, the hairdresser, the shopping, they were easy to drop—I hadn't had those things before. But the servants' salaries, the food to buy for all of us, that couldn't be dropped.

Finally the gardener threatened me with the police about his salary. So Mamacita threatened him and ran him off. She patted me a lot and told me again and again not to have fear, not to have anxiety. But she was anxious, too. Actually I think more for me than for herself. Mamacita belonged in Mexico. I didn't.

Finally she sent her daughters off to other jobs. And at last Mamacita herself left. Once or twice a week she came back to bring me tortillas and beans. I ate tortillas and beans for three months. Not that I'm complaining, I like tortillas and beans—Mexicans eat that way all the time. And there were papayas and bananas and sweet lemons in our garden. I could even have been content if I hadn't kept thinking about those two men. That if they found you, they meant to hurt you. Or worse.

I don't like to say it, Frank, but it's true: alone that way I began to feel clean again. Almost as I used to feel when I was a small girl in my grandmother's house. Often I forgot to think, I'm in love with a racketeer, maybe a criminal. How did someone named Tabitha and raised by her grandmother get mixed up in this?

Six months passed and still you didn't come. It was embarrassing, having the beautiful house and clothes, looking rich, and eating Mamacita's tortillas and beans. So I sold my watch, my camera, some of my clothes. I kept my beautiful diamond ring; you said it was our engagement ring.

Antonio bought the camera. He heard about it through one of Mamacita's daughters. He didn't pay much, only 150 pesos, but it was more than he could afford. With that $12 plus the money I hadn't spent from the other things I sold, I planned to buy a bus ticket to the Border. Back in the States I could find a job. I would leave a letter for you, telling you what I was doing.

One night I packed a small bag, leaving most of my things behind in the hope I would be back. Then early in the morning I left the house and walked down to the locked entrance gate. As I put the key in the lock, Antonio was reaching for the chain which rang the black iron bell above the gate.

"*Buenos dias*, Senorita," he said. Like Mamacita, Antonio knew only Spanish, but by this time I was fairly fluent in it. "Such a beautiful morning, so pretty here, are you leaving, Senorita?"

"Yes," I said. "Yes."

"My heart is grieved," he said, his big brown eyes sad. He was a very handsome boy, just my age he told me later. Even in cotton work clothes he was handsome. Tall for a Mexican, with smooth healthy brown skin, an oval face with strong features. "Acapulco will lose its beauty when you leave." That's the way Mexicans talk; it sounds lovely even when they don't mean it. "Senorita, I came today to fix your garden. The mother of my friend, the one you call Mamacita, tells me your gardener has left, the garden is dry, the weeds grow. I will fix it."

"You're very kind. But I have no money. I couldn't pay the other gardener, that's why he is angry with me. I have only enough money to buy a ticket to the Border. Back to my own country."

A smile flashed and he leaned eagerly toward me. "This could be your country, Senorita. It's true, it is possible. I will arrange it with the mother of my friend, it will be very nice, very respectable. I will marry you, Senorita."

Frank, nothing in me wanted to marry this handsome sweet boy. I knew I would never marry him. Or anybody but you. That isn't why I began to cry. It was because I was so lonely, so lost, so frightened. It was comforting to have someone want to take care of me.

Antonio reached through the iron bars of the gate, took the key from my hand, and unlocked it. He followed me to the tiled garden seat and started to put his arms around me. I shook my head and said, "No. *Siempre no*. Always no. No, no, no." He shook me, gently, and said, "Please, Senorita, I understand, say no more. Be at peace."

He stood aside, placed his hands on his hips, smiled, and tossed his head toward the shaggy dry garden. "I will make it pretty again. You stay. Perhaps—perhaps the Senor will come soon, it's better you wait to see. What if he comes tomorrow? Or next week? If he does not, one can always leave. Senorita, you like chili rellenos, my sister is making chili rellenos today, too many for her family, she give me some, you like them?"

Frank, I was used to being dependent on you. Besides, I'll face it, I'm a dependent person. So it was easy to let Antonio help me. A mirage of safety.

Antonio, I discovered, had a stall in one of the markets. He made beautiful leather sandals, the leather soft and cured, more delicate than most Mexican sandals. He brought me a pair. I couldn't hurt his feelings, could I, by not wearing them?

He was the businessman for his family. His relatives brought their craft work to him to sell—serapes, blankets, pottery, all kinds of things. Actually, even though he was young, the relatives looked on him as their family head because he was so bright and ambitious. He was studying books on mathematics, grammar, and science.

"Someday, Senorita, I will make myself into an educated gentleman," he told me. "You'll see. Like I change stiff leather into a soft beautiful shoe. My family will be proud of me then." He laughed, so natural in the pleasure of what he could become that it didn't sound egotistical. He didn't say it, but I saw it in his eyes: You will be proud of me, too, Senorita.

As head of his family, he could demand assistance from relatives to watch the market stall when he wanted to be away. At those times he made my garden beautiful again. On those days, too, following him shadowlike, one or another shy scrawny little girl of twelve or so would accompany him. A cousin, or a niece, some relative. With rapid Spanish and stern eye he would command the child and off she would scurry to the back patio, gather up pail and mop and clean the floors, or flip a cloth to move the dust from one spot to another.

I protested. I said I had been doing the housework, I was used to work. But I was afraid to protest too much for fear Antonio and the little girls would stop coming.

But when the Mariachi band began to serenade me in the dark predawn morning I knew that all this had to stop, that I must take the bus to the Border. Forget you. Find a job. Forget both you and Antonio.

When I woke from sleep and heard the haunting, lilting song rising from the street outside the garden wall, for the first few minutes I didn't realize what it was. I actually thought I had died and gone to Paradise. But then I noticed my heart pounding, and dead hearts don't pound. Then I wondered if you were dead. That somehow your spirit had sent the Mariachis to tell me that.

But of course Antonio had sent them. He tried to be subtle about it when he came to work in the garden. "Did you sleep well, Senorita?" he asked casually. But his eyes, anxious and shy, gave him away.

"No," I said. "Beautiful music woke me. I thought I had died."

He was stricken. "You were frightened, Senorita Tabby?"

"Yes. Very frightened. Because you are too kind to me and like me too much. The Senor is not going to return. So now I must leave. Tomorrow. This is definite."

So last night I packed my little bag again, ready to leave this morning.

Last night Antonio's large family, along with Mamacita and his relatives, made a fiesta for me. They came weighed down with pots, platters, baskets of food—enchiladas, tamales, chili rellenos, beans, tortillas—and I furnished papayas and bananas. All of us sang and laughed, someone had a guitar. As they left, they wept, embraced me, told me to go with God and to return quickly. Everyone, that is, except Antonio. He wouldn't tell me good-bye. Just bowed and left.

Later, in the dark early morning, the Mariachis came again.

I went out on the bedroom balcony in this lovely filmy robe you bought me. The moon was out, and the street light played tangle-fingers with the leaves of the trees lining the sidewalk, scattering light and shadows over the upturned faces of the musicians. When they saw me on the balcony their voices became softer, more yearning.

I glimpsed Antonio across the street, standing in the shadows, watching to see if I came out to the balcony. He moved from the shadows, into the middle of the street, looking up, taut, leaning forward as if he would walk along his gaze all the way up to me.

I should have gone back inside quickly. Quickly. Antonio was such a nice boy, so sweet. An honorable boy, Frank.

But I didn't. I slipped to my knees by the iron railing of the balcony, weeping, saying, "Oh, Antonio, I'm so lonely, so weak, so lost!"

He ran to one of the musicians, sprang like a cat to his shoulders, and from there to the top of the wall. He grasped the iron spikes on the wall to steady himself, then jumped down into the courtyard. He came beneath the balcony, saying he loved me, he would die for me, please, Senorita, we'll be married.

Then, suddenly, he was on the balcony beside me, murmuring words like honey that blended with the music in the street.

That's all there was to it, Frank. No matter what you thought. That's all. A weak frightened girl kneeling on a balcony and listening to a boy tell her how much he loved her.

We didn't hear the taxi drive up or notice its lights. But we heard the gate open, heard you speak to the driver who carried your bags. I sprang up. All I thought of was, you were back. You hadn't died, you hadn't forgotten me, you were here!

I cried out, "Frank, darling!"

You looked up. I could see your every feature, the moonlight was so bright. Your face terrified me. Partly because you were shockingly thin, your cheeks sunken. But mostly because of the cold rage on your face. "You couldn't wait," you said quietly, dangerously. The musicians had stopped playing and in the still night your cold voice slipped into me like a stiletto blade.

Only then I remembered Antonio beside me. "No, Frank, don't think that! The music, it made me cry. Antonio heard me crying because you were gone and I was afraid you were dead." I thought frantically, what can I say to make him believe me? I said, "Antonio is only a servant."

"Your maid, perhaps?" you said.

Antonio climbed over the balcony railing and dropped lightly into the courtyard. "Senor, a thousand pardons." You didn't understand Spanish, so this is what he said, "A thousand pardons. Not to you, but to the little Senorita whose heart is broken. She weeps for you, not for me. If I had a thousand lives I would give them all if she would but weep for me like that one little hour. So have anger at me, I'm the one with blame."

He raised his voice and called to the musicians, "Go, go! No more music tonight. This is private."

Without taking your eyes off him you paid the taxi driver, waved him away. The gate clanged shut. The lights of the taxi shot up the street.

The night became taut, as though the air was sucked out of it. Every sound hurt the nerves—the feet of the musicians as they shuffled away, the frogs croaking in the fountain's pool, the insects chirping, the breathing of the three of us, the drumming of my heart. It was mesmerizing. I felt outside of everything that was happening, something like when I was a child lying on my stomach on the ground watching ants do funny ant things.

You men stood still, staring at each other. Finally I choked out, "Antonio's the gardener. The only one left."

You said softly, "And the flower is in the house? Upstairs?"

I left the blacony, ran through the bedroom, down the stairs to the front door, drew the bolt, ran to you reaching blindly, like an exhausted swimmer struggling for shore. You held me off, a queer, awkward thing, struggling to touch you, my filmy robe fluttering like a moth.

Finally I gave up and stood back, begging for answers, "Frank, where were you? Why didn't you come back? Please, tell me what happened."

"Troubles. From good friends," you said. "I recovered from them in the hospital. One of the get-well cards read, 'This time the hospital, next time the morgue.' What kind of cards did you want to send to me, Tabitha? 'Having a wonderful time, glad you're not here'? And perhaps this Mexican Romeo is a welcome-home present?"

You sighed then, as though you were tired of everything, too tired even for anger. "Oh, well," you said. "One way or another, I suppose I deserve it." You started toward the house. I followed. You stopped, looked back with a bitter smile, and pointed at Antonio. "Is your friend coming, too?"

Antonio didn't understand English. But the way you looked at him, so contemptuous, he must have believed it a terrible insult to his masculine pride, to his machismo. And Frank, I believe he loved me, truly loved me. He ran at you, grabbed you, threw you to the paved yard. I was shocked when you didn't throw him aside, you were always so big and strong. Later I knew why—when I saw the long scars, the surgeon's stitches on your throat and chest, that had not yet healed.

Antonio was young and healthy. He clutched your throat, suffocating you. Once you rolled him over and were on top, banging his head on the paving stones. Then you were down again and his fingers were at your throat again. I threw myself on him, pulled his hair, raked my fingernails across his face, screaming in Spanish, "Quitate! Leave my man alone! I love him!"

For all the attention he paid I could have been a dream drifting in the night. The crack of your head on the stones came again and again. Your breathing rasped and snuffled.

Then I remembered Mamacita's knife—in the hall cabinet, ready in case of trouble. I ran into the hall, felt in the drawer. For one terrible lost moment in which I saw you dead before I could help, I couldn't find it. Then I did, at the back of the drawer.

I ran back. Antonio still clutched your throat, banging your head. A dark streak poured from your neck. I know now an unhealed scar had burst open.

Antonio's back was to me. For a crazy confused instant I tried

to decide on which side was his heart. Then, with all my force, I
struck the slim sharp blade into his back.

Please, Frank, please talk. Please breathe again. Help me.
I don't know what to do. I never killed anyone before. Should I
call the police tonight? Or wait until daylight? Should the police
see everything just as it is? Two dead men in my front patio and
me with blood all over from pulling Antonio off you. When I
rolled him away, he fell on his back and the knife sank deeper. He
gasped. He gasped once. And that was all.

I never wanted anything like this to happen. How do terrible
things happen to people who don't want them? How can a love
story go so wrong?

Please, Frank, wake up and tell me, tell me.

A GAME IN THE SUN

by John Coyne

This is the 364th "first story" to be published by Ellery
Queen's Mystery Magazine . . . *a story of great tension—vivid,
compelling, frightening . . .*

*The author, John Coyne, was 32 when he submitted "A Game in
the Sun." With degrees from St. Louis University and from
Western Michigan University, he can already claim an interesting
and varied career: caddie, golf professional, high school teacher,
radio writer, foreign service officer, government employee, college
administrator. But his chief ambition has always been to become a
serious full-time writer. Ever since he was 12 he has written short
stories, articles, and novels, all "rejected by nearly every major and*

*minor publishing house in America." Currently, he tells us, his
desk holds six unpublished novels and fifty short stories. His first
published fiction, in this volume, derives from the five years he
spent in Africa, teaching and working for the Peace Corps.*

*Mark our words: some of those fifty short stories and six novels
will, one of these days, see the light of print . . .*

BETSY was not allowed to play croquet with her
husband and the Reverend, so she sat in the shade of the trees at
the top of the mound. The mound overlooked a lush rainforest
which grew thick and dense to the edges of the Mission
Compound. The view was compelling and frightening to Betsy.
The close steamy jungle made her feel insignificant and as she half
listened to Mrs. Shaw's chatter, she watched the bush as if it were
alive.

The Reverend and Mrs. Shaw had started the Mission twenty
years before. Landscaping woods near a village of mud and
cattle-dung huts, they cut into the underbrush, leaving only the
ancient acacias and gum trees for shade, and planting lawns and
gardens. The African laborers had instructions to keep the lawns
neatly trimmed during the rainy season, well watered the
remainder of the year.

The Shaws had been the only white people in the district until
Betsy and her husband arrived with the Peace Corps to teach in
the government school. It was their second year in-country and as
Betsy had calculated that morning, she had only eighteen more
Sundays left in Africa.

"You really won't know Africa for ten years. It takes that long
to get a feel of the land," the Reverend had said when he first
dropped by to say hello and welcome them to the village. He had
crowded himself into their doll-like house, held onto his father's
straw hat, and looked with alarm about the inadequate place.

"The Peace Corps's not giving you much cooperation, are they?"
He shook his head, frowning over the lack of facilities.

He was a big fleshy man, dressed in worn jeans, a tight-fitting
plaid shirt, and heavy-duty boots. His face was burnt from the
long self-appointed days in the African sun. Only his forehead,
protected by the straw hat, was chalky. His eyes were tiny and
squinted against the sun. Dark lines clustered at their corners. The
rest of his face was soft and slightly moist. He kept a white
handkerchief folded in the palm of his hand and continually
wiped the running sweat off his red cheeks, as if he were polishing
them.

"Look, kids, I want ya to come to our place anytime. Anytime.
Come tomorrow for lunch, a game of croquet." He glanced again
about the house. "You're going to need all the comforts of home
you can get. But with the help of God . . . with the help of God."

Before the game the Shaws's houseboys, barefooted and
in starched white uniforms, moved like tropical birds among
them, serving iced tea. The two men talked about the week, the
news from the school and Mission, while Mrs. Shaw took Betsy
through the gardens, the beds of exotic flowers which grew in the
heat and humidity, brilliant and thick.

Mrs. Shaw wore farm gloves and with a gardener's eye clipped
flowers and presented them to Betsy. Mrs. Shaw was also
concerned about Betsy and her husband living in the village, in a
mud-and-dung house, in among the Africans. The flowers were to
pretty up Betsy's life.

Mrs. Shaw lay her scissors on the lawn table and pulled off her
gloves, then she rubbed baby lotion thoroughly into her hands.
The scent was stronger than the flowers and reminded Betsy of
her home, of growing up as a little girl.

"I learned years ago that baby lotion was the answer. Just
ordinary baby lotion keeps me just fine. The weather is so cruel on
people, women especially." Unlike her husband, Mrs. Shaw
looked as if she had never been in the African sun. Her skin was

milky under the protection of a wide-brimmed bonnet and deep in the shadows her eyes flashed like those of a cornered animal. "After a while you learn these little hints. It takes time, of course, but with the help of God." Her voice bore inward like a drill.

Betsy was no longer listening. She had closed her eyes and was leaning back in the lawn chair, resting. She knew she must not begin to cry in front of these people. She must not be vulnerable. There were, after all, only eighteen Sundays left in Africa. She had gone that morning into the bedroom, to her homemade calendar behind the door, and crossed off another day. Briefly she had felt lighthearted, gay, but that exhilaration had slipped away in the hot bedroom, in the heat of the day. Betsy sighed and then, unexpectedly, shivered.

"Are you all right, dear?" Mrs. Shaw reached over. Betsy could feel the damp fingers, the baby lotion sticky on her own arm.

"No—nothing. I'm fine." She gathered herself together, managed a thin smile, blinked away a rush of tears, said quickly, shading her eyes and looking over the lawns, "Are they finished?"

"You've been remembering your quinine, haven't you, dear?" Mrs. Shaw wouldn't let go.

"Oh, of course, it's nothing really, Mrs. Shaw. We'll be into the rainy season soon. Perhaps I'm feeling the first chills. You know how cold it suddenly seems?" She talked rapidly.

"Yes, perhaps even in the hot sun one can feel chilled." And Mrs. Shaw let the subject slip away, as if it were an error.

On the lawns before them the game was drawing to a close. The Reverend was ahead as always, banging his mallet against the wooden ball, moving quickly from one wicket to the next, looking awkward, too huge for the grass game.

"I've gotcha, Jesse. I've gotcha again." His voice was buoyant.

Jesse behind him, struggling, hit the ball. It bounced erratically across the grass, hapless. He followed, thin and undernourished. Jesse had lost weight in Africa and now his trousers were baggy. He laughed at his miscalculations, amused by his inability. She watched him with eyes bled of color, gray and watery, studied him with detachment, as if watching a stranger. Who was this person, she wondered.

The game was over. They came to her through the heat, haze, and sun, their bodies shimmery. Perhaps she was sick. Tentatively she touched herself, felt the clammy skin of her forearm. Her fingers were cold and around her the lawns and gardens were airless.

"Had enough for one day, boys?" Mrs. Shaw grinned. "I'll have lunch ready in minutes." She clapped once, like a single piano note, and the dark houseboys stepped from the shadows and carried food to them on the lawn.

"How's the little lady?" the Reverend asked and spread himself into the lounge chair beside Betsy. "You're lookin' peaked, honey."

"I was just saying so myself, Walter. She doesn't look at all well. Don't you agree, Jesse?"

They wouldn't let her alone. All of them gauged her with worried looks. Her husband stared. His mouth had flopped open, as if half his mind had been blown away. He touched her and she jerked away.

"Betsy, why don't you lie down a while, until the day cools?" Mrs. Shaw was at her side.

Betsy would have to get away from these people. Part of her mind told her she did not know them. And these lawns, the enclosing rainforest, had not happened to her. She would go somewhere cool, somewhere out of the heat. She could hardly breathe. Why won't it rain? The smell of baby lotion again and the touch of warm flesh.

She let herself be guided from the hot gardens into the house where curtains were drawn and there was a bit of air. The bedcovers were soft silk, not the coarse linen from the village. They let her sleep . . .

The rains began the next day. Standing at the windows of the Third Form, Betsy watched it soak into the dry football field. She reached out the window and the cool water soaked her arm. It felt refreshing and she smiled for the first time in weeks.

That afternoon Betsy was going to tell Jesse she wanted a divorce, but he had come home after school—wet and muddy into the tiny house—said something silly about her hair, something she knew was meant to cheer her up; and she had gone into the bedroom, slammed the door, and cried herself to sleep.

It was raining again when she woke. The rain pounded on the tin roof, deafeningly. She jerked the sheets around her without getting up, and slept. When she woke a second time it was dark; he had lit the lamp and made her soup.

"You'll feel better after this." Jesse held out the cup like an offering. His face carried a blankness, like a birthmark. He did not comprehend subtleties, or his wife. She took the soup without speaking, without looking at him, and sipped it. The cup in her fingers was as warm as a small bird and she kept both hands tight around the porcelain, afraid to let it go.

Jesse kept talking, incessantly, afraid of the silence. He had met the Reverend in the village and the Shaws asked about her, wanted to know if Betsy would like to move into the Mission for a few days, until she felt better.

"I feel better."

"Yeah, sure. I told the Reverend you were okay. Told him it was just the heat, you know, Sunday." Jesse perched tentatively, as if he didn't belong, on the edge of her bed.

They had requested a double bed from the Peace Corps early in their tour, but it had never come, and now she was glad of the privacy. If she could only be alone. That was the problem: she couldn't get away.

"I want to sleep." She handed back the cup, careful so their fingers did not touch.

"Again?" He sounded lonely.

She did not respond, but pulled the sheets around her and turned away, dismissing him with silence. This time, however, she did not sleep, only watched the dark room, the dung walls, whitewashed with lime. Jesse left with the shaky yellow lamplight. Betsy could hear him in the other room trying to be quiet, moving carefully, not making noise. She sobbed into the sheets.

Betsy did not go to school the rest of the week. Every morning after he left for school she would wrap herself in a robe and, wearing boots, slip and slide through the mud to the outhouse and throw up whatever little she had eaten into the deep smelly pit. And then, trembling, she'd sit there among the cobwebs and the stink of the tin outhouse until her strength came back and she could make it again through the slush.

Betsy woke from another faulty daytime sleep and found the Reverend and Mrs. Shaw at the foot of her bed, filling the room like massive furniture. They stood tensely, afraid to touch the surroundings. Mrs. Shaw had a giant bouquet of flowers, flaming like a torch in the dark room. The room was as disheveled as a drunk—drawers left open, clothes scattered. It also had a close stale smell. The smell of unwashed bodies.

"My dear, my dear!" Mrs. Shaw rushed through the mess to Betsy, felt her temperature, began fussing with the linen.

"I'm fine; I'm fine. It's just the weather, that's all. I'm feeling better every day." Betsy slipped a smile on and off her face.

The Reverend, with one hand mopping the sweat from his red cheeks, said from the end of the bed, as if calling from a great distance, "We want to see you Sunday. Gotta get you in a game."

Betsy did not respond. She let Mrs. Shaw wipe the perspiration from her face and neck.

"Walter, you go ahead. I'll stay a while with Betsy." She smiled at her patient, then began with busy efficient hands to tidy the covers and make Betsy presentable.

When Betsy woke again, Mrs. Shaw was gone, the room straightened, and her husband home from classes, moving about in the other room. He seemed to bang into everything. Why was he so inept? How did she not know that about him, she wondered. He appeared in the narrow doorway, cautious as a child.

"Bring me the calendar," she ordered, though her weak voice lacked authority. Jesse was happy to help; he hurried to find her magic marker and homemade posterboard.

She took the calendar without thanking him, though he waited for the words, hoped to hear a bit of kindness. She couldn't say thanks, couldn't give him a civil remark. Why didn't he take control, be demanding, take care of her? She slashed black lines through the dates while he stood beside her bed like one of Mrs. Shaw's houseboys.

"I want you to beat the Reverend at croquet," she said, finishing with the calendar.

"Beat the Reverend?" Jesse frowned, moved to look at her face. "But I can't beat him!" His voice touched the edge of alarm.

"You never try. That's your problem." She tossed the calendar aside and continued not to look at him, but to gaze across the room, eyes locked onto a small patch of wall where a chunk of dung had swollen and the whitewash had peeled away, like a scab. "If you had tried we wouldn't need to be in the Peace Corps. You could have gotten out of Vietnam another way."

"It's not a question of trying!" Jesse stuck his small hands into the pockets of his baggy trousers and began to pace. "And you wanted to go too, remember."

"I'm sick of going out there, week after week, talking to that old woman, watching you get beaten—"

"It's a game, Betsy, for God's sake!" He moved about at the end of the bed to catch her eye, but she kept turning away. "You know he likes to win. Croquet is his big deal—the way he takes care of those lawns, sets the wickets."

"You could beat him just once, that's all. No! You're such a damn weak sister." The sentence spilled out, uncontrolled. She watched him hunch up against the words. "Him and his dumb wife, God! How have I stood all of you?" Tears stopped her and she clamped both hands across her mouth to keep from screaming.

Jesse's arms went tentatively around her. He smelled of sweat and the local soap. She did not like his odors. He only washed casually, one bath a week. It was too much trouble hauling and heating water, taking a sponge bath in the kitchen, using the metal tub. There lingered about him a close stale odor, reminiscent, she suddenly realized, of the young sweaty boys in her classes.

"Get away." She pushed him. "Why don't you wash?"

He left, slamming the door. Later, before falling to sleep for the hundredth time that day, she heard him heating and pouring water into the washtub.

Betsy stared across the lawns toward the rainforest, watched the close, creepy jungle while Mrs. Shaw wrapped a shawl about her shoulders, made her comfortable in a lawn chair. Mrs. Shaw's voice rang in her ears. She was full of chatty news from the village, stories of conversions to Christ. Betsy turned her head slowly in the direction of the voice, and Mrs. Shaw's face shimmered.

Betsy felt cold and clammy and the wool shawl was a damp cloth on her shoulders. There was again the oily smell of baby lotion, mixed with the scent of carnations and roses. A gift of flowers, wet with rain, lay abandoned on the table. There were seventeen Sundays left in Africa and Betsy knew now she could not make it.

Bright-colored balls shot over the lawns, trailing sprays of water, and the two men followed from wicket to wicket, halting, swinging fiercely, then hurrying to catch up. The Reverend was ahead, banging the painted balls, shouting, poking fun at Jesse fumbling behind.

Mrs. Shaw leaned over the flowers and whispered, "Dear, are you with child?"

Betsy could feel the breakfast of eggs and toast, of weak tea and lemon, catch like gas in her throat. Mrs. Shaw pressed forward, like a parent. "You're showing all the signs. I told the Reverend. I said, Betsy is with child. I know. I've an uncanny knack for such things." Her eyes flashed.

Tentatively Betsy touched her abdomen, sensed it growing there like fungus inside of her. The Peace Corps had not sent the pills. Days and weeks had passed. She'd kept away from him, begged to be let alone while he panted like a stray dog. It was she who woke one humid night in the single bed, stripped herself naked in the heat, and padding through the house to the refrigerator, drank a cold glass of water that cooled her like rain. She touched the tip of her breast with her wet fingers and shivered. Then she went to Jesse's bed, pulled away the sheet, and woke him with her hands and mouth seeking.

"I've gotcha, Jesse!" The Reverend smashed the ball against the final pole, then turned to her husband still among the pattern of hoops. The Reverend wiped his cheeks with the handkerchief and, laughing, took off the straw hat. He waved to her. "I've got'm, Betsy. I've got'm again. In ten years maybe, in ten years—"

She came running wildly down the soft slope, her face flaming with rage. They dropped the mallets, glanced at each other as if there was some mistake, raised their hands to justify, but she had reached them with the scissors.

OPEN LETTER TO SURVIVORS

by Francis M. Nevins, Jr.

This is the 366th "first story" to be published by Ellery Queen's Mystery Magazine . . .

The author, Francis M. Nevins, Jr., was born in 1943, received his law degree from New York University of Law in 1967, was admitted to the New Jersey bar the same year, has been an editor for a New York City law publisher, has practiced law as a Legal Services "storefront lawyer," and at the time of this writing is Assistant Professor of Law at St. Louis University Law School.

Mike (as he is known to his friends) has already achieved an enviable career in nonfiction areas of the mystery field, and he is only just beginning. He has written numerous articles, including one on "the wild and woolly world of Harry Stephen Keeler." He has edited an excellent book of essays on crime fiction, The Mystery Writer's Art (*Bowling Green University Popular Press,*

1971), and a collection of stories by the late Cornell Woolrich, Nightwebs *(Harper & Row, 1971), which contains an indispensable Woolrich bibliography (the latter compiled in collaboration with Harold Knott and William Thailing). Recently Mr. Nevins finished* Royal Bloodline, *a book-length study of the EQ opera, to be published in 1974 by Popular Press, Bowling Green University. And there are other important projects in the test tubes.*

Now Mr. Nevins has turned to fiction. His first story is a kind of pastiche—strange, unusual, subtle. The case it explores is one of wheels within wheels—a new variant of what might be called a locked room within a locked room; a curious case full of hints, echoes, and intimations of certain books which your editor hopes are familiar to most readers of Ellery Queen's Mystery Magazine . . .

". . . there was the case of Adelina Monquieux, his remarkable solution of which cannot be revealed before 1972 by agreement with that curious lady's executors . . ."

ELLERY QUEEN, *Ten Days' Wonder* (1948)

THE book was conceived only in part, the rest of it was still struggling for conception inside him. A large and vicious neighborhood cat, some lines from Jung, a long wait in a subway station in the stifling postmidnight hours of a torrid summer, were all parts of the organism fighting for birth. But something was missing, some vital element. And when he realized that what he and the book needed was total immersion in the postwar international nightmare, he picked up his phone and called Burt Billings, who was his attorney, his friend, and, as he happened to know, the attorney for Adelina Monquieux.

The indomitable, the inimitable, the incredible Adelina—or, to use her professional name (though she had never married), Mrs. Monquieux, pronounced Mon-Q, not monkey. She was the last of an asset-studded line and the foremost political analyst of the generation. Her gargoyle face with its luminously intelligent eyes had made the cover of *Time* three years earlier, soon after Hiroshima; the artist had sketched endless cameos of death within the tangles of her unkempt henna hair.

The feature story in *Time* had chronicled her travels through Europe and Asia during the Thirties and most of the war years, the disenchanted brilliance of her many books and articles on international politics, and her unrelieved pessimism about mankind. After Hiroshima and Nagasaki she had written an essay boiling with humane fury titled "God Damn Us Every One," had changed her will so that most of her wealth would be left for the care of the bomb's victims, and had retired to the family estate to brood and write.

Billings called back within an hour: the great lady would talk with him the following Sunday at noon.

He drove out of the city early Sunday morning, the cloudless sky like blue glass and promising thick heat before noon. He had spent Saturday rereading the *Time* story and leafing through some of the woman's books. He had learned that she lived on the estate with the three orphans of World War I whom she had adopted as her sons and with a niece who did her secretarial work. He had learned that she had come to believe that no man can govern a modern nation-state without raining hideous atrocities on his own people and on his country's neighbors. He thought he had detected a certain oscillation in her between an idealistic anarchism in the Thoreau tradition and a Swiftian disgust with the entire race. All in all a fascinating woman, combining a large fortune with a desolate philosophy, a dazzling mind with a dumpy body. He looked forward to the meeting with relish.

At 11:00 he spun the new '48 Roadmaster off the Taugus Parkway and the wheels crunched gravel up the steep slope of the drive, which was only five miles beyond where that gas-station attendant had said the turnoff would be. Then suddenly he had crested the peak and a lush cool bed of forest spread below him, with a squarish block of stone seeming no larger than a child's toy in a wide clearing near the center.

Fortress Monquieux.

He descended.

From the radio speaker a voice intoned headlines. Civil war in Greece. Blockade threat against Berlin. Crisis in Czechoslovakia. The infant state of Israel struggling for survival. Truman denounces Stalin. Stalin condemns Truman. God, what a world, he thought. Maybe Adelina's right: who would choose to be born?

On such gloomy reflections he maneuvered the Roadmaster along the curves of the descent and through the tangled green tunnel of forest, finally through a stone archway and into the parking circle at the side of the Fortress. He pocketed his keys and strolled past time-faded classical sculptures in beds of ill-kept greenery. His wristwatch read 11:26, and he hoped he wasn't unconscionably early.

Half a minute after his ring the massive front door opened and he was ushered in by a tall well-built fellow in his early thirties, with crisp dark hair. Over shirtsleeves the young man wore an expensive-looking summer gray dressing gown, monogrammed X at the breast. "Hello and come in," he invited, smiling like a headwaiter. "I am Xavier Monquieux and I've read most of your books at least twice."

"Delighted to hear it. You must be one of Mrs. Monquieux's foster sons."

"Right," Xavier said. "And if you'll step in here"—he led the way into a high-ceilinged room of immense size, filled with books and overstuffed furniture—"you can meet my brothers. This is Yves; and this is Zachary."

Two more tall well-built fellows in their early thirties stepped forward from the mahogany bar, each with crisp dark hair, each with a gin-and-tonic in his hand, each wearing an expensive-looking summer gray dressing gown over shirtsleeves. They were as close in resemblance to Xavier and to each other as three prints of the same photograph. Only the gold letters of their monograms distinguished them: one wore a Y, the other a Z.

"I hadn't realized you were identical triplets," he said inanely as he accepted a light Scotch-and-water from Yves.

"Monozygotic is the technical word, or at least it was when I was in med school," Yves corrected. "Identical down to our fingertips. No one but Adelina can tell us apart and God knows how she does it. We're biological rarities but it's sort of fun, switching on dates and things like that."

"And speaking of girls, *mon frere*," Zachary cut in, "the young ladies ought to be here any minute, so perhaps we should get into our trunks and make sure the liquor cart's stocked up. It was very nice to have met you, sir, and after you've talked to Adelina I'm sure we could find a bathing suit your size if you'd care for a dip." And Zachary and Yves bowed themselves out of the room, the sound of their feet becoming audible a few moments later when they ascended a staircase.

"No sense of the finer things," Xavier clucked disapprovingly. "Imagine preferring a swim to a chat with a famous mystery writer. I'm afraid bookishness has rubbed off only on me. Most of these are mine," he added, sweeping his hand to indicate the crammed shelves.

"Do your brothers have any passions of their own?"

"Oh, yes—we don't have to work for our keep, of course, but all of us got enough boredom in the military during the recent war to ever want to sit around doing nothing again. Yves had a year of medical school before he was drafted and may go back some day, and he's also an amateur concert violinist. Zach is a fanatic stamp collector and he has secret dreams of being a Hollywood star . . . If you'll excuse me I'll go downstairs and tell Adelina you're here." He moved lightly out of the room.

Like most writers and many readers, the guest had an insatiable urge to inspect the contents of all bookshelves that chanced within his eye. He was glancing over a large hand-rubbed cabinet devoted to the modern European novel, with Mann and Sartre and Silone well represented, when a feminine cough behind him gave notice that he was no longer alone. A tall blonde in beige was inspecting him through heavy-rimmed glasses as though he were a signed first edition of something curious.

"Aunt Adelina apologizes," she said, "but she's all tied up in a chapter of her memoirs and won't be free for another little while. I'm Marie Dumont, her niece several degrees removed or something like that. Also her secretary and all-around drudge. She asked me to amuse you for a few minutes."

She said nothing more for about thirty seconds, as though she had no idea how to amuse a male guest. Then, "I understand you want to sort of pick her brains for political atmosphere on a book you're doing? I think you might get more mileage out of her crazy will—you know about that, don't you? When Aunt Adelina dies, the three boys each get half a million outright and the income from another half million held in trust. The remaining twenty million or so after taxes will build and support a hospital to take care of the children we bombed in Japan. But—and here comes the catch—if the safe in her office downstairs is opened by anyone, for any reason, sooner than twenty-four years after her death, all the hospital money is immediately transferred to the Flat Earth Society."

"That *is* a strange will," he commented politely, although something about its terms had already begun to gnaw at him and he was not sure what. "What's in the safe that would lead her to protect it that way?"

"Even I'm not sure and I've been her secretary for twelve years. It's in the manuscript of her memoirs, which she calls *Open Letter to Survivors*, that's all I know. She's writing it in longhand, you see. When she's not actually working on it the manuscript is kept in that safe, and the safe is always locked whether she's working on the book or not. Only she and I and her attorney know the combination. When you think how much of the inside history of the past thirty years must be in those pages, how governments might topple if the secrets leaked out—well, you can see why she takes such precautions."

"Do you inherit anything under the will?"

She shrugged. "A few hundred thousand, I think. Not enough to make up for twelve years of stagnation in this place."

"You could have left."

"You can't pull yourself out of the center of a whirlpool," she said. Which he cynically construed as: you don't throw away free room and board and a guaranteed two or three hundred thousand. "Well, I think she may be done by now, it's almost noon. Let's go down to her office and see."

And she led him along a vast foyer full of Victorian statuary and ancestral portraits and down a steep spiral staircase that ended in the center of a sort of anteroom. A functional secretarial desk, piled with papers and folders, stood against the far wall. A few comfortable chairs, occasional tables holding wrought-iron lamps and current magazines, strategically placed smoking stands—it reminded him somehow of a prosperous dentist's waiting room.

Marie Dumont knocked on the door to an inner office, then poked her head in. "Ready yet?"

"Please show him in," he heard a deep rich voice reply, and a moment later he stood before her teakwood desk in the center of the big windowless room. On the wall to his left, hanging above the squat and forbiddingly shut steel safe, was a tranquil landscape in oils. Adelina Monquieux was seated in a red-leather armchair behind the desk, her henna hair in wild disarray, her spectacles askew on her Roman nose, looking like an intelligent gargoyle.

"I'm so pleased to meet you," she said, touching a thick loose-leaf binder of tough material filled with paper—the only object on the desk except for the blotter, an old-fashioned fountain pen, a small table lamp, and a wicked-looking letter opener. "I'm through writing for the day, and my pen has gone dry anyway. It will take me just a few minutes to read my morning's stint, and I will be glad to give you all the time you desire. Tell me, do you think our survivors, assuming we have any, will appreciate reading the truth about our time?"

She asked the question with mixed bitterness and resignation, as if being witness to three decades of international politics had burned into her the inevitability of man's greed and stupidity and corruption. When she smiled at him it was like the grin he had seen on the faces of the dead.

It was only after he had closed the door gently behind him that he realized he had not said a word to her.

The silence in the anteroom was oppressive and he needed to make conversation. He turned to Marie Dumont who was seated at her own desk. "Does she do all her writing in there?" he asked, not really concerned to know.

"Ever since she inherited the house and had the basement done over. It is a perfect workroom—soundproof, no windows, no distractions, and that door is the only way in or out. Even the bathroom is outside here."

She suddenly gestured up to one of the windows and he heard the noise of splashing and gay squeals coming, he gathered, from the swimming pool. "The girls must have arrived. Peaceful sounds like that drive Aunt Adelina to distraction when she's working, even though she must have been in a dozen air raids in Europe. That's why she had her office soundproofed. By the way, did you notice the English country scene above the safe? That was painted by Churchill."

They both looked up as light footsteps sounded on the spiral stairs and one of the triplets appeared, barefoot and wearing only dark-blue swim trunks. He did not break stride but went right to the inner door, tossing a casual "Have to see Adelina for a minute" over his shoulder.

The triplet gave a perfunctory knock on the inner door and entered, shutting the door behind him. The cuckoo clock on the wall above Marie Dumont's desk announced that the hour was noon. The wooden bird had just cuckooed his last and retreated behind his tiny door when the big door opened again and the triplet walked out and over to the staircase and mounted.

"I wonder what that was all about."

"I don't know," Marie replied. "But I think Aunt Adelina must be through by now. I'll check."

She knocked lightly, stepped in, closed the door, and in less than a minute was back, her face sick-white.

"My God, she's dead," she kept whispering hoarsely.

A wild thought seized him and he knew what had disturbed him about the will: *If she died with the manuscript still on her desk, what good is that crazy twenty-four-year clause? It will protect not the manuscript but just an empty safe.*

He rushed into the office. Adelina Monquieux lay sprawled in her chair, staring sightlessly through spectacles still askew. Blood ran from her heart. The manuscript of *Open Letter to Survivors* was not in sight and the safe was tight shut: he breathed relief.

Then he noticed that the wicked-looking letter opener was not in sight either.

The cuckoo made five noises and popped back into his slot. The body of Adelina Monquieux—according to the medical examiner she had died within a minute after the blade had entered her—had been removed, and when it left most of the police technicians had left, too. The office and anteroom had been searched thoroughly and the letter opener had not been found. A few plainclothesmen still roamed the rooms and grounds haphazardly. Cody, the cigarillo-chewing Taugus County detective in charge, crushed his butt into a smoking stand disgustedly.

"What a cool customer we are dealing with, amigo," he said. "I wish I'd had him in my platoon behind Kraut lines in Normandy! He just walked right past you and the girl, stabbed the old lady to death with one blow of the letter opener, marched out past you again with the weapon, calm as you please, and went out to mingle with the girls at the pool. That, amigo, is a man with guts."

"And with a shrewd sense of psychology," the mystery writer

added. "He figured that with my brief exposure to the triplets I couldn't tell them apart, and he must have known from experience that Miss Dumont couldn't either."

"That," Cody exploded, "is the hell of it. A big whodunit writer like you, a guy who's cleaned up umpteen cases for the New York force, and you can't even tell me what was the monogram on the killer's bathing suit, an X, a Y, or a Z."

"What bothers me more is that the letter opener that killed Mrs. Monquieux is missing. Why did the killer take it? To deprive us of his fingerprints? But why didn't he simply wipe his prints from the weapon right there in the office? Why did he take the much riskier step of removing the knife from his victim and carrying it past two witnesses in the anteroom? Was it impossible or impracticable for him to follow the safer course? Again—why?"

"Very clever, Mr. Genius," Cody snorted. "But changing the subject don't fool me. You didn't notice what monogram the killer was wearing."

"I don't think it would mean anything even if I did. We can't assume the guilty one didn't simply get hold of a monogram belonging to one of his brothers and sew it over his own, or even wear one of his brothers' bathing suits. By the way, what was the result of that test for bloodstains your technician performed on the three dark-blue bathing suits in the household?"

Cody waved a paper from the sheaf on his lap. "Absolutely no dice. My man examined 'em inside and out, and not a trace of a bloodstain. None of the old lady's blood splashed onto the killer's trunks. No, we can't solve this one the easy way, amigo. He killed her with one stab, so we'd have no bloodstains. And he's one of triplets, so for all practical purposes we got no one who saw him!" He cursed while taking out another cigarillo.

"Well, we can at least be thankful that Mrs. Monquieux put her manuscript back in the safe before he walked in and killed her. After all, it was much too thick for the killer to have walked past us with it unnoticed, and there's no way he could have destroyed it in the office itself—even the toilet is out here. So it's got to be back in the safe, and whatever Adelina Monquieux knew will stay under wraps for twenty-four years. Adelina? Pandora would have been a better name. By the way, you will keep a guard on that safe overnight till Mr. Billings and the truck come for it?"

"Damn right I will, I—hey, what's the matter with you?" For the distinguished litterateur across from Cody had suddenly risen and was pacing angrily.

"Scars," he muttered. "Look, the brothers mentioned to me this morning that they were all in the service during the war. Didn't any of them get wounded or scratched or marked somehow, even if only in a tattoo parlor? Can't we eliminate one or even two brothers on the ground that neither Miss Dumont nor I saw any marks on the killer?"

"Hell, no," Cody grunted. "Those boys spent their war in a nice safe psychological testing laboratory stateside. Y'see, they've got something between 'em that the eggheads call tele*pathy*—identical twins and triplets have it fairly often, so I'm told—and the Army had some crazy idea of finding out what causes it and using it to help spring Allied troops from enemy POW camps. The whole thing fell through, of course; there's no way of teaching that stuff to someone who ain't got it in the first place. Hell, if God wanted people to read each other's minds He wouldn't have given us vocal cords. Hey, what's got you now?"

"Don't you see? If each of the triplets can read the thoughts of the others, why can't we simply *ask them* who is the murderer?"

"Oh," Cody rumbled. "Reading your own storybooks again, hey, amigo? Well, first of all, to give you the kinda reason you enjoy, we couldn't rule out that the one guilty brother and one accomplice brother weren't framing the third innocent brother. Second, that tele*pathy* stuff can't be used in court anyway. And third—hell, except for the war I've lived in this community for thirty-seven years. I know those boys. I know they've done everything together their whole lives long. I know as well as I know I'm sitting here that all three of them were in on this murder. They drew straws or some such thing to see who'd do the actual dirty work. But you try to prove that in a court of law, amigo. You storybook writers don't have the first idea in the world the problems of a working cop."

His respect for Cody soared once the truth of a conspiracy among the brothers had sunk home. How could he not have seen it? From the moment he had rung the bell, every word and every action of those three smiling affable brothers had been as carefully calculated as a Broadway stage performance. Dressing identically, speaking with virtually identical modulations, each one doing or saying nothing that would stamp him as an individual in the mind of their guest. He had been manipulated like a puppet and he didn't like it. He stoked his pipe furiously.

Uselessly.

As the sun set he growled a good-bye to Cody and slunk out to his car and drove out of that monstrous valley through a tunnel of darkening forest and mocking bird cries . . .

Next day he read of the murder in the papers, noting idly the news that Adelina Monquieux's private Pandora's box had been crated up by her executors, the law firm of Billings & Krieger, and transferred to a chilled-steel bank vault in the city. *Open Letter to Survivors* having been made doubly inviolable, he tried to dismiss the whole Monquieux affair from his mind as a fiasco.

It was not until two months later that he saw what he should have seen while Adelina's body was still warm.

What triggered it was a piece of research. He had gone to the County Medical Association Library to look up some data on childbirth that he needed for his own novel-aborning; his serendipping eye had wandered from childbirth to infants and from infants to twins and to the precise differences between monozygotic and fraternal twins.

There it lay, buried in a mountain of medical jargon but unmistakable as a gold nugget in a coalpile.

Monozygotic twins, being genetically identical in every respect, are identical in fingerprints also.

His mind took that fact and raced with it.

Three minutes later he was out of the library with a slam of the door and the glares of several peeved medicos behind him.

He dashed into his apartment and dialed Billings & Krieger, demanding to speak to Mr. Billings at once on a matter a thousand times more urgent than mere life-and-death. When he had the attorney on the line he was brief and to the point. "Burt, can we use your office tonight for a conference on the Monquieux case?"

Billings sounded puzzled. "What's up? Why my office?" Then, after a moment, "Hey, you haven't solved the murder by any chance, have you?"

"In one way I think I have, in another way, no . . . I'm sorry, Burt, that's all I can say now. Eight o'clock all right with you? I'll need both you and Mr. Krieger, in your capacity as executors. And I'm going to have Cody there, too—you remember him? Thanks a million, Burt, see you at eight." He hung up and placed a call to Cody who agreed to attend the meeting.

Shortly after dinner he made an excuse to go out, leaving the dishes to his long-suffering father, and paced the neon-washed streets, marshaling his thoughts, until 7:45 when he hailed a cab. Ten minutes later he stepped into the offices of Billings & Krieger. Burt and Cody were already present, and James B. Krieger, who looked like a starving mouse, came in shortly. Introductions were exchanged, hands shaken, chairs pulled up to the conference room's long table.

He began by explaining the fact of identical fingerprints in monozygotics. "Of course the great bulk of mystery stories—my own included, I blush to say—have spread the impression that each set of prints is unique, that no one's prints are the same as any other person's. The man in the street accepts without question that every man's prints are exclusively his own, but, as I've indicated, it's just not so. Therefore we must conclude—of course we can verify this with no trouble at all—that Xavier, Yves, and Zachary Monquieux have identical fingerprints. Now, what follows from that?

"First, it reminded me that all three brothers must be aware of this fact; for it was Yves, talking to me, who used the word monozygotic, and even used the phrase 'identical down to our fingertips,' which is quite literally true.

"Secondly, it satisfied me that we had completely misinterpreted the whole matter of the missing letter opener. We had assumed two things: A, that the person who took it out of the office was the murderer; B, that possibly his motive was to deprive us of his fingerprints, which for some unknown reason he could not simply wipe off on the spot. We now know that B is a completely false assumption: all three brothers know their prints are identical and know, therefore, their prints would be of no use to us. So the killer's reason for taking away the knife could not have been what we thought it was. Gentlemen, can any of you suggest another reason?"

Silence. Cody chewed his cigarillo.

"Nor can I. In fact—and I kick myself for missing this two months ago—not only had he no reason, but it was *physically impossible* for the killer to have taken the letter opener with him!

"Marie Dumont and I observed the killer walk out of his victim's office and he certainly wasn't holding the opener in his hands. Could he have concealed it in his clothes? Well, he was wearing only a bathing suit; the letter opener might have been slipped inside the suit. But you told me, Cody, that there was not the slightest trace of a bloodstain on any of the three dark-blue pairs of trunks that could possibly have been worn by the murderer—*inside or out*. Certainly if he had carried out that bloody weapon inside his trunks, you *would* have found traces. Conclusion: the murderer did not, because he could not, take the weapon away."

"Then what happened to it?" Cody demanded. "Because my men searched that office with a fine-tooth comb and it sure as hell wasn't there!"

"Patience, Cody, patience. Now, let's tackle the problem from another direction. Who had the opportunity to hide or remove the opener between the time I spoke to Mrs. Monquieux a few minutes before her death and the time Marie Dumont and I entered the office shortly after her death and learned that the opener was missing? When I phrase it that way, you can't miss it. *Only one person* set foot in the office during that brief interval. And that was Marie Dumont, who you'll recall was alone in there for almost a minute before she stumbled out to announce that her aunt was dead.

"Now, can the wings of reason bear us any higher? Yes, indeed," he assured his listeners. "Let's go back to your question, Cody—what did she do with the weapon? With me standing right outside the door, would she have concealed it in her clothes and taken a chance she could safely get rid of it later, with the police shortly to invade the premises? Not if she had a safer option, she wouldn't. Was there a safer option in that enclosed office?

"Yes, there was—a safer option, if you'll pardon the pun. Your men searched the entire office, Cody, but in view of the Monquieux will and of your plausible but false conclusions that the killer had taken the opener away with him, you didn't dare tamper with the safe, to which, I remind you, only Mrs. Monquieux and Miss Dumont and you, her attorney, Burt, know the combination.

"And since that safe was under police guard until your truckers removed it to the bank vault, Burt, I'll wager that letter opener is in the safe right now."

"My God," Billings muttered.

"But why would she have hidden the murder weapon like that?" James B. Krieger squeaked.

"If you mean her motive—whether she's in love with the murderer, or hopes to extort money or marriage out of him—I don't know, and its exact nature doesn't affect my analysis. But in a general way her motivation is clear: she intended to protect the murderer. Now, what is presupposed by such intent?"

Again silence.

"Don't you see that it presupposes *she knew which of the triplets* is the murderer?

"Now, did she know prior to the murder itself? Hardly, or she would never have revealed as much information to me as she did. Then she must have learned the truth *after* the murder. But then she had less than a minute, alone in that office, to see the truth, to make a decision, to hide the letter opener in the safe, to return to the doorway. It must have been something instantaneously apparent that revealed the truth to her.

"At this point, gentlemen, we are driven to speculation, but speculation solidly based on facts. Fact: your medical examiner told us, Cody, that Adelina Monquieux lived for perhaps a minute after being stabbed. Fact: Mrs. Monquieux's fountain pen had gone dry shortly before her death, so there was no usable writing implement on her desk. Fact: we don't *know* that it was Mrs. Monquieux herself who put away the manuscript of *Open Letter to Survivors*.

"Hypothesis: In the last moments of her life Adelina Monquieux—the only person on earth who could tell those brothers apart—pulled the knife from her body and slashed into the tough material of the binder of that manuscript the initial—that's all it would take to identify him—of her murderer. X, Y, or Z. This is what Marie Dumont saw when she entered the room. And to protect the murderer she had to conceal that manuscript cover. And being forced to open the safe to place the damning manuscript cover inside, she decided it would be safer to conceal the opener there also. She was counting on being able to remove both objects from the safe later, but circumstances and your truckers, Burt, frustrated her.

"Any questions, gentlemen?"

Cody was now sweating, as if from the strain of following the analysis. "Thank God you lawyers moved that safe to where we can still get at the evidence!"

Billings stared at him as if he had mumbled baby-talk. "But you can't get at it," he pointed out. "Mrs. Monquieux's will provides that the safe cannot be opened for any reason until the twenty-fourth anniversary of her death. If you violate that provision, the hospital for atom-bomb victims will not be built. How many lives is it worth to you to procure your evidence, your *hypothetical* evidence?"

Cody went down fighting. "Can't that will be broken? Hell, this isn't the kind of a situation the old lady had in mind when she made that crazy will."

"You can try to break it in the courts," Krieger said. "My considered opinion is that you won't succeed. And our duty as executors under the will, and as human beings, is to stop you."

Billings nodded. "Something even worse, Cody. Suppose the courts *did* rule that the opening of the safe by the police would not defeat the hospital bequest. If the analysis we've just heard is correct, the opening of the safe would disclose proof positive that the safe had *already* been opened immediately after our client's death. And that prior opening would be beyond the court's power to ignore. The end result being God knows how many dead war orphans, and a windfall for the Flat Earth Society."

Cody leveled a long series of curses at the law. No one in the room was hypocrite enough to contradict him.

"Well, as a professional writer," ventured the only professional writer present, "my hands aren't tied by that will. Why can't I publish my analysis of the case and at least let them know that I know, and maybe make them do something insane like attempting to silence me?"

"You want a million-dollar libel suit slapped against you?" Billings boomed. "You forget you've got no solid evidence—not a shred!"

They sat in silence.

When he could take no more of it he rose, stretched his drained and aching body, and trudged wearily to the door. "I'm not in my dotage yet," he said, "and neither are they. I can wait; and after all, by waiting, we make sure the great bulk of the Monquieux estate goes to a decent cause. But I swear, Burt, that I will be there when you or your successor opens that safe twenty-four years from now. I'm going to see with my own eyes whether or not I was right . . .

"Gentlemen, I'll see you in 1972."

THE PRAYER WHEELS

by Fritzi Franz Lumen

This is the 367th "first story" to be published by Ellery
Queen's Mystery Magazine *. . . mystery and Oriental subtlety in
Tibet, "in the high small world of the Lama Thieh Sang"—an
unusual "first story." No, let's not be parsimonious in praise. An
unusual story whether it happened to be a first, a fifth, or a
fifteenth . . .*

*The author, Fritzi Franz Lumen, has been a farmhand, construc-
tion worker, mechanic, musician, itinerant artist, mountain
climber, airplane pilot, radio engineer, teacher of computer
programming, and business executive. (What stories he has to tell!)
He has traveled extensively—in Europe, Asia, North America—*

and he speaks, among other languages, French, German, Korean, Japanese, and Persian. (What vocational, geographical, cultural, and etymological backgrounds to draw on for the stories he has to tell!) . . .

"WAR CORRESPONDENT MISSING" has become a logo with the hens working it to death. And wearing almost as thin were new leads for my own "Specials from Ernie Cole," with the war in Southeast Asia winding down.

So I used the warming diplomatic trend and a friend in the embassy to wangle a visa and set off for high Tibet. There might be a reheat in the old genocide charges filed with the International Council of Jurists at Geneva; or failing that, a series on happy peasants under agrarian reform, high-altitude style.

And I might still be able to get myself arrested.

Fifty miles in I was "detained" at a C.P. and taken before a painfully polite but positive little Chinese captain. He was over-plump and under strain of some sort, but he was scrupulously correct.

"Arrested? Oh, no, sir. No, indeed, Mr. Cole. Only delayed, shall we say. Until your papers can be confirmed. It is for your own protection, sir. This is a treacherous people, and surly, as you shall see."

His English was excellent—no comic-page clichés of "flied lice"; but what Oriental officer's is not, these days? All of them have studied at Fort Ord or Hood or Benning. Even the enemy—whoever currently he may be. I was warily respectful. A tense fat man always frightens me.

The next morning found me staring from an unglazed window in a tumble of temple buildings, my prebreakfast bowl of salted and buttered tea cooling on the rough stone sill.

Around me hulked the mud-mortar and fieldstone walls of a lamasery. Across from it the Gyangtse road had at this point no shoulder at all. It fell away sheer to the floor of a narrow and arid valley that was little more than a mile-deep crevasse. It was inhabited, though. At its bottom I had glimpsed, while coming in, a scraggle of thatched-roof huts. They were the only evidence of humanity other than the monastery complex itself.

The latter was a semideserted sprawl of buildings, flush to the road at its inner edge, which clung to the mountainside like a sea bird's nest.

South, to my right, the road wound down into Sikkim and India. A traditional invasion route, it was appropriately the way I had come in. North, to my left, it clawed and scrabbled deeper into the "High Land," as the Tibetans call their country, and deteriorated as it went. On policy, I have heard.

Everywhere the horizon was hidden from me by the myriad pinnacles that thrust upward into the chill spring sky. They looked artificial and dangerously innocent, and impossibly high even from my heady perch at 15,000 feet.

Directly in front of me the road was not visible at all. It was too close in to a sort of unrailed sun deck onto which my room on the second floor opened. Behind me, however, the road burst into view beyond the courtyard wall.

There in the thin sunlight I could see a double line of workers and their warders. The guards wore the quilted rag-doll uniform of the Chinese People's Army. They lounged on their rifles or sat on rocks and smoked. The laborers were native villagers, probably brought up from the huts I'd seen. All on the road were males, stooped or sitting to the tedious task of hand-breaking and scattering new roadbed stones. These were brought to them by their cloth-booted and faded women in flat head-held baskets from the slopes above. There was no talk except an occasional guttural command.

Three of the Chinese guards, however, were exceptionally active. They formed a team which moved along the inner ditch, slashing and smashing downward at something with their rifle

butts. I couldn't make out what. They were shouting, gesticu-
lating, jeering mechanically.

The Tibetans seemed to pay no attention to this nameless
vandalism, as though they were too tired to protest. They had
undoubtedly been at their drudgery from dawn on this day and
for many days before and were bone-weary. Even so, as they
crouched there they were proudly tall and thin in their tattered
robes, and their gaunt highland grace made the Chinese look
squat and ugly.

Then I started to sense something else under their listlessness at
the pounding monotony. It appeared from those nearer to me that
the Tibetans were far from aggrieved and might even be gratified
at what was going on. They would glance up furtively from under
their batwing hats at the three-man demolitions team, then smirk
and grin at their nearer neighbors. They exchanged winks, small
signals, and veiled nods. Plainly the unexplained mischief of the
trio of guards was giving the villagers untold glee.

"They think we're damned! And doing it to ourselves!"

I jumped, jostling my tea. It slopped and soaked darkly into the
crude stone sill. The little fat captain had come along the
sun-deck terrace from the left and stopped outside my window.
An arch from the refectory also opened on this balcony, two doors
beyond my chamber.

"Superstition, you know. I'm having their prayer wheels broken
up. They bring them and line the road beside where they work.
I've ordered them all broken."

"Opiate of the people?" I murmured.

"What? Oh. Yes. Well, an enemy to my propaganda, at least.
I've been ordered to convert as well as work them, you see. So I
must."

Peking had spoken.

"And clean them up. They're a filthy lot, morally as well as
physically. Multiple husbands!"

I shook my head, as if sympathetically.

"Anyhow, they think we are courting disaster and will bring down heaven's wrath on our heads."

"And will you?" I said it as mildly as I could but he glanced sharply at me. Then his eyefolds vanished in a grin.

"But you are kidding me, no? Will you join me at breakfast?"

I've never been able properly to dislike these people.

I picked my way through cramped interior passages past a bead curtain of discarded Buddhist rosaries. The captain had said they belonged to all the monks who had ever died here. And he was right. There was an aura of antique filth about them, the feel of centuries of unwashed grime.

He was waiting, and we both watched while an incredibly ancient, stooped, and unclean old woman brought me my morning bowl of Tsamba. It is a concoction of barley laced with the ubiquitous salted and buttered tea and was served with a battered unclean scoop. But it looked hot and so was hopefully sterilized.

The captain sniffled, pressing his temple with pudgy fingers.

"It is high altitude—sinusitis, do you say?" he said when he saw me glance at him.

I nodded. I'd gotten it once covering a copper strike in Quito. "Feels like a screw press clamped to your head."

"And I can't smell anything," he complained.

"You're lucky," I told him, eyeing the old woman. Mixed with her own effluvium she carried a rancid odor of burnt yak fat. From the lamps, perhaps, or the cooking.

He turned for a time to his rice, the food up here only of the rich and of conquerors, concentrating on the steady whip of his chopsticks. He ate with the studied voracity of all Chinese males, drivulets of yak butter from the sauce forming at the corners of his mouth. Finally he flung his chopsticks rattling to the table.

"They sent me up here to fail, Mr. Cole. But I shall not. I will show them, the Long Marchers and old cadre and the rest. We of the Guard can also work and build. I will not only complete this impossible road of theirs, but I shall convert these devil-worshipping heathens. And on time."

Sweat beaded his upper lip, either from pious urgency or his unhealth at this altitude.

"See here," he went on. "I'm distributing these—ten thousand in these valleys the last two months."

He pulled out a leaflet from a bundle beneath his chair and handed it to me. It was brightly printed on one side with Chinese characters, obviously propaganda. The other side was blank.

"Mm-m-m." I didn't want to antagonize him. "But—can they read? And Chinese?"

His fat little fingers waved me off.

"We are having them read aloud while they're working. In translation. And we know it is having an effect. They greatly respect the written word, apparently. Why, do you know we have not found a single one discarded? We have checked most carefully. They are treasuring them!"

Or using them as we once did in rural America. But I held my peace.

"You will report all fairly, I trust, Mr. Cole," he continued. "And that we are doing them no harm, but good. What is wrong, after all? They are dirty, we make them wash. They are lazy, we make them work. Are these not virtues you respect also in the West? They should themselves have made these roads, centuries ago."

To expedite their own conquest? And what of the freedom not to wash?

"You'll find my reporting fair, I think," I said aloud. "As others have. As soon as I can get around." He had commandeered and then sent back my jeep and Sherpa driver.

"The People's Government supplies all transport, to truly and properly neutral journalists."

Or neutralized, I amended silently.

At supper the captain's ebullient certainty was gone.

"How can they do this? How can they resist?" He spoke more to himself than to me.

"What's the matter? What are they doing?"

"We broke up their wheels. You saw?"

"Yes, I saw. What then?"

"They've started setting them up again. Higher, on the hillsides. Beyond our reach."

"I see."

"What bothers me is, where would they get such an idea? They have no leadership."

It was clearly an article of his faith that no one could do his thinking for himself. To act meant there must be leaders to command the act.

"What about their lamas or whatever you call 'em?"

"The jack priests?" He was contemptuous. "We flushed them all out long ago and sent them inland."

"To work on other roads?" I could imagine it.

"Paugh!" Contempt became disgust. "Not them. They would die first. Some did. No, we sent them to prison. They were like princes, it seems, who would not work with their hands. Not even to save their lives. Anyhow, we got them all. Except for the old chief lama, the abbot. One Thich Sang, or Doctor Joy as you would call him in your language. He disappeared just before we arrived here."

"You're sure?"

"Of course!" He was impatient. "We searched the village and this place. And the surrounding range. Though we know he was too old to hide up there." He jabbed a pudgy finger toward the peaks. "We believe he was killed trying to get there, or attempting to flee the country. They have much money, you understand."

"You're sure he's not one of them?" I pointed to the workers on the road. They were being kept at it till well past dusk, apparently as usual.

He snorted. "A full doctor, a lama? At menial labor?" He snorted again and broke into a cough.

In the morning I went out with the captain to inspect the road construction. Seen more closely, the veiled triumph of the Tibetans as they nursed their bruised but beautifully sinewed hands was unmistakable. The old woman was out behind us, serving them with water which was probably dirty.

Near one group—I could not tell from which individual—I caught a strong and acrid whiff of candle wax and incense. Had one of them the strength, after all this, to spend his nights in the vaults and crypts at prayers? I glanced quickly at the captain, but he had smelled nothing. His sinusitis, of course.

The remainder of that day and the next I spent rummaging in the lamasery. In one room there were a number of religious books, many in English and some in French and German. But there was nothing like a full library, and nothing to sustain my treasured misconceptions, gleaned in a lifetime of reading Kipling and Maugham and James Hilton, of super insights and intellects in a timeless capsule world. Only a primal squalor.

I was quite unprepared for the little captain's fury at supper on that second day.

"Those prayer wheels!" he sputtered when I inquired. "I've got to stop them! They're still putting them up!" He bounced and quivered with impotent fervency. "I know! I'll show them! I'll have them shot away!"

He spun and shook his finger at the road outside in malicious exultation.

"I'll blast away their wheels as they are blasting my career. And if some of the lama's precious parishioners happen to be shot by accident—why, that will teach them not to impede the course of history!"

I shuddered, thinking of Far East marksmanship.

Early the next day I was at my window when the firing began. The initial random shots and bursts soon steadied into the dead rhythm of "firing for effect"—which I recognized all too well from Vietnam and the decade of "little" wars that had preceded it.

The captain's whole company was out. Some of the rag-doll soldiers had taken off their padded jackets and stood firing in their droopy britches.

By craning to the right I could just make out a few of the slender targets. They were prayer wheels of the wind-driven type, larger than the others but more lightly built. Even as I stared I saw one shatter and another leap from its propping and spin down the slope toward the road. They would roll and roll until they were caught in a rut or stopped by an obstruction. Many of the marksmen were missing, and I detected several duds.

Down along the road the Tibetans continued their work. They were almost complacent, seemingly paying no attention. Yet that same secret smugness pervaded their entire attitude. Were not the wheels still spinning, the set of their backs and shoulders said?

At noon the captain did not bother to come in. He went without eating, or perhaps ate with his men for their morale's sake.

My own Tsamba wanted to stay not upon the order of its going down, so I spent the afternoon prone and did without supper. But I listened, and all day the firing went on. At dusk it became desultory, then tapered off. I fell asleep.

In the brightness of dawn I awakened, curiously refreshed. There is wine in the high air once you are used to it. The hard trestle bed and the rough yak-wool blankets were suddenly restful and I had slept myself out. I felt extraordinarily well.

The captain was already at his rice in the refectory and also in fine fettle.

"I missed you at dinner, Mr. Cole. Well: you see? That did it! It's settled. I've given the villagers a free day from the road to celebrate. There'll be no more of this—"

He stopped abruptly to listen, but there was no need. There was no way to avoid hearing it. A rattling roar, clearly audible through the heavy mud-stone walls, that rose even as we paused. It swelled perceptibly from an insistent clatter to a din like a giant telling his rosary or shaking an abacus. The volume and momentum of the noise increased, surrounding and pressing in on us.

I looked over at the old woman. She was calmly scooping out my Tsamba.

The captain hurried out onto the balcony. He stood transfixed, staring around to the right and then up behind the buildings, obviously frightened.

"What is it?" I shouted.

There was no answer.

I went as far as the arch. Nothing was visible from there but a few guards, who had apparently run out to look. They were now scurrying back to shelter behind the building and courtyard walls. I edged around to the outer corner of the balcony and looked up.

It was like peering into the maw of an enormous pepper mill. The entire flank of the mountain was alive with tumbling stones, ranging from the size of a fist to a big man's head. They jumped and jounced down the side of the hill like huge hail, in a jumbling roil. With them ran or followed more rocks and gravel and the loose pebbles they dislodged, like progeny. Individual stones sailed through the air with a kind of elephantine grace, or bounded ponderously from ledge to ledge.

The barrage was being constantly renewed. It originated high in a series of crevices near the crest, and each rock appeared to have been wrapped in a separate paper covering. These coverings were twisted at the two ends as one would tissue oranges for crating.

As the stones skittered down the long slope some of them lost their wrappings. The loose papers flew free in the dust above the slide, looking like strange origami birds.

The players of these bizarre bowls were all invisible against the gray blue of the granite crags. The blue robes, I reasoned. And the

Tibetan women and children must all be up there with their men. This incessant rain of rocks argued many more hands than I had seen so far.

By now the captain had recovered the rudiments of locomotion. He staggered forward, his normally gamboge skin so pale it verged on green. Then his round face darkened to maroon with rage. He went jerkily to his hands and knees and peered below, into the shadow of the sheltering overhang. He sighted someone from his cowering company and shouted an angry order.

His answer was a stone the bulk of a coffee mug, still in its paper wrapper. It arced up over the eaves to the flat of the roof, rolled a few feet, and bumped to a stop.

The captain pounced, still ridiculous on all fours. He squatted back, removed the paper, and examined it carefully on both sides. He put it down at his side, appeared to meditate for a time, then lifted the wrapper to look at it again. At last he let his hand, with the paper in it, fall limply away and stared vacantly out at the valley opposite.

Finally he stumbled to his feet. The paper slipped from his nerveless stubby fingers. He tottered to the arch, through the dining hall, and out the bead curtains on the other side.

I picked up the wrapper. It was one of the captain's propaganda leaflets, one side battered but intact. On the other—

On the other side it was a prayer sheet, like those which are put inside the wheels.

Someone had meticulously scrawled over it, from edge to edge, in intricate Burmo-Tibetan script that turned it irrefutably into prayers. Carefully, painfully, on every last square centimeter.

I looked back up the mountain. There were thousands of these flying sheets and stones. Someone had gathered every pamphlet the captain had issued. Someone else had written and written and written through the weeks until now every insane rolling bowl on that slope was itself a prayer wheel, spinning and whirling on its long mad plunge.

Then came a subtle change in the continuum of tumult. A muted rumbling grew under the clacking clatter and threatened to swallow it. The new fuller tone developed into a swollen and earthshaking counterbass.

As I stared, a whole vast sheath of the hillside began to slip and shudder. It looked as though the mountain itself was starting to detach and slide, beyond the knoll that protected the lamasery. Awestricken, I watched an entire layer of rocks and shale, gathering strength and speed with each passing demisecond, pour ponderously down and across the road.

And where it passed, no road was left. Only a great gaping gout, making the mountain continuous with the floor of the valley. At the center was simply a gouged spout which had carried away the roadbed and its supporting shelf for a hundred yards on either side.

In the after-clatter of trickling, clicking pebbles I held my breath. My God! The villagers down there, the huts! I am no Catholic, but I think I crossed myself. Then I remembered. No, no, the Tibetans were safe. They were all up here. Someone had thought of that, too.

Now through the loudness of the sudden silence, lit by shafts of sun through the puffs of dust, there came a new sound. A squeaking, as of a boxed rat trying to clamber out, and with the squeaking, a scrabbling. It was the captain. He came into view, below the balcony overhang. He was again on all fours, whimpering in a hysterical tremolo that no longer sounded human.

He scrambled up the slope to the right, avoiding the area where the Tibetans had been hidden and angling toward the higher ledges and the peaks beyond. He was beginning to pant and sweat. I could hear the interruptions to his whinnying cry and see the glinting in the sun. The pale light caught on flecks of drool that the rising wind whipped from his lips.

How long I watched and listened I don't know. It was hard to take one's eyes from the figure of the frenzied little fat man, shrinking as it mounted ever higher. He climbed and climbed until he was a fly, a specimen insect pinned to the vertical starkness, and still he climbed.

A moment or a millennium later there was a touch on my arm. The old woman was beckoning me inside. Ranged behind the table were a number of the older villagers, indistinguishable from each other in their faded dull-blue robes. At the outer door stood a shaggy Drokpa herdsman.

One of the old men made signs. Was I now willing to go home?

Ah, yes. Why not? There was nothing for me here, an intruder. For the first time in many years I felt like a sneak or snoop and was faintly ashamed of my profession.

Very well. He pointed. The tough-looking tribesman would guide me up and around the slide and south to Sikkim.

I nodded.

The old woman offered me my passport and other papers, retrieved from the captain's effects—and my heart clutched in my chest like a clenched fist.

Just how had she held them out to me? And that odor—of candle wax and incense and burning oil from yak-fat lamps. It reeked from *her!* But there must be proof. Proof—

I was surprised to find the written-over propaganda sheet still in my left hand. I offered it to her.

"Here. This is yours."

I let it slip deliberately, maneuvering so that it planed underneath the table. When she bent to recover it I knew. I had the proof.

"You. It was you, in the crypts at night. It was you who wrote those prayers."

She did not answer immediately, but slowly straightened. The crooked back unwarped. And there was a twinkle in her delicately acanthic eyes.

"Come, now," I persisted. "Your people. How many among them can read at all, much less English? Or write?"

The old woman was now a man, as aged as before but

perceptibly more youthful—taller than the others, erect and spare, with the look of the mountaineer.

He sighed. "It is true. As you say. Unfortunately, few are literate. Tell me: how did you know?"

"I didn't, until you gave me my passport right side up. Courtesy is difficult to disguise. Or to discard."

He sighed again, but the smile deepened on the beautiful old-ivory face.

"But the clincher was your knees."

The amused mouth permitted a faint *moue* of astonishment. "Oh? How so?"

"When a woman in skirts bends to pick up something, she invariably closes her knees and turns them to the side. You squatted, then knelt, with your knees wide-open. Like a man. A principle I learned from our good Mark Twain."

Then something else struck me.

"But how could the captain have failed to find you? Literally underneath his nose? The Commie is no respecter of feminine delicacy; they could easily have checked."

The fine old eyes brightened in the now curiously seamless face.

"It is a principle I learned from your excellent Edgar A. Poe and his purloined letter, and from your excellent G. K. Chesterton and his invisible man. In the Orient, as you know, women are beneath all notice. And as you say, old customs are hard to break."

The Drokpa herdsman shifted uneasily from foot to foot and began to hitch his skirts up under his belt, preparing to depart.

From the doorway I looked back. The old chief lama was still smiling at me.

THE DRIPPING

by David Morrell

This is the 370th "first story" to be published by Ellery
Queen's Mystery Magazine . . . *a story strange in style and
substance, but with a strong emotional impact. An impressive
debut in print . . .*

*The author, David Morrell, was in his late twenties when he
submitted "The Dripping," and he was assistant professor of
American literature at the University of Iowa. He was raised in
Ontario, Canada, and earned his M.A. and Ph.D. at Pennsylvania
State University, where he taught fiction writing. When n₍
teaching or writing he likes riding horses, target shooting, and
scuba diving.*

Shortly before Mr. Morrell's first story appeared in Ellery Queen's Mystery Magazine, *his first novel,* FIRST BLOOD, *was published and became an instant success—Literary Guild Featured Alternate for May 1972, and then purchased by Stanley Kramer for early production as a major motion picture . . .*

THAT autumn we live in a house in the country, my mother's house, the house I was raised in. I have been to the village, struck more by how nothing in it has changed, yet everything has, because I am older now, seeing it differently. It is as though I am both here now and back then, at once with the mind of a boy and a man. It is so strange a doubling, so intense, so unsettling, that I am moved to work again, to try to paint it.

So I study the hardware store, the grain barrels in front, the twin square pillars holding up the drooping balcony onto which seared wax-faced men and women from the old people's hotel above come to sit and rock and watch. They look the same aging people I saw as a boy, the wood of the pillars and balcony looks as splintered.

Forgetful of time while I work, I do not begin the long walk home until late, at dusk. The day has been warm, but now in my shirt I am cold, and a half mile along I am caught in a sudden shower and forced to leave the gravel road for the shelter of a tree, its leaves already brown and yellow. The rain becomes a storm, streaking at me sideways, drenching me; I cinch the neck of my canvas bag to protect my painting and equipment, and decide to run, socks spongy in my shoes, when at last I reach the lane down to the house and barn.

The house and barn. They and my mother, they alone have changed, as if as one, warping, weathering, joints twisted and strained, their gray so unlike the white I recall as a boy. The place is weakening her. She is in tune with it, matches its decay. That is why we have come here to live. To revive. Once I thought to convince her to move away. But of her sixty-five years she has spent forty here, and she insists she will spend the rest, what is left to her.

The rain falls stronger as I hurry past the side of the house, the light on in the kitchen, suppertime and I am late. The house is connected with the barn the way the small base of an L is connected to its stem. The entrance I always use is directly at the joining, and when I enter out of breath, clothes clinging to me cold and wet, the door to the barn to my left, the door to the kitchen straight ahead, I hear the dripping in the basement down the stairs to my right.

"Meg. Sorry I'm late," I call to my wife, setting down the water-beaded canvas sack, opening the kitchen door. There is no one. No settings on the table. Nothing on the stove. Only the yellow light from the sixty-watt bulb in the ceiling. The kind my mother prefers to the white of one hundred. It reminds her of candlelight, she says.

"Meg," I call again, and still no one answers. Asleep, I think. Dusk coming on, the dark clouds of the storm have lulled them, and they have lain down for a nap, expecting to wake before I return.

Still the dripping. Although the house is very old, the barn long disused, roofs crumbling, I have not thought it all so ill-maintained, the storm so strong that water can be seeping past the cellar windows, trickling, pattering on the old stone floor. I switch on the light to the basement, descend the wood stairs to the right, worn and squeaking, reach where the stairs turn to the left the rest of the way down to the floor, and see not water dripping. Milk. Milk everywhere. On the rafters, on the walls, dripping on the film of milk on the stones, gathering speckled with dirt in the channels between them. From side to side and everywhere.

Sarah, my child, has done this, I think. She has been fascinated by the big wood dollhouse that my father made for me when I was quite young, its blue paint chipped and peeling now. She has pulled it from the far corner to the middle of the basement. There are games and toy soldiers and blocks that have been taken from the wicker storage chest and played with on the floor, all covered with milk, the dollhouse, the chest, the scattered toys, milk dripping on them from the rafters, milk trickling on them.

Why has she done this, I think. Where can she have gotten so much milk? What was in her mind to do this thing?

"Sarah," I call. "Meg." Angry now, I mount the stairs into the quiet kitchen. "Sarah," I shout. She will clean the mess and stay indoors the remainder of the week.

I cross the kitchen, turn through the sitting room past the padded flower-patterned chairs and sofa that have faded since I knew them as a boy, past several of my paintings that my mother has hung up on the wall, bright-colored old ones of pastures and woods from when I was in grade school, brown-shaded new ones of the town, tinted as if old photographs. Two stairs at a time up to the bedrooms, wet shoes on the soft worn carpet on the stairs, hand streaking on the smooth polished maple bannister.

At the top I swing down the hall. The door to Sarah's room is open, it is dark in there. I switch on the light. She is not on the bed, nor has been; the satin spread is unrumpled, the rain pelting in through the open window, the wind fresh and cool. I have the feeling then and go uneasy into our bedroom; it is dark as well, empty too. My stomach has become hollow. Where are they? All in mother's room?

No. As I stand at the open door to mother's room I see from the yellow light I have turned on in the hall that only she is in there, her small torso stretched across the bed.

"Mother," I say, intending to add, "Where are Meg and Sarah?" But I stop before I do. One of my mother's shoes is off, the other askew on her foot. There is mud on the shoes. There is blood on her cotton dress. It is torn, her brittle hair disrupted, blood on her face, her bruised lips are swollen.

For several moments I am silent with shock. "My God, Mother," I finally manage to say, and as if the words are a spring releasing me to action I touch her to wake her. But I see that her eyes are open, staring ceilingward, unseeing though alive, and each breath is a sudden full gasp, then slow exhalation.

"Mother, what has happened? Who did this to you? Meg? Sarah?"

But she does not look at me, only constant toward the ceiling.

"For God's sake, Mother, answer me! Look at me! What has happened?"

Nothing. Eyes sightless. Between gasps she is like a statue.

What I think is hysterical. Disjointed, contradictory. I must find Meg and Sarah. They must be somewhere, beaten like my mother. Or worse. Find them. Where? But I cannot leave my mother. When she comes to consciousness, she too will be hysterical, frightened, in great pain. How did she end up on the bed?

In her room there is no sign of the struggle she must have put up against her attacker. It must have happened somewhere else. She crawled from there to here. Then I see the blood on the floor, the swath of blood down the hall from the stairs. Who did this? Where is he? Who would beat a gray, wrinkled, arthritic old woman? Why in God's name would he do it? I shudder. The pain of the arthritis as she struggled with him.

Perhaps he is still in the house, waiting for me.

To the hollow sickness in my stomach now comes fear, hot, pulsing, and I am frantic before I realize what I am doing—grabbing the spare cane my mother always keeps by her bed, flicking on the light in her room, throwing open the closet door and striking in with the cane. Viciously, sounds coming from my throat, the cane flailing among the faded dresses.

No one. Under the bed. No one. Behind the door. No one.

I search all the upstairs rooms that way, terrified, constantly checking behind me, clutching the cane and whacking into closets, under beds, behind doors, with a force that would certainly crack a skull. No one.

"Meg! Sarah!"

No answer, not even an echo in this sound-absorbing house.

There is no attic, just an overhead entry to a crawl space under the eaves, and that opening has long been sealed. No sign of tampering. No one has gone up.

I rush down the stairs, seeing the trail of blood my mother has left on the carpet, imagining her pain as she crawled, and search the rooms downstairs with the same desperate thoroughness. In the front closet. Behind the sofa and chairs. Behind the drapes. No one.

I lock the front door, lest he be outside in the storm waiting to come in behind me. I remember to draw every blind, close every drape, lest he be out there peering at me. The rain pelts insistently against the windowpanes.

I cry out again and again for Meg and Sarah. The police. My mother. A doctor. I grab for the phone on the wall by the front stairs, fearful to listen to it, afraid he has cut the line outside. But it is droning. Droning. I ring for the police, working the handle at the side around and around and around.

They are coming, they say. A doctor with them. Stay where I am, they say. But I cannot. Meg and Sarah, I must find them. I know they are not in the basement where the milk is dripping—all the basement is open to view. Except for my childhood things, we have cleared out all the boxes and barrels and the shelves of jars the Saturday before.

But under the stairs. I have forgotten about under the stairs and now I race down and stand dreading in the milk; but there are only cobwebs there, already reformed from Saturday when we cleared them. I look up at the side door I first came through, and as if I am seeing through a telescope I focus largely on the handle. It seems to fidget. I have a panicked vision of the intruder bursting through, and I charge up to lock the door, and the door to the barn.

And then I think: if Meg and Sarah are not in the house they are likely in the barn. But I cannot bring myself to unlock the barn door and go through. *He* must be there as well. Not in the rain outside but in the shelter of the barn, and there are no lights to turn on there.

And why the milk? Did he do it and where did he get it? And why? Or did Sarah do it before? No, the milk is too freshly dripping. It has been put there too recently. By him. But why? And who is he? A tramp? An escapee from some prison? Or asylum? No, the nearest institution is far away, hundreds of miles. From the town then. Or a nearby farm.

I know my questions are for delay, to keep me from entering the barn. But I must. I take the flashlight from the kitchen drawer and unlock the door to the barn, force myself to go in quickly, cane ready, flashing my light. The stalls are still there, listing; and some of the equipment, churners, separators, dull and rusted, webbed and dirty. The must of decaying wood and crumbled hay, the fresh wet smell of the rain gusting through cracks in the walls. Once this was a dairy, as the other farms around still are.

Flicking my light toward the corners, edging toward the stalls, boards creaking, echoing, I try to control my fright, try to remember as a boy how the cows waited in the stalls for my father to milk them, how the barn was once board-tight and solid, warm to be in, how there was no connecting door from the barn to the house because my father did not want my mother to smell the animals in her kitchen.

I run my light down the walls, sweep it in arcs through the darkness before me as I draw nearer to the stalls, and in spite of myself I recall that other autumn when the snow came early, four feet deep by morning and still storming thickly, how my father went out to the barn to milk and never returned for lunch, nor supper. There was no phone then, no way to get help, and my mother and I waited all night, unable to make our way through the storm, listening to the slowly dying wind; and the next morning was clear and bright and blinding as we shoveled out to find the cows in agony in their stalls from not having been milked and my father dead, frozen rock-solid in the snow in the middle of the next field where he must have wandered when he lost his bearings in the storm.

There was a fox, risen earlier than us, nosing at him under the snow, and my father had to be sealed in his coffin before he could lie in state. Days after, the snow was melted, gone, the barnyard a sea of mud, and it was autumn again and my mother had the connecting door put in. My father should have tied a rope from the house to his waist to guide him back in case he lost his way. Certainly he knew enough. But then he was like that always in a rush. When I was ten.

Thus I think as I light the shadows near the stalls, terrified of what I may find in any one of them, Meg and Sarah, or him, thinking of how my mother and I searched for my father and how I now search for my wife and child, trying to think of how it was once warm in here and pleasant, chatting with my father, helping him to milk, the sweet smell of new hay and grain, the different sweet smell of fresh droppings, something I always liked and neither my father nor my mother could understand. I know that if I do not think of these good times I will surely go mad in awful anticipation of what I may find. Pray God they have not died!

What can he have done to them? To assault a five-year-old girl? Split her. The hemorrhaging alone can have killed her.

And then, even in the barn, I hear my mother cry out for me. The relief I feel to leave and go to her unnerves me. I do want to find Meg and Sarah, to try to save them. Yet I am relieved to go. I think my mother will tell me what has happened, tell me where to find them. That is how I justify my leaving as I wave the light in circles around me, guarding my back, retreating through the door and locking it.

Upstairs she sits stiffly on her bed. I want to make her answer my questions, to shake her, to force her to help, but I know it will only frighten her more, maybe push her mind down to where I can never reach.

"Mother," I say to her softly, touching her gently. "What has happened?" My impatience can barely be contained. "Who did this? Where are Meg and Sarah?"

She smiles at me, reassured by the safety of my presence. Still she cannot answer.

"Mother. Please," I say. "I know how bad it must have been. But you must try to help. I must know where they are so I can help them."

She says, "Dolls."

It chills me. "What dolls, Mother? Did a man come here with dolls? What did he want? You mean he looked like a doll? Wearing a mask like one?"

Too many questions. All she can do is blink.

"Please, Mother. You must try your best to tell me. Where are Meg and Sarah?"

"Dolls," she says.

As I first had the foreboding of disaster at the sight of Sarah's unrumpled satin bedspread, now I am beginning to understand, rejecting it, fighting it.

"Yes, Mother, the dolls," I say, refusing to admit what I know. "Please, Mother. Where are Meg and Sarah?"

"You are a grown boy now. You must stop playing as a child. Your father. Without him you will have to be the man in the house. You must be brave."

"No, Mother." I can feel it swelling in my chest.

"There will be a great deal of work now, more than any child should know. But we have no choice. You must accept that God has chosen to take him from us, that you are all the man I have left to help me."

"No, Mother."

"Now you are a man and you must put away the things of a child."

Eyes streaming, I am barely able to straighten, leaning wearily against the doorjamb, tears rippling from my face down to my shirt, wetting it cold where it had just begun to dry. I wipe my eyes and see her reaching for me, smiling, and I recoil down the hall, stumbling down the stairs, down, through the sitting room, the kitchen, down, down to the milk, splashing through it to the dollhouse, and in there, crammed and doubled, Sarah. And in the wicker chest, Meg. The toys not on the floor for Sarah to play with, but taken out so Meg could be put in. And both of them, their stomachs slashed, stuffed with sawdust, their eyes rolled up like dolls' eyes.

The police are knocking at the side door, pounding, calling out who they are, but I am powerless to let them in. They crash through the door, their rubber raincoats dripping as they stare down at me.

"The milk," I say.

They do not understand. Even as I wait, standing in the milk, listening to the rain pelting on the windows while they come over to see what is in the dollhouse and in the wicker chest, while they go upstairs to my mother and then return so I can tell them again, "The milk." But they still do not understand.

"She killed them of course," one man says. "But I don't see why the milk."

Only when they speak to the neighbors down the road and learn how she came to them, needing the cans of milk, insisting she carry them herself to the car, the agony she was in as she carried them, only when they find the empty cans and the knife in a stall in the barn, can I say, "The milk. The blood. There was so much blood, you know. She needed to deny it, so she washed it away with milk, purified it, started the dairy again. You see, there was so much blood."

That autumn we live in a house in the country, my mother's house, the house I was raised in. I have been to the village, struck even more by how nothing in it has changed, yet everything has, because I am older now, seeing it differently. It is as though I am both here now and back then, at once with the mind of a boy and a man . . .

THE PURPLE SHROUD

by Joyce Harrington

This is the 371st "first story" to be published by Ellery
Queen's Mystery Magazine . . . *the kind of story that the late
Anthony Boucher would have called "lovely," except that you had
to hear him pronounce the word to realize its full meaning . . .*

*The author, Joyce Harrington, admits her age is "no terrific
secret, but let's just say I've been around a while." At the time we
accepted "The Purple Shroud" she had been married for twelve
years to former* Look *photographer, Phil Harrington. The Harring-
tons have two sons, Christopher and Evan. Mrs. Harrington has
"worked at many jobs in many places"—from a doorknob factory
to the U.S. Army Quartermaster Corps. She doesn't have any*

hobbies as such; rather, she does the things that interest her—she climbs mountains, paints pictures, weaves on a loom in her attic. "As you can imagine," she wrote, "I sometimes meet myself coming and going" . . .

MRS. MOON threw the shuttle back and forth and pumped the treadles of the big four-harness loom as if her life depended on it. When they asked what she was weaving so furiously, she would laugh silently and say it was a shroud.

"No, really, what is it?"

"My house needs new draperies." Mrs. Moon would smile and the shuttle would fly and the beater would thump the newly woven threads tightly into place. The muffled, steady sounds of her craft could be heard from early morning until very late at night, until the sounds became an accepted and expected background noise and were only noticed in their absence.

Then they would say, "I wonder what Mrs. Moon is doing now."

That summer, as soon as they had arrived at the art colony and even before they had unpacked, Mrs. Moon requested that the largest loom in the weaving studio be installed in their cabin. Her request had been granted because she was a serious weaver, and because her husband, George, was one of the best painting instructors they'd ever had. He could coax the amateurs into stretching their imaginations and trying new ideas and techniques, and he would bully the scholarship students until, in a fury, they would sometimes produce works of surprising originality.

George Moon was, himself, only a competent painter. His work had never caught on, although he had a small loyal following in Detroit and occasionally sold a painting. His only concessions to the need for making a living and for buying paints and brushes was to teach some ten hours a week throughout the winter and to take this summer job at the art colony, which was also their vacation. Mrs. Moon taught craft therapy at a home for the aged.

After the loom had been set up in their cabin Mrs. Moon waited. Sometimes she went swimming in the lake, sometimes she drove into town and poked about in the antique shops, and sometimes she just sat in the wicker chair and looked at the loom.

They said, "What are you waiting for, Mrs. Moon? When are you going to begin?"

One day Mrs. Moon drove into town and came back with two boxes full of brightly colored yarns. Classes had been going on for about two weeks, and George was deeply engaged with his students. One of the things the students loved about George was the extra time he gave them. He was always ready to sit for hours on the porch of the big house, just outside the communal dining room, or under a tree, and talk about painting or about life as a painter or tell stories about painters he had known.

George looked like a painter. He was tall and thin, and with approaching middle age he was beginning to stoop a little. He had black snaky hair which he had always worn on the long side, and which was beginning to turn gray. His eyes were very dark, so dark you couldn't see the pupils, and they regarded everything and everyone with a probing intensity that evoked uneasiness in some and caused young girls to fall in love with him.

Every year George Moon selected one young lady disciple to be his summer consort.

Mrs. Moon knew all about these summer alliances. Every year, when they returned to Detroit, George would confess to her with great humility and swear never to repeat his transgression.

"Never again, Arlene," he would say. "I promise you, never again."

Mrs. Moon would smile her forgiveness.

Mrs. Moon hummed as she sorted through the skeins of purple and deep scarlet, goldenrod yellow and rich royal blue. She hummed as she wound the glowing hanks into fat balls, and she thought about George and the look that had passed between him and the girl from Minneapolis at dinner the night before. George had not returned to their cabin until almost two in the morning. The girl from Minneapolis was short and plump, with a round face and a halo of fuzzy red-gold hair. She reminded Mrs. Moon of a Teddy bear; she reminded Mrs. Moon of herself twenty years before.

When Mrs. Moon was ready to begin, she carried the purple yarn to the weaving studio.

"I have to make a very long warp," she said. "I'll need to use the warping reel."

She hummed as she measured out the seven feet and a little over, then sent the reel spinning.

"Is it wool?" asked the weaving instructor.

"No, it's orlon," said Mrs. Moon. "It won't shrink, you know."

Mrs. Moon loved the creak of the reel, and she loved feeling the warp threads grow fatter under her hands until at last each planned thread was in place and she could tie the bundle and braid up the end. When she held the plaited warp in her hands she imagined it to be the shorn tresses of some enormously powerful earth goddess whose potency was now transferred to her own person.

That evening after dinner, Mrs. Moon began to thread the loom. George had taken the rowboat and the girl from Minneapolis to the other end of the lake where there was a deserted cottage. Mrs. Moon knew he kept a sleeping bag there, and a cache of wine and peanuts. Mrs. Moon hummed as she carefully threaded the eye of each heddle with a single purple thread, and thought of black widow spiders and rattlesnakes coiled in the corners of the dark cottage.

She worked contentedly until midnight and then went to bed. She was asleep and smiling when George stumbled in two hours later and fell into bed with his clothes on.

Mrs. Moon wove steadily through the summer days. She did not attend the weekly critique sessions for she had nothing to show and was not interested in the problems others were having with their work. She ignored the Saturday night parties where George and the girl from Minneapolis and the others danced and drank beer and slipped off to the beach or the boathouse. Sometimes, when she tired of the long hours at the loom, she would go for solitary walks in the woods and always brought back curious trophies of her rambling. The small cabin, already crowded with the loom and the iron double bedstead, began to fill up with giant toadstools, interesting bits of wood, arrangements of reeds and wild wheat.

One day she brought back two large black stones on which she painted faces. The eyes of the faces were closed and the mouths were faintly curved in archaic smiles. She placed one stone on each side of the fireplace.

George hated the stones. "Those damn stonefaces are watching me," he said. "Get them out of here."

"How can they be watching you? Their eyes are closed."

Mrs. Moon left the stones beside the fireplace and George soon forgot to hate them. She called them Apollo I and Apollo II.

The weaving grew and Mrs. Moon thought it the best thing she had ever done. Scattered about the purple ground were signs and symbols which she saw against the deep blackness of her closed eyelids when she thought of passion and revenge, of love and wasted years and the child she had never had. She thought the barbaric colors spoke of these matters, and she was pleased.

"I hope you'll finish it before the final critique," the weaving teacher said when she came to the cabin to see it. "It's very good."

Word spread through the camp and many of the students came to the cabin to see the marvelous weaving. Mrs. Moon was proud to show it to them and received their compliments with quiet grace.

"It's too fine to hang at a window," said one practical Sunday-painting matron. "The sun will fade the colors."

"I'd love to wear it," said the life model.

"You!" said a bearded student of lithography. "It's a robe for a pagan king!"

"Perhaps you're right," said Mrs. Moon, and smiled her happiness on all of them.

The season was drawing to a close when in the third week of August, Mrs. Moon threw the shuttle for the last time. She slumped on the backless bench and rested her limp hands on the breast beam of the loom. Tomorrow she would cut the warp.

That night, while George was showing color slides of his paintings in the main gallery, the girl from Minneapolis came alone to the Moons' cabin. Mrs. Moon was lying on the bed watching a spider spin a web in the rafters. A fire was blazing in the fireplace, between Apollo I and Apollo II, for the late summer night was chill.

"You must let him go," said the golden-haired Teddy bear. "He loves me."

"Yes, dear," said Mrs. Moon.

"You don't seem to understand. I'm talking about George." The girl sat on the bed. "I think I'm pregnant."

"That's nice," said Mrs. Moon. "Children are a blessing. Watch the spider."

"We have a real relationship going. I don't care about being married—that's too feudal. But you must free George to come and be a father image to the child."

"You'll get over it," said Mrs. Moon, smiling a trifle sadly at the girl.

"Oh, you don't even want to know what's happening!" cried the girl. "No wonder George is bored with you."

"Some spiders eat their mates after fertilization," Mrs. Moon remarked. "Female spiders."

The girl flounced angrily from the cabin, as far as one could be said to flounce in blue jeans and sweatshirt.

George performed his end-of-summer separation ritual simply and brutally the following afternoon. He disappeared after lunch. No one knew where he had gone. The girl from Minneapolis roamed the camp, trying not to let anyone know she was searching for him. Finally she rowed herself down to the other end of the lake, to find that George had dumped her transistor radio, her books of poetry, and her box of incense on the damp sand, and had put a padlock on the door of the cottage.

She threw her belongings into the boat and rowed back to the camp, tears of rage streaming down her cheeks. She beached the boat, and with head lowered and shoulders hunched she stormed the Moons' cabin. She found Mrs. Moon tying off the severed warp threads.

"Tell George," she shouted, "tell George I'm going back to Minneapolis. He knows where to find me!"

"Here, dear," said Mrs. Moon, "hold the end and walk backwards while I unwind it."

The girl did as she was told, caught by the vibrant colors and Mrs. Moon's concentration. In a few minutes the full length of cloth rested in the girl's arms.

"Put it on the bed and spread it out," said Mrs. Moon. "Let's take a good look at it."

"I'm really leaving," whispered the girl. "Tell him I don't care if I never see him again."

"I'll tell him." The wide strip of purple flowed garishly down the middle of the bed between them. "Do you think he'll like it?" asked Mrs. Moon. "He's going to have it around for a long time."

"The colors are very beautiful, very savage." The girl looked closely at Mrs. Moon. "I wouldn't have thought you would choose such colors."

"I never did before."

"I'm leaving now."

"Good-bye," said Mrs. Moon.

George did not reappear until long after the girl had loaded up her battered bug of a car and driven off. Mrs. Moon knew he had been watching and waiting from the hill behind the camp. He came into the cabin whistling softly and began to take his clothes off.

"God, I'm tired," he said.

"It's almost dinner time."

"Too tired to eat," he yawned. "What's that on the bed?"

"My weaving is finished. Do you like it?"

"It's good. Take it off the bed. I'll look at it tomorrow."

Mrs. Moon carefully folded the cloth and laid it on the weaving bench. She looked at George's thin naked body before he got into bed, and smiled.

"I'm going to dinner now," she said.

"Okay. Don't wake me up when you get back. I could sleep for a week."

"I won't wake you up," said Mrs. Moon.

Mrs. Moon ate dinner at a table by herself. Most of the students had already left. A few people, the Moons among them, usually stayed on after the end of classes to rest and enjoy the isolation. Mrs. Moon spoke to no one.

After dinner she sat on the pier and watched the sunset. She watched the turtles in the shallow water and thought she saw a blue heron on the other side of the lake. When the sky was black and the stars were too many to count, Mrs. Moon went to the toolshed and got a wheelbarrow. She rolled this to the door of her cabin and went inside.

The cabin was dark and she could hear George's steady heavy breathing. She lit two candles and placed them on the mantelshelf. She spread her beautiful weaving on her side of the bed, gently so as not to disturb the sleeper. Then she quietly moved the weaving bench to George's side of the bed, near his head.

She sat on the bench for a time, memorizing the lines of his face by the wavering candlelight. She touched him softly on the forehead with the pads of her fingertips and gently caressed his eyes, his hard cheeks, his raspy chin. His breathing became uneven and she withdrew her hands, sitting motionless until his sleep rhythm was restored.

Then Mrs. Moon took off her shoes. She walked carefully to the fireplace, taking long quiet steps. She placed her shoes neatly side by side on the hearth and picked up the larger stone, Apollo I. The face of the kouros, the ancient god, smiled up at her and she returned that faint implacable smile. She carried the stone back to the bench beside the bed, and set it down.

Then she climbed onto the bench, and when she stood, she found she could almost touch the spider's web in the rafters. The spider crouched in the heart of its web, and Mrs. Moon wondered if spiders ever slept.

Mrs. Moon picked up Apollo I, and with both arms raised, took careful aim. Her shadow, cast by candlelight, had the appearance of a priestess offering sacrifice. The stone was heavy and her arms grew weak. Her hands let go. The stone dropped.

George's eyes flapped open and he saw Mrs. Moon smiling tenderly down on him. His lips drew back to scream, but his mouth could only form a soundless hole.

"Sleep, George," she whispered, and his eyelids clamped over his unbelieving eyes.

Mrs. Moon jumped off the bench. With gentle fingers she probed beneath his snaky locks until she found a satisfying softness. There was no blood and for this Mrs. Moon was grateful. It would have been a shame to spoil the beauty of her patterns with superfluous colors and untidy stains. Her mothlike fingers on his wrist warned her of a faint uneven fluttering.

She padded back to the fireplace and weighed in her hands the smaller, lighter Apollo II. This time she felt there was no need for added height. With three quick butter-churning motions she enlarged the softened area in George's skull and stilled the annoying flutter in his wrist.

Then she rolled him over, as a hospital nurse will roll an immobile patient during bedmaking routine, until he rested on his back on one-half of the purple fabric. She placed his arms across his naked chest and straightened his spindly legs. She kissed his closed eyelids, gently stroked his shaggy brows, and said, "Rest now, dear George."

She folded the free half of the royal cloth over him, covering him from head to foot with a little left over at each end. From her sewing box she took a wide-eyed needle and threaded it with some difficulty in the flickering light. Then kneeling beside the bed, Mrs. Moon began stitching across the top. She stitched small careful stitches that would hold for eternity.

Soon the top was closed and she began stitching down the long side. The job was wearisome, but Mrs. Moon was patient and she hummed a sweet, monotonous tune as stitch followed stitch past George's ear, his shoulder, his bent elbow. It was not until she reached his ankles that she allowed herself to stand and stretch her aching knees and flex her cramped fingers.

Retrieving the twin Apollos from where they lay abandoned on George's pillow, she tucked them reverently into the bottom of the cloth sarcophagus and knelt once more to her task. Her needle flew faster as the remaining gap between the two edges of cloth grew smaller, until the last stitch was securely knotted and George was sealed into his funerary garment. But the hardest part of her night's work was yet to come.

She knew she could not carry George even the short distance to the door of the cabin and the wheelbarrow outside. And the wheelbarrow was too wide to bring inside. She couldn't bear the thought of dragging him across the floor and soiling or tearing the fabric she had so lovingly woven. Finally she rolled him onto the weaving bench and despite the fact that it only supported him from armpits to groin, she managed to maneuver it to the door. From there it was possible to shift the burden to the waiting wheelbarrow.

Mrs. Moon was now breathing heavily from her exertions, and paused for a moment to survey the night and the prospect before her. There were no lights anywhere in the camp except for the feeble glow of her own guttering candles. As she went to blow them out she glanced at her watch and was mildly surprised to see that it was ten minutes past three. The hours had flown while she had been absorbed in her needlework.

She perceived now the furtive night noises of the forest creatures which had hitherto been blocked from her senses by the total concentration she had bestowed on her work. She thought of weasels and foxes prowling, of owls going about their predatory night activities, and considered herself in congenial company. Then taking up the handles of the wheelbarrow, she trundled down the well-defined path to the boathouse.

The wheelbarrow made more noise than she had anticipated and she hoped she was far enough from any occupied cabin for its rumbling to go unnoticed. The moonless night sheltered her from any wakeful watcher, and a dozen summers of waiting had taught her the nature and substance of every square foot of the camp's area. She could walk it blindfolded.

When she reached the boathouse she found that some hurried careless soul had left a boat on the beach in defiance of the camp's rules. It was a simple matter of leverage to shift her burden from barrow to boat and in minutes Mrs. Moon was heaving inexpertly at the oars. At first the boat seemed inclined to travel only in wide arcs and head back to shore, but with patient determination Mrs. Moon established a rowing rhythm that would take her and her passenger to the deepest part of the lake.

She hummed a sea chanty which aided her rowing and pleased her sense of the appropriate. Then pinpointing her position by the silhouette of the tall solitary pine that grew on the opposite shore, Mrs. Moon carefully raised the oars and rested them in the boat.

As Mrs. Moon crept forward in the boat, feeling her way in the darkness, the boat began to rock gently. It was a pleasant, soothing motion and Mrs. Moon thought of cradles and soft enveloping comforters. She continued creeping slowly forward, swaying with the motion of the boat, until she reached the side of her swaddling passenger. There she sat and stroked the cloth and wished that she could see the fine colors just one last time.

She felt the shape beneath the cloth, solid but thin and now rather pitiful. She took the head in her arms and held it against her breast, rocking and humming a long-forgotten lullaby.

The doubled weight at the forward end of the small boat caused the prow to dip. Water began to slosh into the boat—in small wavelets at first as the boat rocked from side to side, then in a steady trickle as the boat rode lower and lower in the water. Mrs. Moon rocked and hummed; the water rose over her bare feet and lapped against her ankles. The sky began to turn purple and she could just make out the distant shape of the boathouse and the hill behind the camp. She was very tired and very cold.

Gently she placed George's head in the water. The boat tilted crazily and she scrambled backward to equalize the weight. She picked up the other end of the long purple chrysalis, the end containing the stone Apollos, and heaved it overboard, George in his shroud, with head and feet trailing in the lake, now lay along the side of the boat weighting it down.

Water was now pouring in. Mrs. Moon held to the other side of the boat with placid hands and thought of the dense comfort of the muddy lake bottom and George beside her forever. She saw that her feet were frantically pushing against the burden of her life, running away from that companionable grave.

With a regretful sigh she let herself slide down the short incline of the seat and came to rest beside George. The boat lurched deeper into the lake. Water surrounded George and climbed into Mrs. Moon's lap. Mrs. Moon closed her eyes and hummed, "Nearer My God to Thee." She did not see George drift away from the side of the boat, carried off by the moving arms of water. She felt a wild bouncing, a shuddering and splashing, and was sure the boat had overturned. With relief she gave herself up to chaos and did not try to hold her breath.

Expecting a suffocating weight of water in her lungs, Mrs. Moon was disappointed to find she could open her eyes, that air still entered and left her gasping mouth. She lay in a pool of water in the bottom of the boat and saw a bird circle high above the lake, peering down at her. The boat was bobbing gently on the water, and when Mrs. Moon sat up she saw that a few yards away, through the fresh blue morning, George was bobbing gently too. The purple shroud had filled with air and floated on the water like a small submarine come up for air and a look at the new day.

As she watched, shivering and wet, the submarine shape drifted away and dwindled as the lake took slow possession. At last, with a grateful sigh, green water replacing the last bubble air, it sank just as the bright arc of the sun rose over the hill in time to give Mrs. Moon a final glimpse of glorious purple and gold. She shook herself like a tired old gray dog and called out, "Good-bye, George." Her cry echoed back and forth across the morning and startled forth a chorus of bird shrieks. Pandemonium and farewell. She picked up the oars.

Back on the beach, the boat carefully restored to its place, Mrs. Moon dipped her blistered hands into the lake. She scented bacon on the early air and instantly felt the pangs of an enormous hunger. Mitch, the cook, would be having his early breakfast and perhaps would share it with her. She hurried to the cabin to change out of her wet clothes, and was amazed, as she stepped over the doorsill, at the stark emptiness which greeted her.

Shafts of daylight fell on the rumpled bed, but there was nothing for her there. She was not tired now, did not need to sleep. The fireplace contained cold ashes, and the hearth looked bare and unfriendly. The loom gaped at her like a toothless mouth, its usefulness at an end. In a heap on the floor lay George's clothes where he had dropped them the night before. Out of habit she picked them up, and as she hung them on a hook in the small closet she felt a rustle in the shirt pocket. It was a scrap of paper torn off a drawing pad; there was part of a pencil sketch on one side, on the other an address and telephone number.

Mrs. Moon hated to leave anything unfinished, despising untidiness in herself and others. She quickly changed into her town clothes and hung her discarded wet things in the tiny bathroom to dry. She found an apple and munched it as she made up her face and combed her still damp hair. The apple took the edge off her hunger, and she decided not to take the time to beg breakfast from the cook.

She carefully made the bed and tidied the small room, sweeping a few scattered ashes back into the fireplace. She checked her summer straw pocketbook for driver's license, car keys, money, and finding everything satisfactory, she paused for a moment in the center of the room. All was quiet, neat, and orderly. The spider still hung inert in the center of its web and one small fly was buzzing helplessly on its perimeter. Mrs. Moon smiled.

There was no time to weave now—indeed, there was no need. She could not really expect to find a conveniently deserted lake in a big city. No. She would have to think of something else.

Mrs. Moon stood in the doorway of the cabin in the early sunlight, a small frown wrinkling the placid surface of her round pink face. She scuffled slowly around to the back of the cabin and into the shadow of the sycamores beyond, her feet kicking up the spongy layers of years of fallen leaves, her eyes watching carefully for the right idea to show itself. Two grayish-white stones appeared side by side, half covered with leaf mold. Anonymous, faceless, about the size of cantaloupes, they would do unless something better presented itself later.

Unceremoniously she dug them out of their bed, brushed away the loose dirt and leaf fragments, and carried them back to the car.

Mrs. Moon's watch had stopped sometime during the night, but as she got into the car she glanced at the now fully risen sun and guessed the time to be about six-thirty or seven o'clock. She placed the two stones snugly on the passenger seat and covered them with her soft pale-blue cardigan. She started the engine, and then reached over and groped in the glove compartment. She never liked to drive anywhere without knowing beforehand the exact roads to take to get to her destination. The road map was there, neatly folded beneath the flashlight and the box of tissues.

Mrs. Moon unfolded the map and spread it out over the

steering wheel. As the engine warmed up, Mrs. Moon hummed along with it. Her pudgy pink hand absently patted the tidy blue bundle beside her as she planned the most direct route to the girl in Minneapolis.

EDITORIAL POSTSCRIPT

The story you have just read won the highest possible honor that can be won by a mystery short story. It was awarded the coveted Edgar by MWA (Mystery Writers of America) as the best short story in the mystery field published in American magazines and books during 1972.

A GIRL CAN'T ALWAYS HAVE EVERYTHING

by Tonita S. Gardner

This is the 377th "first story" to be published by Ellery Queen's Mystery Magazine . . . *a most amusing story—bright and breezy, sly, smart, and sophisticated . . .*

The author, Tonita S. Gardner, taught elementary school in the 1950s and at present she alternates between being a housewife (husband an insurance executive; three children) and pecking away at her portable typewriter. She has written "tons" of light verse and much of it has appeared in Good Housekeeping, McCall's, The Wall Street Journal, *etc.*

Mrs. Gardner's hobbies include writing, of course (which she calls "a way of life"), reading, cooking, and "at infrequent

*intervals, hopping a plane with my husband and flying off to
explore some small segment of Planet Earth"* . . .

WHEN Suzy Millette sat down to write her suicide note,
she had no intention of killing herself. She only wanted to scare
her husband into taking her back.

"How do you spell 'desperate'?" she asked—and while I was
considering if the word had an "a" or an "e" after the "p," I must
have looked so serious that she started to grin. "We've got to do
this right or he'll never believe it's a matter of life and death." She
winked at me and laughed so hard that tears rolled down her
cheeks and she had to adjust a false eyelash.

"All kidding aside," she said when she'd recovered from her
giggles, "I mustn't foul up again. Where would I find another
money-machine like Herbert? Ugh, Herbert!" She sighed. "A girl
can't always have everything."

Suzy seemed to have everything, and she usually got what she
wanted. This time she wanted a young computer executive whom
she'd met in a swingers' bar; he was part of the foul-up.

"Still and all," she concluded as she signed the letter and
slipped it into an envelope, "there are certain times, my friend,
when it's inconvenient to have a husband."

But Suzy had always felt this way, even in the beginning, three
years before.

We were roommates then; we shared a small apartment in New
York—a comfortable arrangement because we both had bit parts
in the same off-Broadway play. Suzy's stage name was Suzy Starr;
I used my real name, Patricia Lewis.

Through an actor friend of mine who knew some VIPs, Suzy
convinced me to wangle an invitation to a swanky East Side party.
I'd been told some movie people were going to be there, and
when I mentioned this to Suzy she'd beamed at me and crossed
her fingers. "Opportunity knocks, Pat—we could wind up in
Hollywood!"

It was one of those stand-up cocktail affairs. Suzy immediately began to circulate. I decided to follow her example, and as soon as I spotted Herbert, I was positive I'd found a real live producer. He certainly looked like one: big expensive cigar, balding head, paunchy stomach. I was all set to say hello, but then I chickened out and went to check my makeup.

. When I got back, Suzy was with him. (I couldn't blame her; it was every girl for herself.) But even though I lacked my friend's charisma, I watched her operate and had to admire her technique: her dress was tight enough to show off her marvelous figure, and with her auburn hair, green eyes, and creamy white skin she flattered a man just by giving him her undivided attention.

Herbert was enchanted.

It didn't take Suzy long to discover that our "producer" was actually a toy manufacturer—with factories in four states.

He was also a widower and unattached.

"No wonder he can't take his eyes off me," Suzy confided when we met in the powder room. "He showed me a picture of his dear departed. A face like a broken-down bulldog!" She flashed her brilliant smile. "But this guy is loaded—and I don't mean from drinking."

When a huge bouquet of orchids arrived at our apartment the next day, Suzy knew that Herbert was hooked—hers for the taking. And she took plenty. (Each time she came home with something new, Patty the Pauper tried her best not to drool.) At first there was a series of moderately expensive baubles, then it snowballed into a mink coat and a Thunderbird. ("Quite a haul for a small-time farm girl!" she gleefully informed me.)

Suzy wasn't hepped-up about marriage, but not wanting to lose her golden goose, she said yes. They were married in City Hall, and I was her only attendant; afterward, while Herbert's luxurious penthouse was being completely redecorated for his lucky bride, the honeymooners settled temporarily at the nearby Plaza Hotel, so Suzy could be available in case the decorator needed her. (P.S.: He needed her, she was available.)

As soon as the honeymoon was over, Suzy decided to rejoin the show, mainly because she was having an affair with the leading man; when he left for a more lucrative out-of-town offer, Suzy immediately lost interest in her theatrical career.

"One thing about being married to a rich man," she snickered, "it makes a girl like me lose all her ambition."

"I'd be the same if I didn't have to pay rent every month," I told her, hoping she'd take the hint and spread the wealth.

Instead, she gave me a pep talk: "Your turn'll come too, Pat. And when it does, milk it for all it's worth."

"Sure," I said, "but I'm hardly an expert like you."

"Then for heaven's sake, girl, learn from me! You're only on this earth for a few years—and if you don't grab in some goodies while you're still young enough and pretty enough, you certainly won't be able to when you're older."

I nodded and made a mental note to learn from the Starr of the show.

At this time Herbert was forty-seven to Suzy's twenty-seven, but like a young passionately-in-love bridegroom he confessed his longing to become a father.

"Yi-ich!" Suzy relived the scene for me. "It took all my self-control just to keep from upchucking my fifty-dollar dinner."

"What could you say, though?"

"I'm a better actress than you think, Pat. You should have heard us gooing together about our own little itty-babykins! But if he stuck it out with Dog-Face for nineteen years and she couldn't have kids, he'll also stick it out with me when I give him the same bad news."

"Suppose you become pregnant?"

"Thank God for the Pill! But isn't it a riot?—he thinks I'm going to be a brood mare so he can have a sonny-boy who looks like him"—and she pulled at her jaw to approximate Herbert's jowls. "He's got another think coming!"

Herbert had no way of knowing this. When I called up once and found him home with the flu, he told me Suzy was at her doctor's getting tested to find out why she couldn't conceive. "She wants to become a mother very badly," he said, sounding so wistful I actually felt sorry for him.

Of course he also had no way of knowing that the M.D. whom Suzy was supposed to be consulting was really a chorus boy from a new musical on West Forty-fourth Street. As for the medical bills for her "treatments"—no problem: Suzy knew an expensive Fifth Avenue doctor whom she'd gone out with a few times ("God, he had hands like an octopus!") and who, as a special favor to her, was now willing to mail huge bills to Herbert, which the latter promptly paid. But in spite of her own numerous affairs Suzy kept a shrewd eye on any attractive female with whom Herbert came in contact. (Had she included me, I would have been flattered!)

They say the husband is always the last to know, but Suzy managed so well Herbert might never have found out.

Except for one thing.

It started with a business trip of his down South. Since Suzy went with Herbert only on expensive vacations, she figured this was a good chance to get away to Bermuda for a secret holiday with her newest, the computer executive. (No one she knew ever went to Bermuda, and Herbert thought she was expected at the family farm in Wisconsin: "Too bad you can't call me there, darling. The folks still don't have a phone.")

She packed her bags as soon as Herbert left, and three hours later she and her computer exec arrived at Kennedy Airport. But unknown to them, Herbert's flight had been delayed because of a phony bomb threat, and when they entered the Eastern terminal arm in arm, there was Herbert, almost ready to board his plane.

Suzy was so flabbergasted that for once in her life she didn't know what to say. Not that it would have mattered. Despite her blonde wig and dark glasses, Herbert's vision was 20-20. ("Oh, the look on his face, Pat! The look on his face!") He left on his trip anyway. Suzy, too upset to continue on to Bermuda, went home alone.

That afternoon she called me. "I'm in a terrible mess, Pat," and after spilling the whole story she added, "While I stood there with my mouth hanging open, he told me that as soon as he gets back he's stopping at the house to collect his things. Pat, what should I do?"

She sounded so unhappy that I hurried to her apartment. By the time I got there, she'd regained her usual aplomb. Busily unpacking her suitcase, *she* tried to reassure *me*: "It's not as hopeless as it sounds, old pal. I've got an idea that will work out perfectly. In three words—The Sinner Repents."

"How do you propose to do *that?*"

"By composing a suicide note." Slyly she smiled. "I think I can scare Herbert into taking me back." She reached for some notepaper and a pen and began to write, thanking me profusely when I reminded her to make her hand quiver.

"What would I ever do without you, Pat?"

I smiled back at her. "Suzy, even *you* can't always think of everything."

"And I'm a lousy speller too."

"You need help? Ask *me*."

"How do you spell 'desperate'?" she asked—and while I was considering if the word had an "a" or an "e" after the "p," I must have looked so serious that she started to grin. "We've got to do this right or he'll never believe it's a matter of life and death."

Then, after going through her false-eyelash-giggles routine, and vowing not to foul up again, Suzy signed the letter and slipped it into an envelope, concluding, "There are certain times, my friend, when it's inconvenient to have a husband."

Carefully she addressed and sealed the envelope, and was now ready to launch her plan.

"Listen closely, Pat. On Wednesday, right before Herbert's due back from his trip, I'll go to the Plaza Hotel, get myself a room there, and wait to hear from you. *Your* base of operations will be the drugstore near my apartment; they have plenty of phone booths. What you'll do is start calling Herbert, try to catch him the moment he comes home to pack up and leave for good. His plane lands about five-thirty, so figure he'll be home about seven. As an extra precaution, though, you can begin phoning at a quarter to."

"Why would I call him?"

"To make sure he's there! When he finally answers, hang up. Then, and only then, you can call me at the Plaza. And I can start timing everything."

"Such as?"

"Such as gulping down a bunch of sleeping pills."

"Wha-at!"

"It's part of the plan. If you'll listen I'll explain."

"Suzy, I'd be scared stiff if I were—"

"I am scared—a little."

"Then don't take those things. Just pretend to."

"Uh, uh. It's got to be as real as possible. That's why I'm working out every detail so that nothing can go wrong. Now, the moment you call me with the go-ahead signal, you *immediately* rush up to the apartment and give Herbert my note. Only you're not supposed to know what it says. Meanwhile, I'll wait about ten minutes, then take the pills."

"What do I tell Herbert?"

"Tell him that while you were out making your theatrical rounds, Suzy must have let herself into your apartment with her old key. Because when you got home you found this sealed letter addressed to him in Suzy's handwriting, along with a memo to yourself: 'Dear Pat, Please see that Herbert gets this letter.' Of course you'd be very puzzled by the whole business, and since you thought the letter *must* be important, you hurried right over to give it to him. *Comprende?*"

"I'm beginning to."

"When he opens the letter—wham! And you'll have to pretend to be a little stunned yourself, Pat."

"I'm stunned already."

"Now, if he asks you where in the world I could be, you won't have the slightest idea. But don't ham it up, girl; this is Academy Award time!"

"So how'll he know where to find you?"

"Easy. You'll suddenly remember that I once talked about wanting to recapture the past, or some such goop, and if the dodo doesn't pick up the clue, you then suggest the Plaza Hotel where he and I spent our happy happy honeymoon. Of course he'll grab the phone and ask if a Mrs. Millette is registered, and naturally the answer'll be no."

"No! But I thought—"

"I can't use my *real* name, silly. It wouldn't look like the real thing. But he ought to be smart enough to also try my maiden name and/or my stage name, and if he isn't, you drop another hint and Eureka!—they'll answer that a Miss Starr is registered in room so-and-so."

"So far so great."

"And there's also another valid reason for picking the Plaza," she elaborated. "It's only a block away from our apartment, and since I'll have to gulp down a lot of pills to make the 'suicide' look good, I want to be sure he can get there as soon as possible to slap me awake, et cetera."

"How do you know he won't call for an ambulance instead? Or even call the police?"

"That's where *you* come in, Pat. Just shove him toward the door: 'Hurry, hurry! You've got to save her—I'll call a doctor!'— and start dialing like crazy. Then when he leaves, you wait a few minutes and to really play it safe, call good old Dr. Octopus, who's always dying to take my temperature. His office is near the Plaza, and on Wednesdays he has hours till nine. Hopefully, he'll get to me after Herbie Hero's already saved my life." She looked pleased with herself. "See—no fuss, no muss, no scandal!"

"Suzy," I enthused, "it's terrific!"

"And by the way, Pat, I also plan to leave my hair loose, the way Herbert likes it best, but do you think I should wear a sexy black lace negligee, or maybe a white silk—you know, something pure-looking?"

"Definitely the pure-looking."

Nodding her agreement, she handed me the envelope. "It's going to work like a charm."

Well, to make a long story short—as I said before, when Suzy sat down to write her suicide note, she had no intention of killing herself.

But in life things don't always work out according to plan. Or do they?

May she Rest In Peace.

Of course Herbert said I could have all her expensive clothes and designer furs, but I didn't want them—even though Suzy would think I was a dope for not taking whatever I could get.

"When any opportunity comes along, Pat, just grab it!" she used to say to me. And she was right. (To prove it I now have my own charge accounts at Bergdorf's and Saks Fifth under my new name, Mrs. Herbert Millette.)

Yes, I learned a lot from Suzy. And I'm grateful. That's why I followed her instructions so carefully—right down to the letter. (Or should I say right *up* to the letter?)

How clever of me to have stamped and mailed it.

JERICHO AND THE TWO WAYS TO DIE

by Hugh Pentecost

Portrait of John Jericho: six feet four, 240 pounds, all muscle, red hair and a flaming red beard and mustache; crusader for decency and fairplay, champion of the underdog, fighter against violence who, when necessary, can use the adversary's own weapons; painter who puts on canvas his outrage at man's inhumanity to man . . .

THE place probably had a name, Jericho thought, like Lookout Point or High View or something equally imaginative. The road wound around the side of the mountain, with vertical cliffs on one side and a drop into space on the other. From this particular point there was an incredibly beautiful view of a wide valley below: farming country with fenced-in fields that made it look like a nonsymmetrical checkerboard; cattle looking like tiny toys in the distance and grazing languidly. And color! Autumn glory was at its peak, gold and red and russet brown and the dark green of pines and fir trees.

Jericho had discovered this spot a few days ago and his painter's eye had been caught and held. He'd taken a room in a motel in the nearby town of Plainville and come here each of the last three days with his easel and painting gear.

The town fathers of Plainville had obviously been aware of all this magnificence. The two-lane road had been widened so that visitors in cars could pull out to the very edge of the drop, guarded by a steel-cable fence, park, and take in God's handiwork at their leisure. Jericho had chosen a spot above the road, above the lookout point, to do his painting. He had found a place to pull his red Mercedes off the road, had scrambled up the bank with his equipment, and set himself up for the day. Unless someone was searching for his car or craning his neck to look straight up, his presence would remain unknown.

He was sitting with his back propped against a huge boulder, filling a black curve-stemmed pipe from an oilskin pouch, when he first saw the small sports car with the girl at the wheel. She was driving up from the town, hugging the inside of the road. The car's top was down and he was attracted by the bright blonde hair of the driver that blew around her face, wondering idly if the color was real or if it came out of a bottle. While he watched, the girl stopped the car directly below him and got out. A very short skirt and very nice legs, he thought, and an exquisite figure. She was wearing a pair of amber-tinted granny glasses.

She walked across the road to the lookout area, reached the steel cable of the fence, and instead of looking out at the view she leaned forward and looked down. Some people are fascinated by dizzying heights. She stood there for a full minute, gazing down.

Then she came back to the car, got in, and started the motor. She started, faster than was good for the motor or tires, swung the wheel to the left, and aimed directly at the spot where she'd been standing.

Jericho pushed himself up on his haunches and his mouth opened to shout when she came to a sudden skidding stop, the front bumper of the sports car hard against the steel-cable fence.

"Idiot!" Jericho said out loud, standing up.

The girl got out of the car and went to the fence—staring down again. Slowly she came back and got into the car. She backed across the road, almost in her own tracks, and stopped where she had first parked. Then she started up again, with a spray of gravel from the rear tires, and once more headed straight for the fence. And once again she stopped, just in time.

Jericho went sliding down the bank, braking with his heels. He reached the car and stood gripping the door on the passenger's side, towering over the girl. He was a giant of a man, standing six feet four and weighing about 240, all muscle. He had flaming red hair and a buccaneer's red beard and mustache.

"There are two ways to die," he said in a conversational tone. "One is to give up and kill yourself; the other is to go down fighting whatever it is that has you up a tree." He smiled. "The second way, there's a chance you won't have to die at all."

The eyes behind the granny glasses were wide, frightened. He couldn't tell their color—they were shielded by the amber lenses. The mouth was wide, drawn down at the corners. The face was classic: high cheekbones, straight nose, eyes set nicely apart. She would have been beautiful if something like terror hadn't contorted the features. Her hands gripped the wheel of the car so tightly her knuckles were white knobs.

"Oh, God!" she said in a strangled whisper.

Jericho opened the car door and got in beside her. "This isn't a very heavy car," he said. "I don't know if you could plow through that steel cable or not." He took his pipe out of his pocket and held his lighter to it. "Want to talk about it?"

Her head was turned away toward her target at the lookout point. "You're John Jericho, the artist, aren't you?"

"How did you know?"

"Plainville is a small town. You're a celebrity. Word gets around." Her voice was low and husky. She was fighting for control.

"And you are Miss—?"

"Mrs. Virgil Clarke," she said. She turned to him. "You've heard of my husband?"

He looked at her ringless fingers. "Famous trial lawyer," he said."You live in Plainville?"

"We have a home here, an apartment in New York, an island in the West Indies."

"Nobody can say that crime does not pay," Jericho said. Fragments of memory were falling into place. Virgil Clarke was endlessly in the headlines. His Lincolnesque face was as familiar as a movie star's. He was the Clarence Darrow of the 1970s, the hero of people with lost causes. He must be, Jericho thought, sixty years old, at least twice the age of the girl who sat gripping the wheel of the sports car.

Memory again: a girl charged with murder; a brilliant defense; an acquittal; a headline romance and marriage. It was the first marriage for the noted lawyer; the bride was a widow, accused and acquitted of having murdered her husband.

"You've remembered," she said.

He nodded, his strong white teeth clamped on the stem of his pipe. "Care to tell me why?" he asked.

"Why?"

"Why you were contemplating a plunge into oblivion?"

She looked at him, forcing a smile. "You thought I meant to—?"

"Didn't you?"

"I—I'm not a very good driver," she said. "I wanted to turn around. I couldn't seem to figure out how to—how to do it."

"Have it your way," Jericho said. "It's really none of my business." He opened the car door, swung his long legs out, and stood looking down at her. "At least you've had a chance to think about it twice." His smile was mirthless. "Pull back, cut your wheels right, back up some more, then head for—wherever you're headed for, Mrs. Clarke."

About a hundred yards from Jericho's motel, down the main street of Plainville, was a delightful small country inn. Jericho had tried to get a room there when he decided to stay over but the inn was full. He had discovered, however, that they had an excellent kitchen.

He dined there the evening of the day he encountered the girl at Lookout Point. He had a dry martini, a shrimp cocktail, a very good brook trout helped along by a small white wine, a delicious mixed green salad. He was debating a homemade lemon meringue pie when the boy from the motel came to his table.

"Mrs. Clarke left a note for you, sir," he said. "I knew you were having dinner here."

Jericho opened the pale blue envelope.

Dear Mr. Jericho:

I tried to reach you on the phone without any luck. We are having an open house party tonight and my husband and I would be delighted to have you join us and our guests at any time after eight o'clock.

Janice Clarke

P.S. I hope you won't mind being lionized. Incidentally, anyone can tell you where we live.

People who behave strangely and without explanation were irresistible to Jericho. He went back to the motel, changed into slacks, a blue blazer, and a yellow turtlenecked sweatshirt. At about 8:30 he drove through the big stone gates that guarded the entrance to the Clarke estate. In the moonlight he saw the old Colonial house ideally situated on a hillside, with its magnificent lawns, shrubbery, and gardens. The house was brilliantly lighted and as he came close he saw this was not a small party. There were more than thirty cars parked along the side of the wide circular driveway.

The sound of music and laughter drifted toward Jericho as he approached the front door. The music was loud—rock rhythm. He was admitted by a uniformed maid and found himself in an enormous living room which seemed to occupy most of the ground floor of the house. All the furniture had been pushed to the sides of the room and the floor space was crowded with jumping, gyrating couples. The music came from a bearded trio in a far corner—two electric guitars and drums. There was a bar, loaded with every conceivable kind of liquor. There were two bartenders in scarlet shirts and leather vests. The dancing couples wore every conceivable kind of mod dress.

Jericho, looking around for his hostess, spotted his host standing at the far end of the room, his back to a blazing fire in a huge fieldstone fireplace. Virgil Clarke was unmistakable, tall, angular, with a lock of hair drooping over his broad forehead. He looked wildly out of place in this gathering in his dark business suit, button-down white shirt, and black knitted tie. His attention was focused on his wife who was dancing with a long-haired, not unhandsome young fellow wearing a batik shirt that hung loose outside his trousers. Virgil Clarke's face looked carved out of rock. What he was seeing obviously gave him no pleasure.

Watching the dancers, Jericho thought how things had changed in the last twenty years. When you danced, back then, the music was soft and you held your girl close. Now the music was deafening and the couples danced apart from each other, not touching, each performing a kind of individual war dance.

Jericho's attention was diverted by a luscious blonde girl, not more than twenty, he thought. She was wearing a startling peek-a-boo dress that revealed almost everything of her gloriously suntanned young body.

"Jericho!" There was delight in the young voice and she was instantly clinging to his arm. "Jan is a genius! How did she manage to get you here? I'm Dana Williams, by the way. My father owns two of your paintings."

"Bless your father. And Mrs. Clarke didn't have to be a genius to get me here. She invited me and I came."

"We've been trying to guess how to meet you for the last three days without barging up and brazenly thrusting ourselves on you. How did Jan manage it?"

"She brazenly thrust herself at me," Jericho said, "which is the best and quickest way."

"Does she know you're here? She'll be wild when she sees I've glommed onto you first. Oh, there she is, dancing with Roger."

"Who is Roger?"

"Roger Newfield. He's one of the young lawyers who works in Virgil's office. You'd better have a drink. You're way behind everyone here."

They fought their way around the edge of the dancing throng to the bar. So far Janice hadn't noticed him. She was totally concentrated on the young man opposite whom her body twisted and turned.

Jericho ordered a Jack Daniels on the rocks and Dana a vodka martini. Watching the dancers again, Jericho found himself puzzled. They were all young. There seemed no one here even approaching Virgil Clarke's generation. Jericho suspected that he, at forty, came closest to his host in years. It was odd, he thought, that in the home of a famous man there seemed to be no other famous people, no sycophants, no hangers-on, no yes-men. Clarke, moving away from the fireplace as Jericho watched, seemed out of place in his own home.

"Shall we dance, Jericho?" Dana asked, smiling at him over the rim of her glass.

"It reveals my antiquity," he said, "but I don't—can't—do this modern stuff."

"You want to hold me close we can go out on the terrace," the girl said.

"To dance?"

"No, silly, to hold me close. I like older men, Jericho. Ask and ye shall receive."

"You ought to have your backside paddled," Jericho said.

"Oh, please! I'd love that!"

Before he could reply to that gambit Jericho felt a hand on his arm. He turned to face the uniformed maid.

"Mr. Clarke hopes you will join him in his study for a moment, sir," she said.

"A summons from the All Highest," Dana said. "Maybe he wants to buy a painting, maestro. I'll be waiting on the terrace. You be thinking about what you want to ask me to do."

"I'll be thinking," Jericho said, thinking about a number of ungallant suggestions. He liked to make his own passes.

The maid led him away from the bedlam of the dancers and down a short corridor to an oak door. She knocked and a deep voice invited them in. Virgil Clarke was standing by a far window and looking out over the moonlit lawn.

"Mr. Jericho," he said, as he turned. "Thank you, Millicent."

The maid left, closing the door behind her. The jumping rock rhythms were suddenly silenced. Jericho realized that this room was soundproofed. "Good evening, sir," he said.

At close quarters Clarke was even more impressive. The deep lines at the corners of his mouth were lines of character. The mouth was firm and uncompromising without suggesting vanity or inflexibility. The eyes were deep and dark and somehow tragic, as if he couldn't shake the memory of a thousand violences. Fighting against violence had been his lifework.

"We've never met, Mr. Jericho, but I have been an admirer of yours for some years."

Jericho had noticed the absence of any art in the house. "I hadn't thought of you as being interested in painting, sir."

"I'm not," Clarke said. "Never had a chance to develop a taste for it. I've never seen one of your paintings to know it. I've admired you since the trial of the Faxon brothers."

Jericho frowned. A good part of his own life had been devoted to traveling to the scenes of violence and trying to put on canvas his outrage at man's inhumanity to man. The Faxon brothers had murdered two civil-rights demonstrators. Jericho had been a witness for the prosecution.

"I don't recall your being connected with the case, sir," he said.

"I wasn't, except as a spectator," Clarke said. "I was interested in the defense counsel. I thought of asking him to become a partner in my firm. You broke his back in that case. You stood up under a damn good cross-examination and you broke his back."

"I told the truth."

"You convinced the jury it was the truth."

"It was. Did you hire your man?"

"I did not," Clarke said. "He committed the cardinal sin of getting to admire you while trying to break you down. I would have beaten you, I think, because I wouldn't have allowed myself that luxury. But as a spectator I admired you. There is a good honest man, I told myself. Honest and strong."

"A nice compliment," Jericho said, wondering.

Clarke gestured toward a comfortable armchair. "Can I get you a drink? I noticed you were drinking Jack Daniels out there." He had noticed from across the room. "I'll join you in fruit juice, if you don't mind. I have hours of work ahead of me tonight."

"Lucky your study is soundproofed," Jericho said, smiling. "Thanks. Jack Daniels on the rocks would be fine."

Clarke went to a small sideboard, made Jericho's drink, and poured himself some cranberry juice. He handed Jericho his glass and said, "Why, if I may seem to be impertinent, are you here?"

"Because I was asked," Jericho said.

"What I would like," Clarke said, "is that you, without asking for any explanation, leave this room, go out to your car, and return to your lodgings."

"If you, my host, ask me to leave I will," Jericho said, "but I damn well want to know why. I'm entitled to that, I think."

"I am not your host," Clarke said. "Janice evidently invited you here."

"She did."

"Then go," Clarke said, his voice raised. "You have been asked here to be used. Janice never does anything without a purpose. If you imagine it is your maleness that's attracted her, forget it. Her tastes lie in areas which I suspect would bore you. She has some other reason. I would dislike seeing you used, Mr. Jericho."

"That's a rather extraordinary thing for you to say to a stranger about your wife," Jericho said.

"If you were to say that in front of Janice or that little tramp Dana, you would promptly be labeled a square," Clarke said. His face looked haggard, and there was a kind of frightening bitterness in his voice. Jericho felt acute embarrassment. The man was revealing some kind of deep unhealed wound without hinting how it had been inflicted. Perhaps it was just age, the inexorable process of growing old surrounded by a desirable young wife and her young friends.

But there had been Lookout Point and Janice Clarke's tentative exercise in suicide.

"Perhaps I should tell you how I came to meet your wife, Mr. Clarke," Jericho said. So he told the lawyer about Lookout Point and the little car and the frightened girl and the preparations to die which he had been lucky enough to forestall.

Clarke listened attentively, and when Jericho finished, the lawyer said, "I saved her once and I have been laughed at ever since—betrayed and laughed at. And now, if you don't leave, you will be betrayed and laughed at too. You have already sprouted donkey's ears, Jericho. You have been deliberately made to feel that you were Sir Galahad saving the desperate princess. The next step will be some grotesque practical joke that will have them all laughing at you."

"Why?" Jericho asked.

"It is their prime pleasure," Clarke said.

"Why me?" Jericho asked.

"Because you are a famous man. Because you are a crusader for decency and fair play—causes that seem antiquated to them. Because you are over thirty and your generation must be discredited. Because it will delight them to show you up as a romantic square, to show you up publicly."

Jericho looked at his pipe which rested, cold, in the palm of his hand. "Your wife must be reaching that thirty deadline," he said.

"Which is why she will go to any lengths to show that she is still part of that young world—go to any outrageous lengths, I tell you!"

Jericho looked at the haggard face. "Why do you put up with it?"

"I was once Sir Galahad," Clarke said. "I defended her against a murder charge. I set her free. I was bewitched by her youth, her helplessness, and I wanted to protect her forever. I persuaded her to marry me. And then—then I was laughed at because I couldn't begin to satisfy her needs. Everyone out there knows that, in her terms, I am an inadequate lover. I have no taste for orgies, which makes me a square."

"Why haven't you walked out on her? Your values are sound and you know it. You are miserable, so why do you put up with it?"

"Because there is a bigger joke," Clarke said. "I defended her in court because I believed in her innocence."

Jericho drew a deep breath. "Are you telling me—?"

"That she was guilty," Clarke said, grinding out the words. "I, the Great Defender, was suckered into believing in her innocence. I married her. I showered her with luxuries. I was fooled, blinded."

"But if that's so, she must be ready to do anything you ask. She can't risk your displeasure."

"Double jeopardy," the lawyer said. "There is no new evidence. She can't be tried again. I can bear to be laughed at for my personal inadequacies but there is one area where I can't face public laughter."

"Your legal reputation?"

"It's all I have," Clarke said.

The study door burst open and Janice Clarke swept into the room. "Jericho!" she cried out. "I've been looking for you everywhere! How selfish of you to keep our celebrity to yourself, Virgil." She appropriated Jericho, her arm linked in his. "It's my turn now."

Jericho glanced at the lawyer. Virgil Clarke had turned away. He had revealed himself and issued his warning. Now it appeared he couldn't bear to confront his wife.

Jericho was led out into the hall and instantly assailed by the cacophony of the rock group and the shouting, laughing dancers.

"Take me for a ride in your car," Janice Clarke said. "I need to get away from this for a bit." She looked up at him with a wan smile. "It's been something of a day."

Either Clarke was a vicious liar or this girl deserved an Oscar for her acting talent, Jericho thought. He had a deep instinct for the fake, the phony, but the instinct was blurred at the moment. Someone had lied to him, he knew—either the lawyer in his study tonight or the girl with her performance at Lookout Point this afternoon.

They walked across the lawn to where the red Mercedes was parked. She was hanging onto his arm as though terrified of being separated from him. He helped her into the car and walked around to the other side.

"Where to?" he asked as he settled behind the wheel.

"Anywhere. Just away from here for a while."

"Won't your boyfriend miss you?"

She looked up at him, her eyes wide. "Virgil's been talking to you! Who is alleged to be my boyfriend tonight?"

"My own guess," Jericho said. "The young man you were dancing with when I came in."

"Roger Newfield?" She laughed, a harsh little sound. "Roger is a lawyer on Virgil's staff. He's one of the family. He worships Virgil, not me."

Jericho started the motor and drove the car slowly down the drive and out through the stone gates. He turned right for no particular reason. He wondered if this was part of the "practical joke" that Virgil Clarke had warned him about. Jericho wasn't afraid of laughter, so there was no reason for him to feel uneasy. Yet he did feel uneasy.

"You're too kind to ask me what you want to know," Janice said after a bit.

"Oh?"

"About Lookout Point today. What could have—could have driven me to think—of—of what I was thinking."

Jericho felt the small hairs rising on the back of his neck. "I *was* wondering," he said, looking straight ahead into the cone of light from the car.

"Virgil saved my life, you know," she said, "I owed him everything. I loved him for what he had done for me. I was deeply moved and deliriously happy when he asked me to marry him. I would have married him even if I hadn't loved him. I owed him anything he asked."

"And he's given you a great deal—every luxury you could desire. But not love?"

"Have you never been astonished, Jericho, when the curtains are lifted and you can see inside the house? Virgil, so calm, so cool, so brilliant when he is onstage, turned out to be a sadistic monster in his private world. It is beyond endurance, and yet I owe him my life. Sometimes—and today was one of those times—it seemed I couldn't stand it any longer. If it hadn't been for you—"

Jericho's foot was on the brake. "I think we'd better go back," he said.

"Oh, not yet!" She glanced at her little diamond-studded wrist watch.

"Now," Jericho said, and swung the car in a U-turn.

"Oh, please, Jericho! Let me have a little time to get hold of myself."

The car leaped forward, back toward the stone gates. The girl glanced at her watch again.

"Please, Jericho, not just yet!" she cried out over the sound of the wind and the squealing tires.

They cornered through the gates and up the drive, past the parked cars to the front door. Jericho sprang out of the car and ran into the house, leaving the driveway blocked. He heard the girl call out behind him but he paid no attention. The rock band belted at him, and the almost hysterical laughter.

He ran along the passage to Virgil Clarke's study and put his shoulder to the door as if he expected it to be bolted. There was a splintering sound and he hurtled into the room.

Virgil Clarke was sitting at his desk, his eyes wide with astonishment. Standing beside him was Roger Newfield, the young lawyer in the mod clothes.

"What in the name of—"

Clarke was staring at the door bolt which hung ripped from its fastenings.

"I'm afraid the joke—a very grim joke—was to be on you, sir," Jericho said, rubbing his shoulder.

"Joke?"

"Death is a joke played on all of us, sooner or later," Jericho said. He moved slowly toward the desk, aware that Janice Clarke had come through the door behind him. She was standing there, her face a white mask, gripping the doorjamb to steady herself.

"Do you own a gun, Mr. Clarke?" Jericho asked.

"Why, yes, I do," Clarke said, bewildered.

"Where do you keep it?"

"Here. Here in my desk."

"May I see it?"

Clarke was not a man to take orders, but something of Jericho's violence had thrown him off balance. He opened the flat drawer of his desk and fumbled inside it. Then he looked up.

"It seems to be gone," he said. "I must have—misplaced it."

Jericho took a stride forward and was facing Roger Newfield. He held out his hand. Newfield stared at him, a nerve twitching high up on his cheek. Then Jericho stepped in and started to pat at Newfield's batik shirt. The young lawyer sidestepped and swung at Jericho.

Jericho's left hand blocked the punch and his right swung with crushing force at Newfield's jaw. The young man fell, his eyes rolling up into his head. Jericho bent down, searched the pockets, and came up with a small handgun. He dropped it on the desk.

"Is that yours, Mr. Clarke?" he asked.

The girl in the doorway screamed and ran to the fallen Newfield, crooning his name. "Roger! Roger!"

Clarke had picked up the gun. "It's mine," he said, in something close to a whisper.

"Suicide is the name of the game," Jericho said. "A fake suicide. Two fake suicides, in fact."

"I don't understand," Clarke said. His eyes were fixed on his wife, fondling the unconscious Newfield.

"You and the Williams girl both told me something I wasn't supposed to know," Jericho said, his voice hard. "You both implied that Mrs. Clarke was aware I was painting above the bank at Lookout Point. That meant the whole suicide gambit there was a fake, a setup. I was to stop her. I was to feel sorry for her. I would almost certainly be curious as to what had driven her to contemplate suicide, so I would accept her invitation to the party.

"You almost told me why, without knowing the reason yourself. I was to be the object of a practical joke, you said. But why me? Yes, I'm well known, but not to this crowd. What could she possibly do to me that would make me the butt of laughter? And then, when she asked me to take her away from here, I began to wonder. And when I suggested coming back she instantly looked at her watch. We hadn't, it seemed, been gone long enough. Long enough for what?"

"I don't follow you," Clarke said.

"Why the elaborate scheme to get me here? What could my presence here tonight possibly do for her? It suddenly hit me. I could provide her with an unbreakable alibi. Her friends might not be trustworthy. Her friends might be suspected of playing along with her, lying for her. But I, God help me, am a solid citizen with a reputation. If I testified she was with me it would hold fast."

"But why did she need an alibi?" Clarke asked.

"Because you were going to commit suicide, sir," Jericho said. "You were going to be found here, shot through the head with your own gun. The gun would be found in your hand with your fingerprints on it. But there was bound to be at least a faint suspicion. People close to you must know that your marriage isn't a happy one, and your wife was once charged with a murder. There are people who must still wonder if she was innocent of that crime or if it was your brilliance that set her free. They might ask if a woman who might have killed one husband might not have killed another. She didn't dare have that question asked. I could prevent it. I, the solid citizen, the stranger who had no past connections with her. I could have provided her with the perfect alibi if I hadn't insisted on coming home too soon."

Janice Clarke looked up from where she was cradling Newfield in her arms. "It isn't possible for you to prove a word of this insane theory," she said. "Surely, Virgil, you can't believe—"

"It's not my job to prove it, Mrs. Clarke," Jericho said. "Your husband is the legal expert here. Maybe if he can stop feeling sorry for himself long enough, he'll know how to deal with you."

Jericho turned toward the door and then backed again. "You

were right, Mr. Clarke. I was asked here to be used. I trust my donkey's ears have disappeared."

He walked out into the night, the rock band hurting his ears. He was eager to get away, as far and as fast as he could.

THE THEFT FROM
THE EMPTY ROOM

by Edward D. Hoch

In this, the fifteenth recorded case in the career of Nick Velvet, the unique thief accepts what seems to be a "simple enough" assignment—an easy job and a quick $20,000. But the assignment proves to be something else—one of the most unusual, if not the most unusual, Nick has ever tackled. And once again Nick has to succeed first as a detective before he can succeed as a thief . . .

NICK VELVET sat stiffly on the straight-backed hospital chair, facing the man in the bed opposite him. He had to admit that Roger Surman looked sick, with sunken cheeks and eyes, and a sallow complexion that gave him the appearance of a beached and blotchy whale. He was a huge man who had trouble getting around even in the best of condition. Now, laid low with a serious liver complaint, Nick wondered if he'd ever be able to leave the bed.

"They're going to cut through this blubber in the morning," he told Nick. "I've got a bet with the doctor that they don't have a scalpel long enough to even reach my liver." He chuckled to himself and then seemed about to drift into sleep.

"You wanted to see me," Nick said hastily, trying to focus the sick man's attention.

"That's right. Wanted to see you. Always told you if I needed a job done I'd call on you." He tried to lift his head. "Is the nurse around?"

"No. We're alone."

"Good. Now, you charge twenty thousand—that right?"

Nick nodded. "But only for unusual thefts. No money, jewels, art treasures—nothing like that."

"Believe me, this is nothing like that. I'd guess it's one of the most unusual jobs you've ever had."

"What do you want stolen?" Nick asked as the man's head bobbed again.

"First let me tell you where it is. You know my brother Vincent?"

"The importer? I've heard of him."

"It's at his country home. The place is closed now for the winter, so you won't have any trouble with guards or guests. There are a few window alarms, but nothing fancy."

"You want me to steal something from your brother?"

"Exactly. You'll find it in a storeroom around the back of the house. It adjoins the kitchen, but has its own outside door. Steal what you find in the storeroom and I'll pay you twenty thousand."

"Seems simple enough," Nick said. "Just what will I find there?"

The sick eyes seemed to twinkle for an instant. "Something only you could steal for me, Velvet. I was out there myself a few days ago, but the burglar alarms were too much for me. With all this fat to cart around, and feeling as bad as I did, I couldn't get in. I knew I had to hire a professional, so I thought of you at once. What I want you to steal is—"

The nurse bustled in and interrupted him. "Now, now, Mr. Surman, we mustn't tire ourselves! The operation is at seven in the morning." She turned to Nick. "You must go now."

"Velvet," Roger Surman called. "Wait. Here's a picture of the rear of the house. It's this doorway, at the end of the driveway. Look it over and then I'll tell you—"

Nick slipped the photo into his pocket. The nurse was firmly urging him out and there was no chance for further conversation without being overheard. Nick sighed and left the room. The assignment sounded easy enough, although he didn't yet know what he'd been hired to steal.

In the morning Nick drove out to the country home of Vincent Surman. It was a gloomy November day—more a day for a funeral than an operation—and he wondered how Surman was progressing in surgery. Nick had known him off and on for ten years, mainly through the yacht club where Nick and Gloria often sailed in the summer months. Surman was wealthy, fat, and lonely. His wife had long ago divorced him and gone off to the West Indies with a slim handsome Jamaican, leaving Surman with little in life except his trucking business and his passion for food and drink.

Surman's brother, Vincent, was the glamorous member of the family, maintaining a twelve-room city house in addition to the country home. His wife Simone was the answer to every bachelor's dream, and his importing business provided enough income to keep her constantly one of New York's best-dressed women. In every way Vincent was the celebrity success, while

Roger was the plodding fat boy grown old and lonely. Still, Roger's trucking business could not be dismissed lightly—not when his blue-and-white trucks could be seen on nearly every expressway.

Nick parked just off the highway and walked up the long curving driveway to Vincent Surman's country home. The place seemed closed and deserted, as Roger had said, but when Nick neared it he could see the wired windows and doors. The alarm system appeared to be functioning, though it wouldn't stop him for long.

Following Roger's directions and referring to the marked photograph, he walked along the driveway to where it ended at the rear of the house. There, next to the kitchen door, was the storeroom door that Surman had indicated. Both the door and the single window were locked, but at the moment Nick was mainly anxious to see what the room contained—what he'd been hired to steal for $20,000.

He looked in the window and saw a room about twenty feet long and fourteen feet wide, with an inside door leading to the kitchen.

The room, with its painted red walls and white ceiling and wooden floor, was empty. Completely empty.

There was nothing in it for Nick Velvet to steal.

Nick drove to a pay telephone a mile down the road and phoned the hospital. They could tell him only that Roger Surman was in the recovery room following his operation and certainly could not talk to anyone or receive visitors for the rest of the day.

Nick sighed and hung up. He stood for a moment biting his lower lip, then walked back to the car. For the present there was no talking to Surman for a clue to the puzzle. Nick would have to work it out himself.

He drove back to the country home and parked. As he saw it, there were only two possibilities: either the object to be stolen had been removed since Roger saw it a few days earlier, or it was still there. If it had been removed, Nick must locate it. If it was still in the room, there was only one place it could be—on the same wall as the single window and therefore out of his line of vision from the outside.

Working carefully, Nick managed to bypass the alarm system and open the storeroom door. He stood just inside, letting his eyes glide across every inch of the room's walls and floor and ceiling. The wall with the window was as blank as the others. There were not even any nail holes to indicate that a picture might have once hung there.

And as Nick's eyes traveled across the room he realized something else: nothing, and no one, had been in this room for at least several weeks—a layer of dust covered the floor from wall to wall, and the dust was undisturbed. Not a mark, not a footprint. Nothing.

And yet Surman had told Nick he was there only a few days ago, trying to enter the room and steal something he knew to be in it—something he obviously was able to see through the window.

But what was it?

"Please raise your hands," a voice said suddenly from behind him. "I have a gun."

Nick turned slowly in the doorway, raising his hands above his head. He faced a short dark-haired girl in riding costume and boots, who held a double-barreled shotgun pointed at his stomach. He cursed himself for not having heard her approach. "Put that thing away," he said harshly, indignation in his voice. "I'm no thief."

But the shotgun stayed where it was. "You could have fooled me," she drawled, her voice reflecting a mixture of southern and eastern origins. "Suppose you identify yourself."

"I'm a real-estate salesman. Nicholas Realty—here's my card."

"Careful with the hands!"

"But I told you—I'm not a thief."

She sighed and lowered the shotgun. "All right, but no tricks."

He handed her one of the business cards he carried for just such emergencies. "Are you the owner of this property, Miss?"

She tucked the card into the waistband of her riding pants. "It's Mrs., and my husband is the owner. I'm Simone Surman."

He allowed himself to relax a bit as she stowed the shotgun in the crook of her arm, pointed away from him. "Of course! I should have recognized you from the pictures in the paper. You're always on the best-dressed list."

"We're talking about you, Mr. Nicholas, not me. I find you here by an open door that should be locked, and you tell me you're a realtor. Do they always carry lock picks these days?"

He chuckled, turning on his best salesman's charms. "Hardly, Mrs. Surman. A client expressed interest in your place, so I drove out to look it over. I found the door open, just like this, but you can see I only took a step inside."

"That's still trespassing."

"Then I apologize. If I'd known you were in the neighborhood I certainly would have contacted you first. My understanding was that the house had been closed down for the winter."

"That's correct. I was riding by, on my way to the stables, and saw your car on the highway. I decided to investigate."

"You always carry a shotgun?"

"It was in the car—part of my husband's hunting equipment."

"You handle it well."

"I can use it." She gestured toward the house. "As long as you're here, would you like to see the inside?"

"Very much. I gather this room is for storage?"

She glanced in at the empty room. "Yes. It hasn't been used in some time. I wonder why the door was open and unlocked." She looked at the alarm wires, but didn't seem to realize they'd been tampered with. "Come around to the front."

The house was indeed something to see, fully furnished and in a Colonial style that included a huge brick oven in the kitchen. Nick took it all in, making appropriate real-estate comments, and they finally ended up back at the door to the storeroom.

"What used to be in here?" Nick asked. "Odd that it's empty when the rest of the house is so completely furnished."

"Oh, wood for the kitchen stove, supplies, things like that. I told you it hadn't been used in some time."

Nick nodded and made a note on his pad. "Am I to understand that the house would be for sale, if the price was right?"

"I'm sure Vincent wouldn't consider anything under a hundred thousand. There's a great deal of land that goes with the house."

They talked some more, and Simone Surman walked Nick back to his car. He promised to call her husband with an offer in a few days. As he drove away he could see her watching him. He had no doubt that she believed his story, but he also knew she'd have the alarm repaired by the following day.

The news at the hospital was not good. Roger Surman had suffered postoperative complications, and it might be days before he was allowed visitors. Nick left the place in a state of mild depression, with visions of his fee blowing away like an autumn leaf.

He had never before been confronted with just such a problem. Hired to steal something unnamed from a room that proved to be completely empty, he had no way of getting back to his client for further information. If he waited till Roger was out of danger and able to talk again, he would probably jeopardize the entire job, because Vincent Surman and his wife would grow increasingly suspicious when no real-estate offer was forthcoming during the next few days.

Perhaps, Nick decided, he should visit Roger Surman's home. He might find some clue there as to what the fat man wanted him to steal. He drove out along the river for several miles, until he reached a small but obviously expensive ranch home where Roger had lived alone for the past several years.

Starting with the garage, he easily opened the lock with his tool kit. The car inside was a late-model limousine with only a few thousand miles on it. Nick looked it over and then went to work on the trunk compartment. There was always the possibility, however remote, that Roger had succeeded in his own theft attempt, but for some reason had not told Nick the truth. But the trunk yielded only a spare tire, a jack, a half-empty sack of fertilizer, and a can of red paint. The spotless interior of the car held a week-old copy of *The New York Times,* a little hand vacuum cleaner for the upholstery, and an electronic device whose button, when pressed, opened or closed the automatic garage door. Unless Nick was willing to believe that the fertilizer had been the object of the theft, there was nothing in the car to help him.

He tried the house next, entering through the inside garage door, and found a neat kitchen with a study beyond. It was obvious that Roger Surman employed a housekeeper to clean the place—no bachelor on his own would have kept it so spotless. He went quickly through the papers in the desk but found nothing of value. A financial report on Surman Travelers showed that it had been a bad year for the trucking company. There were a number of insured losses, and Nick wondered if Roger might be getting back some of his lost income through false claims.

He dug further, seeking some mention of Roger's brother, some hint of what the empty room might have contained. There were a few letters, a dinner invitation from Simone Surman, and finally a recent bill from a private detective agency in New York City. After another hour of searching, Nick concluded that the private detective was his only lead.

He drove down to Manhattan early the next morning, parking in one of the ramps off Sixth Avenue. The Altamont Agency was not Nick's idea of a typical private eye's office, with its sleek girl secretaries, chrome-trimmed desks, and wide tinted windows overlooking Rockefeller Center. But Felix Altamont fitted the setting. He was a slick, smooth-talking little man who met Nick in a cork-lined conference room because a client was waiting in his office.

"You must realize I'm a busy man, Mr. Velvet. I can only give you a few moments. Is it about a case?"

"It is. I believe you did some work for Roger Surman."

Altamont nodded his balding head.

"What sort of work was it?"

The detective leaned back in his chair. "You know I can't discuss a client's case, Mr. Velvet."

Nick glanced around at the expensive trappings. "Could you at least tell me what sort of cases you take? Divorce work doesn't pay for this kind of layout."

"Quite correct. As a matter of fact, we do not accept divorce cases. The Altamont Agency deals exclusively in industrial crimes—embezzlement, hijacking, industrial espionage, that sort of thing."

Nick nodded. "Then the investigation you conducted for Roger Surman was in one of those fields."

Felix Altamont looked pained. "I'm not free to answer that, Mr. Velvet."

Nick cleared his throat, ready for his final bluff. "It so happens that I'm in Roger Surman's employ myself. He hired me to try and clamp a lid on his large insurance losses. The company's threatening to cancel his policy."

"Then you know about the hijackings. Why come to me with your questions?"

"Certainly I know about the hijacking of Surman trucks, but with my employer in the hospital I thought you could fill me in on the details."

"Surman's hospitalized?"

"He's recovering from a liver operation. Now let's stop sparring and get down to business. What was hijacked from his trucks?"

Altamont resisted a few moments longer, then sighed and answered the question. "Various things. A shipment of machine tools one month, a load of textiles the next. The most recent hijacking was a consignment of tobacco leaves three weeks ago."

"In the south?"

"No, up here. Shade-grown tobacco from Connecticut. No crop in the nation brings as high a price per acre. Very valuable stuff for hijackers."

Nick nodded. "Why did you drop the investigation?"

"Who said I dropped it?"

"If you'd been successful, Surman wouldn't need me."

The private detective was silent for a moment, then said, "I told you we don't touch divorce cases."

Nick frowned, then brightened immediately. "His sister-in-law, Simone."

"Exactly. Roger Surman seems intent on pinning the hijackings on his brother, apparently for the sole purpose of causing a divorce. He's a lonely man, Mr. Velvet. He'll give you nothing but trouble."

"I'll take my chances," Nick said. "Thanks for the information."

When Nick arrived at the hospital late that afternoon he was intercepted by a brawny thick-haired man who bore more than a passing resemblance to Roger Surman.

"You're Velvet, aren't you?" the man challenged.

"Correct. And you must be Vincent Surman."

"I am. You're working for my brother."

"News travels fast."

"You were at my country house yesterday, snooping around. My wife caught you at it. This morning you were in New York, talking to that detective my brother hired."

"So Altamont's on your side now."

"Everyone's on my side if I pay them enough. I retain the Altamont Agency to do periodic security checks for my importing company. Naturally he phoned me after you left his office. His description of you matched the one Simone had already given me."

"I hope it was flattering."

"I'm not joking, Velvet. My brother is a sick man, mentally as well as physically. Anything you undertake in his behalf could well land you in jail."

"That's true," Nick agreed with a smile.

"Whatever he's paying you, I'll double it."

"My work for him is just about finished. As soon as he's well enough to have visitors I'll be collecting my fee."

"And just what was your work?"

"It's a confidential matter."

Vincent Surman tightened his lips, studying Nick. "Very well," he said, and walked on to the door.

Nick watched him head for the hospital parking lot. Then he went up to the information desk and asked for the doctor in charge of Roger Surman's case. The doctor, a bustling young man whose white coat trailed behind him, appeared ten minutes later, and his news was encouraging.

"Mr. Surman had a good night. He's past the worst of it now. I think you'll be able to see him for a few minutes tomorrow."

Nick left the hospital and went back to his car. It was working out just fine now—the money was as good as in the bank. He drove out the country road to Vincent Surman's place, and this time he took the car into the driveway, around back, and out of sight from the road.

Working quickly and quietly, Nick bypassed the alarm and opened the storeroom door once more. This time he knew what he was after. On his way to the hospital he'd stopped to pick up the can of red paint from the trunk of Roger's car. He had it with him now, as he stepped across the threshold into the empty room. He stood for a moment staring at the red walls, and then got to work.

It had occurred to him during the drive back from New York that there might be a connection between the can of red paint in Roger Surman's trunk and the red walls of the empty room. Roger had driven the car to the country house a few days before his operation to attempt the robbery himself. If the paint on the walls had been Roger's target—the paint itself—he could have replaced stolen paint with fresh red paint from the can.

Nick had stolen strange things in his time, and taking the paint from the walls of a room struck him as only a little unusual. The paint could cover any number of valuable things. He'd read once of a room that had been papered with hundred-dollar bills from a bank holdup, then carefully covered over with wallpaper. Perhaps something like that had been done here, and then a final layer of red paint applied.

He got to work carefully scraping the paint, anxious to see what was underneath; but almost at once he was disappointed. There was no wallpaper under the paint—nothing but plaster showed through.

He paused to consider, then turned to the paint can he'd brought along. Prying off the lid, he saw his mistake at once. The red in the can was much brighter than the red on the walls—it was an entirely different shade. He inspected the can more closely and saw that it was marine paint—obviously destined for Roger Surman's boat. Its presence in Roger's trunk had been merely an annoying coincidence.

Before Nick had time to curse his bad luck he heard a car on the driveway. He left the room, closing the door behind him, and had almost reached his own car when two men appeared around the corner of the house. The nearer of the two held a snub-nosed revolver pointed at Nick's chest.

"Hold it right there, mister! You're coming with us."

Nick sighed and raised his hands. He could tell by their hard icy eyes that they couldn't be talked out of it as easily as Simone Surman had been. "All right," he said. "Where to?"

"Into our car. Vincent Surman has a few more questions for you."

Prodded by the gun, Nick offered no resistance. He climbed into the back seat with one of the men beside him, but the car continued to sit there. Presently the second man returned from the house. "He's on his way over. Says to keep him here."

They waited another twenty minutes in silence, until at last Surman's car turned into the driveway. Simone was with him, bundled in a fur coat against the chill of the autumn afternoon.

"The gun wasn't necessary," Nick said, climbing out of the car to greet them.

"I thought it might be," Vincent Surman replied. "I had you tailed from the hospital. You're a thief, Velvet. I've done some checking on you. Roger hired you to steal something from me, didn't he?"

"Look around for yourself. Is anything missing?"

"Come along—we'll look."

With the two gunmen staying close, Nick had little choice. He followed Vincent and Simone around to the storeroom door. "This is where I found him the first time," she told her husband, and sneezing suddenly, she pulled the fur coat more tightly around her.

"He was back here when we found him too," the gunman confirmed.

Vincent unlocked the storeroom door.

The walls stared back at them blankly. Vincent Surman inspected the place where the paint had been scraped, but found nothing else. He stepped outside and walked around, his eyes scanning the back of the house. "What are you after, Velvet?"

"What is there to take? The room's empty."

"Perhaps he's after something in the kitchen," Simone suggested.

Vincent ignored her suggestion, reluctant to leave the rear of the house. Finally, after another pause, he said to Nick, "All right. We'll look through the rest of the house."

An hour later, after they'd convinced themselves that nothing was missing, and after the gunmen had thoroughly searched Nick and his car, Vincent was convinced that nothing had been taken. "What's the paint for?" he asked Nick.

"My boat."

The dark-haired importer sighed and turned away. "Roger is a madman. You must realize that. He'd like nothing better than to break up my marriage to Simone by accusing me of some crime. Altamont was hired to prove I was hijacking Roger's trucks and selling the goods through my import business. He hoped Simone would quarrel with me about it and then leave me."

Nick motioned toward the gunmen. "These two goons could pass for hijackers any day." One man started for him, but Vincent barked an order. Simone's eyes widened, as if she were seeing her husband's employees for the first time.

"You don't need to hold them back," Nick said.

This time the nearer man sprang at him and Nick's fist connected with his jaw. The second man had his gun out again, but before he could bring it up Simone grabbed his arm.

"Simone!" Vincent shouted. "Stay out of this!"

She turned on her husband, her eyes flashing. "I never knew you used hoods, Vincent! Maybe Roger knows what he's talking about! Maybe you really are trying to ruin him by hijacking his trucks."

"Shut up!"

Nick backed away, his eyes still on the two hoods. "I'll be leaving now," he said. "You two can fight it out."

Nobody tried to stop him. As he swung his car around the others in the driveway he could see Vincent Surman still arguing with his wife.

The next morning Roger Surman was sitting up in bed, just finishing a meager breakfast, when Nick entered the hospital room. He glanced at the paper bag Nick was carrying and then at his face. "I'm certainly glad to see you, Velvet. Sorry I didn't have a chance to tell you what I wanted stolen."

"You didn't have to tell me," Nick said with a grin. "After a couple of false starts I figured it out."

"You mean you got it?"

"Yes, I've got it. I had a few run-ins with your brother and his wife along the way, but I got the job done last night."

"How did you know? How *could* you know?"

"I talked to your detective, Altamont, and learned about the hijackings. Once I started thinking about it—the country place, the driveway leading to the storeroom—my reasoning must have followed yours quite closely. Vincent's hired hijackers were bringing the loot there and leaving it in the storeroom for transfer to his own importing company trucks."

The fat man moved uncomfortably under his blanket. "Exactly. I tried to tell Simone, but she demanded proof."

"I think she's got it now. And I think you have too. It wasn't easy finding something to steal in an empty room—something that would be worth $20,000 to you. First, I considered the room itself, but you would have needed heavy equipment for that—and you told me you'd hoped to accomplish the theft yourself. That led me to your car, and I found the paint can in your trunk. Next, I almost stole the paint off the walls for you, until I ruled that out too. Finally, I remembered about the last shipment that was hijacked a few weeks ago. It consisted of bundles of valuable tobacco leaves, and certainly such a shipment would leave traces of its presence. Yesterday, out at the house, Simone walked into the storeroom and sneezed. Then I remembered something else I'd seen in your car."

Roger Surman nodded. "The little hand vacuum cleaner. I was going to use it if I got past the alarms."

Nick Velvet nodded and opened the paper bag he was still carrying. "I used it last night—to steal the dust from the floor of that empty room."

THE COLDNESS OF
A THOUSAND SUNS

by Celia Fremlin

What a special quality Celia Fremlin has! . . . Which do you believe in? Death in life? Life in death? Or in both? . . . Another haunted and haunting story by a writer whose work is always fascinating, thought-provoking, and in the end, however elusive the deeper meaning, touching . . .

HOW warm the water still was, after nearly thirty years! Through the shallow pools left by the falling tide her feet slid, white and mysterious in the starlight, like some strange new species of fish. Quiet, too, just the way fish are quiet; scarcely a ripple stirred the stillness of the summer night as she waded softly on, across the dark sands which had once been golden in the noonday heat as her children scampered across them all those years ago, those many years ago.

"Mummy!" they had shrieked. "Mummy, look! Look at my starfish . . . Look at my castle, it's much bigger than Janie's castle, isn't it? . . . Mummy, look, is this a hermit crab? . . . Look at my shell, Mummy, it's all pink inside! Look, Mummy, look!"

Oh, she had been a goddess then: dispenser of buns and knowledge and ginger beer, provider of towels for shivering little bodies; comforter of bruised toes; inventor of enchanted games. She had known then what it was to reign over sea and sand and summer. She had been "Mummy."

Now her fingers tightened round the bottle of pills in the pocket of the thick winter coat she had chosen, summer through it was, to come here and die in. A winter coat, and once she had worn so little and had run across the sands with her squealing children: "I can race you, Mummy! Look, Mummy, look, I can run faster than you can!"

And then the sandwiches and the crisps and the fizzy drinks, and after that the guessing games and the story games as they lay, drunk with sunshine, in the hot sandy hollow mid the marram grass. She remembered the feel of sand and salt drying on her skin in the benign, endless afternoon heat; she remembered how the damp, sandy little bodies pressed up closer: "Another story, Mummy! *Please*, Mummy, just one more!"

And now the voices were silent, her children vanished; grown, long since, into mere people, as surely as if they had died. And she was Mummy no longer, and the glory had gone from her. She was an aging woman, a nuisance to her doctors who could do no more for her, and to her friends whose sympathy for her eternal aches and pains was beginning to wear thin.

The pain! Aaaah, it was coming back now—not just the weary gnawing that went on all the time, but a heavy bloated agony that twisted her over double, brought her to a standstill. Oh, God, oh,

God, no, no! Oh, please! Clutching herself in a half hoop, she saw her white quivering feet, with the water trembling over them; swollen, grotesque, like the intensity of pain itself.

And then the spasm passed, grew weaker, and she straightened up again. Now that it had gone away, she was glad—yes, glad—that the pain had returned, if only for a minute. For it had been strange the way it had ceased completely, for a whole afternoon, once she had decided to make an end to it. Just the way a tooth stops aching the very moment you step into the dentist's waiting room.

It had shaken her resolve, this eerie cessation of pain, after all the unrelenting months of it. The absence had left room for the fear of death to come flooding back, and she had sat in the cheap boardinghouse lounge, her winter coat already on, and had cried with the uncertainty and the fear of it all. And then it was evening, and she didn't go in to dinner; and presently there were her landlady and the woman from the first floor back, asking her what was the matter. "Nothing," she'd said, and had to turn her tear-stained face away and fuss with her handbag. Nothing, nothing at all; she was just going out to post a letter, that's all, before turning in.

Under the pitying, guarded gaze of both of them she had managed to get herself out of the front door; and then, somehow, there was no turning back. On, on, past the last of the dark houses, past the straggling beach huts, past the silent, salty little pleasure boats, upended under the stars. Soon her feet were gliding over the gray glimmering sand left by the falling tide, and she had known that she would never rest, now, until she had reached the Place.

The Place.

Our Place. The picnic place. The hollow in the sandhills sacred to Us.

Us? There is no such thing now. We are gone, finished. Gone like all the summer noondays of the vanished years. There is no Us now, there is only me, a dreary middle-aged woman, riddled with death, padding through the dark still-warm shallows, dragging herself here, here to Our Place, to die.

Nothing had changed. Even in the darkness of the moonless night she recognized the slope of dry sand and sea thistle that led up to the dunes. Black against the stars, she could see the spiked marram grass, could hear its dry whispering in the night air. Once it had been astir with insects, with galloping children, under the blazing August sky.

All gone. The sun, the children, the insects of long ago. The dry powdery sand, once so warm to bare brown holiday feet, was cold now, cold like death; and the marram grass, as it stirred and rustled against her calves, was cruel in the darkness, sharp and vicious against her flabby aging skin.

And how cold, cold Our Place had become after thirty years! Bare, like a crater on the moon, and only eight feet wide! The marram grass on the rim bent stiffly to her passing, then raised itself and seemed to watch, grave and hostile, as she slithered and stumbled down to the very heart and center of Our Place.

Once there she sat down in the darkness; and the coldness of the soft deep sand sent a shudder of foolish dismay along her thighs. Somehow she had not thought that the warmth would be *all* gone, but it was. Our Place knew her no more.

Well, and why should it? Why had she imagined it would still welcome her after all the years? She, who had once brought laughter here and delicious food and happy sunburnt children— now, she was bringing to Our Place only death, and her pain-racked body.

She was a pollution, a blasphemy, a sin against the golden days that were gone.

And yet . . . The impulse to die in the place where one has truly lived is strong in all of us. So she stayed sitting there, right in the center of Our Place, just where she had once sat in her glory, dispensing chocolate and ideas for games and bottles of lemonade. Now she took from her coat pocket a bottle of plain water. It gleamed eerily in the starlight, and the water glugged and gurgled as she swallowed it, mouthful by mouthful, with one handful after another of the long blue pills. And when she had finished them all, she lay back on the same soft deep sand where she had once basked, and waited for death to come.

She could hear the tide, at its lowest ebb now, murmuring far off in the darkness across the flat sands; and as the pain ebbed slowly, and for the last time, from her tormented body, she could almost imagine she heard her children's voices, far off, playing at the water's edge. And as the night breeze moaned above her she could almost fancy beyond her closed eyelids the hot blue sky blazing.

And this strange drowsy warmth stealing over her, it was like the warmth of the sun. No, of a thousand suns, the suns of all the long-dead summer days, beating down upon her from far, far away across the years . . .

"Mummy! Mummy! Wake *up!* We're *starving!* You've been asleep for so *long!*"

Their laughter, their mock reproaches, broke through the strange light feeling in her head. Damp, eager little hands were tugging at her, urging her into a sitting position; shrill voices clamored in her ears.

Dazed, almost incredulous with joy, she shook the sleep from her eyes. What a ghastly dream! Thank goodness the kids wakened her before it had got any worse! For a few moments she lay still, ignoring their clamor, and gave herself up to the incredible sensation of being *young!* Of having a body that was *well!* The miraculous, unbelievable sensation of health, of organs working exactly as they should, all of them, in magical, effortless harmony.

"*Mummy!* You *said* we could have the picnic straight after our swim! You *promised!* Oh, Mummy, come *on!*"

And slowly, still dizzy with sun and sleep, and with a stupefying sense of relief, she scrambled to her feet, the dry powdery sand scattering this way and that from her sun-warmed limbs. How marvelous her body felt, so strong, so lithe, and with only the ridiculous barrier of a bikini between it and the glory of the sun!

And now she was standing up; and as she stood there, her littlest child, her berry-brown little four-year-old, ran up, squealing with excitement.

"Look, Mummy!" she cried, "look, everybody! I'm going to go bye-bye in the sand, like Mummy did!" And so saying, she flopped down onto the patch of sand her mother had just vacated, then leaped up, as if she had been stung.

"Mummy! Mummy! It's so *cold* where you've been lying! Mummy, why is it so cold?"

THE PANIC BUTTON

by Michael Gilbert

Mr. Calder and Mr. Behrens are back—and glory be they are still around! For this time they are involved in an affair in which the fate of the world (no less) is at stake. Literally, the fate of the world. Will there be a nuclear war? Will someone press the panic button that could result in the destruction of millions of human beings? . . . Watch the moves and countermoves—and hold your breath . . .

MR. CALDER first met Colonel Garnet in 1942 in the Western Desert.

The colonel, who had commanded an armoured regiment with such dash that it had lost most of its tanks, was doing a stand-in job as G.S.O.2 at Corps. He had acquired the reputation of turning up more often at the dangerous end than was usual with staff officers. Nevertheless, it did surprise Mr. Calder to see him at that particular time and place; seeing that the infantry regiment to which he was attached was about to do one of the things which infantry regiments dislike greatly. It was due, in five minutes' time, to advance over a stretch of open desert which was certainly registered by enemy mortars and was probably full of anti-personnel mines.

Colonel Garnet had engaged Captain Calder in a learned discussion on modern theories of artillery support, while Captain Calder kept an anxious eye on his watch. When the whistle blew and he climbed cautiously out of the line of slit trenches, he was staggered to observe that the colonel was climbing out with him. It appeared that there were some additional observations on artillery support which the colonel had not had time to finish, and that he saw no reason these contributions to military thought should be lost.

"Just exactly," as Mr. Calder said afterward to his C.O., "as though we were out for an afternoon stroll. And the odd thing is that the mortars didn't open up, and if there were any mines we, at least, didn't step on them. In fact, we had remarkably few casualties. When we reached our objective the colonel said, 'Well, I must get back, I suppose. Can't stand about all day gossiping.'"

"He's quite mad," said the C.O. "That's why he's collected two D.S.O.'s already."

Later on, Colonel Garnet went to Burma and finished up with a Brigade and a second bar to his D.S.O. His rise after that was steady, if not spectacular, and it was generally felt that he had reached his limit as G.O.C. Southern Command, when he was unexpectedly appointed Vice Chief of the Defence Staff. This was not, normally, a very exacting job, but became so when his Chief, Air Marshal Elvington, had to retire to a nursing home with a heart condition, brought on, it was rumored in Whitehall, by his attempts to cope with a government which thought that free wigs and dentures were more important than fighter aircraft.

On the other hand, the career of Arnold Litman had been a good deal less exciting. A member of the merchant-banking family, with offshoots on both sides of the Atlantic, he had entered politics in the late forties, had won a marginal seat in the 1951 election, and had risen in his party's counsels by a mixture of financial shrewdness and political tact. Why he should have been made Under-Secretary for War was far from clear. But once installed in office he had delighted his masters by abolishing several ancient and expensive regiments.

His only known indiscretion had been his marriage to Rebecca, a dreamy girl with a weakness for picking up fads and a habit of discussing them with the press. In a private citizen this would not have mattered; in the wife of a public man it could, and did.

Sue Garnet read the article, first to herself and then to her father, over the breakfast table. It was headed "The Lion and the Virgin" and it started: "In a special interview given to *Daily News* man Frank Carvel yesterday, Mrs. Litman, wife of recently appointed Under-Secretary for War, Arnold Litman, gave it as her view that all great wars were likely to break out between late July and early September. She pointed out that it was at this period that the two most exciting signs in the zodiac come into conjunction. Leo and Virgo, the Lion and the Virgin. It could hardly be a coincidence, she said, that every major war in history had started at this time. The Under-Secretary refused to comment on this remarkable prediction."

"Bloody fool," said General Garnet.

"Which?"

"Both of them."

"What could he have done except refuse to comment?"

"Not asked the brute into his house."

"I expect his wife did the asking."

"I don't doubt it. She's a stupid bitch."

"Daddy!"

"*He's* not stupid, though. I'm beginning to think he's a crook."

Sue Garnet was hardened to her father's methods of discourse and argument. These, as she had warned Terence Russel when he became her father's military secretary and her fiancé, resembled a machine gun firing on fixed lines interspersed with casual grenade throwing. But even she was taken aback by this last comment.

She said, "You can't really mean that!"

"Can't I," said the general, decapitating his second breakfast egg with the same zeal and expertise that he had once decapitated a Japanese officer with his own Samurai sword. "What about that fight we had last month with the Americans over the ground-to-air ballistic missile? Our prototype was years ahead of theirs and a bloody sight cheaper. So why did we have to give them the contract?"

"Well, why did we?"

"If you want my guess it's because Litman, or his associates, have got a big holding in the American company."

"If you can prove it," said Sue, "you ought to do something about it. If you can't you ought to be jolly careful about saying it. After all, he's your boss."

"My boss," said the general, "is the Queen, and not a jumped-up Jack in office who'll probably be Deputy Postmaster General next time they reshuffle the Cabinet. Dammit, where's Terence? I want to see those papers before the meeting."

"He's *your* secretary. You ought to know where he is."

"He's your fiancé. You ought to keep him up to the mark, the idle young beggar. What are you laughing at?"

"I saw your last confidential report. You said that he was a keen and promising young officer."

"Are you aware, Miss," said the general, filling his mouth with toast, "that you can be prosecuted under the Official Secrets Act for disclosing the contents of a confidential document?"

"And did you know," said Sue unrepentantly, "that you can be cashiered for leaving them lying about? You never lock anything up. Anyone could read them. Our charwoman might be an agent of the Chinese Secret Service."

The idea so tickled the general that he roared with laughter while trying to swallow the last piece of toast. In the middle of this complicated situation the telephone rang.

The general listened, spluttered, listened some more, and then said, "All right. I'll be there." And to Captain Terence Russel, who had hurried in carrying a brief case, "The meeting's postponed."

"I heard," said Russel. He was a large blond young man who wore his service dress with the swagger expected of a cavalry officer. "The emergency meeting's at the Foreign Office. You're to go in quietly by the Charles Street entrance, not the Downing Street one. I've ordered a car."

"What the hell did they think I'd do?" bellowed the general. "Walk in with a banner saying, 'Armageddon Is at Hand'??"

Mr. McAlister, the head cashier at the Westminster Branch of the London & Home Counties Bank, greeted Mr. Calder and Mr. Behrens as old friends and explained that the manager, Mr. Fortescue, was engaged, but would be free soon.

"What's happened to the stock market, Mac?" said Mr. Behrens.

"We've all been asking ourselves the same thing. Fifteen points down yesterday and twenty-five over the weekend. We haven't seen anything like it since August 1939. Ah, there's his light. He's disposed of his visitor. Go straight in."

Mr. Calder had sometimes wondered how Mr. Fortescue "disposed" of visitors whose identities he wished to conceal. One never saw them come out. He concluded that there was either a hidden door in the paneling behind his desk, or an oubliette in the floor.

"I've not much time," Mr. Fortescue said. "I have to be at the Foreign Office at eleven. If you have been reading your papers you must have seen what is happening."

"You could hardly miss it, could you?" said Mr. Calder. "What are we supposed to do about it? Soothe the shattered nerves of Lombard Street?"

"The reactions of the City," said Mr. Fortescue coldly, "are not a cause of alarm. They are a symptom of it. The real reason for their uneasiness is that Interstock has started selling heavily."

"Interstock?"

"I'm not at all surprised that you haven't heard of them, Calder. They take pains to avoid the limelight. They're a group of people, based in Switzerland, who handle much of the floating money of the world. Their funds come mainly from Kuwait, Abu Dhabi, the Argentine, Greece, and South Africa. They are very large sums of money indeed, and Interstock's job is to keep them in an optimum state of investment. This means reasonably high interest rates. But above all, absolute safety."

"And they're selling us short, are they?"

"They're not selling us short. They're selling us *out*."

"Where's the money going?"

"Most of it to Canada."

"What on earth's got into them?"

"That is exactly what we have to find out. The most probable explanation is that someone has deliberately started a scare. There could be financial as well as political reasons for it. There's a lot of money to be made in a falling market, if you happen to know when it's going to *stop* falling."

Mr. Behrens said, "I have, as it happens, a wartime acquaintanceship with Grover Lambert. I understand he's the London representative of Interstock. But it's a fairly casual connection. Even if I could get in to see him, I can't think I'd get much of an answer if I just said, 'Why are you selling us out?'"

"I have often found that a direct question gets a direct answer."

"Only if backed by force. In some countries, no doubt, the authorities would string him up by his thumbs and prod him with a white-hot knitting needle until he volunteered the desired information. But we can't do that here."

"No," said Mr. Fortescue. "No." His listeners thought they detected a note of disappointment in his voice.

Arnold Litman said to his wife, "I don't think you quite realize what you've done. I had to make a personal explanation to the Cabinet this morning. It was accepted. As far as they're concerned this particular episode is over. But people aren't going to forget it. In politics it's fatally easy to pick up labels. Look at Winnie and Tonypandy. In a few months' time no one's going to remember precisely what happened. But I shall be permanently labeled as an alarmist."

Rebecca Litman said, "I'm terribly sorry, my darling. But was I really to blame?"

"What do you mean?"

"When I told that young man that I thought war was coming, was it *me* talking? I wonder."

"For God's sake—"

"Do you think someone was using me as a mouthpiece? Speaking through me?"

"And who do you think was speaking through you?"

"It's a wild idea. But it did occur to me it might have been you. After all, if war was coming, you'd know about it, wouldn't you?"

Litman had stopped pretending to smile, and his blue-gray eyes were as cold as the snow-fed lakes of his fatherland. He said, "I suppose you haven't by any chance passed on *that* interesting idea to the papers, too."

"Oh, Arnold. As if I would."

Litman said, "No. I don't think even you would be stupid enough to do a thing like that."

Terence Russel and Sue Garnet were sitting on a bench in St. James's Park, watching the ducks. They, too, were discussing the crisis.

"Daddy's been very funny lately," said Sue. "You know he promised me a month in Florence. The thing was practically fixed and now he's back-pedaling. It's almost as though he doesn't want me out of his sight. In case anything starts."

"Nothing's going to start."

"Well, that's a comfort," said Sue. "If anyone knows, you ought to."

"I'm only a junior captain."

"Said he modestly. You also happen to be military secretary to someone who is notoriously the least security-minded officer in the three services. Daddy doesn't just leave confidential papers in taxis. He discusses their contents with the taxi driver."

Terence grinned and said, "If you're not going to go to Florence, why don't we get married?"

"Right away?"

"As soon as possible."

"Have we enough money?"

"I've a feeling we shall manage all right."

"Well," said Sue. "It would be rather nice."

Mr. Calder had not found General Garnet as hard to approach or as difficult to talk to as he had anticipated. The general had not pretended to remember him, but had greeted him as a former comrade in arms. He had also, clearly, seen his DMI file and was quite willing to talk.

"What we really want to know, sir," said Mr. Calder, remembering Mr. Fortescue's dictum about direct questions, "is whether there really is a chance of someone pressing the panic button, or whether the whole thing's a manufactured scare."

The general paused before answering. Then he said, "When I was a young soldier I was told that an ounce of demonstration was worth a pound of explanation. I was just about to make a visit of a routine nature. If you will come with me I will try to convince you that, although a nuclear war *could* start at any moment, it is extremely unlikely that it *will* do so."

The staff car took them westward toward Holborn, then stopped in a quiet side street. The general unlocked a metal grille which led into a small concrete yard. On the other side of the yard was an insignificant-looking concrete building, the size of a large toolshed. Using a second key, the general unlocked the door of this, and Mr. Calder saw that it housed an elevator. They stepped inside. The general pressed a button, and the elevator started slowly to descend. Mr. Calder looked at him.

"How far does this go down?"

"A hundred and fifty feet. The people who built them had to get through the London clay and into the rock."

"There's more than one, then?"

"There are six in the London area and eight in the home countries. Here we are. Good morning, Sergeant-Major. This is Mr. Calder. You have his clearance?"

"Just came through by telephone, sir. Shall I open up?"

"Please."

The sergeant-major evidently released some switch under his hand and a steel partition behind him slid up. He then rose to his feet, saluted the general punctiliously, and ushered him and Mr. Calder in, remaining outside.

Mr. Calder's first reaction was one of disappointment. He saw that the general was smiling.

"Well," he said, "what did you expect?"

"I don't really know," said Mr. Calder. "Masses of complicated machinery. Shining steel. Winking lights."

"You've been reading too much science fiction. This is a communication center. The machinery it controls is all over the place. The Norfolk coast, Dartmoor, the lochs of Scotland. This place is in contact with them all. Triple cable, buried in concrete. That set of telephones links with the Defence Ministry and the Prime Minister. The other lines are to service headquarters. And to Strike Force."

"And the system is in operation?"

"Naturally. The exchanges at the other end are permanently manned."

"And either of us could give the order for a nuclear attack right now? This moment?"

"I could. You couldn't," said General Garnet with a grin which emphasized rather than softened the fact that he was talking about the possible destruction of millions of human beings. "There's a code word which has to precede the order. It's changed every day. There are precisely ten people at any one time who know what it is."

"Nine too many," said Mr. Calder.

"Perhaps. It's a question of immediacy. Suppose the enemy started a conventional air raid. Enough to block roads and cause confusion. If only two or three men knew the word for launching Counter Strike, none of them might temporarily be in a position to do it. And ten minutes could make all the difference."

Mr. Calder thought it was one of the most disturbing conversations he had ever had. He was not a man who suffered much from nerves, but the smallness of the room, the enormous physical presence of the general, and the 150 feet of earth on top of him were bringing on symptoms of claustrophobia.

He said, "You talk about the enemy, General. Had you anyone in mind?"

"Naturally. I mean the Chinese."

This forthright statement took Mr. Calder aback even further. "Do you think they would?"

"I put the point to Litman at the meeting this morning. Do you know what he said? He said, 'Their civilization is two thousand years older than ours. Why would they want to destroy the world?' The only answer I could think of was a rude word beginning with 'b'."

The general rocked with sudden laughter at the recollection. Then he said, more seriously, "Of course they'd do it. The moment they were convinced it would pay them. They're logical—a damn sight more logical than we are in the West. They know that the only thing that counts in world politics is results.

Legality and illegality don't come into it. That's a conception confined to a country with laws. It cuts no ice in the international sphere because, in that sphere, there are no laws. If the Chinese could blast the rest of us off the face of the earth and get away with it, they'd do it tomorrow. The rate they're growing they'd repopulate the world quick enough on their own."

"But they can't get away with it?"

"Not as long as Counter Strike is manned here and in the United States. Our detection apparatus is far more sophisticated than that of the Chinese. We could wipe them out, every mother's son of them. If not by direct blast, inevitably by nuclear fallout."

"Do you know," said Mr. Calder, "this seems to me to be about the most dangerous thing I've ever heard of. Ten men know the code word. If one of them was a traitor, or even a fool, he could start a nuclear holocaust."

"He'd have to get down here first."

"If I had the keys I could do it easily enough. I'd simply step out of the lift and shoot the sergeant-major."

"That wouldn't get you very far. Did you notice that he didn't get up when I came in?"

"Yes. It seemed rather curious."

"He was making quite sure of our identity. He'd been given instructions from the Ministry of Defence to let the two of us in. If anyone turned up without that instruction—even me—he wouldn't let him past. And he was sitting with his hand on the spring lever. If he let it go, the door into here would have permanently locked. And I mean permanently. It would need a breakdown squad to get it open."

"I see," said Mr. Calder thoughtfully.

"The situation is becoming ludicrous," said Mr. Fortescue. "None of our normal intelligence agencies knows anything. The international situation generally has never been quieter."

Mr. Calder said, "Things seem to be hotting up in China."

"Internally, yes."

"I see our legation has been attacked again. They caught the First Secretary in the street and beat him up."

"I'm very sorry for the First Secretary. But it doesn't alter the situation. Someone, for some inexplicable reason, has made up his mind that we are going to be subjected to a nuclear attack. And—possibly by accident, but more likely deliberately—that person allowed the news to leak out. With the result that the pound is under severe pressure, the bottom has fallen out of the stock market, and now our allies are beginning to get worried. The American Ambassador saw the P.M. yesterday."

"And everyone," said Mr. Calder, "is damn certain who's responsible. If it wasn't for the law of libel the papers would print what's being said in every club in London—that Litman started the rumor, helped by that pea-brained wife of his, so that his friends in the City and in Wall Street could make a killing in a bear market. And it's got out of hand."

"You realize that we've no option. We've got to do something about it," said the general.

"I'm not sure what you mean," said Litman.

The two men were alone in the room overlooking the Horse Guards Parade. The Undersecretary was entrenched behind his desk, looking as though he was glad it was broad enough to afford him some physical protection. The general was standing by the window. He had not sat down since he entered the room.

"You've read Foster's report, I take it," said the general.

"Yes. I don't necessarily agree with it."

"Foster says that the attacks on British lives and property have now reached a point where it goes far beyond casual hooliganism."

"As I said, I've read the report."

"He thinks it's an organized campaign designed to provoke retaliation which could, in turn, be used by the Chinese as an excuse for hostile action."

"I'm afraid I don't agree with him."

"For God's sake," said the general savagely. "What do you know about the Chinese?"

"At first hand, nothing."

"Well, I do! I've fought with them, as nominal allies, in Burma. They're treacherous as hell. Do you realize that they—or some friend of theirs"—as the general said this he put both hands on the desk and his knuckles showed white—"have fixed things so that an actual *date* for their attack is now on everyone's lips. July 17."

Litman said, "*If* this is a deliberate plot, which I don't believe, why on earth would they warn us of when to expect the blow?"

"The oldest trick in war. Get your opponent's eyes fixed on one particular date. Then hit him the day before. A nuclear attack on this country will start on July 16. I am completely certain of it."

When the general had gone, Arnold Litman's hand went out to the green telephone on his desk, which carried the direct line to Downing Street. He hesitated for a long time before he picked it up.

"Our instructions," said Mr. Fortescue to Mr. Behrens, "have been changed. They are now categorical, and quite clear. We are to find out—*by any means we choose to employ*—from what source Interstock first received information that a nuclear attack was possible." He paused, then repeated, "*By any means.*"

"A few days ago," said Mr. Behrens, "I contrived to run into Grover Lambert. Our acquaintanceship dates from 1940, when we worked together at Blenheim. I suggested that we might have dinner one night at the Dilly. I told him he would meet some of his old friends. Sands-Douglas and Happold particularly. He jumped at the idea."

"Then I suggest," said Mr. Fortescue, "that the reunion take place as soon as possible. Today is July 10. We haven't a lot of time—only a few days."

The Universities, Legal and Professional Classes Club is never referred to by that full and cumbersome title. Its members long ago rechristened it the Dons-in-London, abbreviated to the D.I.L. or the Dilly Club. It occupies two houses on the north side of Lords Cricket Ground, has an unrivaled library of classical pornography, the best cellar in London, and the worst food.

As old Mr. Happold explained to Grover Lambert over the port in the small private dining room, it was a very useful *pied-à-terre* for impoverished senior members of Oxbridge and the Bar. Having been handsomely endowed by that eccentric millionaire, Professor Goodpastor, it could afford to limit both its charges and its membership.

"It is open to all senior members of Oxbridge, I suppose," said Grover Lambert.

"In theory," said Mr. Behrens, "it's open to anybody. There's only one limitation. *All* the existing members have to approve a new nomination."

"That must make it rather a close circle."

"It's very cosy," agreed Commander Sands-Douglas. He was large, red-faced, and had a mop of snowy-white hair, in curious contrast to Mr. Happold who looked like a very old snapping turtle. "The hard core are people who worked together in Intelligence during the war. Most of them came from the Universities and the Bar. Incidentally, it makes *you* eligible—if you could stand the food."

"It was fairly plain," agreed Grover Lambert politely, "but more than compensated for by the wine. I think that Corton was the finest I've ever drunk. By the way, didn't I recognize your wine waiter?"

"Applin. Sergeant Applin when you were at Blenheim."

"Circulate the port, Behrens," said Mr. Happold. "It's taken root in front of you."

As Grover Lambert took up the decanter his hand slipped and he put it down, spilling a few drops.

"I'm sorry," he said. "Stupid of me. It must be the heat."

"It is warm," agreed Mr. Behrens, studying his guest's face, which was now red and sweating. "Would you like to sit outside for a moment?"

Sands-Douglas said, "Let me give a hand," and both men helped Grover Lambert carefully to his feet, supporting his weight between them. That weight became heavier as his knees buckled and his eyes turned glassy.

"Put him on the sofa," said Behrens.

"I thought for one terrible moment," said Mr. Happold, "that he was going to upset the port. How long have we got?"

"The staff would normally knock him out for fifteen minutes. Then he'd start to come round with nothing worse than a hangover."

"Better lock the door," said Sands-Douglas. "Applin wouldn't let anyone in, but we can't be too careful. What next?"

"What I'm going to do—" began Mr. Behrens. "I say, prop his head up, would you, Happold—is to put a regulated dose of scopalamine-dextrin into him. It should wake him up enough to make him talkative, but not enough to remember things afterwards."

"Inject him, you mean."

"Good heavens, no," said Mr. Behrens. "What's he going to think if he wakes up with his arm full of holes? It might get the Club a bad name. No, the modern method is to inhale it." He was breaking a capsule under Grover Lambert's nose as he spoke. "It's quicker and more effective that way."

The unconscious man's eyelids fluttered. Mr. Behrens was perched on the couch beside him and said in a loud voice, "Wake up, Lambert. You are Lambert. Grover Lambert."

"I am Grover Lambert," said the man sleepily.

"You work for Interstock."

"I work for Interstock."

"Your directors have told you to sell your British holdings."

"Sell British holdings."

"Why? Why are you to sell British holdings?"

"War. Because of war."

"Who told you war was coming?"

"Who told me war was coming."

"Who told you?" said Mr. Behrens, very sharply.

The young man behind the counter in the travel agency looked superciliously at Mr. Calder and said, "I'm afraid we aren't allowed to give information about other customers."

Mr. Calder leaned forward across the counter and spoke without heat. "You have a telephone. That is the private number of Scotland Yard. You can ring it, if you wish, and ask for Extension 05. That is Commander Elfe, head of the Special Branch. He will confirm my authority."

"Well—" said the young man uncertainly.

"But if you hold me up for more than three minutes I will have this branch closed for a week while we investigate your reasons for obstructing the police."

"I'm sure I didn't mean to be obstructive."

"Then answer my question."

The young man turned to a filing cabinet behind him. His hand was shaking slightly as he pulled out a folder and opened it. He was not the first man to find Mr. Calder unnerving. He said, "General Garnet booked the ticket through this agency two days ago."

"For his daughter?"

"Yes. Air travel. London to Montreal. Montreal to Ottawa. Rail to Pettawawa. That's quite a small place, outside Ottawa. I believe it used to be an army camp."

"Single?" said Mr. Behrens. "Not return?"

"That's right. We thought it a bit odd."

"It would have been odder still if he had booked her a return ticket," said Mr. Calder, and left the shop without further comment.

Mr. Fortescue looked at the calendar on his desk. It was held by a large white china cat, with a blue ribbon round its neck, and it showed July 16.

He glanced at his watch, picked up one of the telephones on his desk, and dialed a number. The voice at the other end said, "C.M.P. Duty Officer."

"Please get Colonel Jackson."

It took a few minutes to find Colonel Jackson.

Mr. Fortescue said, "Colonel Jackson? Fortescue here. Send an officer and a sergeant—the officer must be of the rank of captain or above—to detain Captain Terence Russel. He's military secretary to General Garnet. You'll find him in his room at the Defence Ministry. The charge will be under the Official Secrets Act. I'll have the details in your office by the time you bring him back."

"Good afternoon, Sergeant-Major," said the general. "You look worried. Nothing amiss with your family, I hope?"

"No, sir. Not that I know of."

"I'm glad to hear it. Now, if you wouldn't mind—?"

The sergeant-major looked even more worried, but remained seated, his right hand out of sight down by his side. He said, "You know the drill, sir. I'm not allowed to let anyone in, even yourself, sir, until I've had a telephone call from headquarters."

"Quite right. But this is a surprise visit. To keep you on your toes."

"I see, sir."

"Then unless you think I'm an enemy agent in disguise, perhaps you'll be good enough to open the door."

"I can't do it, sir."

"Are you questioning my order?"

"Not without authority."

The general smiled, a ferocious grin which lifted his upper lip and showed a fine pair of incisor teeth. He said, "You have a telephone by your left hand, Sergeant-Major. Perhaps you'd care to ring my assistant, Captain Russel. You have his number. Well, what is it?"

"It's the lift, sir. It's just gone up. I expect this will be your authorization."

The general said thoughtfully, "Ah. Yes. I expect it is. That will save us all a lot of trouble, won't it?"

After that they waited in silence for what seemed to both of them to be an uncomfortably long time before the elevator reappeared and Mr. Calder stepped out of it. He said to the general, "I'm sorry I'm late. My car got held up in the traffic." And to the sergeant-major, "There seems to have been some break in the line between the Ministry and this post. They thought the general might have some trouble getting in, so they sent me with written authority."

The sergeant-major read the document carefully, right through, and then said slowly, "I see, sir. Yes. That clears everything up. I'll unlock the door."

"After you, General," said Mr. Calder.

The door closed behind them as silently as it had opened. The general sat down on the edge of the table, with his back to the door, swung one leg a couple of times as though to shake the stiffness out of it, and said, "Now, perhaps, Captain Calder, you will be good enough to tell me the truth. Since no one knew that I was coming here, how could they have sent you after me with a written authority?"

Mr. Calder was standing, his feet apart, his arms hanging down at his sides. It was an attitude of apparent, but deceptive relaxation.

He said, "I took the liberty of following you, General. As soon as we found out you were planning to send your daughter away to Canada. Even before that, some of the things you've been doing and saying have been worrying your superiors."

"My superiors are a lot of weak-kneed old women who'd be scared if you came up behind them and said 'boo'."

"They haven't got a row of medals for gallantry, I agree."

"I'm not talking about gallantry. I'm talking about guts. A few years ago we wouldn't have allowed a crowd of half-educated Chinese Reds to jump us. But then, at that time, the war machine was being run by Churchill. Not by a long-haired Lithuanian gutter-snipe."

"What do you think Churchill would have done?"

"What I'm going to do. Hit them first, and hit them for keeps. And no one is going to stop me. I take it you can see this."

Mr. Calder said sadly, "Yes, General, I can see it. A .455 automatic. In my opinion, the best weapon the British army ever produced."

"You're on top-secret Defence Ministry premises. You got in here by telling lies. I should be entirely justified in shooting you. And I will if I have to. You understand?"

"Perfectly, General."

"Then proceed. You say I've been worrying my superiors. How?"

"It wasn't only you. Your military secretary, Captain Russel, has been under arrest since midday. He has already admitted that some weeks ago he communicated to an acquaintance in the City, a Mr. Grover Lambert of Interstock, the view that this country would be at war with Communist China before the end of July."

"Nonsense."

"It's been confirmed by Mr. Lambert. He—er—happened to let it out after a very good dinner at my club."

"Why would anyone listen to what a captain said?"

"In the ordinary way, of course, they wouldn't. But Captain Russel was able to quote certain facts and figures in a private memorandum you had written for the Cabinet. Written, but not yet, I think, delivered. You really should have been more careful with such a potentially inflammatory document."

"Continue," said the general. He was smiling in a way which Mr. Calder found disturbing.

"What happened then might even have been funny if it hadn't been so bloody dangerous. In the eighteenth century, I understand, this country went to war because a Captain Jenkins had his ear cut off. We very nearly went to war because Captain Russel wanted to get married. He was innocent enough to think that his communication to Lambert would cause a sharp but temporary fall in the market. His naive scheme was to buy at the low point and then revive the market by telling Lambert that it was all nonsense, when he could sell at a handsome profit. I think he rather fancied himself as a financier. In fact, he was a babe-in-arms playing with high explosives. He had started a chain reaction which he had no way of stopping."

"I can't help noticing," said the general, "that while you have been speaking, you have been edging closer. If you come any nearer I will shoot your right knee off. But do go on with your story."

"What happened then is that the Chinese took fright. They don't understand a free press. When a senior war minister's wife foretold war in July and then the big boys started selling their British holdings, they reckoned they could read the signs. They got frightened, and they got angry. They still didn't really believe we would attack them, but if we did they were going to be ready to hit back."

"I've always been told that you chaps had vivid imaginations," said the general. "You've made up a very good story. It might even convince a weak-kneed pacifist like Litman. But it doesn't convince me. You're completely wrong. This whole business started in China. It was worked out by them, from beginning to end, like a game of chess. Move and countermove. I'm not a chessplayer. That's why I'm going to kick the board over, before we get to checkmate. Do you think you can stop me?"

Mr. Calder was trying to do three things at once. He was keeping the whole of his apparent attention on the general and he was watching the door which had started to open very slowly and he was also trying to work out certain angles and possibilities.

The general had picked up the telephone. Still keeping Mr. Calder carefully covered, he lifted the receiver and spoke into it.

"Counter Strike Headquarters. General Garnet speaking. Code word *Cromwell.* Action immediate. Full scale. I'll give you the countdown. Ten—nine—eight—"

The door was open now and the sergeant-major was inside the room. He knew exactly what to do, because Mr. Calder had written it all down on the paper he had given him and he had now had time to counter-check it by telephone.

"Seven—six—"

Mr. Calder noticed that sensibly the sergeant-major had taken his shoes off and was moving in stockinged feet. The overhead light would throw no shadow.

"Five—four—

"Three—two—*one*—"

The sergeant-major whipped one arm round the general's throat from behind. As his gun went up, Mr. Calder plunged forward in a dive for the general's knees.

Neither of them could have done it alone, but together they managed it. After they had lashed his hands and feet, the general spat in Mr. Calder's face and said genially, "It must be a comfort to you to know that you're too late. Nothing can stop it now."

"Do you think," said Mr. Fortescue, "that he realized the telephone had been disconnected?"

"I don't think so," said Mr. Calder. "But it's always difficult to know what a madman does grasp and what he doesn't."

"When did you realize he was mad?"

"In 1942," said Mr. Calder. "But I didn't realize how far his madness had gone. However, I'm very glad he didn't shoot me at that particular moment."

"Why at that moment?"

"I had an urgent telephone call to make to my stockbroker. You remember what you told us. There's a good deal of money to be made in a falling market if you happen to know when it's going to *stop* falling."

THE GOOD COMPANIONS

by Dana Lyon

Susie was alone in the world, an embittered old maid, with no friends, no relatives, no one even to talk to. She lived mostly on the pittance from her dead sister's insurance. She desperately needed a change, but of course she couldn't afford to go away. So when Anne and Greg, her former next-door neighbors, asked Susie to look after their house and two friendly dogs while they took a trip—well, Susie's loneliness tipped the scales and led her to what was waiting beyond the door . . .

GREG and Anne Hayward were the only friends I had at the time they moved away from the city, and that left me with none. My sister Rose had been the one who made all the friends, working in an office the way she did with me staying home and keeping house for her; but when she died last year none of her fine friends bothered to come around and see me or invite me to their homes after they'd paid their condolence calls. So there I sat, alone, living on Rose's pittance from her insurance and the remains of our father's legacy, until Anne and Greg moved in next door; and why they paid so much attention to someone like me I'll never know—maybe just because they were kind and felt sorry for me.

Well, of course I was kind to them, too, like the time I took Greg some of my homemade soup when he had the flu and Anne was working—he was a writer, so he didn't have to go to work—and I guess some other times, too, though I can't place them. They were young folk, in their late twenties, and they didn't have too much of a social life; they seemed to be satisfied just to be with each other, except they'd drop in to see me quite often—to borrow an egg or use my phone if theirs was out of order or chat a bit . . .

I missed them badly when they left but they said they couldn't stand the city noises any longer, they just had to get away, and they'd write.

Anne wrote shortly after they'd left:

Dear Susie,

We've found the most wonderful bit of land, a little clearing in some trees with a tank house (the regular house burned down some time ago) on it and real privacy. We're camping out now, but we're going to fix up the tank house until it's *darling* and then you must come to visit us.

Best—
Anne and Greg

Well, I didn't hear from them after that for ages, and then along came a letter from them special delivery:

Susie dear—

We're about to ask a great favor of you, though we think you might enjoy it, too. Greg has got to take a trip up north to see his family—his father is quite ill—and we don't want to leave the place alone, now that we've fixed it up. Especially our two darling dogs—of course we wouldn't leave them alone under any circumstances, but they hate the kennels where we take them occasionally when we go into the city, and they droop around for days afterwards.

How would you like to have a little vacation here amidst the pines and sycamores or whatever, in the company of two wonderful dogs? They are no trouble at all, are wonderful protectors and good companions. Do say yes and let us know as soon as possible. Would have called, but we can't get a phone this far out. Will be waiting to hear.

Love,
Anne and Greg

Well, of course I said yes, even though they hadn't invited me to visit until I could be of some service to them. I hadn't been away from the apartment overnight since I could remember and I felt I needed a change but couldn't afford to go away, of course. Besides, I was curious to see what kind of place they had; no doubt they had exaggerated, young people being what they are, always talking about their wonderful experiences and opportunities that usually boil down to nothing much. So I took a bus and three hours later I was there.

Everything was as they had described it: the small two-storey tank house was now painted a pale blue with white trim, with pink geraniums planted all the way around it; the small clearing; the pine trees rising in the distance. And the dogs, who were introduced to me as Rex and Regina, one a huge German shepherd, the other a small, prancing, beautiful collie. They came up to me, while Anne and Greg looked on smiling, and I reached out a hand to touch the big dog on his head. He had been standing there looking amiable but now suddenly he changed, without seeming to move a muscle; there was something different and withdrawn about him, like a polite child you're going to kiss who doesn't want to be kissed.

I turned to little Regina, who had been dancing alongside him, also seeming amiable, but she too had changed although I hadn't made a move to touch her. It was as if she were blindly following the other dog's lead.

Now I can't say I don't like dogs, it's just that I've never had any experience with them, having lived in an apartment for the last thirty years, and I can't say my experience with other people's dogs has been too good. They always jumped up on me or growled or made messes in the wrong place or something, and I got so I couldn't help feeling that people who devoted their lives to their animals had something a little bit wrong with them, like not liking people but needing something to love.

Anne showed me around. "All you have to do," she said, "is feed the dogs morning and evening and they'll be happy. Oh, and keep their water dish full outside. Here's the dog door"—a big square hole in the back door with a flap over it—"where they can come in and out as they please." She laughed. "We let them sleep wherever they want, usually in the living room, but they're very neat, perfectly housebroken, they don't claw the furniture or get it dirty, so they have their way with us." She paused. "I hope you won't get too lonely here—the freezer is stocked with all kinds of food and everything is in good working order—"

She led the way up the narrow spiral stairs and showed me to one of the two bedrooms—the smaller one, naturally—which was clean as a whistle and fresh with sunshine. "You'll have to go through our bedroom to get to the bath—this place is so tiny, that's the only way we could manage a bath at all," she added apologetically. "I do hope you'll have a good rest while you're here. If you want to walk in the woods take the dogs with you; there's nothing to be protected from, really, but they're good company. Have fun."

Later the two of them waved good-bye and were gone in their

little compact car, disappearing almost instantly through the tall dark trees.

There were plenty of things for me to do, as Anne had pointed out: walks in the woods, a color TV set although it could receive only two channels—but color! I'd always wanted one but couldn't afford it—and there were shelves full of books in the tiny living room, also a small fireplace to sit in front of during the chilly evenings.

I roamed outside and poked around a bit; I could see trees spreading off in all directions with only a narrow dirt road leading to the highway, and I couldn't help wondering why some people have all the luck. I would have loved a home like this—well, just for summers, perhaps—with a little car of my own and fresh air and country living. I couldn't help the touch of bitterness in me at the thought that people like Anne and Greg, so young and beautiful and free, with their lovely homemade house and beautiful surroundings, seemed to have everything. While I had nothing.

I looked through the books in the living room and selected a mystery that was years old. I sat down with it but couldn't put my mind on it. Restless, I got up and went to the kitchen, fixed myself a can of soup and some buttered toast, then went back to the living room where I turned on the TV—and a whole new world opened up before me. I'd never enjoyed Westerns in black and white, but now with the color, the landscapes, the mountains in the distance, all the blues and greens and yellows seemed to fill the room; I was lost in another dimension, far from the city and my dingy apartment and my colorless life as housekeeper for my busy sister, now gone. So dull since she died, so almost poverty-stricken. Again the thought came, why couldn't I have something like this all my own?

Then suddenly there was a dark shadow in front of the set, blotting out the picture, and I was frightened until I realized that it was Rex, the German shepherd, just standing there looking at me. Regina moved up beside him and they both stared at me. What on earth, I thought, then glanced at my watch. Eight-thirty, the windows dark now, no light in the room except from the flickering screen.

"Get out of the way," I said to the dogs, but they sat there, unmoving. Oh, good heavens, I suddenly remembered, I forgot to feed them! Anne had said, "First thing in the morning you give each of them some canned dog food, and at five o'clock a dish of kibble." And now it was more than three hours past their suppertime.

I got some kibble out of the large paper sack under the sink, plunked down their dishes, then rushed back to the TV set.

Next morning when I came downstairs, there was a horrid smell. On the living-room rug was a mess that one of the dogs had left, and I can tell you I was furious. Anne had assured me they were housebroken. They sat and looked at me and I could feel the contempt in their whole beings—an extension of what caused the mess in the first place—which enraged and frightened me at the same time. I picked up the nearest thing I could find, the hearth broom, and chased them out of the house.

"You nasty creatures!" I yelled. "Get out of here if you can't behave yourselves!"

They scurried out through the dog door and I decided to punish them by not giving them their breakfast; they'd just have to wait until suppertime. That would teach them.

I cleaned up the mess and settled down to the TV again, though there wasn't much on except children's shows and women interviewing other women. All young, of course, nothing to interest a woman in her fifties. Well, I'd just have to wait until night to see a good show.

After the first day or two there wasn't much to do. I went for walks in the woods and the two dogs trailed behind me, but when they chased a skunk right across my path and I tried to get them to go after it, they just sat there and did nothing. Nothing but stare at me.

Weeks of waiting here, I was beginning to think, before Anne and Greg would be back. No human company. No traffic sounds. No one to talk to. Nothing to do but look at TV and read old books. Well, I decided after a few hours of idleness, maybe I'll make myself a pie with some of the berries in the freezer—Anne had told me that she and Greg had picked them themselves.

I spent the whole morning on two pies and put them on the table to cool, then went back to TV again—even the silly woman shows were better than nothing. Vaguely, through my absorption, I heard a slight noise in the kitchen but when I went out there later I didn't notice anything at first. Then—my pies! They had been carefully eaten down to the tin plates.

"Get out of here," I screamed at the two skulking dogs, beating them with the broom. "Get out and stay out!"

But I couldn't make them stay out because there was no way to lock the dog door. They came in again and sat looking at me. I tried to stare them down but they just sat there and looked at me; then Regina touched her nose to Rex's—communicating, I suppose—and went outside and I could hear her lapping water. She came in and sat down, staring at me again, and Rex went out and had some water.

"All right," I said at last, "if that's the way you want it, you can just go to bed tonight without your kibble. That ought to teach you."

After supper I sat down in front of the TV again and the dogs were quiet. Suddenly I remembered having seen a bottle of sherry in the kitchen, and I thought maybe a little would quiet my nerves, so I stood up to get it. The result was disastrous, for Regina had been sleeping at my feet, almost as if keeping watch on me; but I hadn't known she was there and as I stood up I stumbled over her and she yelped and I lost my balance and started to fall. As I did so I grabbed the floor lamp beside me but it wasn't enough to stop my fall, and it came down with me.

I sprawled out on the floor with the dogs carrying on, the lampshade broken, and me with a bruise on one leg. I was frightened and terribly nervous and, most of all, enraged. "Get *out* of here!" I yelled at the dogs. And hardly knowing what I was doing, I kicked out at Regina, hit her in the ribs, and she yelped again and the two dogs ran out of the room and through the dog door to the outside.

I got up, too shaken to know what I was doing, and limped my way to the kitchen where I had half a glass of sherry to quiet my nerves. Then I went upstairs to bed.

It was quiet during the night.

Next morning, when I came down, the two dogs were waiting for me at the foot of the stairs. Just sitting there silently, as if they had been waiting for me a long time. I was in no mood for amiability.

"Get out of the way," I said, but they didn't move and I started to go past them. Rex stirred slightly and the way was blocked, so I stepped past Regina, but Rex was there, too. "You crazy dogs! Don't you want me to feed you?"

Again I tried to move past them, but they didn't budge. "Get out of my way!" I said again, raising my voice. "Move! Out of the way!" They didn't stir.

I started to push past them, and now there was a long deep growl, the first I had heard from Rex, and when I looked at him his eyes seemed almost red. He pulled back his lips a bit and I could see the long fangs. I tried to push past Regina; she didn't growl, she simply snapped her sharp little teeth together, and it made a dreadful sound. Now they inched closer to me; now they were the aggressors, not I; now they were not blocking my way to the lower floor, they were pushing me upstairs.

"No," I said. "No. Good dogs, good dogs. I want to feed you, let me come down," and I moved down the stairs again; but there was that little collie snapping at my ankles and the big dog with the low growl in his throat. I moved back. This wasn't enough. Again the snapping and the growl until, step by step, I backed up into the hall above and was pushed against my bedroom door.

The dogs were on both sides of me now. Growl, snap; snap,

growl—and finally I was in my room, the door closed quickly behind me, and those two terrible beasts on the other side. Now I breathed more easily, though I was still shaken and trembling.

Why hadn't Anne and Greg told me they were dangerous? How dare they leave me alone and unprotected with these dreadful creatures? What did they have against me that they must lure me here and leave me at the mercy of two dangerous beasts? I tried opening the door a wedge several times, but there were my antagonists, just sitting and looking at me.

After a while I grew hungry. And thirsty. I opened the door carefully, wider this time, but again came the low growl and I could see them both sitting there, watching, waiting. I closed the door again. Now that I knew I couldn't reach water, my thirst became acute. I must get to the bathroom off the other bedroom.

I put my ear to the door and heard nothing. But I felt the two uncanny creatures on the other side. There was silence, but they were there. Why? Why were they keeping me imprisoned like this? What did they want?

I thought, I must get out of here! Perhaps if I made a break for it? Opened the door suddenly and ran down the stairs? No, that wouldn't do, they could tear me apart. I'd just have to try my luck getting into Anne's and Greg's room where the bathroom was so that I could get some water for my parched throat.

I opened the door a crack, slowly, carefully. A growl, a snap. They were still there. But *they* would have to eat! They needed food even more than I did, for by now my appetite was gone though I still craved liquid. I would wait until they went for food; perhaps they'd finally realize that I was the one who fed them and would let me out for that purpose. They'd have to.

Or would they? They surely couldn't get at the canned dog food, but now I had a sudden picture of the large paper sack of kibble in the cupboard under the sink. And the cupboard door did not quite close. They could eat the kibble and they had water in the pan outside. How long would the kibble and water last?

My watch had stopped—I had forgotten to wind it. I did not know what time it was although I could see the shadows changing when I glanced out the window. My thirst grew, and now I was also beginning to feel the first pangs of hunger. I looked out the window again and there was Regina, capering about as if she had just eaten and now felt active and playful.

I opened my door. Rex sat there. Later I opened it again and Regina sat there. Alone. While Rex was eating, I suppose. "Nice doggie," I said, reaching out a hand to pat her on the head. The snap was sudden and dangerously close to my hand. She seemed to be smiling—although I know, of course, that dogs can't smile; but her eyes, those golden eyes into which one could gaze forever without reaching the bottom of the pit, were not smiling; they were deadly.

And so the two dogs imprisoned me, in shifts. Always one of them was outside my door. Rex could have torn me apart; Regina could not have done this but she could have ripped my legs to shreds. Singly or together, they were my keepers.

I could not last long without water. Often I went to the door and listened, afraid to open it, but I always knew one of them was there. I could hear the soft shhh-ing sound when they stirred, I could almost hear their breathing. I did not know how much time had passed; I knew that there was daylight and then dark, twice, and my throat was parched and my body weak.

Then, one day, the sky clouded over and grew dark and off in the distance I heard the rumble of thunder and saw an occasional flash of far-off lightning. I stood dully at the window, thankful for anything to break the monotony, too far gone in despair to realize what this storm could mean to me. But suddenly, when the huge drops spattered down, I came back to myself and reached my hands out frantically, cupping them for the cherished water. So little of it could I catch! I looked frantically about the room for any kind of receptacle and my eyes fell on a small, pretty glass bowl meant for flowers but now empty. I reached it out through the window and the rain lasted until the bowl was half full and then I sipped, rationing the water until I could plan some way out of my prison.

Occasionally, when there was complete quiet beyond the door, I would open it a crack; but instantly both dogs, or one of them when the other was busy eating or drinking or exercising, would leap up and stand there, no longer growling or baring fangs but looking like polite, well-trained pets. Smiling at me. It seemed. Once I tried opening the door enough to let myself through and I could feel, rather than see, the tenseness in their bodies, the preparation for attack, the guardedness that came over them when they sensed that I might escape.

Another time, when there had been quiet for several hours outside my door, an idea came to my mind. I went to the window and looked down at the ground: fifteen feet? Too far to jump with safety, but—I ran to the bed, ripped the sheets off, tore them into strips, knotted them together, then tied one end to the foot of the bed and threw the other out the window; it dangled to within a few feet of the ground. I pulled hard on my self-made rope and it held.

Then I went to the window and leaned over the sill and looked down, and there was Rex, sitting below, looking up at me, looking pleasant, looking amiable, smiling, smiling . . .

I do not know how long it has been now.

The weakness of hunger pervades me, now that the greater pain of thirst had been relieved, and I move about listlessly, or else sit on the bed and do nothing. There is no TV here, no radio, no reading material. Nothing but quiet and stillness and loneliness, and death by inches.

Once I came out of my lifeless lethargy at a sound outside my window. A horrible sound. Ravening. I went and looked out and Rex was below and he was tearing a small animal apart, blood on both of them. So the kibble must have given out, but that still wasn't important enough to those two creatures to cause them to let me out so that I could feed them.

Strangely, hungry as Rex must have been, he did not devour all the rabbit, but left part of it and trotted off around a corner of the house. In a moment Regina came capering around, full speed ahead, and fell on the meat that Rex had left for her. She glanced up once, as if to say, *See what you're missing?*—and went on with her meal.

They survive well.

I do not. I am unkempt, with no way to clean myself, and with hope deteriorating fast. I am hungry, I am growing thirsty again as the water slowly disappears from my bowl, and there is nothing to occupy my mind.

Except one thing: why are the dogs doing this to me? Revenge? Fear? Savagery? Mindless behavior of the jungle? No, not this last. Their behavior is not mindless . . .

My thoughts wander, then center on the one thing that is beginning to take over all that is left of my mind: *Why?* Rex could have killed me at any time, with one leap at my throat. He could have crunched my ankle when they were herding me upstairs. Regina could have torn my legs to shreds if she had wished. But instead they are keeping me here as a prisoner, not knowing or perhaps not caring, that I can die here, die on the wrong side of a door that can lead to freedom.

The thought keeps coming back, over and over again—for what else do I have to think about? They could have killed me at any time, so why didn't they? Because they need me to feed them in order to keep themselves alive? No. They are managing without me, they can survive without my ministrations, they are totally self-sufficient. Then why don't they kill me, any time I open the door, kill me and be done with it?

Finally I knew. The reason they didn't kill me outright was that then there would have to be an accounting. When their masters returned and found me dead in my room, they would not blame the dogs; they would only be sorry the dogs had been neglected while poor Susie lay dead of natural causes in their absence. But if I were found torn apart by their darlings' fangs, then there would be retribution, perhaps even execution. Like humans, I thought, the idea coming slowly and painfully into being—like humans. Like humans. *Do your deed, evade the consequences.*

THE NIECE FROM SCOTLAND

by Christianna Brand

What have you come to expect from Christianna Brand? Unobtrusive mastery of technique. Interesting plots. A flowing, almost enthusiastic style. Credible characters. Yes, all that—and more. The "more" are rare ingredients: the unusual, the unorthodox, the out of the ordinary, and often the flick or even the whiplash of surprise.

Here is a new story by Christianna Brand—about the theft of a pearl necklace from a house in a London cul-de-sac, only a stone's throw from the police station itself. Yes, once again you'll find the twists and turns—the rare ingredients . . .

"WELL, fancy meeting you again!" the pleasant stranger exclaimed, all flattering astonishment. (And about time, too, old girl! he thought to himself. Kept him hanging about a solid two hours for this "chance" encounter.)

Gladys had first met him last week here in The Green Man at the mouth of the cul-de-sac. She'd been sipping a dry sherry before going home to cope with her ladyship and he'd happened to sit down at the same table. Such a nice man! He'd seemed so interested in her, thought her far too good to be just a housekeeper, wanted to know all about where she worked and for whom. She'd soon found herself pouring out all her little personal troubles; if Gladys had a fault it was perhaps that she was rather too unreticent about the problems of life with Lady Blatchett.

And now here he was again, just dropped in for a quick one and insisted on her joining him. "Well, all right, but I *must* be home on the hour. If I'm not she locks the door and then hides the key and by the time she's had a couple of drinks, she can't find it again and I'm done for."

"Surely there must be other ways you could just nip in? You've got the run of the place. You could leave something unlocked."

"Unlocked! She goes over every door and window even when I'm there; you never know when she'll go round checking. If I *wasn't* there . . . I tell you," said Gladys, "the house is like a beleaguered castle." Guilelessly she described its inner fortifications. "She lives in terror, poor old thing, especially after dark."

It was all on account, it seemed, of Lady Blatchett's Past. She'd done something shady—fiddled a Trust or something—and so all the family money had come to her and now she went in fear of vengeance at the hands of cheated relatives. "Especially one of them. 'My niece from Scotland,' she calls her. It must have been the niece who should have got most of the money. She's built up this niece into some sort of terrible ogre; I really think she believes she'll be murdered in her bed." She supposed, said Gladys, that was what had turned her to drinking.

"A proper old lush, she sounds to me. I wonder you stay with her," said the sympathetic stranger.

A new look came into Gladys' sad middle-aged eyes. "I get very good wages. And I've got my poor brother, you see. I'm not having him put in any public institution. With his background and living with a lot of patients beneath his proper station—" She was back on a well-worn hobby-horse. Mr. "Smith" looked at his watch and warned her that the hour was approaching.

Patsy was waiting for Mr. "Smith" when he returned from seeing Gladys safely through the front door of Number 20, at the bottom of the cul-de-sac. Patsy looked exhilarated. Her blue eyes were shining, her feather-cap of dusty gold hair seemed to be standing on end with excitement and gaiety. "You look somewhat lit," he said, climbing into the driver's seat of the little car.

"Oh, Edgar, he's such a pet! And fallen for me like a ton of bricks; poor lamb—quite defenseless."

"You are speaking of Dr. Fable, I take it," said Edgar, not quite so pleasant now.

"At Number 10—slap opposite Lady Blatchett's. We did agree, dear heart, that I should go to work on him?"

"Well, you did go to work then? And it went off all right?"

"Like a bomb. I was the last patient, all as arranged. 'Stay and have a glass of sherry, my dear Miss Comfort?' 'Hey, hey,' I said, 'watch your doctor-patient relationship—it's slipping!' "

"Despite all this wit, however, you stayed for the sherry?"

"Yes, I stayed. And who else do you think stayed, too? The Desiccated Receptionist. Now, wasn't that a masterstroke? I made her join us; and now I've got not one of them eating out of my hand, but two." She wriggled complacently in her seat. "So how's about the housekeeper?"

Edgar told her his own news. "It's true all right, blast it! The place is like a fortress. Bolts, keys—I heard the very rattle of the chains as the drawbridge went up. And what's worse, they've got it so fixed that once inside you can't get out again. Self-locking doors and whatnot. You have to have special keys." Though why she should want to cage herself *in* with thieves and murderers, he couldn't imagine. "I tried advising dear Gladys to leave a few orifices open, but she literally dared not. The old woman lives in terror." He expanded on Lady Blatchett's reactions to her niece in Scotland.

"Oh, well, revenge is sweet, no doubt," said Patsy equably. "Personally, I'll be quite content with the pearls."

"You'll have to be—everything else she's got is kept in the bank vault," said Edgar.

Their plan went into operation the following evening. Gladys, patently rattled, answered the front door and beheld the friendly stranger from The Green Man. "Do forgive my disturbing you at such an hour—" he began.

"You shouldn't be calling here at any hour," said Gladys, glancing fearfully back to the closed drawing-room door.

"It was only that I mislaid my lighter last night. Sentimental value, you know; I couldn't bear to lose it. I wondered if by any chance you'd happened to notice—"

"I noticed nothing," said Gladys, beginning to close the door.

"It's nowhere in the pub. I suppose—" He had unconsciously moved a step forward so that she could do nothing without physically pushing him backward. "You couldn't possibly have picked it up, without thinking, and dropped it with your other things into your handbag?"

In his anxiety the gentleman had begun—quite unconsciously again, of course—to raise his voice. Gladys glanced back over her shoulder again. "No, no, of course. No such thing!"

"If you wouldn't mind just looking? So sorry to trouble you."

"*Please* keep your voice down; she'll be coming out into the hall." Gladys dithered doubtfully. "Well, I'll just go and make sure."

She hurried off toward the kitchen and in her agitation she never thought of asking him to wait on the step outside. And extraordinary to relate, what he had suggested must have happened; for there at the bottom of her neat vinyl handbag was a rather cheap silver lighter.

He thanked her effusively and went away. She listened for a moment at the drawing-room door, but except for the clinking of glass against bottle all was peace.

Gladys' room was on the third floor; her ladyship never climbed that high—couldn't manage the stairs, these days; and one way and another Gladys had got it very comfortable and cosy. With an occasional glance down from the top landing to see that all was well, she spent the rest of the evening with her knitting and the television.

Patsy slipped out of the dining room, once Gladys was gone, and went quietly up to the second floor. She located her ladyship's bedroom—really, the amount Edgar had got out of that house-keeper!—and inspected the others. There were two unused rooms, their keys in the doors. She chose the more remote, went in, locked the door behind her, and put herself very comfortably to bed. There would be the whole night to wait; and who ever looked into a locked spare room?

At midnight Lady Blatchett, propelled by the patient Gladys, reeled uncertainly up to bed. She would remain there till lunchtime—so Gladys had confided to her sympathetic friend in the pub—"She never thinks *I've* got to get up, after waiting up for her till all hours!" Patsy did not hear them. She was snuggled up under the spare-room eiderdown, deep in untroubled slumber.

At eleven the next morning Gladys, according to her custom, inched open the bedroom door and peeked in, before going to the kitchen for coffee and a biscuit. Lady Blatchett was still fast asleep and snoring. The pearls were kept under her pillow but in her late-evening condition her ladyship hadn't been too careful about concealing them; Gladys could see their gentle gleam, tumbled half out from under the crumpled linen. A choker of pearls, not many of them and not very large—but perfectly matched, they said, of a wonderful quality and worth a small fortune.

At that moment Gladys heard the milkman's knock and went down to the back door. Patsy had checked on this being settling-up day. Gladys would be kept occupied for several minutes.

Gladys came back into the house to hear muffled squeals and the sound of her ladyship's bell ringing violently. Lady Blatchett had been shocked awake to find her head and shoulders enveloped in a tangle of draperies; and by the time she managed to get free to summon help, the front door had closed and the pearls were gone.

Gladys spent some time in calming her ladyship's agitations, which centered largely on the threat of the niece from Scotland, and then she telephoned the police.

The station was at the mouth of the cul-de-sac, just opposite The Green Man; and a constable on duty outside was able to report that though many people had gone in and out of the cul-de-sac in the course of the morning, in the few minutes since the theft of the pearls, not a soul had left it. Unless egress had been effected through one of the other houses—which on a rapid mental reconnaissance seemed most unlikely—it was safe to assume that both the plunder and the plunderer were still safely bottled up inside. A police officer made good time to the scene of the crime.

Patsy, meanwhile, had trotted calmly out of the front door of Number 20 (it now being daylight, its defenses were down) and across to the front door of Number 10.

The Desiccated Receptionist was all of a flutter. "Oh, Miss Comfort, you're early."

"Am I?" said Patsy. "That's not like *me*. I'm usually late."

"Well, you aren't due today until half-past eleven."

"Oh, aren't I?" said Patsy. "Well, never mind. I'll just have to sit in your lovely waiting room and wait."

She was at leisure, therefore, to observe the antics of the patient who emerged from Dr. Fable's consulting room five minutes later and she could therefore describe them in full when the police subsequently made their inquiries.

In the interim, however, she had been in to see Dr. Fable and assure that infatuated practitioner that her headaches were, alas, no better. He showed no marked distress at this information and agreed that she'd have to come back several times—several times—for more treatment. Meanwhile: "Have you got another box of the pills for me, like you promised? Oh, you *are* a sweetie!—lovely sample ones again so I shan't have to pay for those either?"

He handed them over in their round white cardboard box, faintly rattling, the box plastic-covered and sealed. "It'll have to be a prescription after this, I'm afraid," he said. "That's the last of the lot they sent me. Let me know next time how much good they've done you."

"I'll make it an evening appointment and scrounge another drink from you," said Patsy, cheerfully departing. "With you and your nice Miss Hodge," she added, just loud enough for nice Miss Hodge to hear.

What with putting down her gloves on Miss Hodge's desk while she ruffled through her handbag for her diary, and riffling through the diary for a suitable date for the evening appointment, it was not surprising that when at last she left, in a near hysteria of jokes and farewells and thank-yous, Miss Comfort should have forgotten to take her box of pills with her. She was making such good time up the cul-de-sac that Miss Hodge could not catch her. The receptionist put the box on her shelf where it merged very nicely into the clutter of professional samples common to any doctor's office—and forgot all about them.

The police intercepted Patsy at the mouth of the cul-de-sac. She was highly entertained to learn of the theft of pearls from the house opposite the doctor's: just like on the telly, she said— weren't they all thrilled, right here under the nose of their own dear little police station, in their own dear little cul-de-sac? Was she a suspect? Were they going to search her? She simply longed to be searched—only promise not to tickle!

The police compromised by inviting her into their own dear little station where a young policewoman obliged with the searching. Neither Miss Comfort's charming person nor her handbag offered up anything of interest, except that, mixed up with the exotic clobber in the latter, there appeared a round white box of pills. The police broke the seal and glanced at the pills, even breaking one or two of them across; but they proved to be just pills. Since they showed so little eagerness, Patsy apparently thought it not worth while to mention that while one pillbox now appeared in her handbag, another had been left behind on Miss Hodge's desk. Instead she trailed a pretty little red herring.

"I suppose the thief must have been the funny man with the medicine?"

What funny man with what medicine?

"Well, he came out of Dr. Fable's examining room while I was waiting, but instead of leaving he sat down while Miss Hodge was busy with the next patient and pulled a bottle of pink medicine out of his pocket and started taking it. I mean, poured it down his throat straight out of the bottle."

Police interest perked up. The man was still in the station, having just come through, unscathed, a fairly thorough searching.

"Yes, and then he jumped up and went over to one of the pictures on the wall and began looking at it, terribly intent—I mean, sort of looking at the frame and feeling behind it in a funny sort of way. A frightful picture, too! Personally, I think Dr. Fable's got it upside-down, poor love. Perhaps the man thought so, too. Anyway, he took some more medicine and then went away."

The officers went away, too, legging it down the cul-de-sac as fast as they could. The picture was there all right and, upside-down or not, simply covered with glove prints, the gloves having been liberally dribbled over with the pink medicine. Apart from these, however, it all proved unrewarding.

There seemed little doubt about the genuineness of Lady Blatchett's loss. The police went about the busy elimination of suspects. Gladys the housekeeper had an unsullied ten-year record and a further twelve years to her credit of faithful if not devoted service to her ladyship.

Dr. Fable appeared to be a blameless practitioner, debonair and extremely well-to-do, hardly susceptible to suspicion of an elaborate and well-planned theft.

Desiccated Miss Hodge had been twenty years in the service of this doctor or that, without a blot on her escutcheon.

Inquiries in neighboring houses were in progress, of course; but meanwhile all that remained was the little clutch of patients. And one was Miss Comfort, limpidly innocent; one was an ultra-respectable mother-to-be from an address in Kensington; and the third was the funny man with the bottle of pink medicine. The police may be forgiven for concentrating with some intensity on the man, and since he had not gone at all into Miss Hodge's room, for saving this sanctum to the very last in their investigations of Dr. Fable's premises.

Miss Comfort slid up close to Miss Hodge as they sat awaiting dismissal from the police station. "I say, Miss Hodge, it's a little bit awkward. But I seem to have left my pills in your room."

"Yes, I found them," said Miss Hodge. "I put the box on my shelf."

"The thing is—well, it's because of Dr. Fable," said Patsy, raising troubled blue eyes to Miss Hodge's sharp, gray, elderly ones. "I mean, they're—well, you know, sort of pep pills. I don't think he really ought to have given them to me only I—I pleaded with him. I'm trying to fight it. I told him—well, he doesn't know I'm not supposed to be on them." She insisted: "It would be so awful if through helping me he got any kind of horrid publicity. You know how ugly it can be and the reporters will be swarming around here soon."

"What can *I* do about it?" said Miss Hodge.

"If you just wouldn't mention my having left them? Could you perhaps sort of whisk them out of sight before they start looking round your office? It's for his sake, you know. I do like him so much. And I think you do, too?" said Patsy, half tender, half teasing.

"I'll see that it's all right," said Miss Hodge gruffly.

"And not say a word to him? I swore to him I wouldn't tell a soul, not even you."

"I'll keep it to myself," said Miss Hodge.

A further examination, increasingly penetrating, produced nothing in the man that might have been "taken internally" along with the pink medicine. His fingerprints on the other hand were highly revealing. For Mr. Smith, the agreeable stranger of The Green Man, proved to be none other than Edgar Snaith, jewel thief, with a long and unbeautiful history behind him.

He appeared to have arrived but recently in London, though he had a familiar face—and a set of fingerprints—farther up north. Usually he worked with accomplices, varying them frequently. Certainly he was not known ever to have associated with Dr. Fable, Miss Hodge, the pregnant patient, or Miss Comfort. He had, however, scraped up an acquaintance with the now deeply penitent Gladys (currently under notice of dismissal) and had certainly elicited from her a great deal of information about Lady Blatchett's ménage and regime.

Witnesses attested to his having been seen at Gladys' front door the previous evening, but agreed with her indignant avowal that he had been (almost) immediately sent away; and both Gladys and Lady Blatchett herself could testify to the pearls having been in her ladyship's possession long after he had gone. He had turned up at Dr. Fable's two mornings earlier, declaring himself the victim of mysterious pains, his regular doctor having been left behind when Snaith came south. He had been a little insistent on a second appointment being fixed for eleven o'clock this morning.

By this time it was not remarkable that the vivacious and gregarious Miss Comfort, still caged up—though with all courtesy —at the police station, had fallen into a chat with her fellow sufferers. The pink-medicine man, however, proved impervious to her blandishments. "A fine mess of things you've made for *me*, Miss! The pain come on frightful and I took a swig of me stuff to ease it. What else do I carry it around for? And as for the picture, it's my belief he's got it upside-down, so I was trying to see how it'd look if I righted it."

Miss Comfort sh'sh'd him, to the great disappointment of everyone else present, and his voice died away to a reproachful grumble. Miss Comfort seemed to be defending her actions. In fact, she was whispering, "It all went fine, Edgar. The Desiccated One's got them. You've drawn off the hunt beautifully."

"When can you get hold of them?"

"As soon as the police stop harassing *you*. And they soon must—there's nothing to hold you on. Get in touch like we arranged and we can get on with it."

"No tricks meanwhile," warned Edgar.

"Of course not," said Patsy warmly. And she meant it. He deserved his share.

When some days later she judged the time was ripe, she went back to Dr. Fable's office. Miss Hodge was in the act of shrugging on her outdoors coat. "The doctor's left, I'm afraid."

Patsy knew that. She had not come to see Dr. Fable.

Miss Hodge took off her coat and led the way back to her room. "You've come for the pills?"

"I've tried to hold out. But the craving—it's terrible," said Patsy, going into her act. "I just simply must have them."

"No doubt," said Miss Hodge. She had turned and now half sat on the edge of her desk and was looking straight at Patsy. "You see, Miss Comfort, I know what the pills are."

Patsy played for time. "Well, I explained to you—"

"I mean I know that they're *not* pills," said Miss Hodge.

"Oh," said Patsy. It did seem rather final.

"You see," said Miss Hodge, "you made one small mistake. Yes, I am in love with Dr. Fable; to anyone of your age, no doubt that's very amusing. But it does mean something: it means that Dr.

Fable knows he can trust me, that I'd never ever let him down. He would never in his life have warned you not to tell *me.*"

So she'd looked in the box. But having looked there, reflected Patsy, taking heart, she had done nothing—hadn't gone at once to the police. Perhaps even the Miss Hodges of this world had their price? "Have you told this to anyone?" Patsy asked.

"No, I haven't," said Miss Hodge. (Was the glass of sherry paying dividends?) "I thought—well, you have shown yourself very—friendly—towards me, Miss Comfort. And I know Lady Blatchett, she's a patient of ours—and I know she's a horrid old woman. So I thought I'd wait and hear your side of the story."

"Let's sit down and have a nice natter, Miss Hodge," said Patsy, and she began to explain. "You see, Lady Blatchett is my aunt. And when my uncle died she sort of fiddled things—nothing illegal that anyone could get hold of—just worked on our doddering old family solicitor till she'd done us out of something like twenty thousand pounds. Well, that was too bad; but now my father's dead and my mother's ill—so beautiful, she is, Miss Hodge, and still quite young—and so dreadfully ill! And twenty thousand pounds—or ten thousand or five, for that matter—might make all the difference in her living a little longer and living that little in comfort. So . . .

"Well, one day our little house in Scotland was burgled and I caught the thief—no one more surprised than I was, unless it was him!—and I locked him up in a room. And then, instead of sending for the police, I had a little chat with him. I mean, suddenly I saw that if I could bring in a professional I might get some of my own back—and I do mean that, Miss Hodge," said Patsy, "get my *own* back. The pearls would be only a part of the value of what she's robbed us of. So we went into partnership. His name, no doubt you realize, was Edgar Snaith."

And Patsy went off into fits of giggles describing the alternative plans she and Edgar had devised for drawing the fire of the police. "*He's* safe enough. He never touched the pearls, and they can't pin anything on him for drinking pink medicine and staring at a picture. Unless, of course," she asked, raising her sweet blue eyes, half alarmed, half smiling, "you're going to give us away?"

"You mean," said Miss Hodge, "that I'm simply to hand over the pearls to you!"

Patsy half opened her mouth to propose a cut, but knew better and closed it again. "Would you—please?" she said.

Miss Hodge got up and fetched the round white box with its green lettering. She sat nursing it in her hand. Then she suggested pleasantly, "Fifty-fifty?"

"Fifty-fifty!" said Patsy.

"Twenty-five percent for you and the same for Mr. Snaith. The other half to me."

Patsy made a wild snatch at the box. It was empty. "I was expecting that," said Miss Hodge. She added that Miss Comfort need not worry; the pearls were quite safe—but not where Miss Comfort could ever find them.

"Fifty-*fifty*?" said Patsy.

"Make up your mind," said Miss Hodge.

Patsy's quick little mind shifted—she had spotted a discrepancy. "Possession is nine points of the law," she said. "You have possession of the pearls. Why divvy up? Why not scoop the lot for yourself?"

"I am not an habitual criminal," said Miss Hodge simply. "I wouldn't know how to dispose of them."

"Impasse," said Patsy.

"Impasse," agreed Miss Hodge.

And yet, not quite.

"Possession's nine points of the law," said Patsy again. "But the law will not allow you to keep possession of Lady Blatchett's pearls. Suppose I cut my losses and inform the police?"

"You do just that," said Miss Hodge, growing alarmingly less desiccated every minute, "and see where it will get you."

"It won't get me anywhere, except one up on *you*. And if I can't have my proper share of the pearls that'll do next best for me. Twenty-five percent of what a fence will give for them!—it'll be worth that much to me to see you doing time. And don't think you won't. You can say what you like to them about me—I haven't got them, I'm in the clear; they don't even know I know Edgar.

"But Edgar was at that house last night and he was here the next morning. You wait till Edgar starts coming clean to the police—how you bribed him to take care of the sale of the pearls, which you'd already stolen on one of the old woman's visits here, replacing them with false ones; perfectly easy while the doctor was examining the patient. You'd have told Edgar to look for them behind the picture frame," said Patsy, warming to her theme, "and to swallow them down with some medicine and so smuggle them out."

Patsy shrugged. "Lots of holes, but Edgar will stop them up, never fear! He's a past-master, is Edgar, at conning the police. And there'll still be nothing against him—he won't ever have touched the pearls; he'll tell them you have them, and that'll be true. And against me—also nothing."

"Except, of course," said Miss Hodge, "that the most casual inquiry will reveal that you are the niece from Scotland, with a grudge against Lady Blatchett and a well-founded conviction that whatever she possesses is rightfully yours."

"Oh, that!" said Patsy. "No dice there, I'm afraid, love! You didn't really fall for that, did you?"

"Well, no," said Miss Hodge. "You cooked it all up on the spur of the moment from what poor Gladys had confided to your friend, Mr. Snaith. You thought such a story must surely win my sentimental spinster's heart and that I'd turn over the pearls to you."

"But you didn't believe it?"

"Lady Blatchett is an old woman," said Miss Hodge. "So odd for her to have a niece of your generation, especially as your poor dying mother is still so young." She smiled at Miss Comfort with the smile of a crocodile. "So much more likely, don't you think, that the niece from Scotland is by now at least a middle-aged woman."

Miss Comfort saw the light immediately. "Like you?"

"That's right, my dear," said Miss Hodge. "Like me."

The niece from Scotland: obliged to earn her own living, wangling herself at last with her excellent references into a position where she might observe the old aunt at close quarters, might even ingratiate herself into her favor. The older one became, the more frequent one's visits to the doctor—chosen because his office was so conveniently just across the way—and the more necessary the attentions of the doctor's kindly receptionist.

Miss Comfort bowed to necessity. "*You* are the niece from Scotland."

"And *you* are a professional thief," said Miss Hodge, "and that's that." She rose, dusted her charmless dress. "So I think fifty-fifty is a very fair division. Where do we begin?" she said.

At Number 20, Lady Blatchett rang the bell for Gladys. She continued a serial lecture on the sins and follies of careless talk in public. "But I have decided after all to retain you."

Gladys was not exactly astonished; not for nothing had she made herself indispensable over all these years. She said, "Thank you, my lady."

"I have had a nice check from the insurance people, so I feel rather better."

"Oh, I *am* glad," said Gladys, much relieved. "Now your ladyship can have some pearls again." Then she said humbly for in some mysterious way the theft was acknowledged to have been all her fault, "Always seeing you with them—I've missed them, my lady."

"I hadn't intended—" But Lady Blatchett looked into the mirror. "Perhaps I do need something."

Bare, ancient, crepey throat, where the dewlap hung unlovely and the "bracelets" deepened with each succeeding year.

"I was even thinking that your ladyship might get a double row, this time. You'll never match the last, I know, but perhaps two rows not quite so good—?"

Her ladyship thought that might be a good idea. After all, a nice bit of jewelry was better for her, really, than all that money lying in the bank.

Better for Gladys, too. What a blessing the burglary had been! Not that she hadn't been, for simply ages, working toward something of the sort—all that carefully indiscreet talk in the pub! She'd been beginning to feel a bit desperate by the time Mr. "Smith" turned up; the money from the first pearls wouldn't last forever—and if she died for it, her poor brother wasn't going to be moved to some public institution where he wouldn't have his proper privacy; a man of his background mixing with just ordinary patients—no, it just wouldn't do.

Behind the shop front of a respectable jeweler's, Miss Hodge, Miss Comfort, and Mr. Snaith stood aghast at an offer of £25 for some nice cultured pearls; and up in her comfortable room Lady Blatchett's well-paid housekeeper was writing off to an address in Scotland.

THE RESURRECTION MEN

(as told by James Boswell; Spring, 1776

by Lillian de la Torre

In Queen's Quorum *(1951) we wrote: "Late in 1943 Ellery Queen's Mystery Magazine had inaugurated a series of historical detective stories by Lillian de la Torre. These tales had as their protagonist the Great Cham of Literature, the Sage of Fleet Street, the jovial, Jovian Dr. Sam: Johnson who devoted his prodigious learning to the detection of Eighteenth Century crime and chicanery. The origin of the series is interesting: one day it dawned on the author that James Boswell—the immortal Bozzy— was in reality the greatest of 'Watsons.' Immediately stories in detective form began to shape themselves around every queer personality and dubious event in Dr. Johnson's lifetime . . . the author re-created that grand old gentleman-and-scholar in all his glory and produced . . . the finest series of historical detective stories ever written—in scholarship, humor, flavor, and compelling detail."*

In his recent and excellent Mortal Consequences *(1972), Julian Symons wrote that the Dr. Sam: Johnson stories "are perhaps the most successful pastiches in detective fiction . . . Miss de la Torre caught most happily the tone and weight of Johnson's conversation . . . [the pastiches are] certainly done on a high level."*

The last Johnson-Boswell adventure to appear in Ellery Queen's Mystery Magazine *prior to this story was "The Banquo Trap," in June 1959—nearly fifteen years ago. Welcome, now, the return of Dr. Sam: Johnson, Detector—and enjoy, enjoy! . . .*

"BODY-snatchers and Resurrection Men, 'tis a scandal!" growled Dr. Sam: Johnson in his loud bull's mutter.

"Oranges! Sweet Chaney oranges!"

The call of the orange-girl rose, filling the theatre in the interval between the tragedy and the after-piece. 'Twas at the after-piece that my philosophical friend had taken umbrage, for it was announced as *The Resurrection of Harlequin Deadman*, a theme which Dr. Johnson considered both sacrilegious and inopportune.

"What are these mountebanks thinking of," he demanded, "to give us another dead man, when the whole town reeks with the grave and the vault, when ghouls and Resurrection Men lift our dead from the earth [shuddering] to be sacked and carried off by night, and carved like mutton by the Anatomist in the morning!"

"Oranges! Sweet oranges!"

The orange-girl was before us, a trim little piece with a dimple beside her bee-stung lip. I longed much to try her mettle, but set up there on publick view, so to speak, in a forward box at Drury Lane Theatre, between two weighty and well-known personages, I hesitated, and she passed on.

Dr. Sam: Johnson, burly and broad, his little brown wig clapped carelessly askew on his head, was known to every tavern and tea-table in town as Ursa Major, the Great Bear, the Grand Cham of Literature.

Our companion, Mr. Saunders Welch, tall, robust, and powerful, with his snowy poll and his round benevolent face, was recognized by the upper crust and the under world alike as the incorruptible Westminster magistrate, second in command to the Blind Beak of Bow Street himself. Often had the world seen him leading the procession to a Tyburn hanging, black-clad, stately on his white horse, bearing his black baton of office tipped with silver.

Nor was I, I flatter myself, unknown on the London scene: James Boswell, Esq:, of Auchinleck in Scotland, advocate and man of the world, chronicler of the *detections* of Dr. Sam: Johnson: very much at your service. Many an eye from the stalls was marking my elegant bloom-coloured attire, my swarthy visage set off by powdered clubbed wig, my genteel bearing and complaisant air.

"And what does Bow Street," my worthy friend was demanding, "to quell these grave-robbing scoundrels?"

"What can Bow Street do?" rumbled Mr. Welch. "These involuntary levitations of inhumated decedents—" He paused impressively, for he loved to outdo Dr. Sam: Johnson himself in the matter of sesquipedalian terminology.

"By which you mean, digging up the dead?" suggested Johnson with a half smile.

"Just so, sir. We do what we can to prevent it. The vaults are concealed, but the Resurrection Men find them out; coffins are sealed, but somehow come unsealed; guards are set, but the Resurrection Men prove stronger. They are persistent, for the traffick is very profitable. The Anatomist pays high for the fresh bodies he dissects."

"Too much of this," growled Johnson in revulsion. "Harlequin Deadman, pah! Let us go."

I had got my friend to visit the theatre by promise of a tragedy of a moral tendency, *The Distrest Mother*; and now it was over he was little disposed to wait for the harlequinade. But I found myself reluctant to leave my bee-stung charmer unattempted.

"Do, sir," I perswaded, "do sit on with us, for they say Mr. De Loutherbourg back stage has outdone himself with his scenes and his transformations, his opticks and his mechanicks, his grand effects of light and dark."

"Well, well, I'll humour you, Bozzy. Let us see what this Dutchman can do."

This complaisance enabled me to close with the pretty orange-girl, and privily purchase from her at an inflated rate not only a regale of oranges, but a rendezvous for a later hour at a bagnio hard by Covent Garden. I devoured my orange well pleased.

Suddenly, with a loud groan of the tuba, the musick banged up a grotesque dead march. Salt-box and cleaver beat time, and nimble fingers made the marrow-bones to rattle. Ropes creaked, and the scene-curtain rolled up in Mr. De Loutherbourg's new manner. The stage lay in darkness. All the candles, at the front and in the wing-ladders alike, had been snuffed. Only a large opal moon gleamed of itself in a black velvet sky.

" 'Tis some chymical substance makes it glow," observed Dr. Johnson, his interest engaged, for he dabbled in chymical experimentation himself.

The dead march swelled, torch-light appeared, and a grotesque funeral procession stalked into view. The children of the company, inappropriately attired as Cupids, capered on first, scattering flowers. Harlequin's bier was borne on shoulder high, under a diamond-chequered pall. There followed his friends and enemies as mourners, Columbine in her gauzy skirts supported by the noted Grimaldi as Pantaloon, Clown with white-painted face wringing his floury hands, and the rest of the farcical rout. Dr. Johnson snorted. He hates to be reminded that man—even Harlequin—is mortal.

Harlequin under his pall was laid in his grave—that is to say, in the Cauldron Trap, depressed just deep enough—and the mourners footed it off to a quickstep. De Loutherbourg's opal moon precipitously declined and set.

In the dead darkness there was a stir. A sheeted figure, gleaming with a luminous moony glow, sat up in the grave. 'Twas startling. Ladies shrieked, men cursed in admiration. Then the figure straightened and stepped up, the glowing cerements were cast aside, and Harlequin stood before us—a skeleton! Every bone gleamed with that same mysterious moonlight glow, the palms of his hands shone, and where the face should have been shimmered the grin of a skull.

"Bravo, De Loutherbourg!" muttered Welch.

"Tschah!" said Johnson, "black body hose and bright paint!"

The musick struck up a weird melody. Wright was Harlequin that night, and his Deadman's Dance was a triumph of loose shank-bones and prodigious leaps. But Dr. Johnson, finding in it no moral content, could not sit still. When the foolery ended, we hardly stayed to hear tomorrow's bill announced (*Venice Preserved* and *Harlequin Cherokee*) before we escaped ahead of the press.

Outside the theatre, as usual, a mob of riff-raff was gathered, chairmen, link-boys, night-walking wenches, ready-handed rapparees, pimps and pickpockets.

Past us as we left the play-house strolled a youth who engaged my regard, fresh of face, erect of form, lace-ruffled, clad in ivory brocade. Striding easily forward, he came up against a knot of blackguards. There was a jostle. The boy seized a collar and shouted. I thought the word was "Murder!" He was fatally right. A knife flashed, the boy fell, the brawlers melted from sight.

"Halt!" shouted Welch, and gave chase, but in vain. They were gone.

"Zookers, my cousin!" ejaculated a flash-looking bystander in a bag-wig, starting forward. "He's in a fit! Quick, lads, bear him to the tavern!"

Several hands were reaching for the boy, when past my elbow sped a lady in rose-coloured lutestring, small and daintily formed, her grey eyes enormous in her pale delicate face.

"Stand off!" she cried, and the would-be helpers fell back.

"Patrick!" she breathed, and knelt beside him. He lay as the dead, no breath, no motion. She wrung her hands.

"My son!" she wailed. "What shall I do? He's dead as his father died, and the body-snatchers will have him as they had his father, and what will become of me?"

"Give place," said a resonant voice. "I am a surgeon, madam, John Hardiman, at your service. Pray permit me, milady."

He knelt beside her, a military-looking man of middle height. Soon he rose, shaking his head.

"Lend a hand here," he cried, "and bear him to my surgery in White Hart Yard, where I may apply my skill to restore him."

"Never!" cried the lady. "He shall go home, for my house is hard by. Summon a chair!"

"A chair for Lady Julia Fitzpatrick!" voices took up the cry.

"Who is this lady?" I wondered aloud. "And what means her talk of the bodysnatchers?"

"Why, all the world knows Lady Julia Fitzpatrick," replied Dr. Johnson, "sister to an Earl, wife to the late Fighting Fitzpatrick, the notable Irish duellist. He died last year in a brawl at a tavern, and yon boy, his son, saw him fall. The tale they tell is strange. Fitzpatrick had, they say, his heart misplaced in his breast, an opponent could never nick it. You may imagine how the Anatomist would desiderate such a rarity."

"Preposterous!" I ejaculated.

"That may be; but preposterous or no, what the world believes, as I observed in the matter of the Monboddo Ape Boy, is a sharp-edged fact upon which a man may cut himself. So it was, perhaps, with Fighting Fitzpatrick. As the story goes, an assassin, instructed by the Anatomist, put a quarrel on him and struck the right spot, ending his days and producing the desiderated cadaver. I know the Sack-em-up Men lifted him, for I saw the empty grave

myself, passing by the churchyard of St.-Mark-in-the-Fields, with
the coffin riven and empty and the winding-sheet thrown down
beside. Small wonder if Lady Julia dreads the Resurrection Men."

"A shocking story!"

"It is so. And who knows? If Fighting Fitzpatrick proved in fact
an anatomical rarity, might not the same Anatomist have a mind
to have the boy on his dissecting table, to see if such misplace-
ment runs in families?"

As we spoke thus, two burly bearers edged a sedan-chair with
difficulty through the press. Many hands lifted the fallen boy, his
brocades now blotched with crimson. The lady ascended the
chair, received the inert form beside her, the half-door was
fastened, and the chairmen heaved up the poles. The attentive
surgeon walked beside.

"Let us go along," said my benevolent friend with concern, "for
I perceive this lady needs a friend."

I followed along towards Covent Garden; but I had another
kind of friend waiting in a bagnio there, and at Lady Julia's door
in Russell Street I parted for the night.

Frustration ensued. My little Cytherean with the dimple,
after all, embezzled my gold and left me standing, no doubt
following some deeper purse to a more fashionable bagnio; and
thus she passes from my story. I went late to my lodging in an evil
mood, slept but ill, and rose to melancholy. Then when I called in
Bolt Court, looking for the consolations of philosophy, Dr.
Johnson was from home.

Not until evening did we meet. We dined together at the Mitre.
I was silent as to the perfidious orange-girl; but over a mighty cut
off the joint, my benevolent friend adverted to the tragedy at the
theatre, and imparted something of its consequences.

"At my urging," he remarked with satisfaction, "little Davy
Garrick at Drury Lane has consented to lay upon the shelf the
resurrection of Harlequin Deadman as long as the publick is
shocked by the doings of the real Resurrection Men."

"And what of the bereaved mother, Lady Julia?"

"Calling in Russell Street, I found her resolved that these ghouls shall not have the remains of Patrick. She fears that they may snatch him from the very house of mourning, and perhaps justly so, for certain it is, that it was a body-snatcher's trick, almost successful, when yon bravo in the bag-wig claimed kin and would have carried him off but for Lady Julia's arrival. She is made wary. The body has been shrouded and coffined, and the lid made fast, by her own hands. The wake is in progress, and in the morning the body will be consigned to earth, to be kept under strong guard while the cadaver is fresh. Pah! It destroys the appetite!"

My sturdy friend, falling silent, applied an undestroyed appetite to the demolishing of a toothsome veal pye. I lent a hand. Not 'til it was consumed did he lean back with a sigh.

"Come, then, Mr. Boswell, we are expected at Lady Julia's."

"What, sir, will *you* make one at a wake, and join in the pillaloo or Irish howl?"

"I will do more than that for a distrest mother."

We found Lady Julia's house decked in deep mourning. Sable crape draped the doorway and muffled the knocker. The door was opened to us by a sombre-clad footman with a pugnacious bog-trotter's face, and we stood in an entrance hall hung from ceiling to floor with rich mourning trappings laced with silver. From within sounded the low moans and loud howls of the Irish pillaloo.

"Dr. Johnson, Mr. Boswell, your servant!"

It was the undertaker, swelling and grand in black broadcloth.

"What, good Mr. Blackstock, sir, yours!"

The man was known to us, for we had met at Dilly's, under more congenial circumstances. Mr. Blackstock, the society undertaker, broad in the shoulder and short in the leg, had a face that reminded me of that pair of Greek masks, one broad grin alternating with a professional countenance of distress. He wore the latter now, mouth corners turned down and eyes turned up.

"A sad occasion, sir," he intoned; "and," he added in a confidential murmur, "a strange one. These Irish are too much for me! No expense spared on trappings of woe—" He glanced with approval at the costly velvet hangings. "—night made hideous by heathenish howlings—" The pillaloo rose to a loud keen, wavered. and fell. "No wax figure to display as in my father's time; nc hatchment, no loved countenance preserved through my art; but shrouded, coffined and screwed down in haste, and hugger-mugger off to the grave in the morning! I'll never understand the Irish!"

"Lady Julia is apprehensive for the safety of the remains," remarked Dr. Johnson. "And she has cause, sir, she has cause."

Mr. Blackstock looked put about.

"Most unfortunate, that, sir, last year," he muttered, "but I did all I could, the usual guards at the grave, spring-guns, and so on; and so I shall again, with close supervision too. Lady Julia may make herself easy."

"I will tell her so," said Dr. Johnson.

Mr. Blackstock bent his weeds in a bow that would have done honour to an archbishop, and we passed withinside.

In a parlour hung with black, the coffin stood dark, covered with a rich sable velvet pall. Candles flickered at head and foot. Around it knelt the inferior Irish females of the household, tearing at their dishevelled locks and ululating with a will. Even ladies of the better sort moaned into their pocket handkerchiefs, and gentlemen stood by looking grave. A strong posse of rough-cut Irish footmen put about the consoling glass, and often retired to the kitchen, there presumably to console themselves with similar potations.

In all the hullabaloo, little Lady Julia sat erect, silent, dry-eyed and grim. To my surprise, Dr. Hardiman the surgeon h ingratiated himself, for he stood by her, gently smiling, v hartshorn bottle at the ready, and when her duties called away, he supported her steps.

With doleful countenance, Mr. Blackstock tiptoed softly among us, distributing the trappings of woe. Elaborate "weepers," white bows fluttering fringe, soon adorned every arm. Rich mourning garments were passed out, black shammy gloves, Italian crape hat-bands, silk mourning scarves, and the finest of funereal cloaks, black broadcloth from neck to heel, and deep-hooded, to hide the ravages of tears. Tearless, the bereaved mother submitted to be swathed in a long black crape veil.

As the candles paled with the waning of night, the bearers shouldered the coffin and bore it out in the grey of dawn. At the door six black horses waited with the hearse, of carved wood black-painted, and surmounted by a sooty solemn crest of tall nodding feathers. The coffin was slid in. We mounted the mourning coaches, and the cortège paced off to the tolling of the church bells, bearing the slain boy to his resting-place in the churchyard of St.-Mark-in-the-Fields.

St. Mark is no longer in the fields, for the city has moved out that way; but the churchyard still extends alongside massy wall, ivied lych-gate, solemn yew-tree, old grey tombstones, all very fit for our melancholy obsequies.

Of the funeral sermon, whined out with a snuffle by a pursy divine, I say nothing; but at last we stood by the opened grave. A wall-eyed sexton and his muscular helper stood by, looking, I thought, rather too pleased for the nature of the occasion; but no doubt they had been well fee'd.

"Ashes to ashes, dust to dust—" The first clods fell upon the coffin, and the sexton and his man wielded spades with a will to close the grave. I wondered how soon it would be opened in unholy resurrection.

The mourning coaches departed, but a knot of us lingered: the sexton, Mr. Blackstock and his men, Mr. Saunders Welch, Dr. Johnson and myself. We remained to observe as Mr. Blackstock took his measures for the safety of the cadaver. With his own hands he set the mechanism of a wicked-looking spring-gun. As the wall-eyed sexton stacked his shovels against the wall, still grinning, two rough-clad fellows took up their post by the raw grave. Each was armed with a blunderbuss; but they looked neither intelligent nor resolute. Would they avail to stand off the body-snatchers?

My gorge rose as I imagined to myself the horrid scene—the loose earth shovelled away in hurried silence in the dark of the moon, the rending sound as the coffin is riven, the pallid form torn from its winding sheet, huddled by brutal hands into a sack; the chink of the Anatomist's coin as he pays off the criminals, his indecent satisfaction as he bares his scalpel and carves his silent victim like butcher's meat. No endeavour, no expense, seemed too much to avoid such a fate.

These gloomy reflections haunted me as the daylight hours passed in indifferent affairs. Waiting on Dr. Johnson in Bolt Court as twilight fell, I found that he had apprehensions as gloomy. Trusting as little as I to the abilities of the fellows on guard, he proposed that we should add ourselves, unheralded, to the churchyard watch. Sore against my inclination, but much by my will, I repaired with him to Saint Mark's.

There, unseen, we took up our watch in a corner of the ivy-covered church wall, where in a niche some by-gone vicar had concealed a chill stone seat in the yew-tree's dusky shade. Our mourning cloaks clothed us from top to toe in impenetrable shadow. In the moonless night I dimly saw the shape of the fresh grave close by, where in silence the watchers passed and repassed like Sentinels.

As the hours rolled around, to my imagination the darkness seemed astir all around us. Vapours arose like ghosts and walked among the gravestones. Once I thought I saw a knot of cloaked figures flit through the lych-gate and silently enter the church porch. Once a black-swathed shape rose tall like a spectre behind me. My hair stood up on my head, and my tongue clove to my palate.

"Abate your horripilation, Mr. Boswell," breathed the apparition, "for I am no noctambulant, only your friend, Saunders Welch, come to bear you company."

We sat on. The church bell's solemn chime told hour upon hour. At the dead time of night, at last, a chaise drew up outside the churchyard wall. A moment later, dimly seen figures came over the wall, there was a stir by the grave-side, and we heard the whisper of shovels in loose earth.

"The body-snatchers!" I gasped. "What, sir, shall we not fall upon them?"

"No, sir. To abate this nuisance, we must take them red-handed. Let them dig."

Mr. Welch growled in his throat, but made no move. In the faint starlight, shovels swung. Piled earth rose. At last, we heard shovel strike upon plank. Then followed the shriek of riven wood. Hands reached down, and slowly the sheeted form rose out of the earth, gleaming with an eerie light. One of the body-snatchers cried out.

"Pah! Afraid of moonlight?" sneered a voice. "Off with the winding, man, make haste!"

Many hands tore at the winding sheet. The gleaming cerements fell away, and there appeared a thing of horror—not a body fresh in its youthful beauty, but a skeleton shining as with the phosphorescent light of decay.

There was a scream, an oath, and the Resurrection Men scattered.

"After them!" I cried.

"Be easy, sir," said tall Welch. "My men are ready for them. Come along."

Outside the lych-gate there was a confused scuffle, oaths, the sound of blows. As we passed through, we were surrounded by dark forms of captors and captured.

"You mistake me, good fellows," cried a resonant voice, "I am no body-snatcher, but Lady Julia's friend Dr. Hardiman, come hither in her interest."

"The surgeon! A friend!" exclaimed the Bow Street man who held him pinioned. "A likely story!"

"See," said the surgeon with a smile, "my hands are clean."

In that darkness it was hardly to be seen whether they were or no; but Dr. Johnson assented at once: "They are so. Unhand him, good fellow."

"And me," exclaimed another captive whose voice I knew. The starlight fell on the lugubrious face of Mr. Blackstock the undertaker.

"Mr. Welch!" he cried. "Bid these boobies release me, for I come on the same errand as you and the surgeon, to see to my dead-watch and baffle the Sack-em-up Men, and I desire you'll release me at once."

"Stay," said Dr. Johnson, "look at his hands."

"They are clean!" cried Mr. Blackstock.

They may have been clean of graveyard mold, but as tall Welch turned up the palms, they glowed weirdly in the dark.

" 'Tis enough," said Dr. Johnson with satisfaction. "You are caught, sir, if not red-handed, yet with traces on your palms put there by Harlequin's chymically glowing shroud. You are detected, sir; you have gone about to rob your own grave!"

Other glowing palms told the same tale, and soon the whole squad of Sack-em-up Men stood detected. Among them, not at all to my surprise, grinned the sexton. Of course it was he who had disconnected the spring-gun.

"Bravo, Dr. Johnson!" cried a soft voice, as a black-cloaked figure emerged from the church porch. "Your stratagem has succeeded!"

Putting back the mourning hood, Lady Julia stood revealed, smiling and sparkling in the faint light that began to grey the East.

"Shall I have no credit?" A second form stood forth. I stared in disbelief—the fine eyes, the fair face—there stood young Patrick Fitzpatrick, whom I thought I had seen laid in the grave!

"I'm not so easy killed," the boy grinned at my astonishment, "more especially when I find a skilled surgeon to nurse my wound—"

"A mere scratch," murmured Dr. Hardiman. "And the heart's in the right place too."

"To nurse me like a friend," said the youth with emotion, "nay, like a father—"

"Which I yet shall be," smiled the surgeon, and the Lady Julia gave him smile for smile.

"So I mended, and 'twas but lying low for some thirty hours by Dr. Johnson's plan. Nay," said the youth with a schoolboy's relish, " 'twas a splendid bam! Building up a dummy inside Harlequin's gear, with my lady mother's wig stand for a head—and so trapping the villain that stole my father's body!"

The undertaker cursed to himself.

"And there"— the young voice hardened— "there stands the scoundrel that murdered him!"

The body-snatcher he pointed to started back with an oath.

"I recognized him in the throng at the theatre, lying in wait for me, I doubt not. But before I could collar him, he nicked me and got away; and hence comes all the rest of this comedy of Dr. Johnson's devising."

"Retribution shall be exacted," said Mr. Welch. "Conduct them to the round-house."

"So, boy," said Dr. Johnson, "our task is done. Thanks to Mr. De Loutherbourg's chymical paint, which I had of Davy Garrick along with Harlequin's gear, Mr. Blackstock's villainy is detected. He will snatch no more by night the bodies he buries by day; and so farewell to the Resurrection Men!"

DON'T WORRY, JOHNNY

by Robert L. Fish

Another story from the darker side of Robert L. Fish . . . No bright humor this time, no outrageous puns, no slapstick burlesque. Still, you might find humor in this story about ex-con Johnny Daniels, but it won't be humor to laugh by . . .

THE small statuette of blindfolded Justice stood on the side table in her office, flanked by neatly piled legal abstracts. The statuette had been a gift from some colleague; there had been admirers to bestow gifts, she remembered, but somehow they had never given themselves.

She brought her attention back to the parole officer facing her. Johnny, she thought, should have known he couldn't really keep it a secret from her.

The parole officer reached out and crushed his cheap cigar in the ashtray.

"He'll be in trouble again in no time, Miss Benson," he said. His voice recognized the inevitability of trouble with ex-cons; like sunrise and sunset—into prison, out of prison, into prison.

"You say you know the girl?"

"Yes, ma'am. She's a—a tramp."

"What's her name?" A pencil came into her hand automatically.

"Mavis Gallagher. She's got a room at the Glenmont, you want to call it a room. She sure isn't the one to straighten Johnny out. No morals plus expensive tastes."

Like Johnny, Lauretta Benson thought. She forced herself to smile enigmatically across the desk, hiding the pain.

"I'm just the boy's lawyer," she said, turning up the palms of her well-manicured hands. "Not his guardian."

"I know," the parole officer said, "but I thought I ought to mention it to you." He came to his feet, brushing ash from his wrinkled suit, looking down at her neatly coiffed head with sympathy. "He's wild, Johnny is. You've been more than a lawyer to him, Miss Benson, you been like a mother to him. And it's only because of your defending him in court that he's only been sent up once." He shook his head. "Now the kid's got a record, he won't be so easy to get off in the future."

"I know," she said softly, but she was saying it more for herself than for the officer.

She watched him tug his misshapen hat into place and move to the door, watched him nod and then close the door behind him. She stared at the blank panel of the door, not seeing it, seeing only Johnny as she had first seen him six years before. She closed her eyes, fighting down the panic that rose at thought of losing him.

More than a lawyer to Johnny? Yes. But a mother? God, no!

It had all started when the court had appointed her to act as Public Defender in the case of the State of New York vs. John Daniels in Juvenile Court on a charge of breaking and entering, plus felonious assault on the elderly woman who had come downstairs to find her small shop being ransacked. Johnny Daniels, age sixteen, orphan. Handsome, reckless, brash—and also amoral, dangerous. And she a respectable lawyer, age thirty-six, a spinster lady, as she called herself wryly, although she had had opportunities. But she had also had a fear of men.

She had arranged bail for the boy and had taken him home to wash up before the trial—at least, he would come into court with clean hands in one respect if not in the other. And Johnny, swaggering into the living room draped only in a towel and asking her if she'd like to help him take his bath!

Her first reaction had been shock, followed by an almost irrational anger, and then there had been the shame of knowing her own desire. Could she possibly lose that fear with this child? This child! She still felt that flush of shame, but also the painful want, as he came up to her, reaching for her almost casually.

"You ain't a bad-looking chick, you know?" he said. "Not bad at all."

They had been lovers for three years. Discreet, but lovers. Under Johnny's tutelage—learned where, and when and from whom?—she had come to appreciate the infinite capacity of her still-youthful body. And in return Johnny had his own apartment, his clothes, and an ample allowance which he allowed people to believe came from his skill at gambling.

But Johnny had not been satisfied. He had tried to rob a bank, overlooking the hidden cameras, and despite all of Lauretta Benson's ability, Johnny had been convicted by the photographic proof. He had pulled down a big five but had come out in three, being bright, but for those three years her bed had been empty. And now he had come out of prison, outfitted himself in style once again at her expense, and had avoided her.

She had thought it was merely getting accustomed to civilian life, but now she had been told it was another woman. She felt ill at the thought; she came to her feet suddenly, bending to the intercom.

"Dorothy?"

"Yes, Miss Benson?" Her personal secretary's voice was incurious.

"I—I'm not feeling well at the moment. I'm going home. I'll take some work with me in case I feel better later on, but please cancel the rest of my appointments for today."

"Yes, Miss Benson." The sympathy subtly changed to a more businesslike tone. "I hope you feel better by tomorrow. You're due in court in the afternoon."

"I know. I'll be there."

She shoveled papers in her attaché case like an automaton, closed it with a snap, and let herself out a side door of her office, leading directly to the corridor. She didn't feel like facing her office staff; she didn't feel like facing anyone. The elevator pointer was rising rapidly in her direction; she hesitated one moment and then pushed through to the stairwell. Even the thought of possible commiseration in the eyes of the old elevator man was too much for her at the moment.

She let herself into her dim shade-down apartment, dropping her attaché case, and walked a bit unsteadily toward the sideboard. She poured herself an unaccustomed drink and raised it to her lips with shaking fingers. There was the calculated clearing of a throat from the depths of an easy chair. Her drink jerked and spilled.

Johnny Daniels was smiling at her easily. "Hi, Lorrie."

"Johnny!" She put her glass down shakily. "You startled me!" Her eyes moved about. "How did you get in?"

He raised a thin strip of celluloid casually; his smile was cold.

"You changed the lock since I went away, eh? But you forgot I just graduated college up the river. You ought to double-lock them doors, Lorrie, a smart woman like you—" He tilted his handsome head toward the sideboard. "Go ahead, don't mind me. I'm a couple up on you, anyways."

"I really didn't want a drink." All I wanted, she added silently, was for you to tell me the parole officer was lying; or mistaken. And I only changed the lock because I lost my keys, Johnny, not to keep you out. She walked over to his easy chair and sat down gracefully on the arm, looking down at him possessively, running her fingers through his hair.

He shook her hand away, trying to do it lightly.

"Hey, don't bruise the dandruff. It takes time for that Sing Sing trim to grow out. Give it air."

She tried to smile but it was a grimace. Her hand moved from his hair to stroke his cheek; the contact brought desire against her wish. "Johnny—would you like—?"

He pushed himself from the chair abruptly, almost putting her off balance. He looked down at her, his face expressionless, and shook his head.

"Not today, Josephine. I ain't in the mood."

She knew then it was no mistake. Johnny would never be in the mood again. She forced herself to seeming calmness, walking across the room to a sofa there. She sat down and crossed her legs, aware that her ankles were still trim, her legs still lovely.

"Then what are you doing here?"

Johnny studied her for several minutes, then walked back to his chair and sat down. He leaned toward her.

"I want a favor, Lorrie."

"*You* want a favor? Another?"

"This will be the last one." There was a final cutting of ties in his tone. "I want an alibi for tomorrow afternoon. One o'clock."

At first the words did not make sense, although after short consideration she realized they had not unduly surprised her. She was beyond surprise; she was rapidly getting beyond hurt.

"You know, Johnny, you never asked me for an alibi before."

The smile was cruel, instantly removed. "I was saving you, Lorrie. For the big one. This is it."

"Why don't you ask your new girl friend to give you your alibi?"

If she hoped to startle him she failed. Johnny grinned at her derisively. "So you heard about Mavis, huh? Well, what the hell did you expect? I'm young, and so is she." He shrugged. "Anyways, she couldn't alibi a priest. She's got a reputation worse than my own. But you—"

Lauretta Benson felt an almost hysterical urge to laugh.

"Johnny, Johnny! What makes you think I would alibi you?"

"Because you're a pigeon, Lorrie. Think a bit. You ain't stupid. Think how it would look in the papers, a sixteen-year-old kid seduced by a woman of—" He frowned at her. "What were you then, Lorrie? Forty?"

"Thirty-six," she said faintly.

"You looked older, but never mind," Johnny said. "It's the same thing. A client of yours—juvenile case—poor dumb kid, no relatives, no mama to teach him better, no experience. Court says you got to defend him. Kid don't know which end is up. You take him home and make him do what you want—because if he don't, you'll see to it he gets the works. Kid got no choice, see? And for three years running." His cold eyes looked at her curiously. "How does it read? Do you want me to draw you a diagram?"

She stared at him, numb with disbelief.

"What do you think?" he asked again. "Picture it in the *Daily News*."

Lauretta Benson took a deep breath. It didn't seem possible this was happening, not to her.

"I would deny it, of course."

Johnny laughed, a genuine laugh.

"You? Man, Lorrie, you come alive for the first time in your life that first time." He chuckled at the memory. "You think nobody noticed? The difference in you, I mean?" She felt her face reddening. Had they noticed, she wondered?

Johnny seemed to read her mind. He leaned forward, a friend. "Lorrie, take my word, you're a lousy liar, especially about how you feel when I just touch you. Don't put it to the test, because you'd lose. Believe me."

Lauretta Benson tried to believe she was actually engaged in this monstrous dialogue.

"I can't alibi you. I've got to be in court tomorrow afternoon."

"So be in court," Johnny said with sudden ease. He took a cigarette from a box on the end table, lit it, and tossed the match carelessly toward an ashtray. "All you got to do is be here at one o'clock, in case the phone rings, or some nosey neighbor happens to be looking this way. After that, do what you want." He shrugged. "The story is I got here at one o'clock on the button, and you had to go to court, like you say, so you left me here. And I hung around for a while and then I got tired of hanging around, so I blew." He smiled at her, her former intransigence forgiven. "I knew you wouldn't let an old pal down."

"Johnny."

"Yeah?" His face hardened, prepared for argument and prepared to deal with it.

"You wouldn't do anything—well, foolish?"

He mimicked her. "No, Johnny, I wouldn't do anything—well, foolish."

He came to his feet, pinched out his cigarette, and slid the blackened butt into his pocket, prison-style. He walked to the window and pulled the heavy drapes aside, letting in the late-afternoon light, and then moved to the door. He opened it and stared at her, a sardonic twinkle in his eye.

Lauretta Benson felt as if she were being undressed; her hand tugged at her skirt. Johnny grinned derisively. "Have fun," he said, and winked at her. The door closed quietly behind him.

Through the open curtains the shadows of coming evening enclosed the room; the cries of children in the street filtered past the locked window frames, echoing faintly in the darkening room. She came to her feet slowly and found her way to the sideboard without lighting a lamp, pouring a large whiskey, sipping it gratefully, her mind at work.

An alibi for Johnny tomorrow afternoon at one o'clock or—what? An end to her career? Disgrace? Did it really matter? Could anything she did make her feel more ashamed than she felt at this moment? She sipped the whiskey and then poured another.

She found herself with the classified section of the telephone directory in her hand, searching lists, flipping pages. She reached up and switched on a lamp; in the sudden light the number she wanted seemed to spring at her from the printed page. She took a deep breath and dialed, listening to the telephone at the other end begin to ring.

Oh, Johnny! Why are you making me do it?

It was amazing to her, the following afternoon, that her session in court, short as it was, could possibly have passed without the judge noticing her inner conflict, or her opposing attorney—a legal enemy of long standing—both recognizing and taking advantage of her obvious confusion. Obvious to her but apparently not to them. *I must be a better actress than I realized,* she thought, and paid off the taxi before her apartment door, relieved that the court session had finally been overcome. She tipped accurately and slid from the cab seat to the sidewalk, aware of the driver's admiring glance.

There was a car parked in front of the building, apparently undisturbed by the No Parking sign beside it. She passed it without paying any attention; the three men in the rear seat and the two in front registered on her mind merely as part of the street scene. It was only as she was in the process of taking her key ring from her purse that she became aware of the car door opening and a man approaching. He seemed to wait until she had found the proper key and then tapped her diffidently on the shoulder.

"Miss Benson?"

She swung about, startled. "Yes?"

"Police." An identification card was held for her inspection. Her eyes automatically swept the car at the curb; Johnny was sitting calmly in the rear seat between two quite-obvious detectives. As she watched, Johnny raised his wrists and shook the handcuffs, grinning at her derisively. She was suddenly aware of the parole officer looking at her sadly from the front seat. She turned abruptly to the detective at her side.

"What trouble is Johnny in?"

He tucked the card carefully back into his wallet. "Could I have a moment of your time, Miss Benson?" He saw the direction of her eyes. "They'll wait. In your apartment?"

Her eyes turned to Johnny's face. He raised his shoulders humorously.

"Of course," she said, and managed the key into the keyhole. She led the way to the stairway and made her way up to the second floor. The detective climbed behind her, his eyes studiously avoiding the trim legs above him. They turned into a corridor and paused before a door.

Lauretta Benson fitted the key into the lock, turning it twice to unlatch it. She swung it open and flicked on a light, staring about, as if something might have changed since she had last seen it; but the room was quiet and neat. She turned, looking at the respectful man behind her.

"I saw your identification card, but I forget your name."

"Sergeant Collier." The sergeant closed the door gently, glancing around the room. His eyes came back to hers. "Miss Benson, would you care to sit down?"

"I'm fine." Her tone was businesslike. "What kind of trouble is Johnny in?"

Sergeant Collier looked at her. "Quite a bit, I'm afraid," he said, and dug into his pocket. "Miss Benson, I'll try and waste a minimum of your time. I want you to look at some photographs."

"Photographs?" She was honestly surprised.

"Three of them." He brought them from his pocket. "Please."

"Of course," she said, and took them. "What am I supposed to be looking for?"

"Just look, please."

She stared at the top one. It showed a typical scene in a bank, except that a crouched man broke the normal harmony. He was holding a revolver, pointing it stiff-armed toward the teller's cage. The teller could not be seen in the picture. The crouched man had a woman's nylon stocking pulled over his head with eyeholes cut in it; he wore gloves and the collar of his windbreaker was pulled to his ears.

In the background a guard had half turned, one foot lifted as if starting in a walking race. Spectators stood with frozen faces; one woman, obviously unaware of what was happening, stood patiently making out a slip at a counter.

Lauretta Benson looked up. "Yes?"

"Would you look at the next picture, please?"

She shifted the top one to the bottom and studied the second photograph. It was the same scene, but taken by a different camera from a different angle. Now the teller was visible; he was twisted unnaturally on the floor behind his cage, his legs drawn up, his hands on his stomach. Lauretta Benson drew in a sharp breath.

"Yes," the sergeant said quietly. "He died an hour ago in White Plains General. In the Emergency." His finger rested on the photograph over her shoulder. "See the clock? One o'clock— that's when it took place. Now, would you please look at the last picture?"

She shifted pictures again. This one seemed to be a duplicate of the first, except in this picture the man did not have the stocking mask on or the gloves. She saw with a start that the man was Johnny, and then realized the picture was both old and familiar. It had been the State's prime evidence at Johnny's trial three years before. Her eyes rose.

"Yes?"

Sergeant Collier looked at her quietly.

"We picked Johnny Daniels up at his apartment about a half hour ago. He was packing. We found a pair of gloves and a lumberjacket jammed down in a rubbish barrel in the basement of his apartment building; they match the ones in the picture. You'll say they're common enough items, and others live in the apartment as well—both true statements. Still . . .

"It's also true we haven't found the gun, or the money. Yet. But we say the man is the same height and build as Johnny Daniels, and that the men in both the picture taken today and the one taken three years ago hold their arms out the same way, stiff, like on a pistol range."

He took a deep breath and continued, "Johnny Daniels says he was here, coming into this apartment, at one o'clock today. We say he was at the Mamaroneck National Bank at one o'clock, and we say these pictures prove it."

Lauretta Benson remained silent, waiting. Sergeant Collier's eyes were steady on her face.

"Miss Benson, we know you're a friend of Johnny Daniels, and we know you practically adopted him and that you are his lawyer. But we also know you're a respectable member of the bar and an officer of the law yourself. This is a capital offense. Daniels claims he was with you at one o'clock. Is that true?"

She could feel the lash of Johnny's words the day before. She could see him sitting downstairs now, between two detectives. She could hear the threat in his voice.

"Miss Benson?"

She took a deep breath. "It's true, Sergeant. I was on my way out when Johnny came. I told him to go in and make himself comfortable, that I was due in court."

Sergeant Collier's face fell. "That's what he said."

"That's what it was."

The detective frowned. "Miss Benson, are you sure of your times?"

"I'm—well, I suppose nobody is ever too sure, especially in a case like this." Lauretta Benson shrugged diffidently. "If you have any doubts as to the accuracy of my clocks, you're welcome to check them. I remember looking at the one on my bedroom dresser just before I left, and I'm sure it said one o'clock, or a few minutes to one."

Sergeant Collier shrugged helplessly. "I suppose I'd best," he said, and walked from the room looking beaten.

Lauretta Benson wanted a drink but she felt she could hardly take one at this moment. In the silence of the room the ticking of the clock on the mantel seemed to emphasize the alibi she had provided for Johnny Daniels. It was with a slight sense of awakening that she became aware the detective had returned and was addressing her.

"Your bedroom clock checks with my watch, and that's as accurate as the one at the station. And at the bank." He walked to the window, opened it, and leaned out, bellowing "Mike!"

A car door opened and a head poked out. "Yeah?"

"Bring him up!"

Sergeant Collier stood facing the door, his eyes expressionless. Lauretta Benson wanted a drink more than ever. There was the sound of scuffling feet in the corridor and the two policemen edged their way past the pale woman, bringing Johnny into the room. The parole officer followed, shutting the door behind him. Johnny was half seated, half thrown into an easy chair. He started to remonstrate, then shrugged and subsided.

"You're cute, Johnny," Sergeant Collier said.

Johnny Daniels frowned. He didn't like the tone of voice, the confidence in the detective's voice. He hid his sudden tenseness with belligerency. "She didn't support my alibi?"

"Did I say she didn't?" Sergeant Collier asked. "One o'clock, wasn't it?"

"One o'clock!" Johnny said. "I've only said so a hundred times!"

"Who's arguing with you?" Sergeant Collier looked at his seated prisoner with near-admiration. "You're cool, Johnny. I've got to give you that." He leaned over the prisoner, his voice curious. "Did you really think Miss Benson would cover for you? On a murder charge, Johnny? That was stupid."

"What do you mean? I was here, I tell you!"

"At one clock. I'm sure," Sergeant Collier said softly. He held up a wrinkled piece of paper he had been palming in his hand and read it. "*564 Thistlewood Drive. Meet Johnny one o'clock.*"

Lauretta Benson stared. "But that's this address! Where did you get it?"

Sergeant Collier folded the paper carefully and slid it into his billfold. His eyes came up to study Johnny. There was satisfaction in his voice as he spoke to the handsome woman over his shoulder.

"I found it in a pocketbook on the floor of your bedroom, Miss Benson. It apparently belonged to a girl named Mavis Gallagher." He heard the indrawn breath behind him and felt sorry for the further shock he was about to afford her. "I'm sorry, Miss Benson, but she's in your bathroom. Stabbed to death."

Johnny Daniels stared wordlessly across the room, straining against the strong hands of the masklike plainclothes policeman on either side of him. His lean handsome face was pale, outraged.

"Don't worry, Johnny," Lauretta Benson said soothingly. "I've always taken care of you, and I'll see to it you're taken care of this time. Don't worry, Johnny."

WINNER TAKES ALL

by Patricia McGerr

A terrific suspense story—also destined, we're sure, to become an anthology favorite . . . Husband, wife, lover—and a deadly game of cyanide roulette. Each man had a 50-50 chance to survive and have everything his heart desired. Which one would it be? The old man, Zeus? The young man, Apollo? . . .

PHILIP WADE sat at the desk in his study and read the note he had just written.

My darling Laura,
  What I am about to do will cause you shock and, perhaps, pain.

But I know that you love someone else and you are more dear to me than my life. So tonight I shall toast you for the last time with a glass of poisoned cognac. Do not grieve for me, my sweet. In the four years you have been my wife you have given me great happiness. I choose this way to set you free with the hope that you too will be happy.

Yours till death,
Philip

Not, he thought, one of my best literary efforts. A bit oversentimental. Some might even call it corny. But it should bring a tear to the eyes of readers of the morning tabloid if it is ever printed.

If. He spoke the word aloud, then inhaled deeply. Is this, he asked himself, my final hour? Will tomorrow's papers carry my obituary? He closed his eyes to visualize the headline. BEST-SELLING NOVELIST, AGE 54, TAKES OWN LIFE. What will they say of me? Which book titles will they list? How will they appraise my artistic worth? Or will they dwell instead on my folly in marrying a girl young enough to be my daughter?

He smiled grimly, shaking off the questions. He would not, after all, be there to read his last reviews.

But it was not too late to draw back. When Don Talbott arrived, he could say he'd reconsidered, did not wish to play this game of cyanide roulette. And then what? They'd be back at the beginning, as they were six days ago when he'd confronted his wife and secretary with evidence of their adulterous relationship. He could divorce Laura and fire Talbott. Then Wade would be alive and rich and alone. And the other two would be together and poor. Because that solution satisfied none of them, Talbott had suggested tonight's trial.

"Let's meet," he said, "and set out two glasses, one containing poison. Then you and I, Mr. Wade, will both drink and one of us will die. The survivor will have Laura."

"And my money," Wade snapped. "That's at the heart of it, isn't it? If I use this evidence to get a divorce, Laura will have nothing. But if I die, she'll be a wealthy widow."

"That's true," the younger man admitted. "Since she married you she's grown used to luxury. I don't want to deprive her of that. But we love each other. It's not something we planned, it just happened. And now we're trapped."

You've lain in bed, Wade wanted to say, now try to make it. Good riddance to you both. But he could not bring himself to speak the words. It was too easy to understand their situation and see his own mistakes. It was his wealth and fame that had attracted Laura. But she had been a loving and faithful wife until, a year ago, he had brought into their household this handsome virile young man.

Looking at Talbott, Wade was painfully aware of the contrast between them. He could not wholly blame Laura. Nor could he take pleasure in seeing her reduced to penury. And he had an anguished awareness of how bleak his own future would be without her. It was then that he began to take seriously the other man's bizarre proposal.

In the week that followed they worked out the details. Talbott was to supply the poison, an insecticide concentrate whose taste and smell could be masked by brandy. Laura would pour the drinks, poison one, then set the glasses in front of them.

"Laura," Wade objected, "is not a neutral party. She'll let you know which drink is safe."

"I don't blame you for being suspicious," Talbott conceded. "But we can't bring in an outsider. And if you have the first choice of glasses and I take the one that's left, there's no way we can make you the loser."

Wade thought it over and subdued his doubts. It was, as Talbott said, a gamble. A 50–50 chance, winner takes all. Laura had promised, if he lived, to stay with him and try to make their marriage work. That was a gamble too, but with her lover permanently removed, a fresh start was possible. He weighed the alternatives—to risk death or let her go—and agreed to try his luck.

The test was set for 8:00 P.M. on Sunday evening. Each man

was to prepare a suicide note to forestall any police investigation or talk of murder. Now it was nearly 7:30 and Wade, his own note ready, had nothing to do but wait. He laid the paper on the desk top, straightened it until it was in the exact center of the blotter. Half an hour, he thought, half an hour and then—

A light tap on the door made him jerk erect. "Yes?" His voice was pitched unnaturally high. "Who is it?"

"It's me, Phil." Laura opened the door, slipped inside, and closed it behind her. "I've been going crazy, waiting alone, wondering what was going to happen."

"It'll be all right," he said ineptly. Looking at her, he was once more sure of the rightness of his decision. She was as small and soft and tawny as a kitten. A strand of fair hair drooped over one eye and she pushed it back with a characteristic gesture that made his loins tighten; then she came to kneel beside his chair and look trustingly up at him. She's still a child, he thought, and touched her cheek with a comforting pat. He could not, even now, condemn for her infidelity.

"I'm frightened, Phil," she said. "All the time you and Don were talking about tonight, it seemed like—well, like some game you were playing. But it's real, isn't it? You're actually going to do it?"

"Yes, it's real. But it's also a game. One with very high stakes. My note is finished. Would you like to read it?" He handed her the paper and watched with a certain pride of authorship as she scanned the words, then looked at him with brimming eyes.

"Oh, Phil, I can't bear it. It's so beautiful. How can you be so kind to me when I've been so wicked?"

"You're not wicked. You met a man your own age, an attractive man, and you fell in love."

"That's not true. It's you I love. What I feel for Don is ugly and cheap—it has nothing to do with love. I was too dumb to see the difference till this week when you've been so good, so forgiving. Then when I realized that you might—that I might lose you, that's when I knew how much I love you, need you. Phil, you mustn't be the one to die."

"If that's how you feel"—he smiled with a sudden lightening of spirit—"then nobody will die. We'll send the young man packing and you and I will have a special celebration. Where would you like to go, my dear? Name any place on the globe and we'll have a second honeymoon."

"I wish it were that simple." She lowered her head till her brow rested on his knee and her voice was muffled. "You don't know what he does to me. It's not love, not love at all, but I have this terrible longing. From the time it began I tried to stop him, tried to break it off, but I'm too weak. When he touches me, or even looks at me, it's like I was on fire. Oh, it's awful to say these things. I hate myself for hurting you, but I have to make you see how it is. Whatever promises I give you, I couldn't keep them. Not so long as Don's alive and wanting me."

"And if he were dead?"

"Then you and I could be happy again—the way we were before he came and spoiled things." She raised her head to look up at him. "Please, Phil, we've got to arrange it so he's the one to die."

"I'm afraid that's in the hands of Fate."

"It doesn't have to be. I've been thinking and thinking about it. You get first pick of the glasses, don't you? And he's obliged to drink from the other one."

"That's the way we planned it."

"Because you didn't trust me. But Don does. It will never enter his head that you and I might plot against him."

"So?" He waited for her to continue.

"Which glasses are you going to use? Have you decided yet?"

"Yes, they're set out and ready. The big ones with the drawings of gods and goddesses that you've always found so amusing."

"Then it will be easy." She scrambled to her feet, moved swiftly to the alcove that was fitted with a small bar. On its top Wade had placed a decanter filled with cognac, a small silver tray, and a set of six snifters. Into the bowl of each was etched a mythological divinity. Laura picked out two and brought them back to place on the desk in front of him.

"Here's what I'll do." Her face was alight with youthful enthusiasm. "I'll pour your drink in this one." She pointed to the bearded image of Zeus. "And the poison will go in here." Her fingernail made a faint *ting* as it tapped the curly head of Apollo. The old man and the young, Wade thought wryly. Easy enough to remember which is which.

"He'll never suspect," she said eagerly. "Even after he's drunk the poison, he'll think it was just bad luck. And then—oh, darling, it will be the way it was before, only better. I'll make it up to you, I swear I will." She leaned close and pressed her mouth on his with a fervor that bordered on fierceness. The doorbell pealed and she broke away. "Oh, God, he's come. I'd better get out of here. We don't want him to know I've been talking to you."

She hurried away. Wade, moving more slowly, returned the glasses to the bar and went to answer the door. He felt a little stunned by the swift change of events. She loves me, he thought, she's never stopped loving me. With Talbott it was only a physical thing, a kind of enslavement. But that's over and she'll be all mine again.

Yet when he opened the door to admit his young rival, the figures of Zeus and Apollo came unbidden to his mind and the doubts began. Am I, he asked himself, an utter fool to believe she prefers me to him? Were all her protestations, her tears even, a well-rehearsed act, one the two of them had planned together to make sure I would take the poison?

He led the way toward the study, stopping at the foot of the stairs to call up to her. "Laura, Talbott's arrived. Will you join us, my dear?"

"No use wasting any time, I guess." Talbott was nervous. He took from his overcoat pocket a small bottle filled with dark liquid. Walking over to the bar, he put it beside the glasses. Then he removed his gloves, thrust them into his coat pocket, took off the coat and hung it on the rack in the corner.

"You've written your note?" Wade asked.

"Yes, it's here." Talbott reached inside his jacket for an envelope which he gave to Wade.

"Mine's on the desk." Wade read the inscription on the envelope, To Whom It May Concern, and took out a folded sheet.

The woman I love doesn't love me and I don't want to live without her. My will is made and I'm going to take poison. Good-bye to all.

Donald Talbott

Not much style, Wade thought critically, but it will serve the purpose. At any event, Talbott was too obscure for the press to be interested in his death. If it got a brief mention it would be due only to his association with Wade.

"That says it all." Talbott turned from the desk where he too had been reading. "If you're satisfied with mine, we can get on with it. Ah, Laura, come in. We're just ready for you."

She entered silently, her eyes cast down, not looking at the young man. Is she afraid, Wade wondered, that he might read her treachery in her eyes? Or is it the other way? Does she fear my intercepting a glance that will reveal their conspiracy?

"I'll put this on the desk too." Talbott took his own note from Wade and slid it back into the envelope. "You can say I gave it to you just before I drank the poison. And of course after—after it happens—the one who's still alive must be sure to destroy his own note before he calls the doctor. Once that's done, there shouldn't be any problems."

"You—you brought it?" Laura asked. She still didn't meet his eyes.

"Yes," Talbott answered. "The bottle's on the bar. Empty it, all of it, into one of the glasses. Then put in enough brandy to reach a level of one inch. Be sure the level in the other glass is exactly the same. We'll turn our backs so we can't see what you're doing."

"When the drinks are poured," Wade added, "put the two glasses on the small tray and set it down on my desk. Then we'll make our choice."

They watched her walk toward the alcove. As soon as she reached it both men turned round to face the door.

"It should be quick," Talbott said, "and, I hope, fairly painless."

Wade said nothing. His mind was circling like a rat in a cage. Was she lying? Can I trust her? Is she putting poison into Zeus or into Apollo?

He heard a clink as the decanter struck the rim of one of the glasses, then a gurgle as the brandy was poured. A few seconds of silence and the sounds were repeated. Live or die, he told himself, it will soon be over.

Laura's light steps, behind them, approached the desk and the two men turned round again. The girl's hands shook as she put down the tray. The liquid sloshed in the bottom of the glasses.

"Better pour one for yourself," Talbott advised her. "Our story is that the three of us were having a drink together when it happened. There should be three glasses to bear it out."

Obediently she turned back to the bar. Wade studied the two snifters standing side by side on the silver tray. Each held the same quantity of liquid. There was, so far as he could see, no variation in color. They differed only in the decorations. Zeus and Apollo. Apollo and Zeus. If Laura was honest, Apollo held the poison and Zeus was harmless. But if Laura had deceived him—

He looked again at Don Talbott, whose attention was fixed on Laura's back as she poured the third drink. They've been lovers for six months. Compared to him, I'm old and worn and have nothing to offer her but wealth. By putting the poison in Zeus's glass, she can have both my money and the man she loves. But by choosing Apollo, I can spoil their plans, dispose of him, win her back.

And yet—suppose she told me the truth. She cared for me

when we were married, I'm sure it wasn't all pretense. She was faithful for more than three years. The affair with Talbott may be an aberration. She understands her own weakness, knows that only his death can free her. Can I believe her, take Zeus's glass and live?

Laura came toward them, carrying her drink in one hand. She stopped a few feet away and gazed at her husband—a lingering look full of promise that made his pulse race. How could I not believe her? he asked himself.

"Ready, Mr. Wade?" Talbott broke the silence. "Your choice."

"Yes, I—I'm ready."

He moved close to the tray, put out a hand, and hesitated.

Zeus or Apollo?

Apollo or Zeus?

He could feel the other two holding their breath and at last he reached a decision. Better to die, trusting her, than to live with the knowledge of her betrayal. Worst of all would be to doubt her wrongfully and die for his lack of faith.

He picked up the glass that bore the image of Zeus. By force of habit he cradled the bowl in his hand to warm it and passed it beneath his nose to savor the bouquet. Is it cyanide, he wondered, that smells of bitter almonds? Inhaling deeply, he got only the aroma of his own best brandy.

Talbott had taken the other glass. He raised it, looked over its rim at Wade. "To the woman we both love," he said.

"To Laura," Wade seconded.

Simultaneously the two men put the glasses to their lips, swallowed the contents in a single gulp, then stood still, waiting. Wade felt a sudden chill, a churning in his stomach, a weakness in his knees. His mind whirled with panicky questions. Am I poisoned? Are these the symptoms? How soon will it take effect?

He wanted to look at Laura, to seek in her face an answer, but he could not turn his head. Then Talbott cried out.

"Oh, my God! My throat—it's on fire!" The glass dropped from his hand, rolled toward the desk. He clutched his throat with one hand, covered his mouth with the other, and dropped to his knees. His body formed an arc.

"Please—somebody—help—" Talbott slid slowly down and forward till he was lying prone. His shoulders arched convulsively, then fell, and he was still.

"That's it," Laura said. "It's all over."

"Yes." Wade put his empty glass back on the tray and ran a dry tongue over drier lips. Averting his eyes from the body on the rug, he took an unsteady step backward to drop into the leather chair beside the desk. His whole body was drenched in cold sweat.

"Darling, pull yourself together." Laura came close to him. "We've got to be sure our stories are straight and everything's in order before the doctor comes."

He looked at her, amazed at her self-control. Her lover was dead, by her arrangement, and she was completely calm. But she was right. They must both keep their heads until after their stories were told, until after the authorities had come and gone.

"I'm all right," he said, but he had to clench his jaw to keep his teeth from chattering.

"Here, drink this." She handed him her own untouched brandy. "You mustn't go to pieces now."

He took the glass, drank quickly, and tried to give her a reassuring smile. But there was something in her gaze that made him colder than before. She turned away from him.

"It's done, Don," she said. "He drank it."

Unbelievingly, Wade watched the man on the floor lift his head and start to rise. Then Wade's vision blurred, the room seemed to spin, and pain struck deep in his stomach. They've won, he thought. It didn't matter which glass I chose. Laura poisoned her own drink.

He sank back in his chair with his head lolling forward, staring down at the glass in his lap. The last thing he saw was the figure etched on its surface. A scantily clad nymph with bow and arrow. Diana, the huntress.